STORY AND ART BY
NORIYUKI KONISHI

ORIGINAL CONCEPT AND SUPERVISED BY LEVEL-5 INC.

YO-KAI WATCH
Volume 5
SUMMON YOUR COURAGE
Perfect Square Edition

Story and Art by Noriyuki Konishi
Original Concept and Supervised by LEVEL-5 Inc.

Translation/Tetsuichiro Miyaki
English Adaptation/Aubrey Sitterson
Lettering/William F. Schuch
Design/Izumi Evers
Editor/Joel Enos

YO-KAI WATCH Vol. 5
by Noriyuki KONISHI
© 2013 Noriyuki KONISHI
©LEVEL-5 Inc.
Original Concept and Supervised by LEVEL-5 Inc.
All rights reserved.
Original Japanese edition published by SHOGAKUKAN.
English translation rights in the United States of America and
Canada arranged with SHOGAKUKAN.

Published by VIZ Media, LLC
P.O. Box 77010
San Francisco, CA 94107

10 9 8 7 6 5 4 3 2 1
First printing, May 2016

www.perfectsquare.com

www.viz.com

PARENTAL ADVISORY
YO-KAI WATCH is rated A
and is suitable for readers
of all ages.
ratings.viz.com

YO-KAI WATCH 5™

STORY AND ART BY
NORIYUKI KONISHI

ORIGINAL CONCEPT AND SUPERVISED BY LEVEL-5 INC.

CHARACTER INTRODUCTION

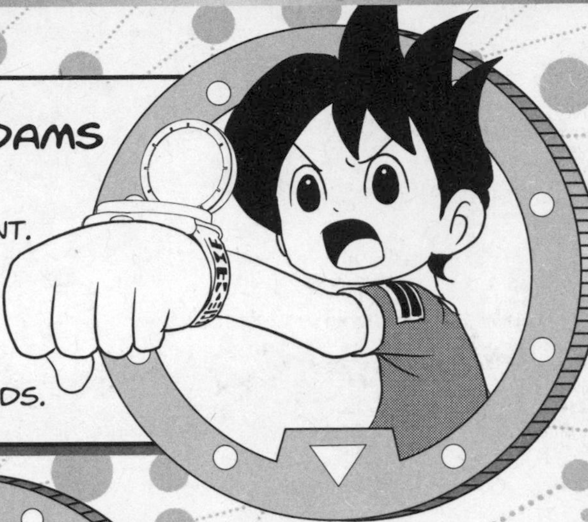

NATHAN ADAMS

AN ORDINARY ELEMENTARY SCHOOL STUDENT. WHISPER GAVE HIM THE YO-KAI WATCH, AND THEY HAVE SINCE BECOME FRIENDS.

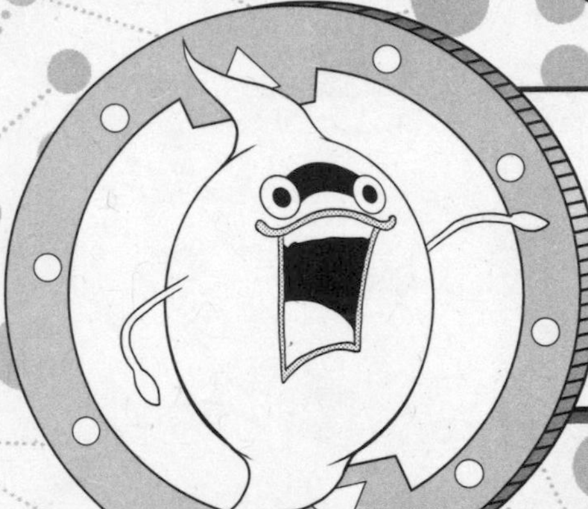

WHISPER

A YO-KAI BUTLER FREED BY NATE, WHISPER HELPS HIM BY USING HIS EXTENSIVE KNOWLEDGE OF OTHER YO-KAI.

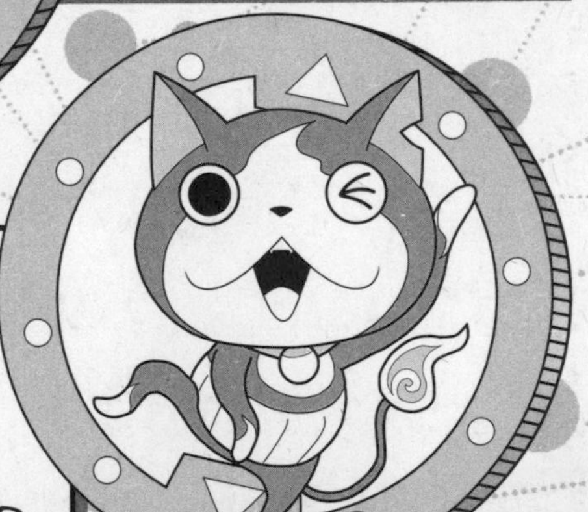

JIBANYAN

A CAT WHO BECAME A YO-KAI WHEN HE PASSED AWAY. HE IS FRIENDLY, CAREFREE AND THE FIRST YO-KAI THAT NATE BEFRIENDED.

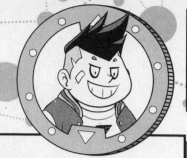

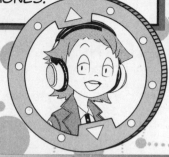

BARNABY BERNSTEIN
NATE'S CLASSMATE.
NICKNAME: BEAR.
CAN BE MISCHIEVOUS.

EDWARD ARCHER
NATE'S CLASSMATE.
NICKNAME: EDDIE. HE
ALWAYS WEARS HEAD-
PHONES.

TABLE OF CONTENTS

CHAPTER 35: THE GIRL WITH FROZEN BREATH

FEATURING ICY YO-KAI FROSTINA

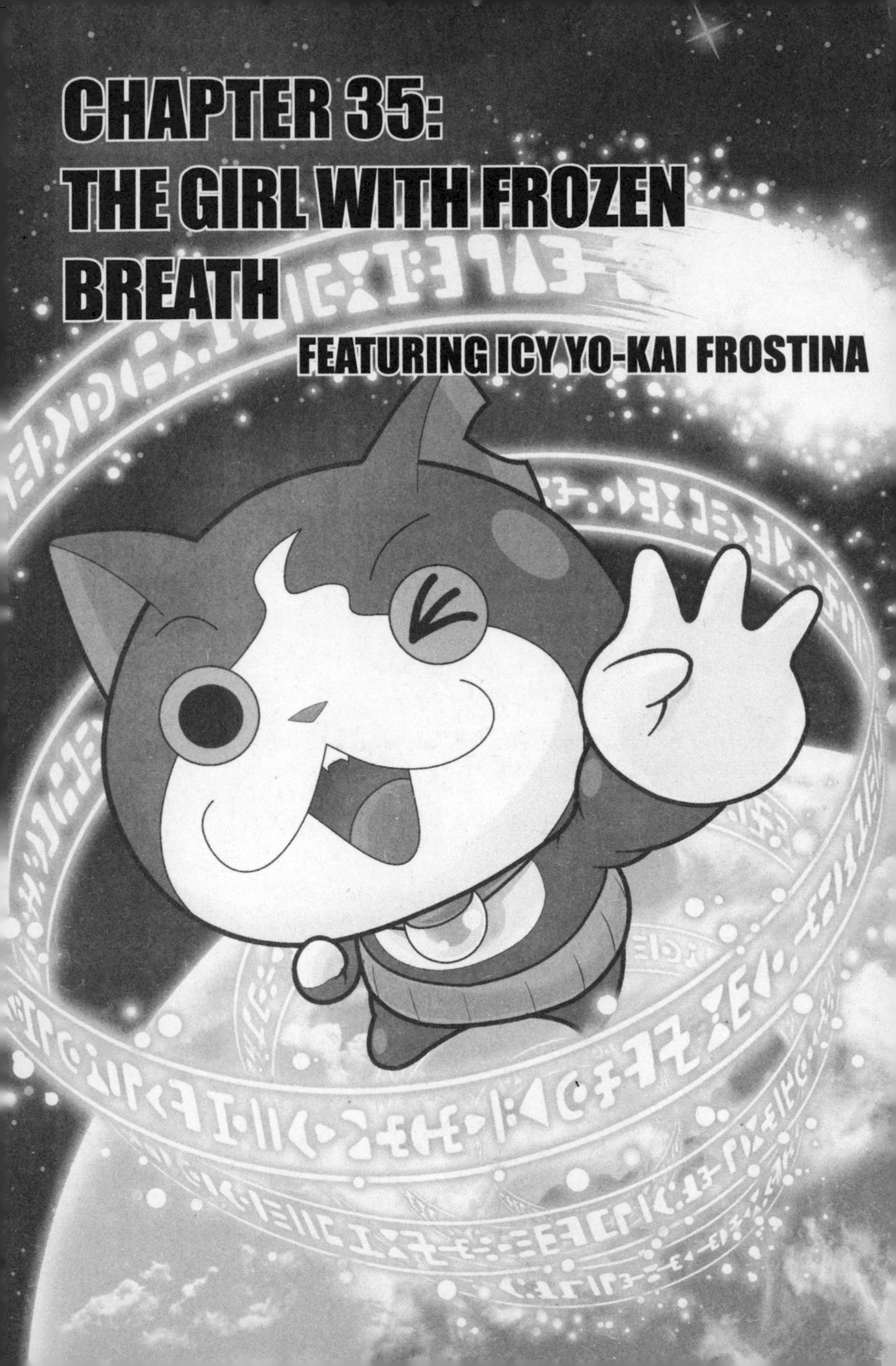

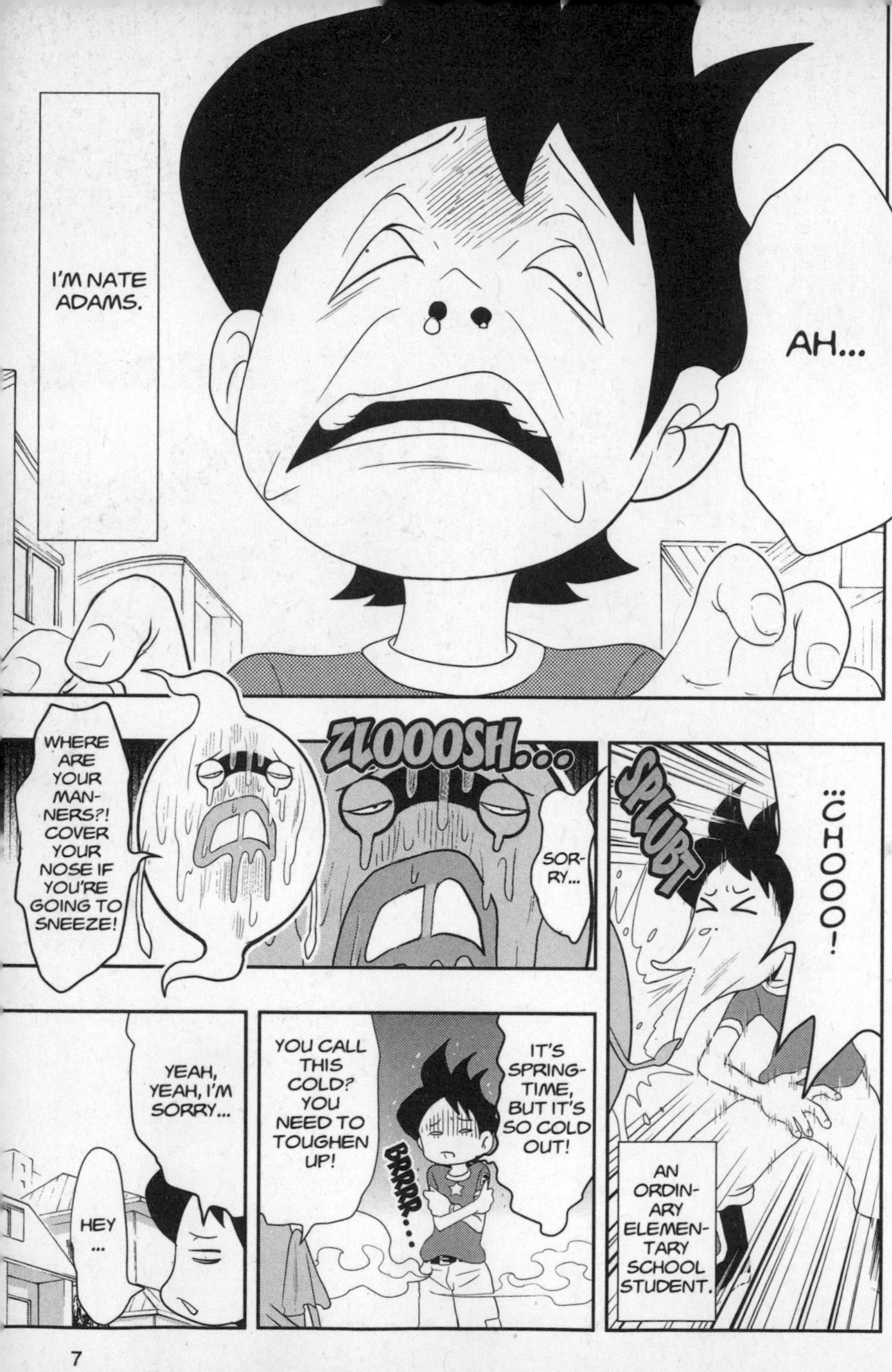
I'M NATE ADAMS.
AH...
...CHOOOO!
SPLUBT
AN ORDINARY ELEMENTARY SCHOOL STUDENT.
ZLOOOSH...
SORRY...
WHERE ARE YOUR MANNERS?! COVER YOUR NOSE IF YOU'RE GOING TO SNEEZE!
IT'S SPRINGTIME, BUT IT'S SO COLD OUT!
BRRRR...
YOU CALL THIS COLD? YOU NEED TO TOUGHEN UP!
YEAH, YEAH, I'M SORRY...
HEY...

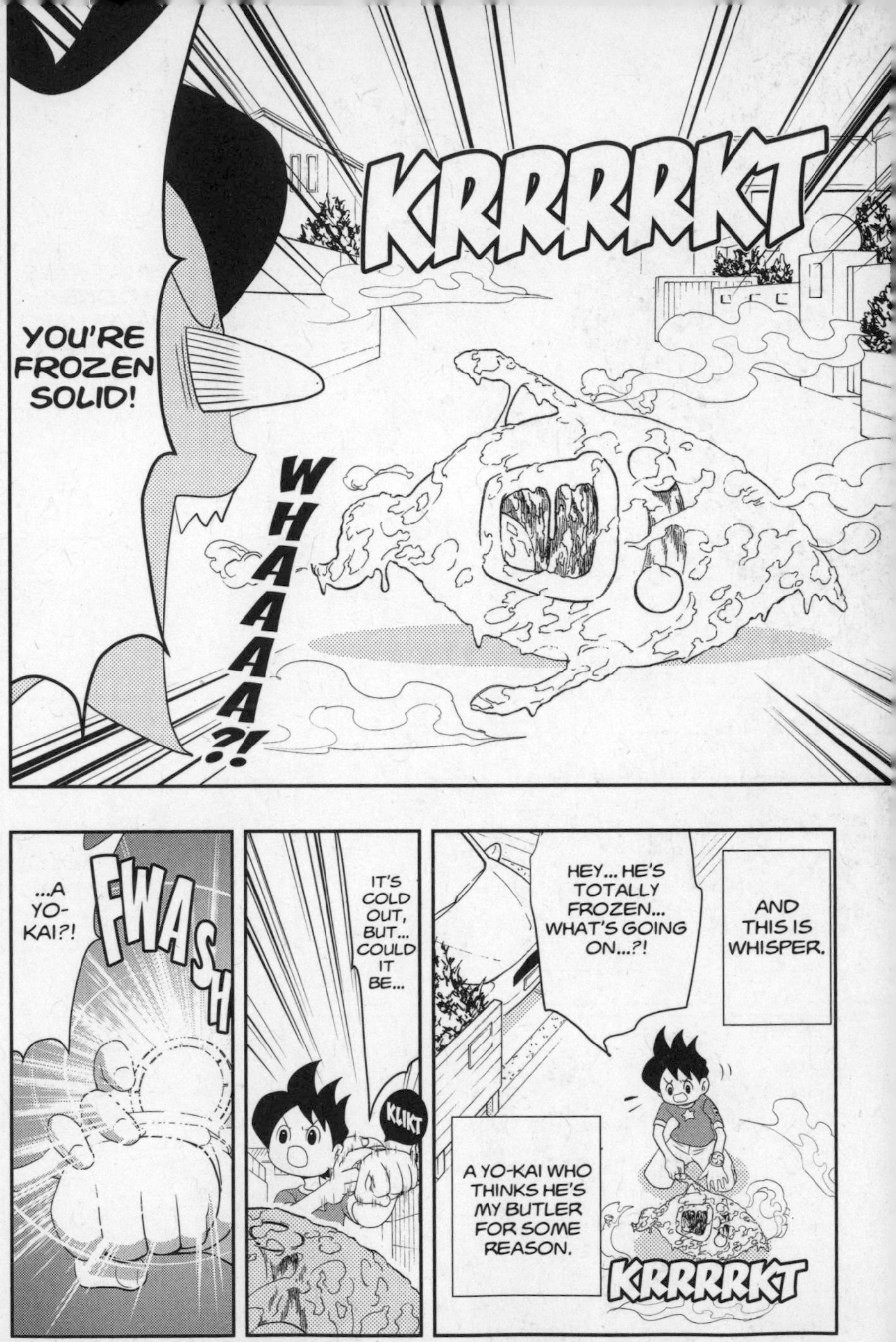
KRRRRRKT
YOU'RE FROZEN SOLID!
WHAAAAAA?!
AND THIS IS WHISPER.
HEY... HE'S TOTALLY FROZEN... WHAT'S GOING ON...?!
A YO-KAI WHO THINKS HE'S MY BUTLER FOR SOME REASON.
KRRRRKT
IT'S COLD OUT, BUT... COULD IT BE...
KLIKT
FWASH
...A YO-KAI?!

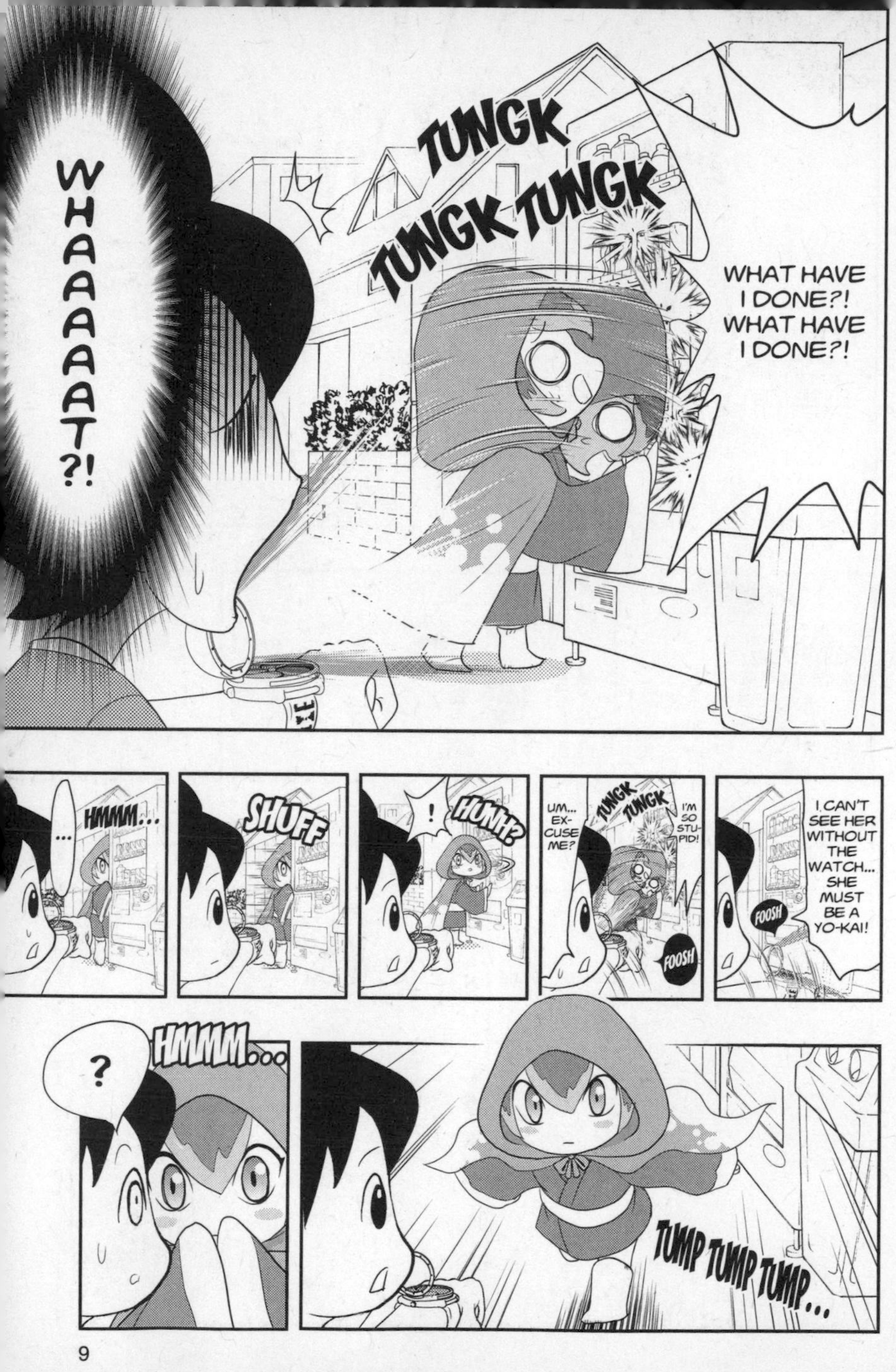
TUNGK
TUNGK TUNGK TUNGK
WHAT HAVE I DONE?! WHAT HAVE I DONE?!
WHAAAAAT?!
FOOSH
I CAN'T SEE HER WITHOUT THE WATCH... SHE MUST BE A YO-KAI!
I'M SO STUPID!
TUNGK TUNGK
UM... EXCUSE ME?
FOOSH
HUNH?
!
SHUFF
HMMM...
...
TUMP TUMP TUMP...
HMMM...
?

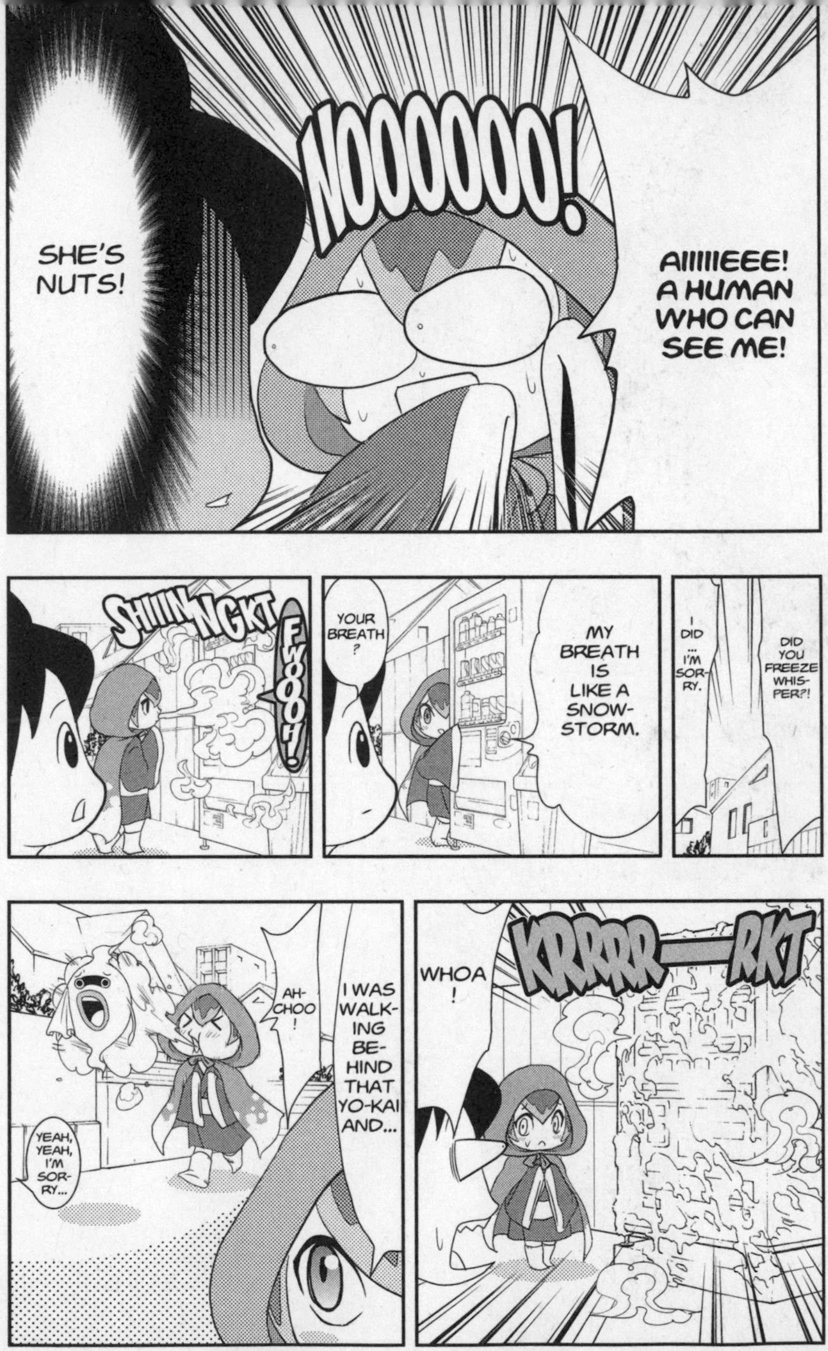
AIIIIIEEE! A HUMAN WHO CAN SEE ME!
NOOOOOO!
SHE'S NUTS!
DID YOU FREEZE WHISPER?!
I DID... I'M SORRY.
MY BREATH IS LIKE A SNOWSTORM.
YOUR BREATH?
FWOOOH!
SHIIINNGKT
KRRRRR—RKT
WHOA!
I WAS WALKING BEHIND THAT YO-KAI AND...
AH-CHOO!
YEAH, YEAH, I'M SORRY...

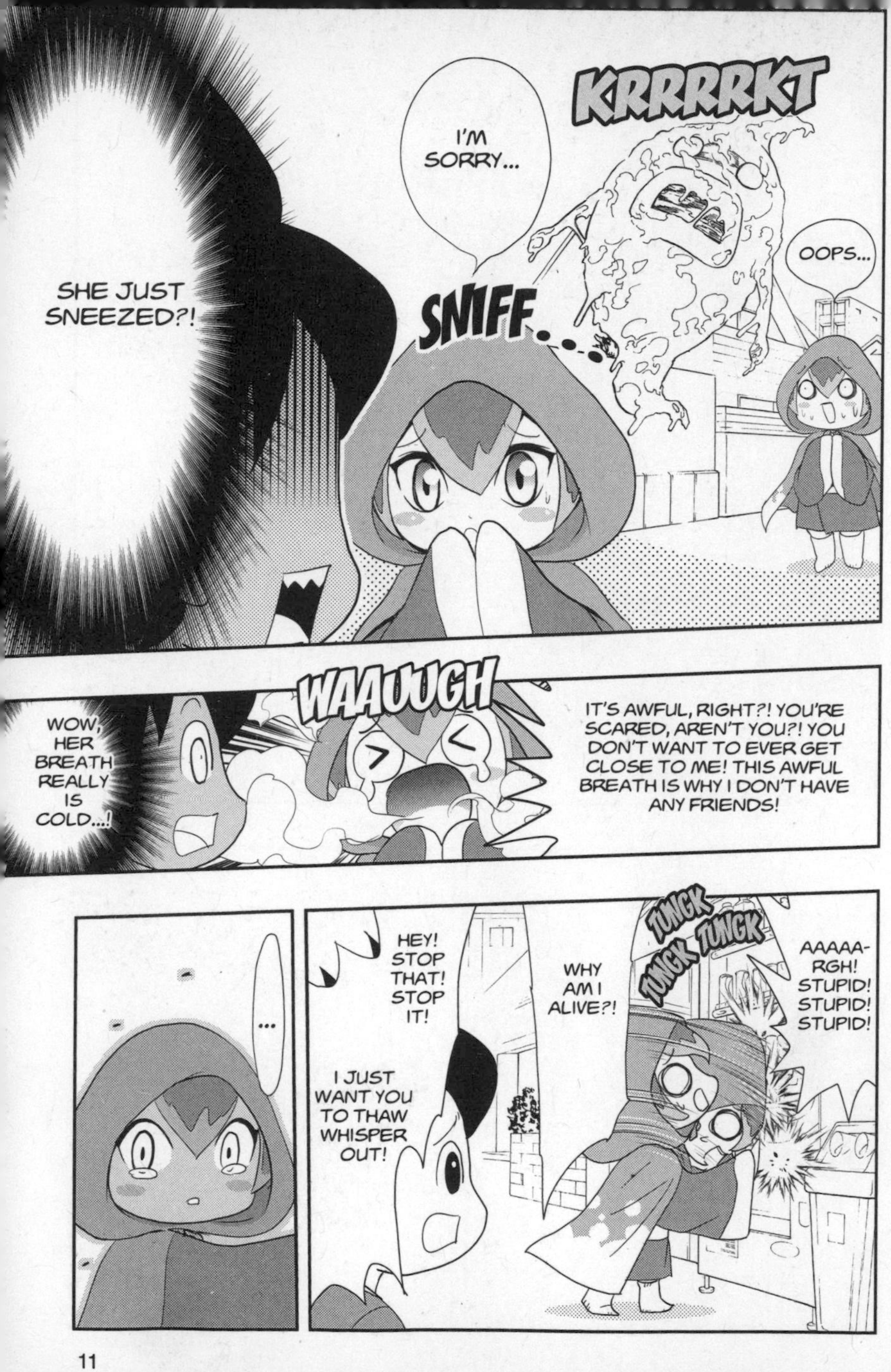
KRRRRRKT
I'M SORRY...
OOPS...
SNIFF...
SHE JUST SNEEZED?!
IT'S AWFUL, RIGHT?! YOU'RE SCARED, AREN'T YOU?! YOU DON'T WANT TO EVER GET CLOSE TO ME! THIS AWFUL BREATH IS WHY I DON'T HAVE ANY FRIENDS!
WAAUUGH
WOW, HER BREATH REALLY IS COLD...!
AAAAA-RGH! STUPID! STUPID! STUPID!
TUNCK TUNCK TUNCK
WHY AM I ALIVE?!
HEY! STOP THAT! STOP IT!
I JUST WANT YOU TO THAW WHISPER OUT!
...

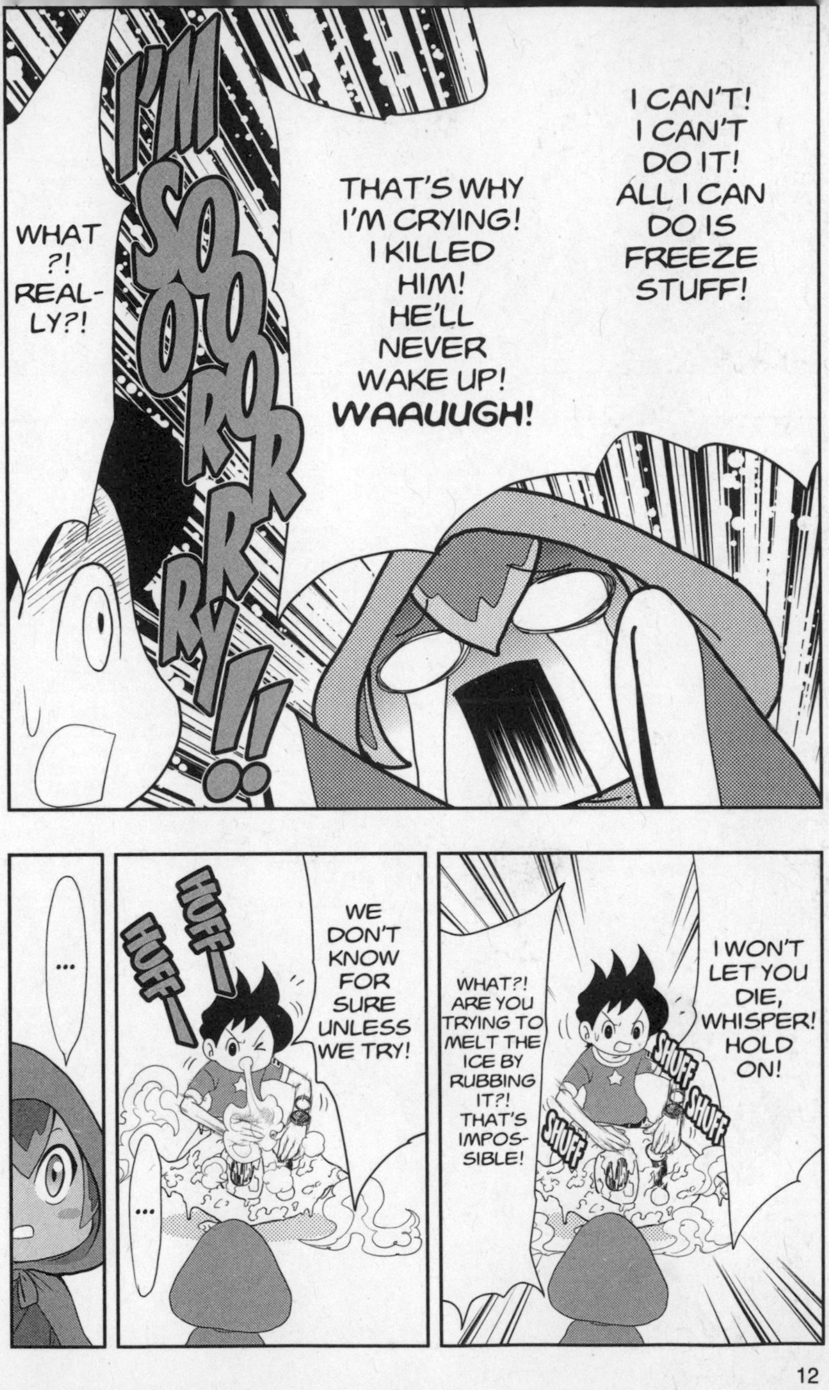
I CAN'T! I CAN'T DO IT! ALL I CAN DO IS FREEZE STUFF!
THAT'S WHY I'M CRYING! I KILLED HIM! HE'LL NEVER WAKE UP! WAAUUGH!
I'M SOOORRRRY!!
WHAT?! REAL-LY?!
I WON'T LET YOU DIE, WHISPER! HOLD ON!
SHUFF SHUFF
SHUFF
WHAT?! ARE YOU TRYING TO MELT THE ICE BY RUBBING IT?! THAT'S IMPOS-SIBLE!
HUFF HUFF
WE DON'T KNOW FOR SURE UNLESS WE TRY!
...
...

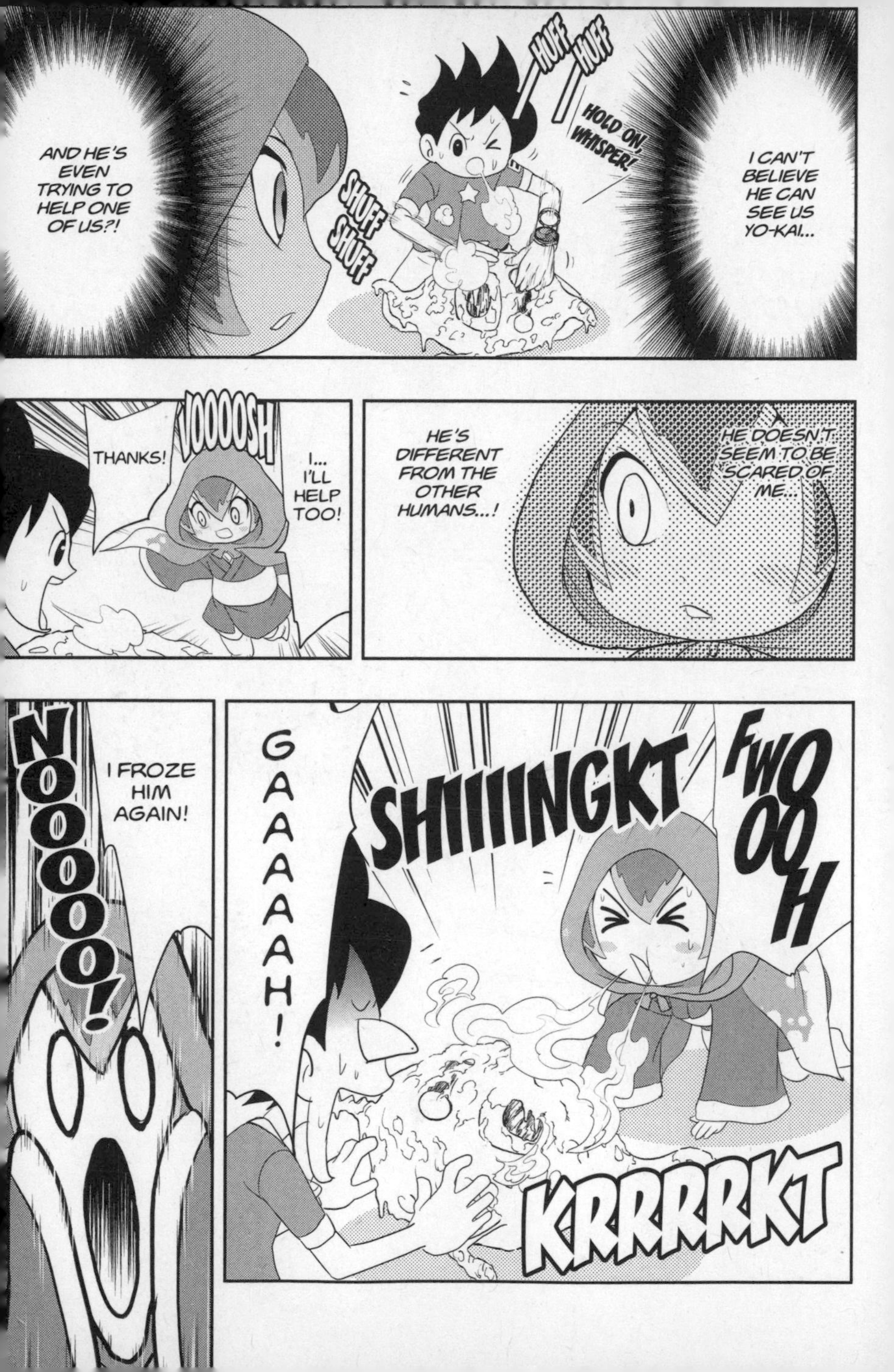
I CAN'T BELIEVE HE CAN SEE US YO-KAI...
HUFF HUFF
HOLD ON, WHISPER!
SHUFF SHUFF
AND HE'S EVEN TRYING TO HELP ONE OF US?!
HE DOESN'T SEEM TO BE SCARED OF ME...
HE'S DIFFERENT FROM THE OTHER HUMANS...!
I... I'LL HELP TOO!
VOOOOSH
THANKS!
FWOOOOH
SHIIIINGKT
GAAAAAAH!
KRRRRRKT
I FROZE HIM AGAIN!
NOOOOOO!

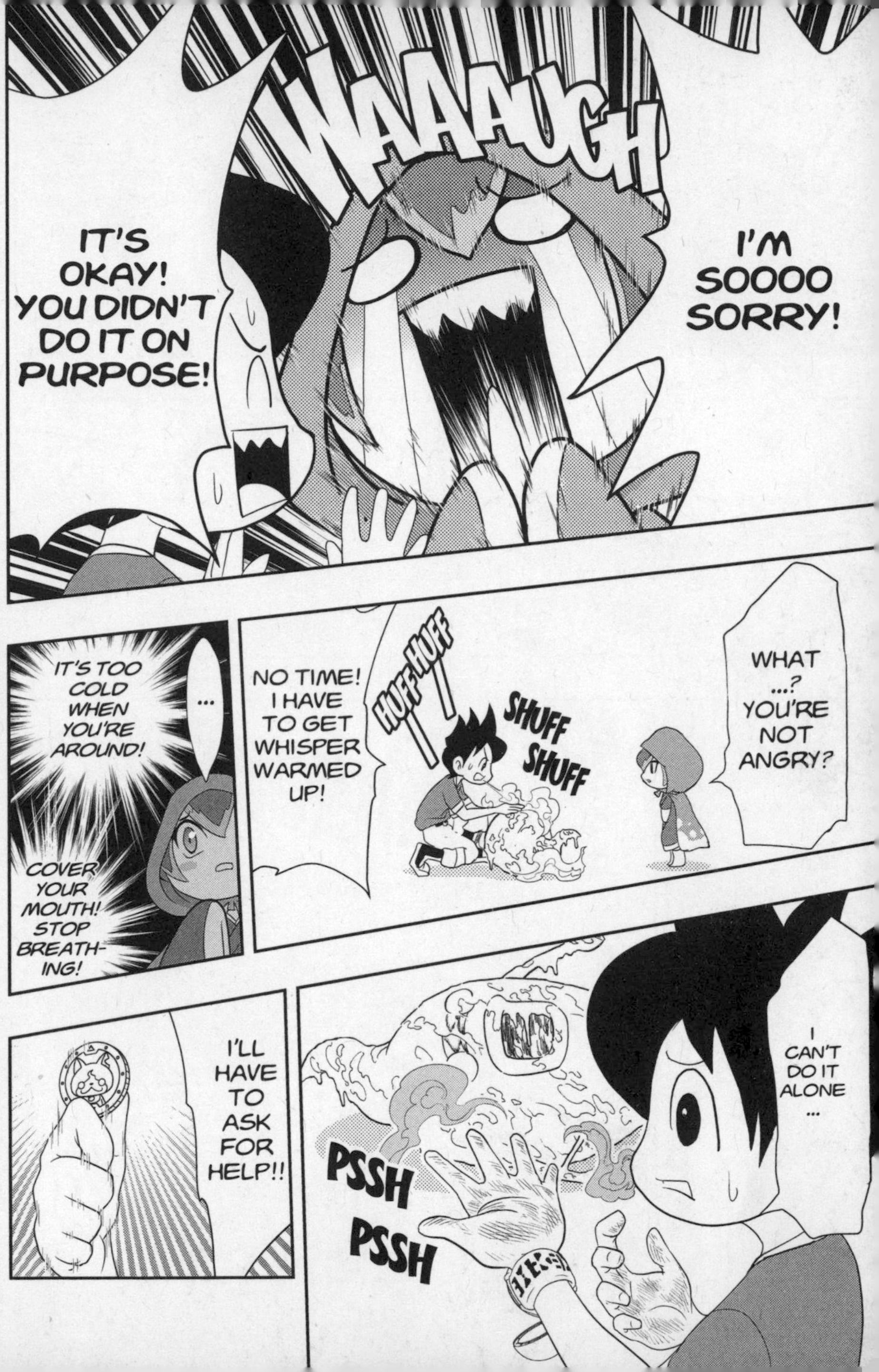
WAAAUGH
I'M SOOOO SORRY!
IT'S OKAY! YOU DIDN'T DO IT ON PURPOSE!
WHAT ...? YOU'RE NOT ANGRY?
SHUFF SHUFF
HUFF HUFF
NO TIME! I HAVE TO GET WHISPER WARMED UP!
...
IT'S TOO COLD WHEN YOU'RE AROUND!
COVER YOUR MOUTH! STOP BREATHING!
I CAN'T DO IT ALONE ...
PSSH
PSSH
I'LL HAVE TO ASK FOR HELP!!

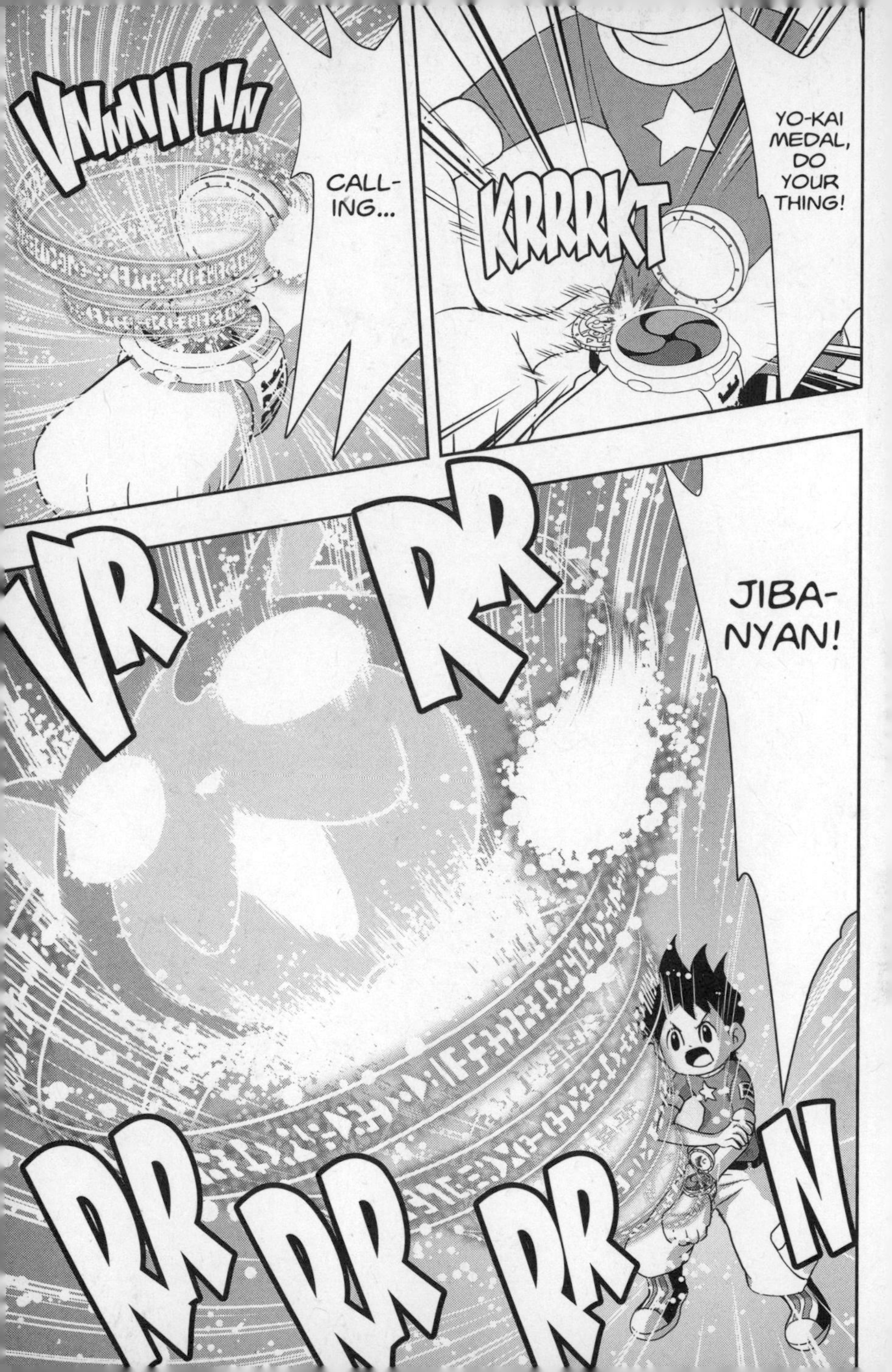
YO-KAI MEDAL, DO YOUR THING!
KRRRKT
VNNNN NN
CALL-ING...
JIBA-NYAN!
VRRR
RRRRRRN

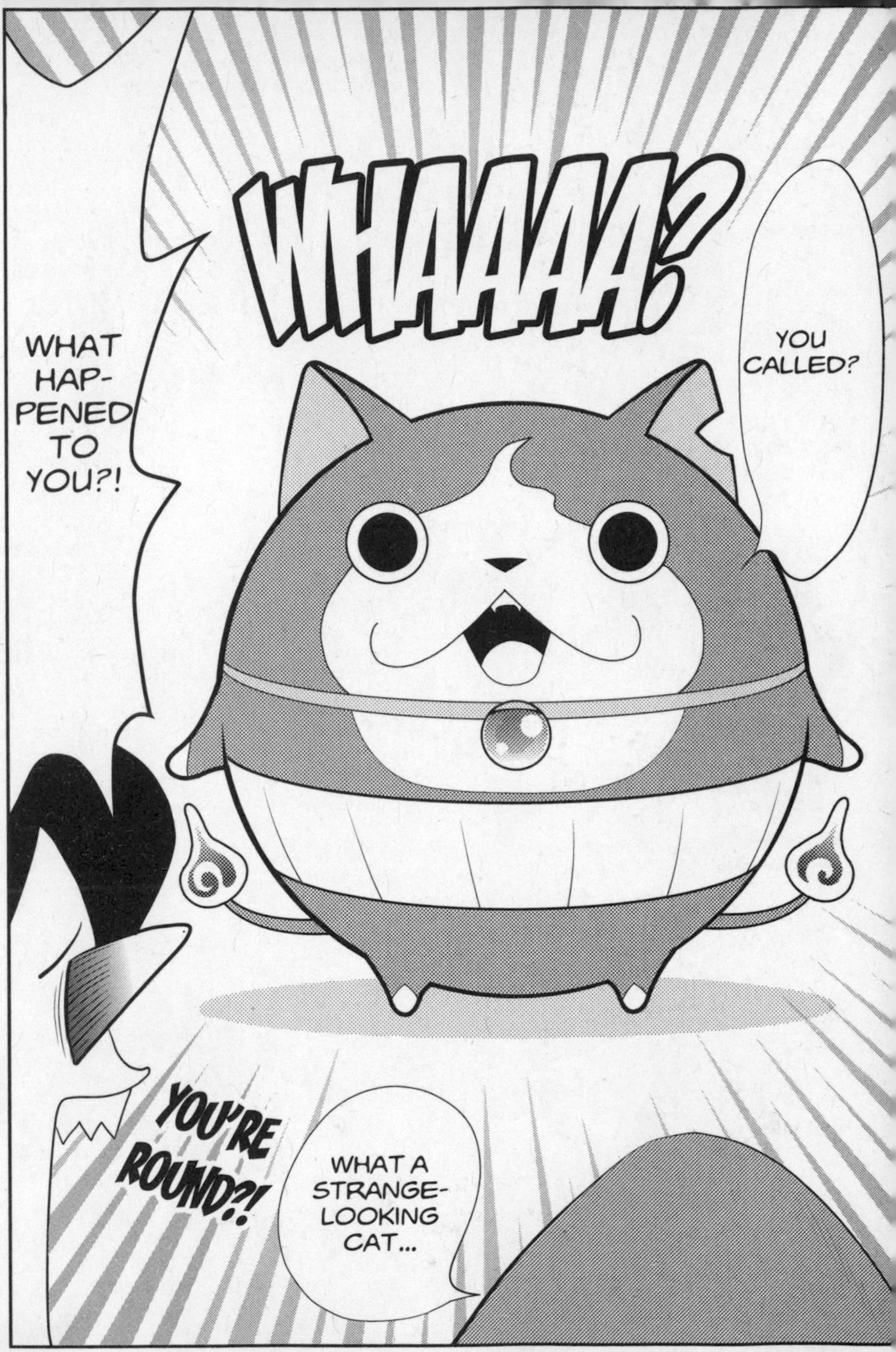
YOU CALLED?
WHAAAAA?
WHAT HAP-PENED TO YOU?!
WHAT A STRANGE-LOOKING CAT...
YOU'RE ROUND?!

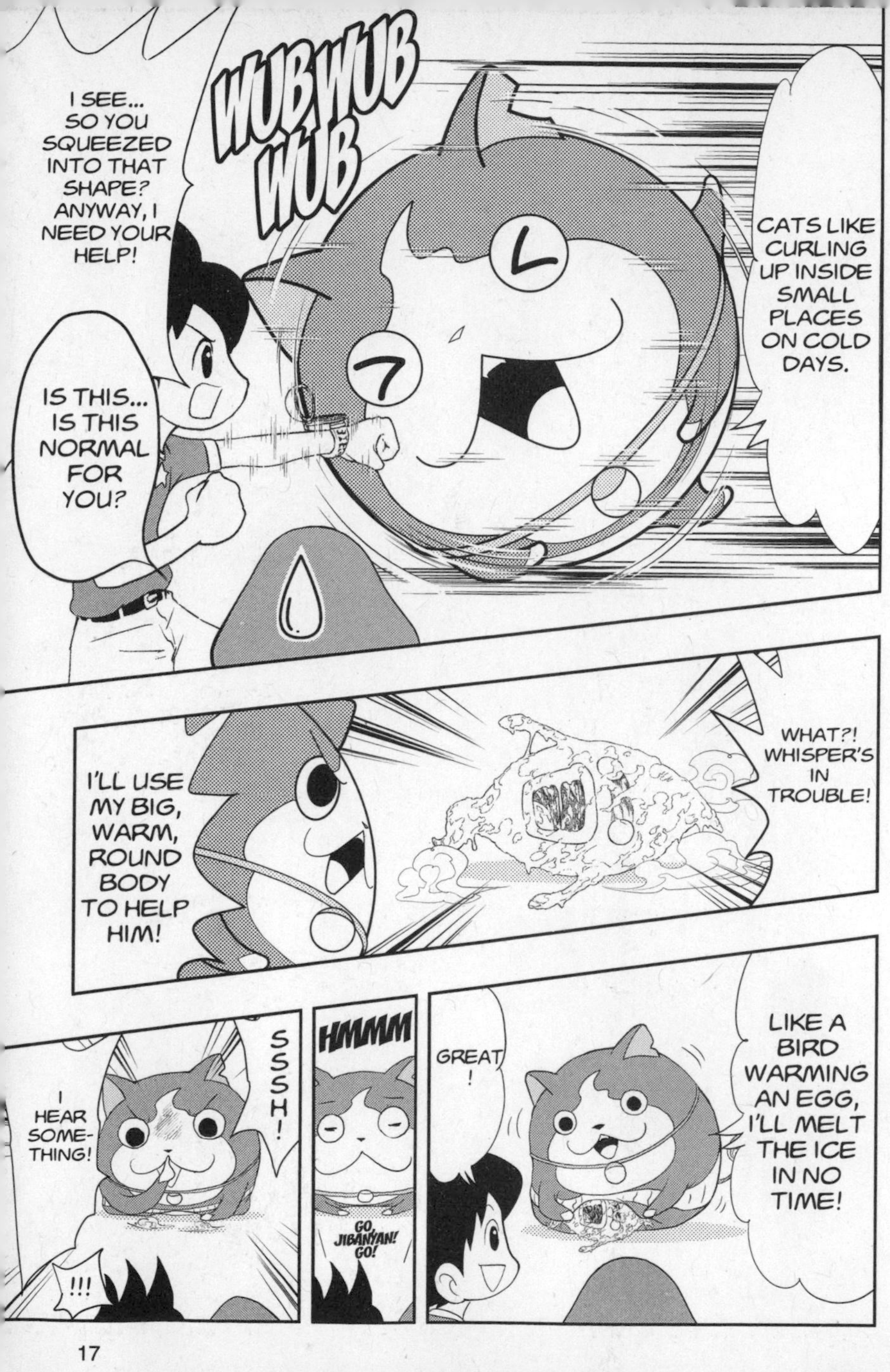
CATS LIKE CURLING UP INSIDE SMALL PLACES ON COLD DAYS.
WUB WUB WUB
I SEE... SO YOU SQUEEZED INTO THAT SHAPE? ANYWAY, I NEED YOUR HELP!
IS THIS... IS THIS NORMAL FOR YOU?
WHAT?! WHISPER'S IN TROUBLE!
I'LL USE MY BIG, WARM, ROUND BODY TO HELP HIM!
LIKE A BIRD WARMING AN EGG, I'LL MELT THE ICE IN NO TIME!
GREAT!
HMMM
GO, JIBANYAN! GO!
SSSH!
I HEAR SOME-THING!
!!!

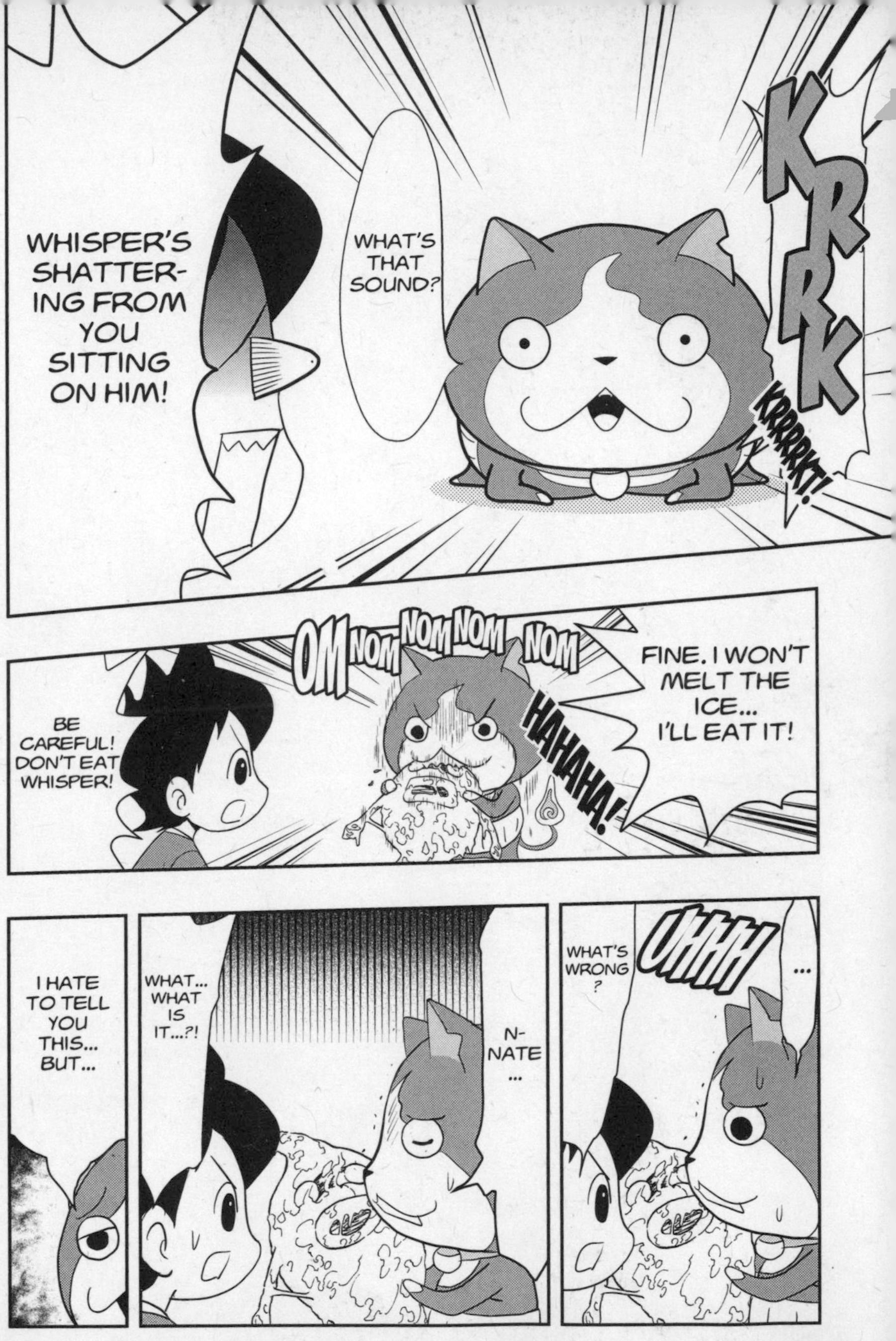
KRRK
KRRRRK!
WHAT'S THAT SOUND?
WHISPER'S SHATTER-ING FROM YOU SITTING ON HIM!
FINE. I WON'T MELT THE ICE... I'LL EAT IT!
HAHAHA!
OM NOM NOM NOM NOM
BE CAREFUL! DON'T EAT WHISPER!
UHHH
...
WHAT'S WRONG?
N-NATE...
WHAT... WHAT IS IT...?!
I HATE TO TELL YOU THIS... BUT...

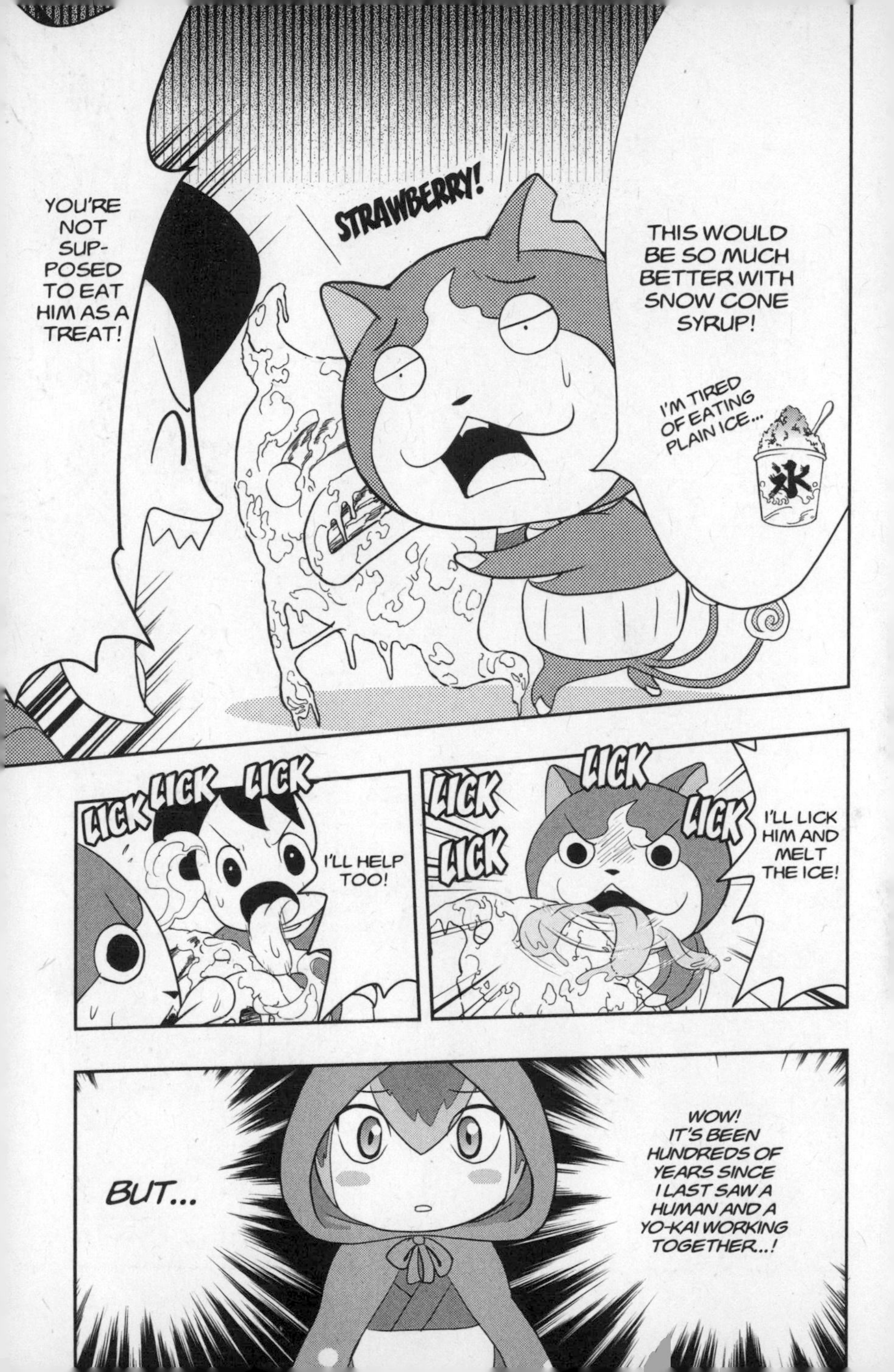
THIS WOULD BE SO MUCH BETTER WITH SNOW CONE SYRUP!
I'M TIRED OF EATING PLAIN ICE...
氷
STRAWBERRY!
YOU'RE NOT SUP-POSED TO EAT HIM AS A TREAT!
LICK
LICK
I'LL LICK HIM AND MELT THE ICE!
LICK
LICK
LICK
LICK
LICK
I'LL HELP TOO!
WOW! IT'S BEEN HUNDREDS OF YEARS SINCE I LAST SAW A HUMAN AND A YO-KAI WORKING TOGETHER...!
BUT...

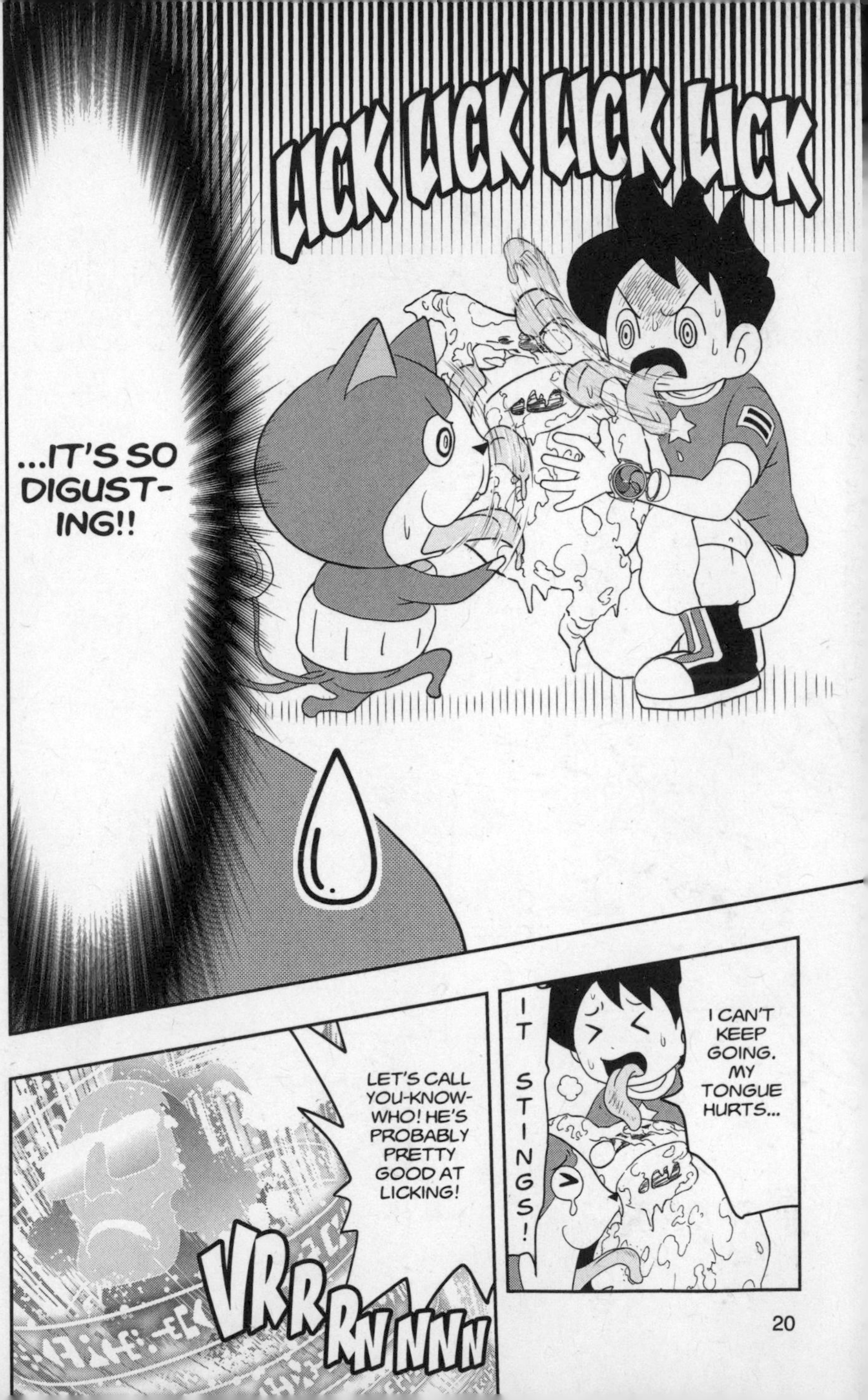
LICK LICK LICK LICK LICK
...IT'S SO DIGUST-ING!!
I CAN'T KEEP GOING. MY TONGUE HURTS...
IT STINGS!
LET'S CALL YOU-KNOW-WHO! HE'S PROBABLY PRETTY GOOD AT LICKING!
VRRRNNNNN

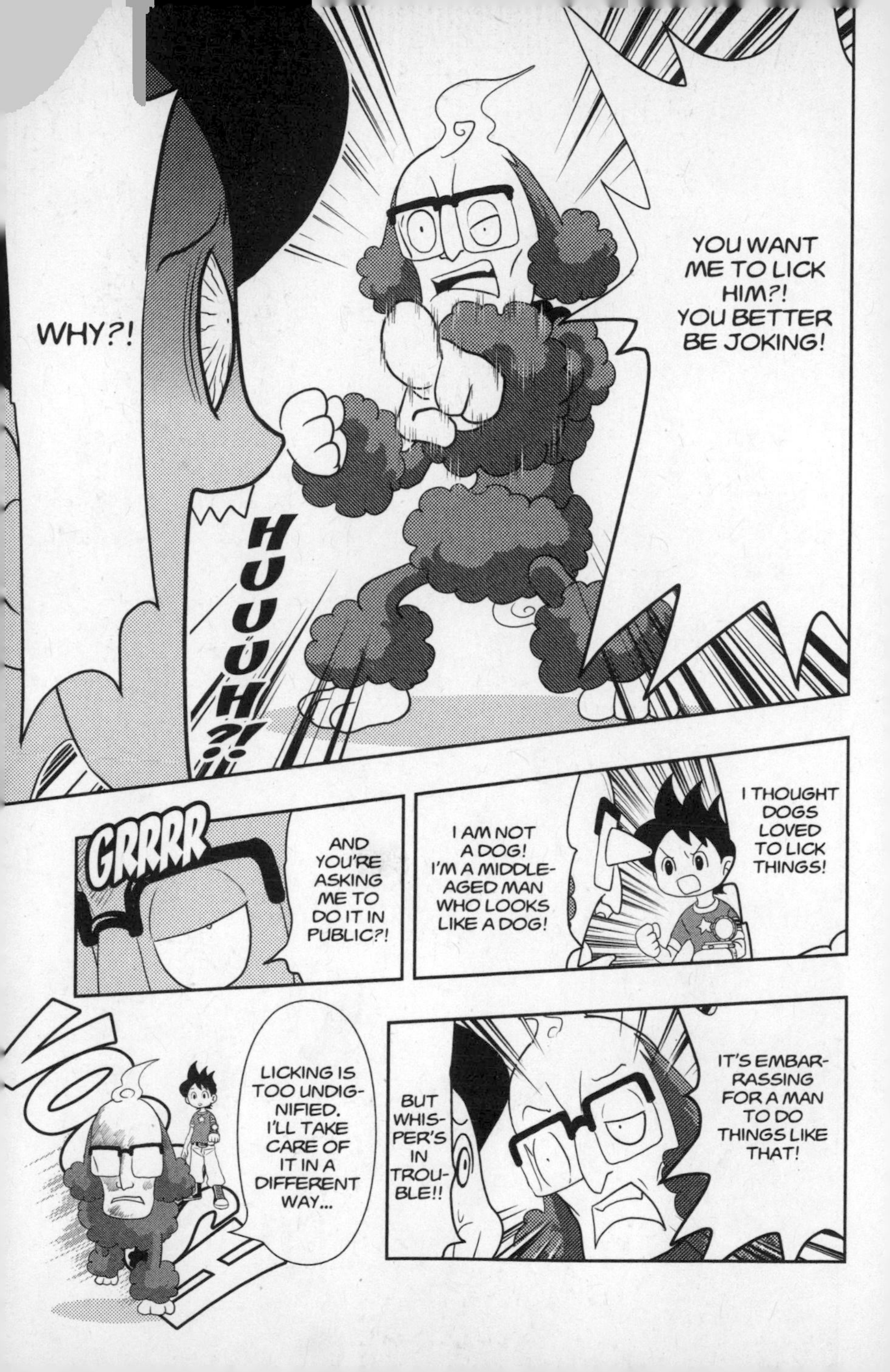
YOU WANT ME TO LICK HIM?! YOU BETTER BE JOKING!
WHY?!
HUUUUH?!
I THOUGHT DOGS LOVED TO LICK THINGS!
I AM NOT A DOG! I'M A MIDDLE-AGED MAN WHO LOOKS LIKE A DOG!
AND YOU'RE ASKING ME TO DO IT IN PUBLIC?!
GRRRR
IT'S EMBARRASSING FOR A MAN TO DO THINGS LIKE THAT!
BUT WHISPER'S IN TROUBLE!!
LICKING IS TOO UNDIGNIFIED. I'LL TAKE CARE OF IT IN A DIFFERENT WAY...

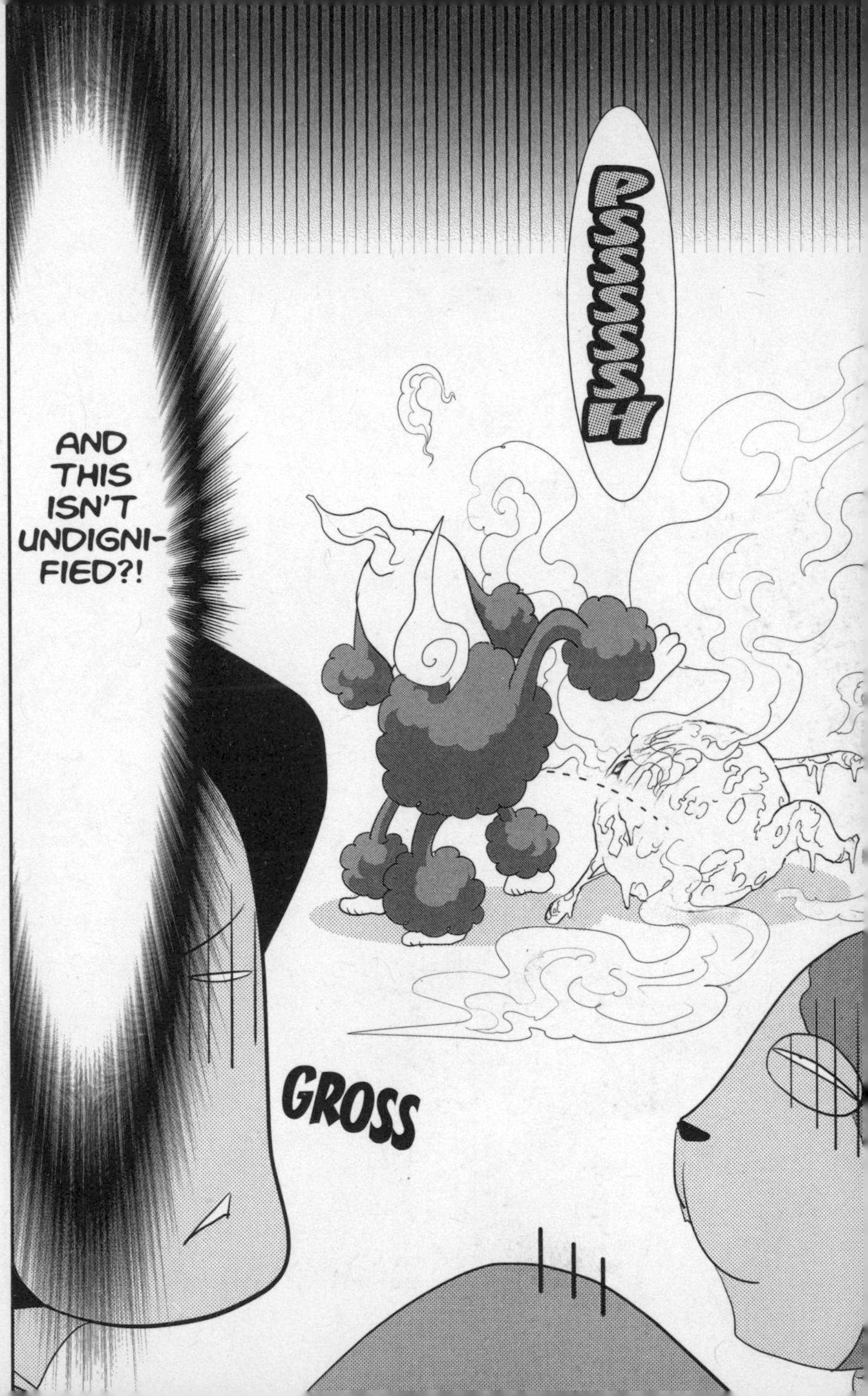
PSSSSSH
AND THIS ISN'T UNDIGNIFIED?!
GROSS

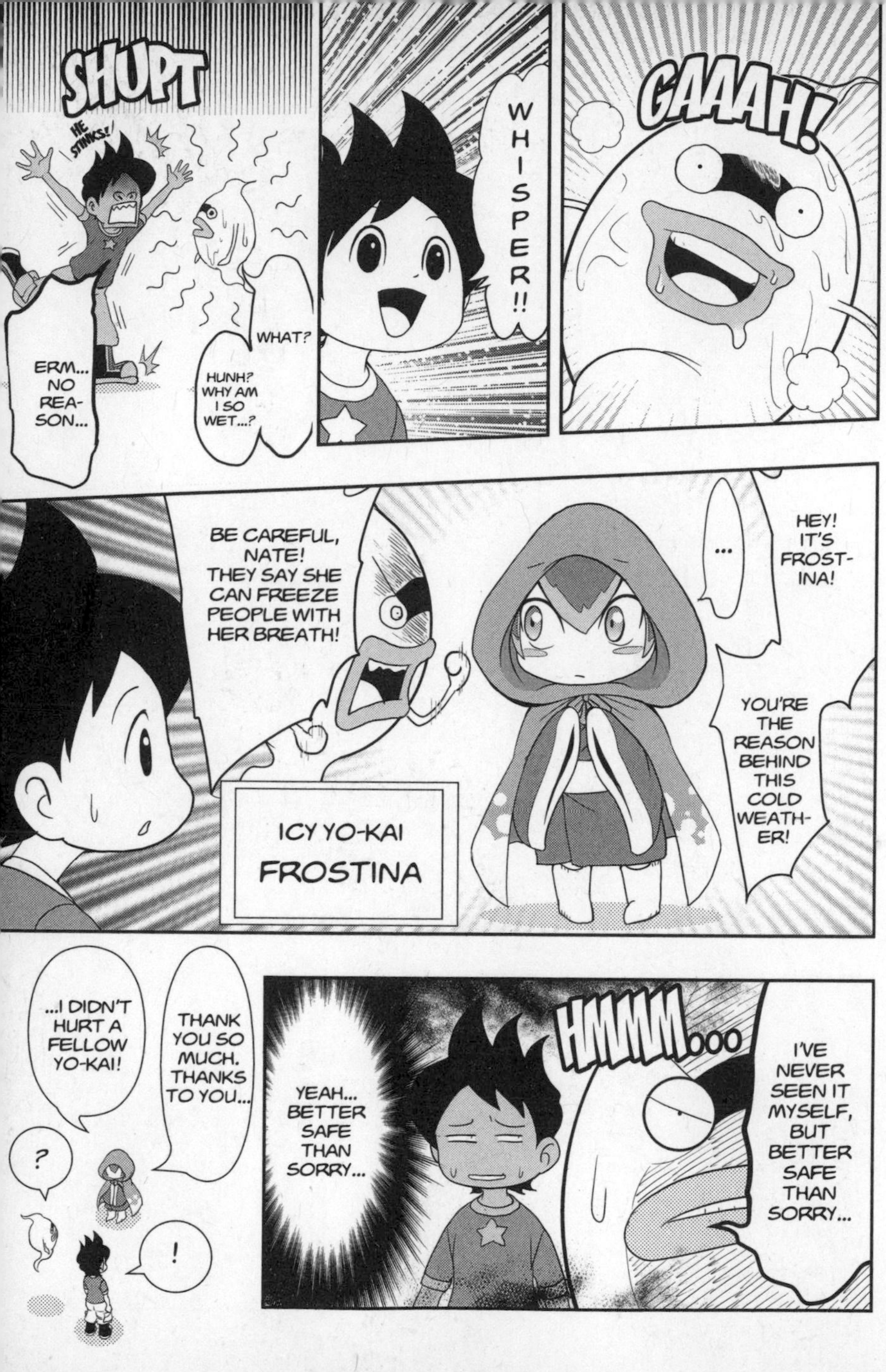
GAAAH!
WHISPER!!
SHUPT
HE STINKS!
WHAT?
HUNH? WHY AM I SO WET...?
ERM... NO REA-SON...
HEY! IT'S FROST-INA!
...
BE CAREFUL, NATE! THEY SAY SHE CAN FREEZE PEOPLE WITH HER BREATH!
YOU'RE THE REASON BEHIND THIS COLD WEATH-ER!
ICY YO-KAI
FROSTINA
HMMM...
I'VE NEVER SEEN IT MYSELF, BUT BETTER SAFE THAN SORRY...
YEAH... BETTER SAFE THAN SORRY...
THANK YOU SO MUCH. THANKS TO YOU...
...I DIDN'T HURT A FELLOW YO-KAI!
?
!

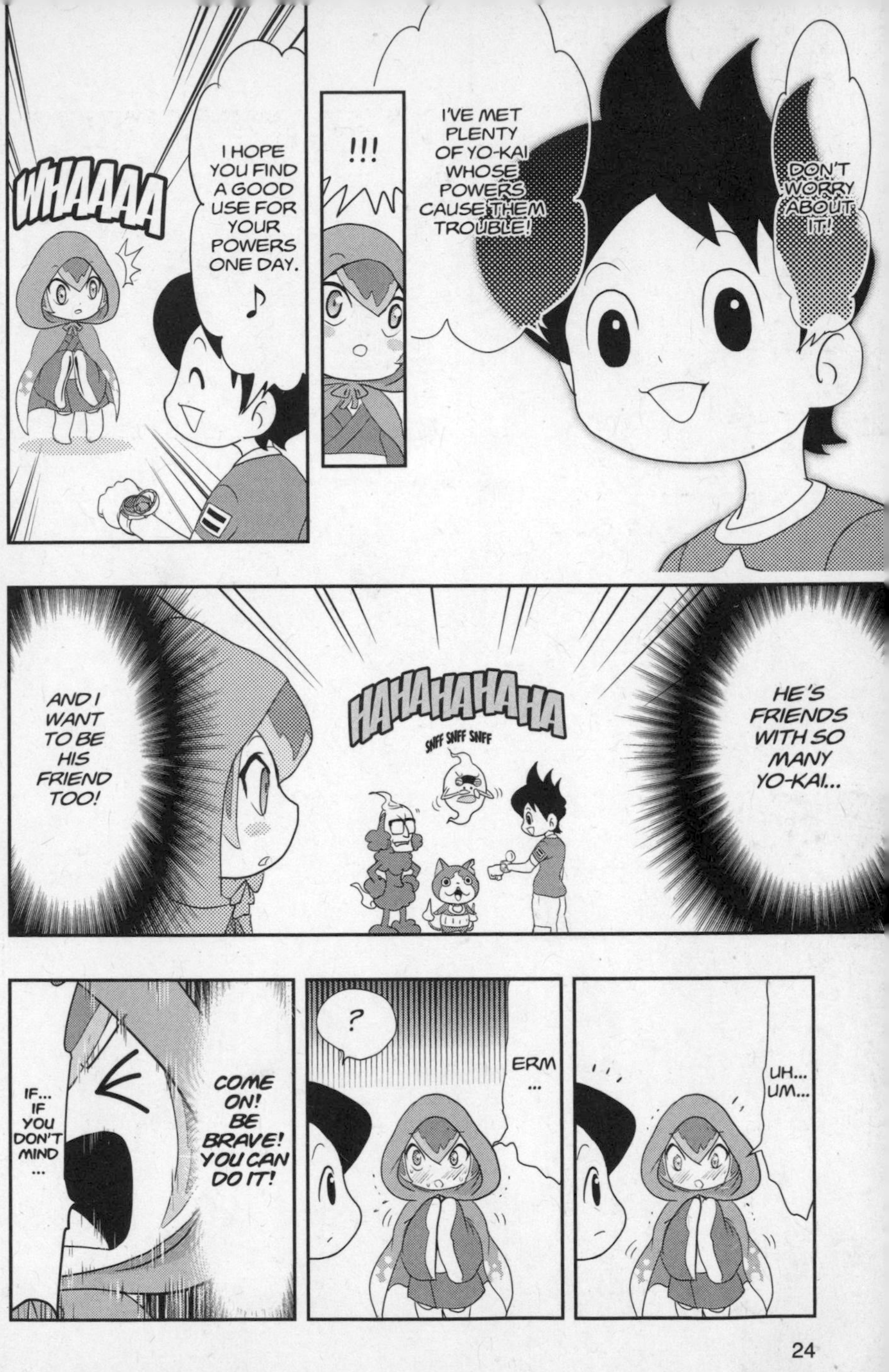
DON'T WORRY ABOUT IT!
I'VE MET PLENTY OF YO-KAI WHOSE POWERS CAUSE THEM TROUBLE!
!!!
I HOPE YOU FIND A GOOD USE FOR YOUR POWERS ONE DAY. ♪
WHAAAAA
HE'S FRIENDS WITH SO MANY YO-KAI...
HAHAHAHAHAHA
SNFF SNFF SNFF
AND I WANT TO BE HIS FRIEND TOO!
UH... UM...
ERM ...
?
COME ON! BE BRAVE! YOU CAN DO IT!
IF... IF YOU DON'T MIND ...

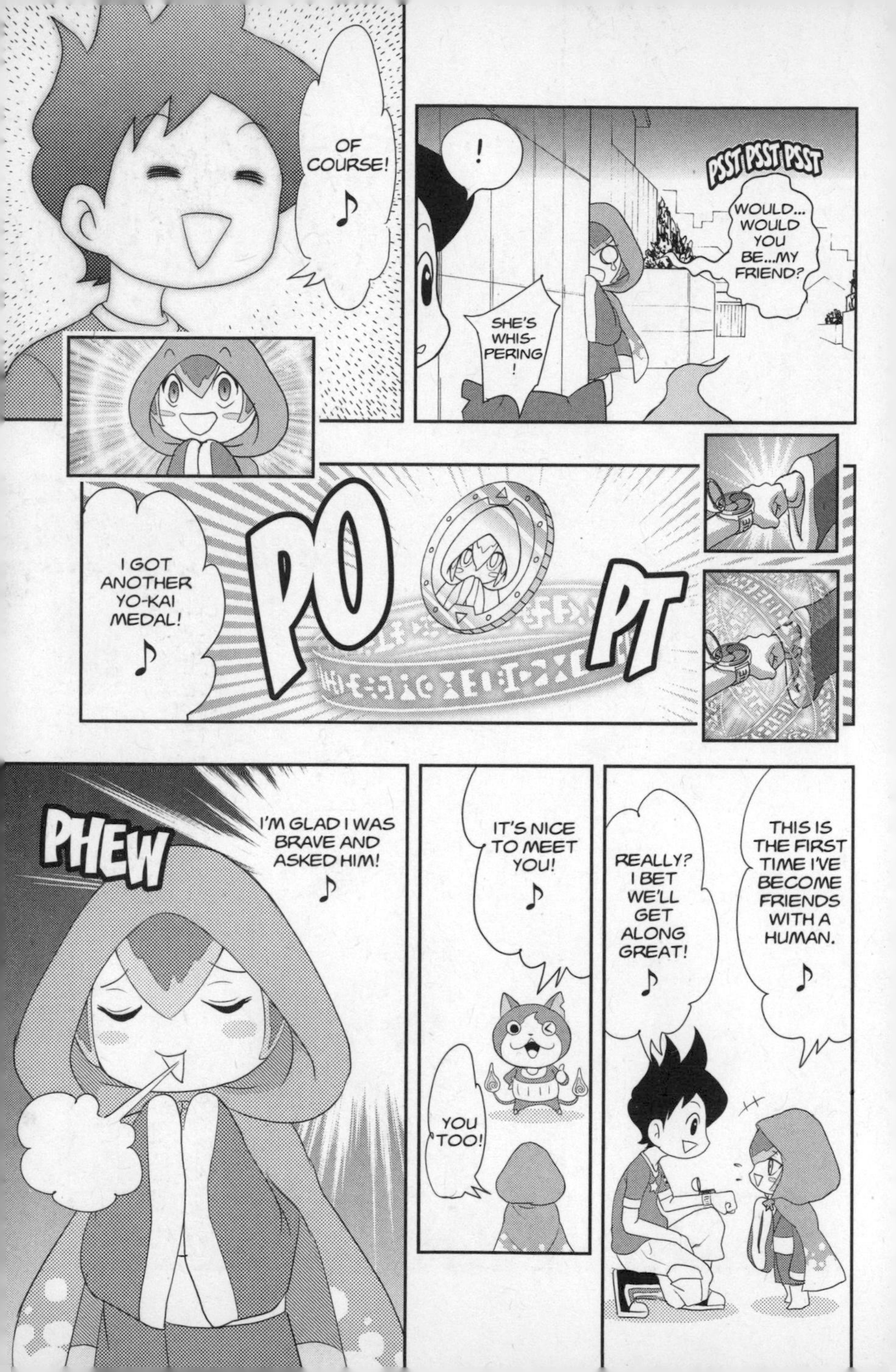
PSST PSST PSST
WOULD... WOULD YOU BE...MY FRIEND?
!
SHE'S WHISPERING!
OF COURSE! ♪
POPT
I GOT ANOTHER YO-KAI MEDAL! ♪
THIS IS THE FIRST TIME I'VE BECOME FRIENDS WITH A HUMAN. ♪
REALLY? I BET WE'LL GET ALONG GREAT! ♪
IT'S NICE TO MEET YOU! ♪
YOU TOO!
I'M GLAD I WAS BRAVE AND ASKED HIM! ♪
PHEW

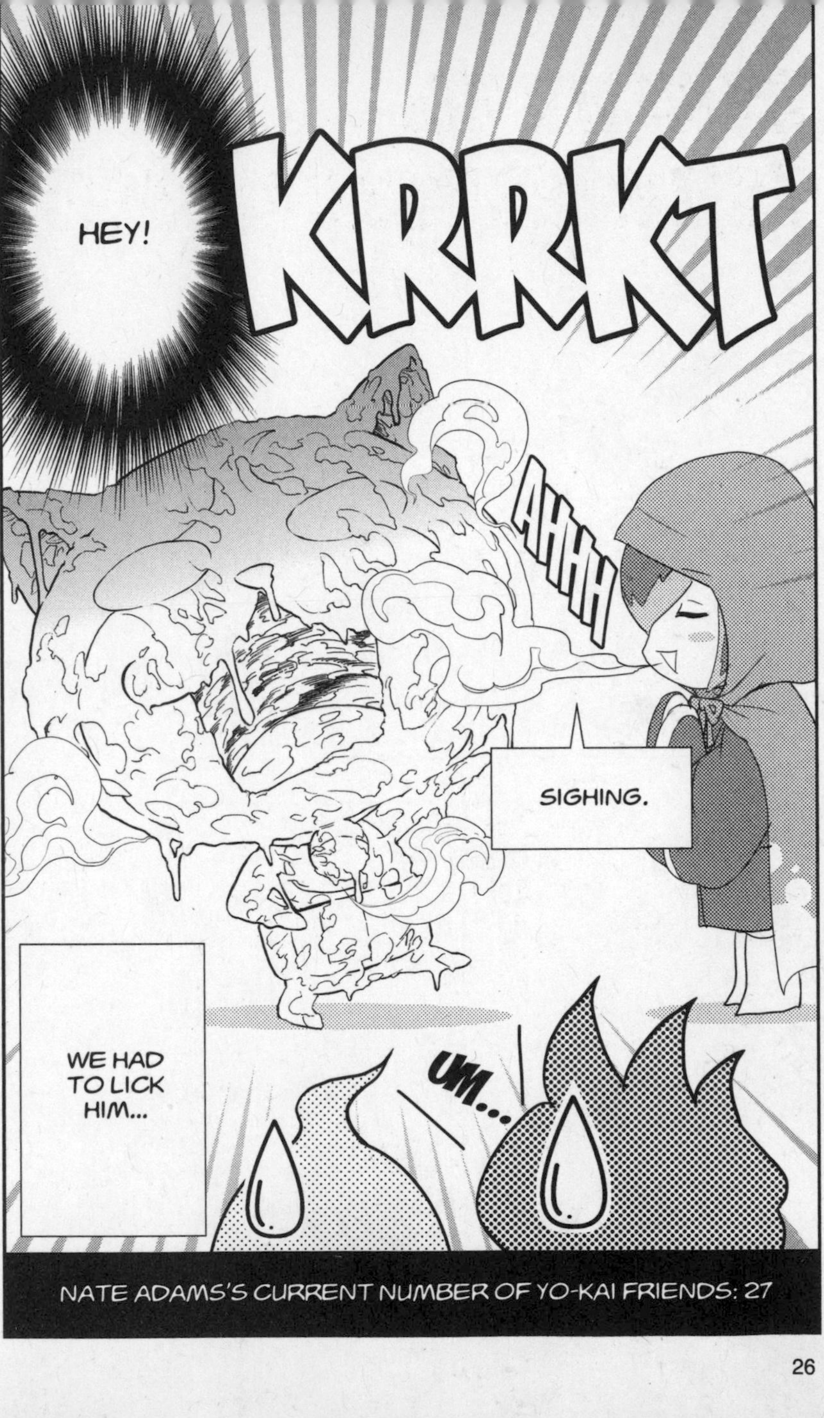
KRRKT
HEY!
AHHH
SIGHING.
UM...
WE HAD TO LICK HIM...
NATE ADAMS'S CURRENT NUMBER OF YO-KAI FRIENDS: 27

CHAPTER 36: SUMMON YOUR COURAGE!

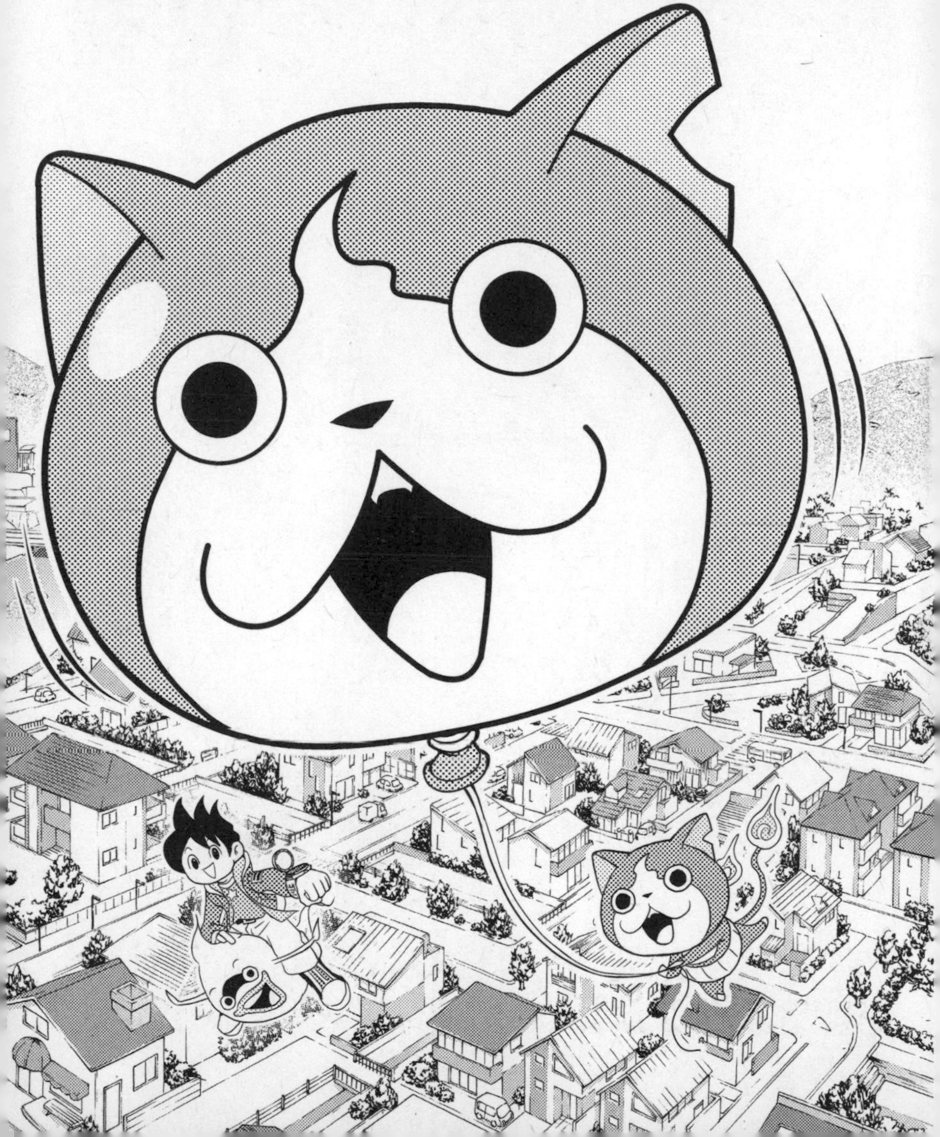

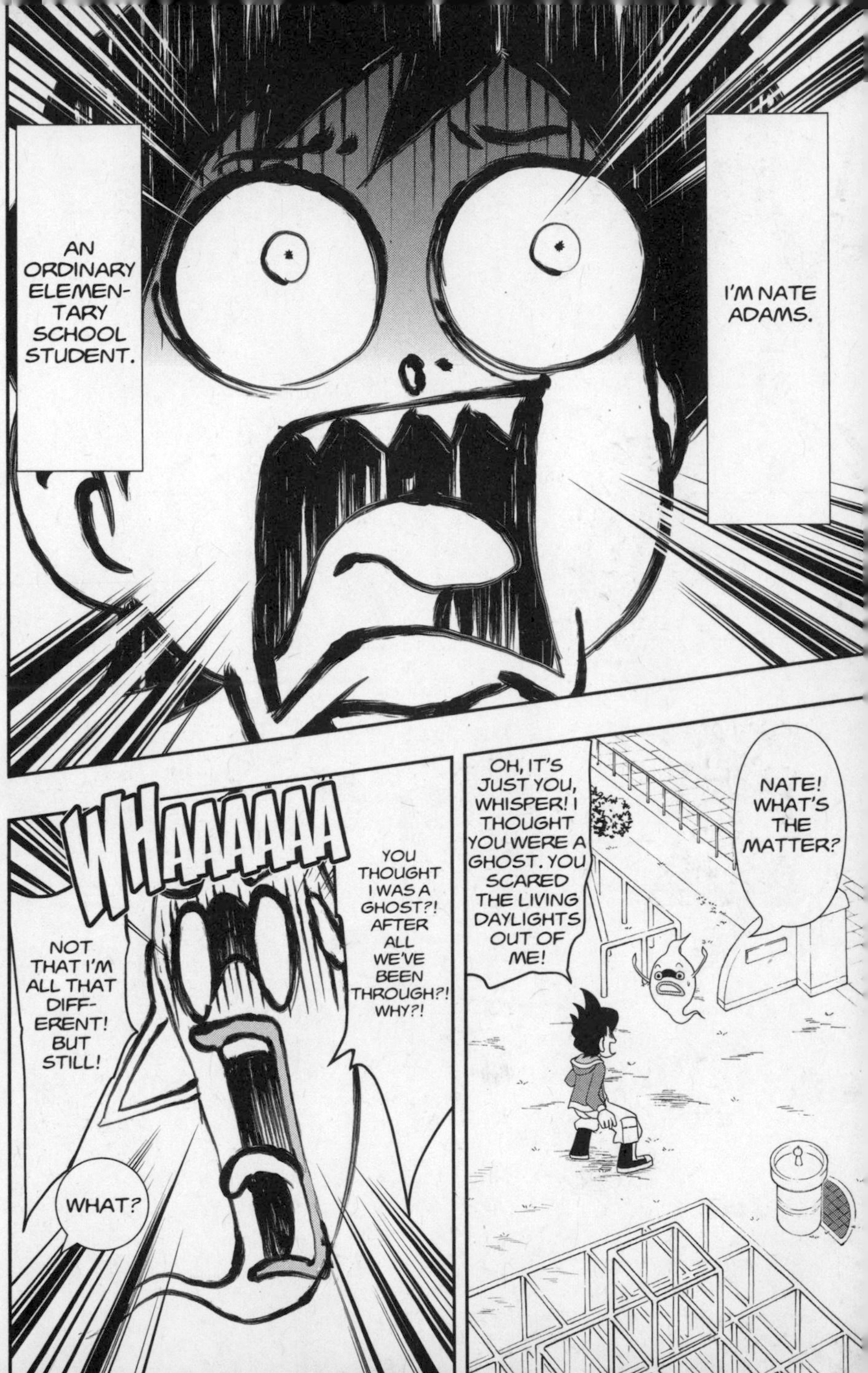
I'M NATE ADAMS.
AN ORDINARY ELEMENTARY SCHOOL STUDENT.
NATE! WHAT'S THE MATTER?
OH, IT'S JUST YOU, WHISPER! I THOUGHT YOU WERE A GHOST. YOU SCARED THE LIVING DAYLIGHTS OUT OF ME!
WHAAAAAA
YOU THOUGHT I WAS A GHOST?! AFTER ALL WE'VE BEEN THROUGH?! WHY?!
NOT THAT I'M ALL THAT DIFFERENT! BUT STILL!
WHAT?

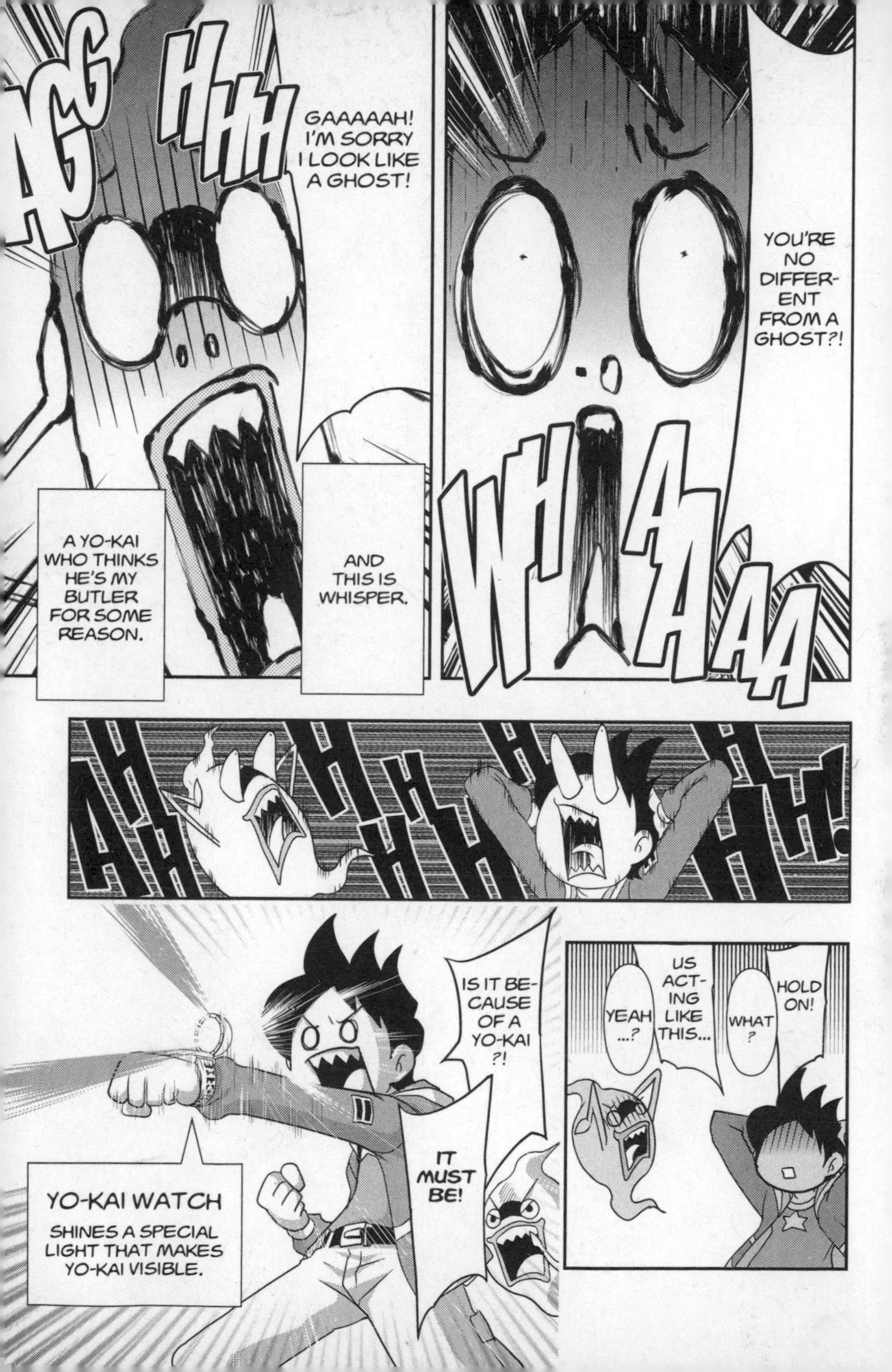
YOU'RE NO DIFFERENT FROM A GHOST?!
WHAAAA
GAAAAAH! I'M SORRY I LOOK LIKE A GHOST!
AGGHHH
AND THIS IS WHISPER.
A YO-KAI WHO THINKS HE'S MY BUTLER FOR SOME REASON.
AHHHHHHHHH!
HOLD ON!
WHAT?
US ACTING LIKE THIS...
YEAH...?
IS IT BECAUSE OF A YO-KAI?!
IT MUST BE!
YO-KAI WATCH
SHINES A SPECIAL LIGHT THAT MAKES YO-KAI VISIBLE.

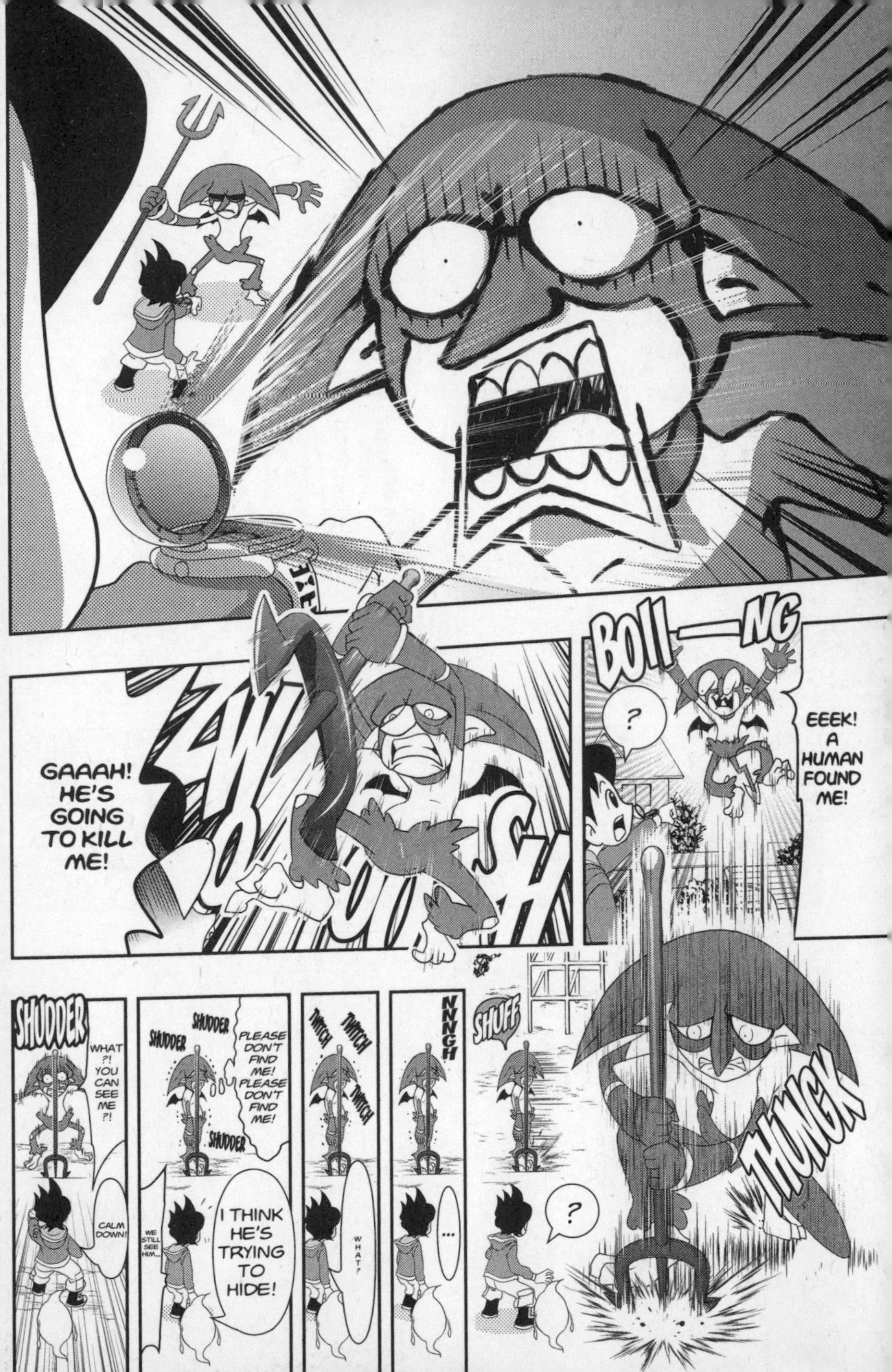
BOII—NG
?
EEEK! A HUMAN FOUND ME!
GAAAH! HE'S GOING TO KILL ME!
ZWOOSH
THUNGK
SHUFF
?
NNNGH
...
TWITCH TWITCH TWITCH
WHAT?
SHUDDER SHUDDER SHUDDER
PLEASE DON'T FIND ME! PLEASE DON'T FIND ME!
I THINK HE'S TRYING TO HIDE!
WE STILL SEE HIM...
SHUDDER
WHAT?! YOU CAN SEE ME?!
CALM DOWN!

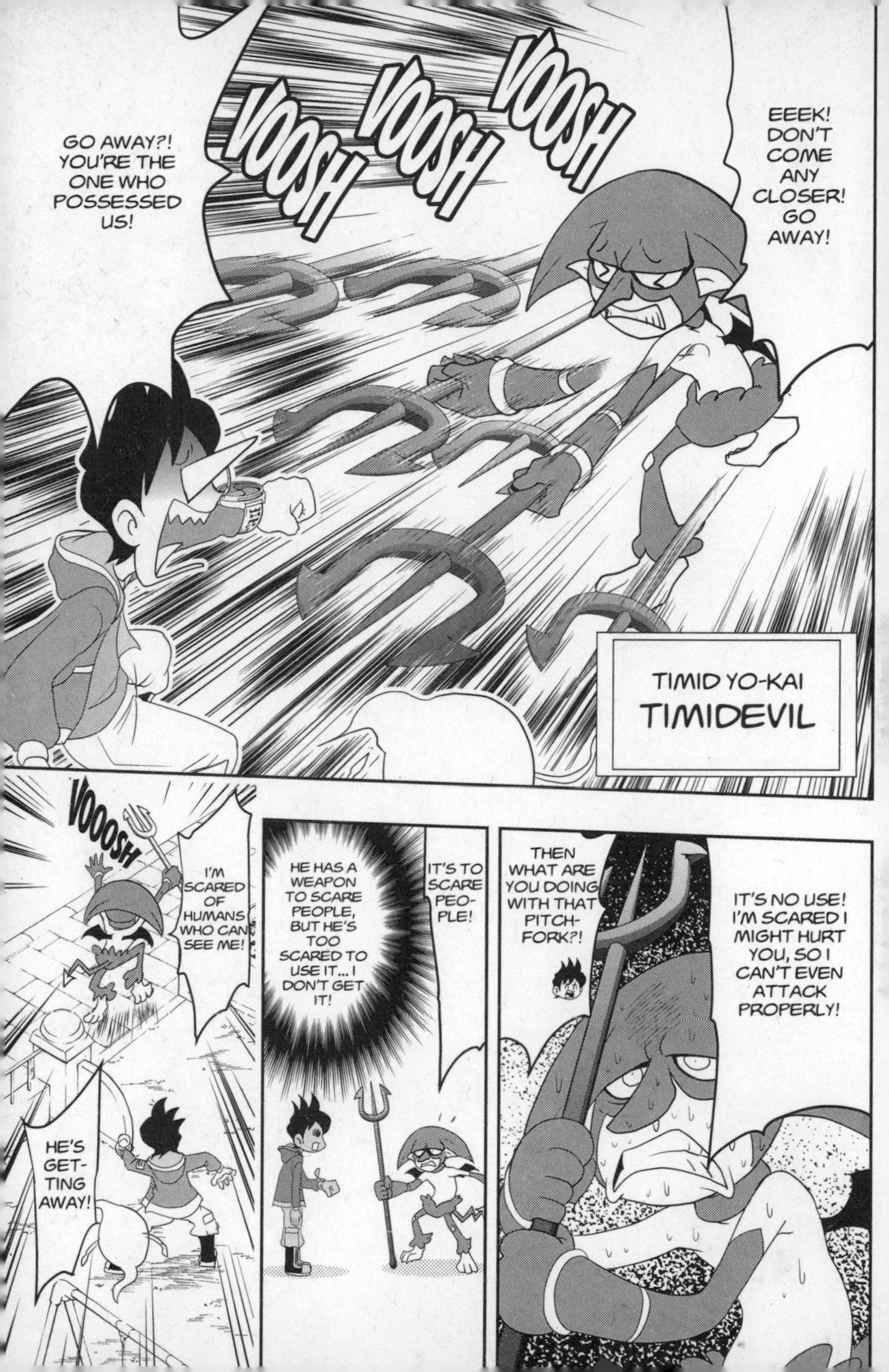
EEEK! DON'T COME ANY CLOSER! GO AWAY!
VOOSH
VOOSH
VOOSH
GO AWAY?! YOU'RE THE ONE WHO POSSESSED US!
TIMID YO-KAI
TIMIDEVIL
THEN WHAT ARE YOU DOING WITH THAT PITCH-FORK?!
IT'S NO USE! I'M SCARED I MIGHT HURT YOU, SO I CAN'T EVEN ATTACK PROPERLY!
IT'S TO SCARE PEO-PLE!
HE HAS A WEAPON TO SCARE PEOPLE, BUT HE'S TOO SCARED TO USE IT... I DON'T GET IT!
I'M SCARED OF HUMANS WHO CAN SEE ME!
VOOOSH
HE'S GET-TING AWAY!

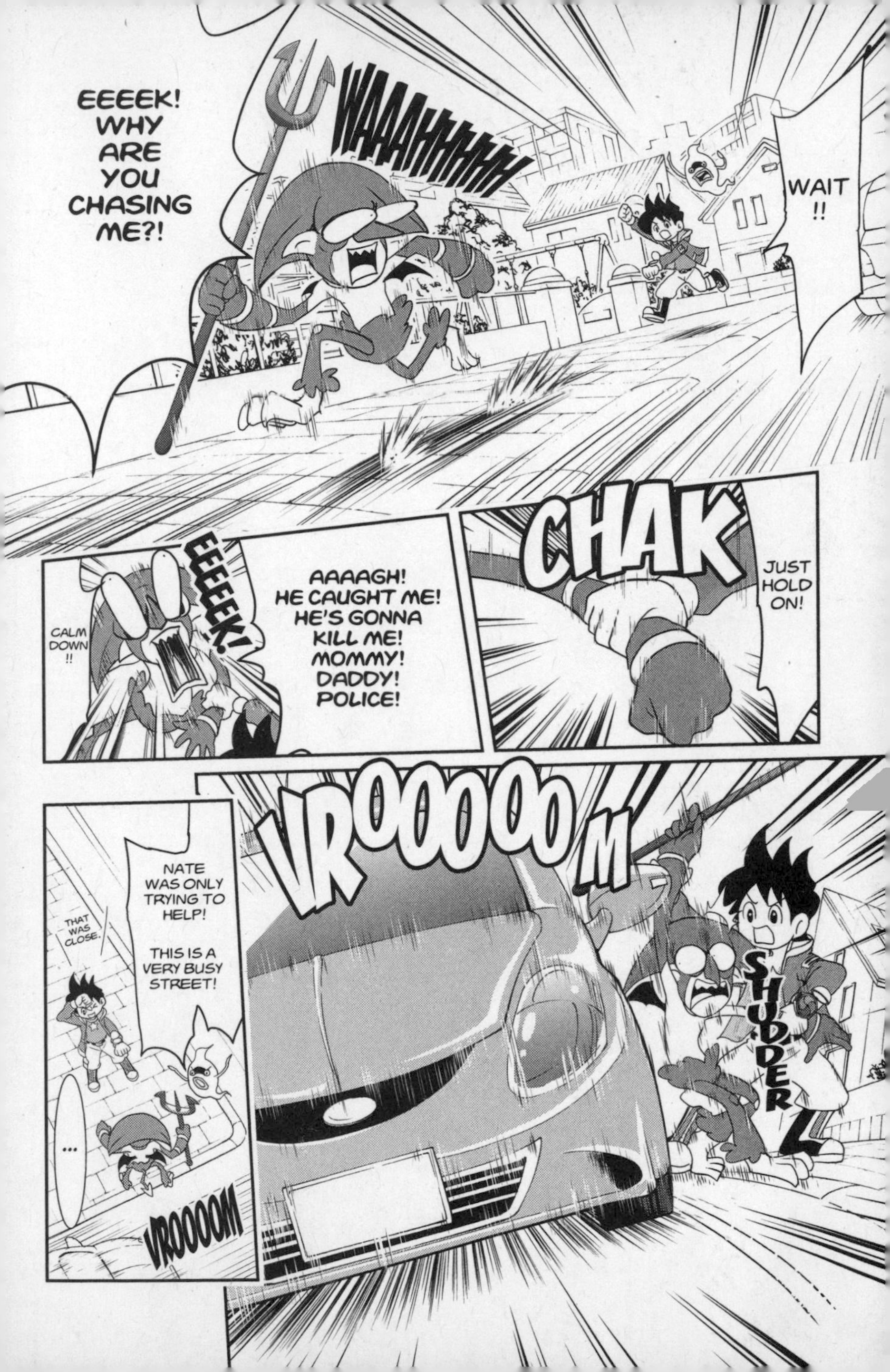
WAIT !!
WAAAHHHHHHH
EEEEK! WHY ARE YOU CHASING ME?!
CHAK
JUST HOLD ON!
EEEEEK!
AAAAGH! HE CAUGHT ME! HE'S GONNA KILL ME! MOMMY! DADDY! POLICE!
CALM DOWN !!
VROOOOOOM
SHUDDER
NATE WAS ONLY TRYING TO HELP!
THIS IS A VERY BUSY STREET!
THAT WAS CLOSE.
...
VROOOOM

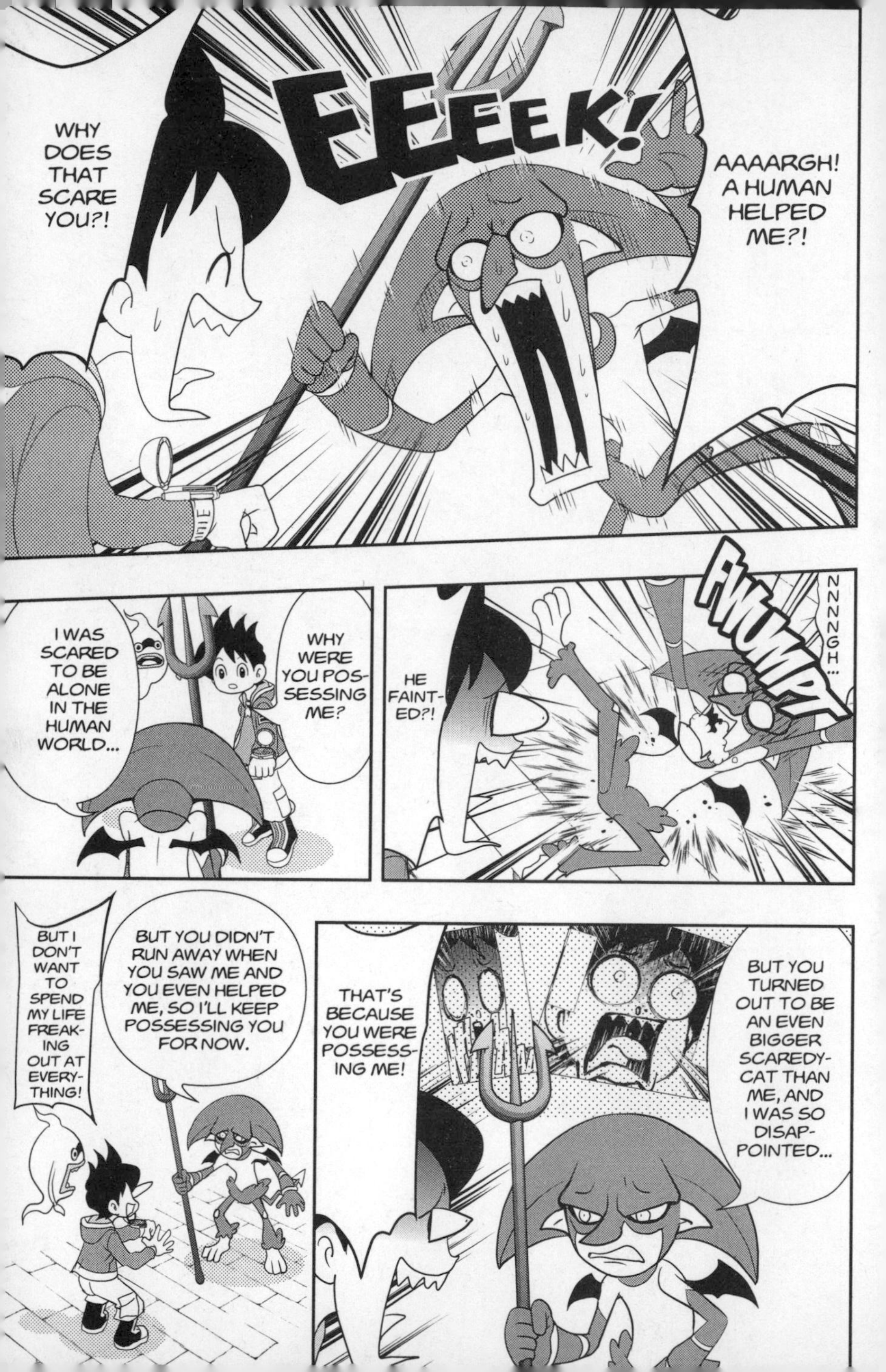
AAAARGH! A HUMAN HELPED ME?!
EEEEK!
WHY DOES THAT SCARE YOU?!
FWUMP!
NNNNGH...
HE FAINTED?!
WHY WERE YOU POSSESSING ME?
I WAS SCARED TO BE ALONE IN THE HUMAN WORLD...
BUT YOU TURNED OUT TO BE AN EVEN BIGGER SCAREDY-CAT THAN ME, AND I WAS SO DISAPPOINTED...
THAT'S BECAUSE YOU WERE POSSESSING ME!
BUT YOU DIDN'T RUN AWAY WHEN YOU SAW ME AND YOU EVEN HELPED ME, SO I'LL KEEP POSSESSING YOU FOR NOW.
BUT I DON'T WANT TO SPEND MY LIFE FREAKING OUT AT EVERYTHING!

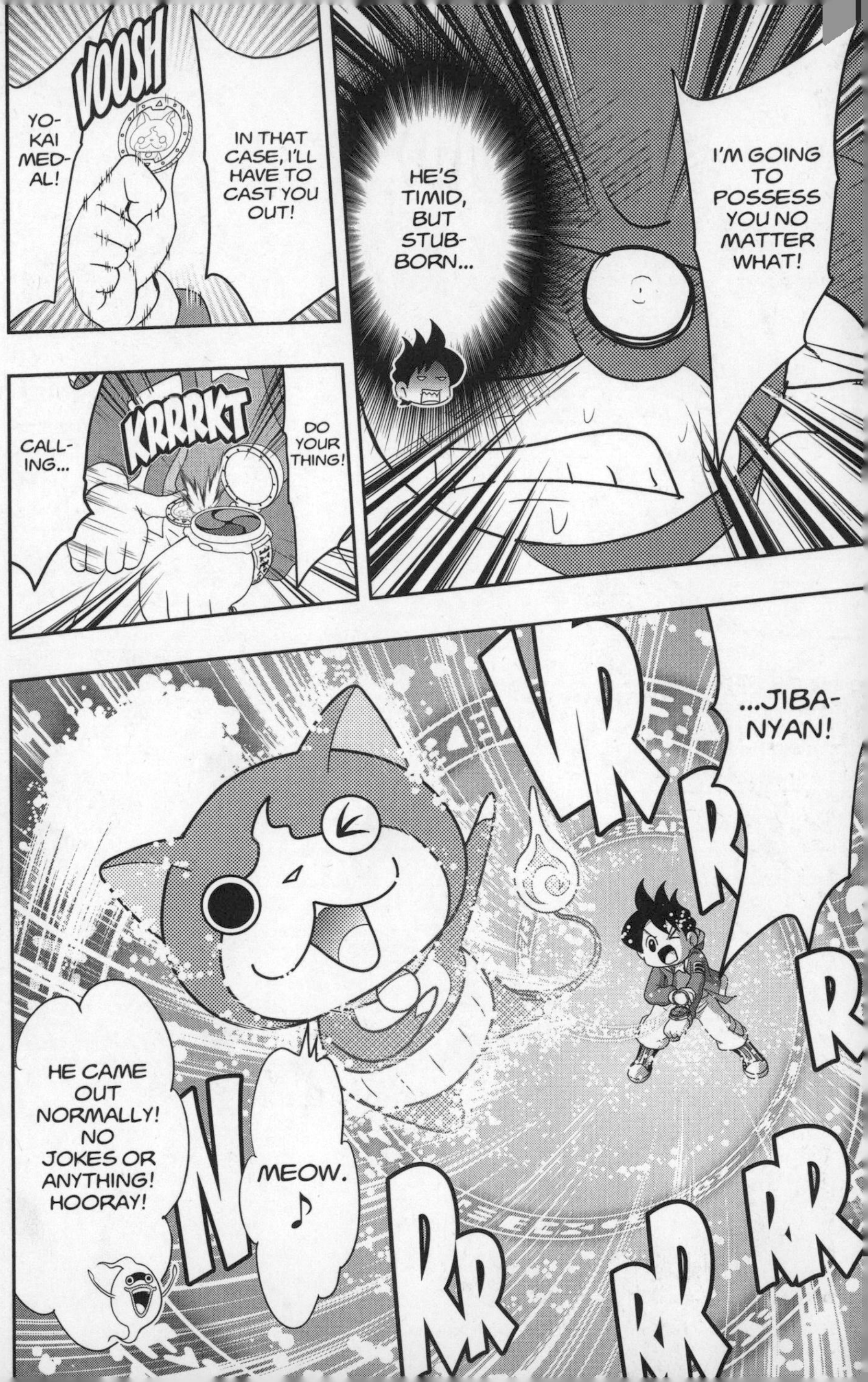
I'M GOING TO POSSESS YOU NO MATTER WHAT!
HE'S TIMID, BUT STUBBORN...
IN THAT CASE, I'LL HAVE TO CAST YOU OUT!
VOOSH
YO-KAI MEDAL!
DO YOUR THING!
KRRRKT
CALLING...
...JIBANYAN!
VRRRR
MEOW. ♪
NRRRRRR
HE CAME OUT NORMALLY! NO JOKES OR ANYTHING! HOORAY!

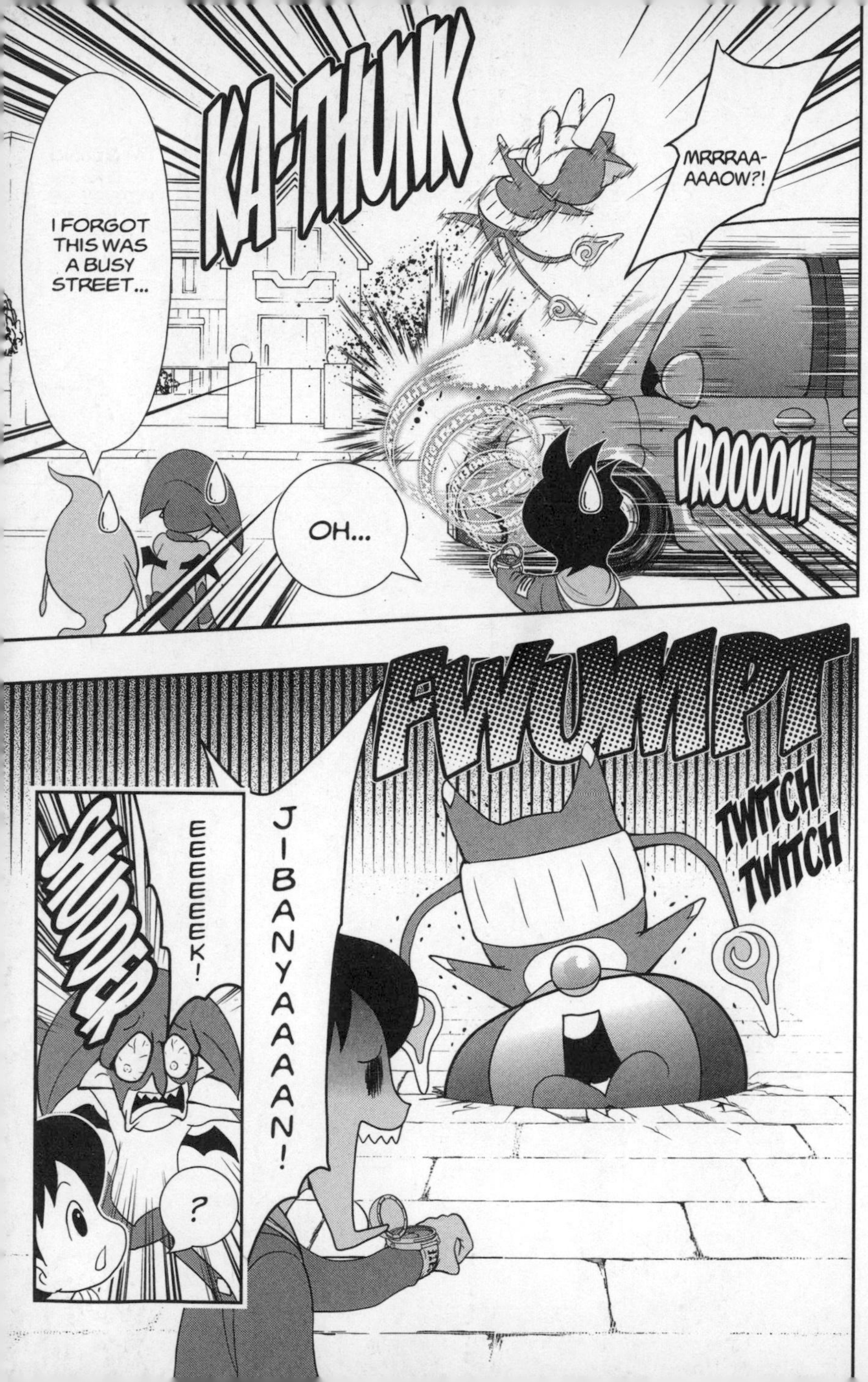
MRRRAA-AAAOW?!
KA-THUNK
I FORGOT THIS WAS A BUSY STREET...
VROOOOM
OH...
FWUMMPT
TWITCH TWITCH
JIBANYAAAAAN!
EEEEEEK!
SHUDDER
?

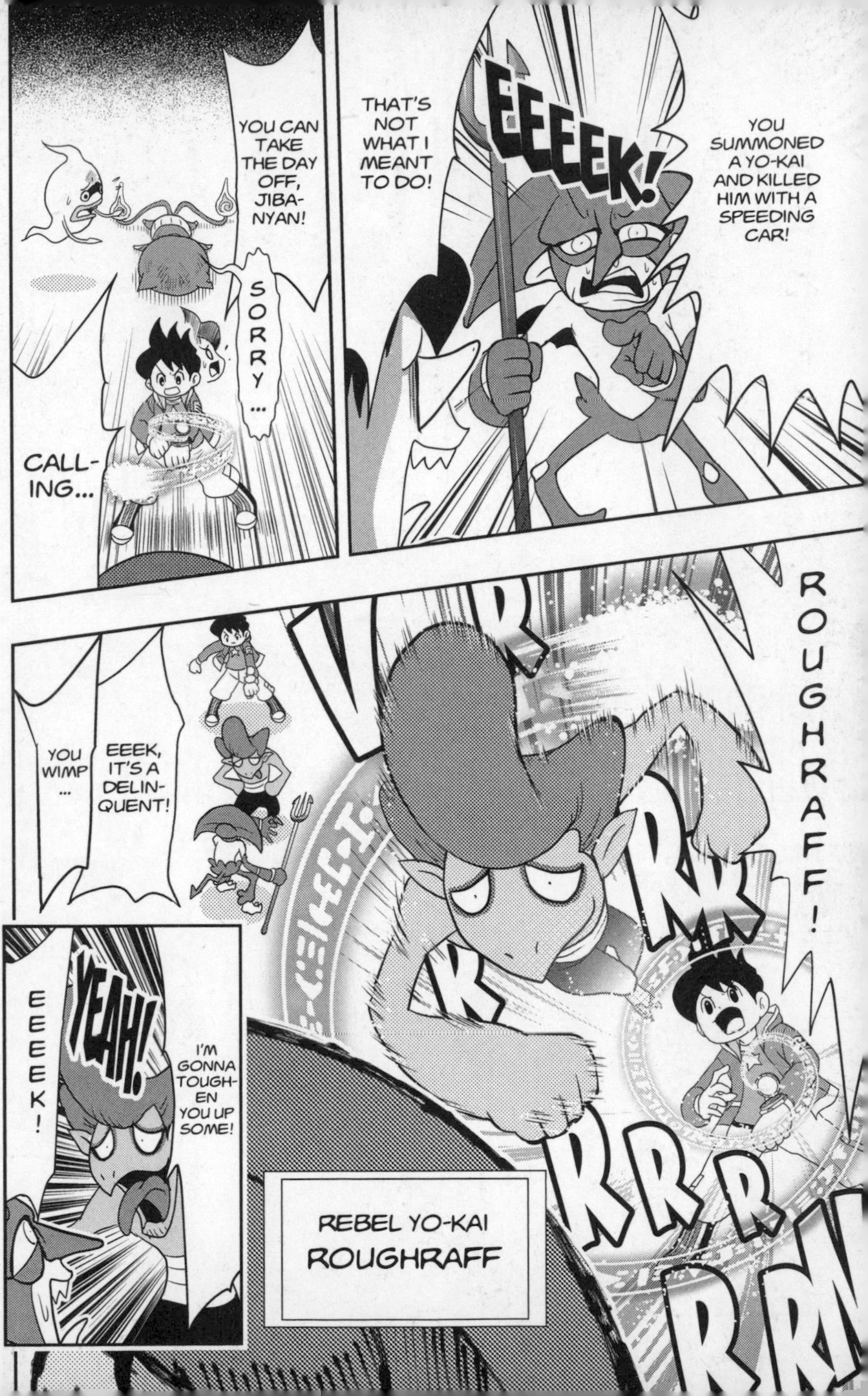

YOU SUMMONED A YO-KAI AND KILLED HIM WITH A SPEEDING CAR!
EEEEK!
THAT'S NOT WHAT I MEANT TO DO!
YOU CAN TAKE THE DAY OFF, JIBA-NYAN!
SORRY...
CALLING...
ROUGHRAFF!
REBEL YO-KAI ROUGHRAFF
EEEK, IT'S A DELIN-QUENT!
YOU WIMP...
YEAH!
I'M GONNA TOUGH-EN YOU UP SOME!
EEEEEK!

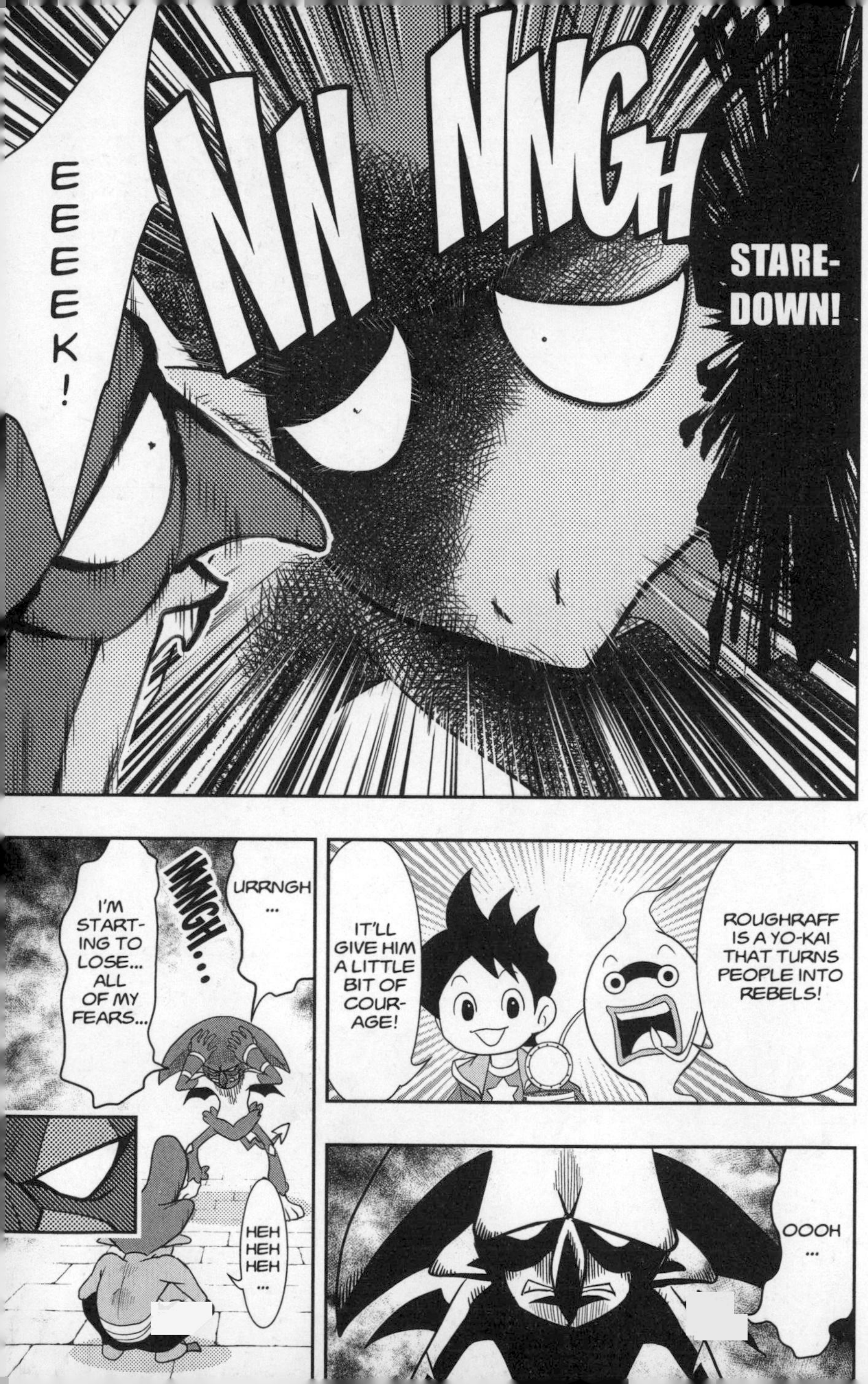
STARE-DOWN!
NN NNGH
EEEEEK!
ROUGHRAFF IS A YO-KAI THAT TURNS PEOPLE INTO REBELS!
IT'LL GIVE HIM A LITTLE BIT OF COURAGE!
URRNGH ...
NNNGH!...
I'M STARTING TO LOSE... ALL OF MY FEARS...
OOOH ...
HEH HEH HEH ...

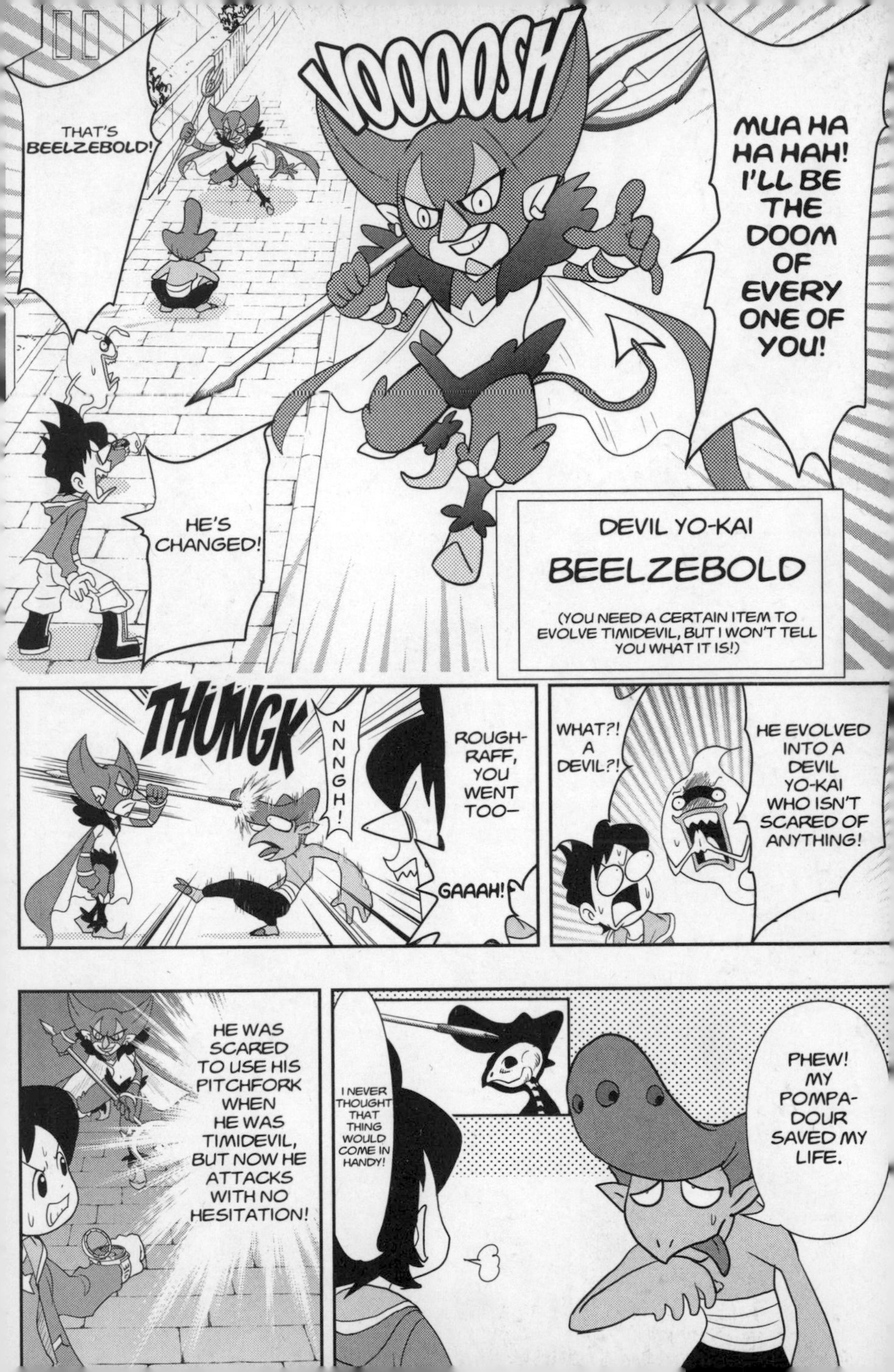

VOOOOSH
MUA HA HA HAH! I'LL BE THE DOOM OF EVERY ONE OF YOU!
THAT'S BEELZEBOLD!
DEVIL YO-KAI
BEELZEBOLD
(YOU NEED A CERTAIN ITEM TO EVOLVE TIMIDEVIL, BUT I WON'T TELL YOU WHAT IT IS!)
HE'S CHANGED!
HE EVOLVED INTO A DEVIL YO-KAI WHO ISN'T SCARED OF ANYTHING!
WHAT?! A DEVIL?!
ROUGH-RAFF, YOU WENT TOO—
NNNGH!
THUNGK
GAAAH!
PHEW! MY POMPA-DOUR SAVED MY LIFE.
I NEVER THOUGHT THAT THING WOULD COME IN HANDY!
HE WAS SCARED TO USE HIS PITCHFORK WHEN HE WAS TIMIDEVIL, BUT NOW HE ATTACKS WITH NO HESITATION!

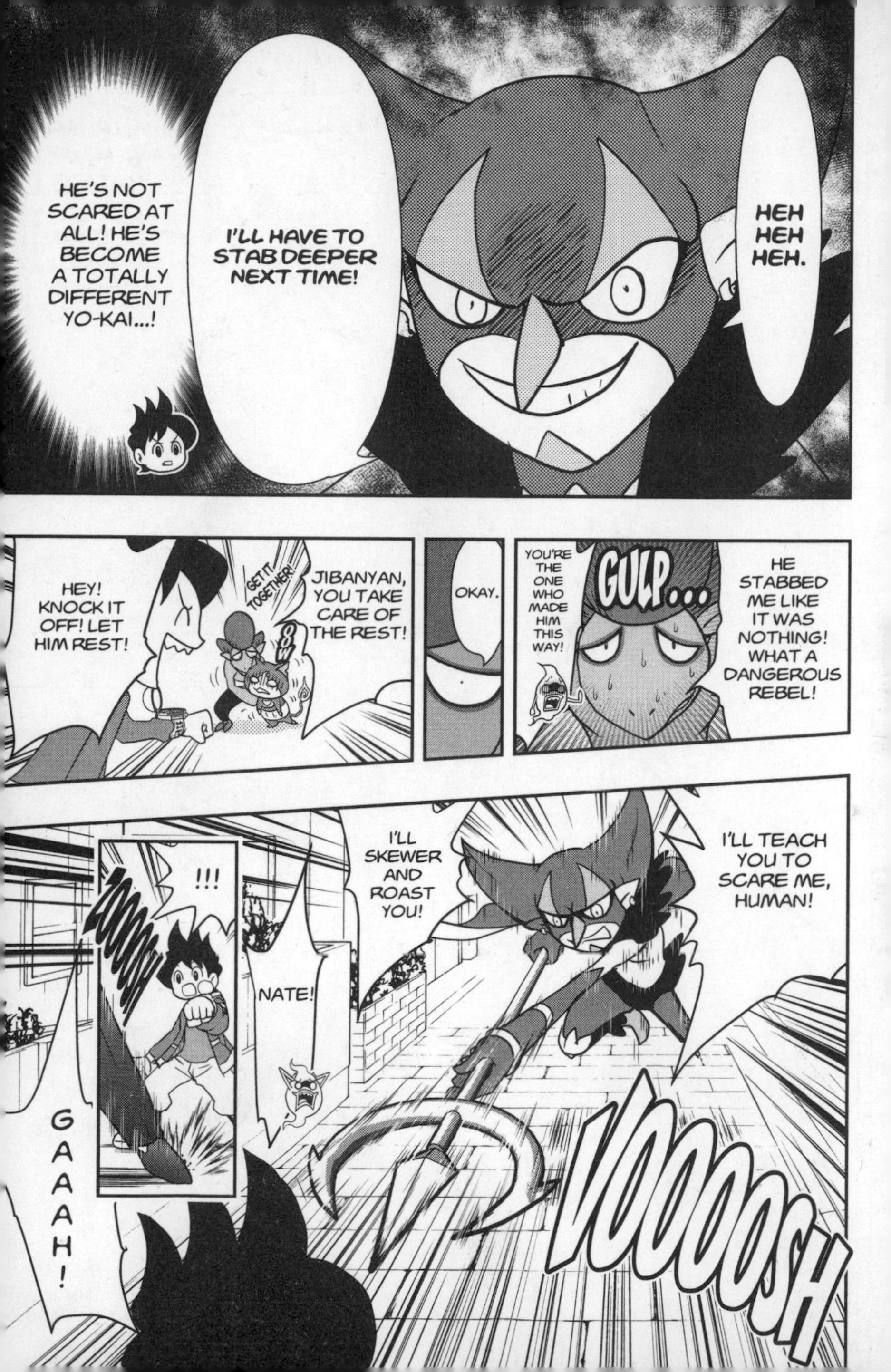
HEH HEH HEH.
I'LL HAVE TO STAB DEEPER NEXT TIME!
HE'S NOT SCARED AT ALL! HE'S BECOME A TOTALLY DIFFERENT YO-KAI...!
HE STABBED ME LIKE IT WAS NOTHING! WHAT A DANGEROUS REBEL!
GULP...
YOU'RE THE ONE WHO MADE HIM THIS WAY!
OKAY.
JIBANYAN, YOU TAKE CARE OF THE REST!
GET IT TOGETHER!
HEY! KNOCK IT OFF! LET HIM REST!
I'LL TEACH YOU TO SCARE ME, HUMAN!
I'LL SKEWER AND ROAST YOU!
VOOOOSH
NATE!
!!!
GAAAAH!

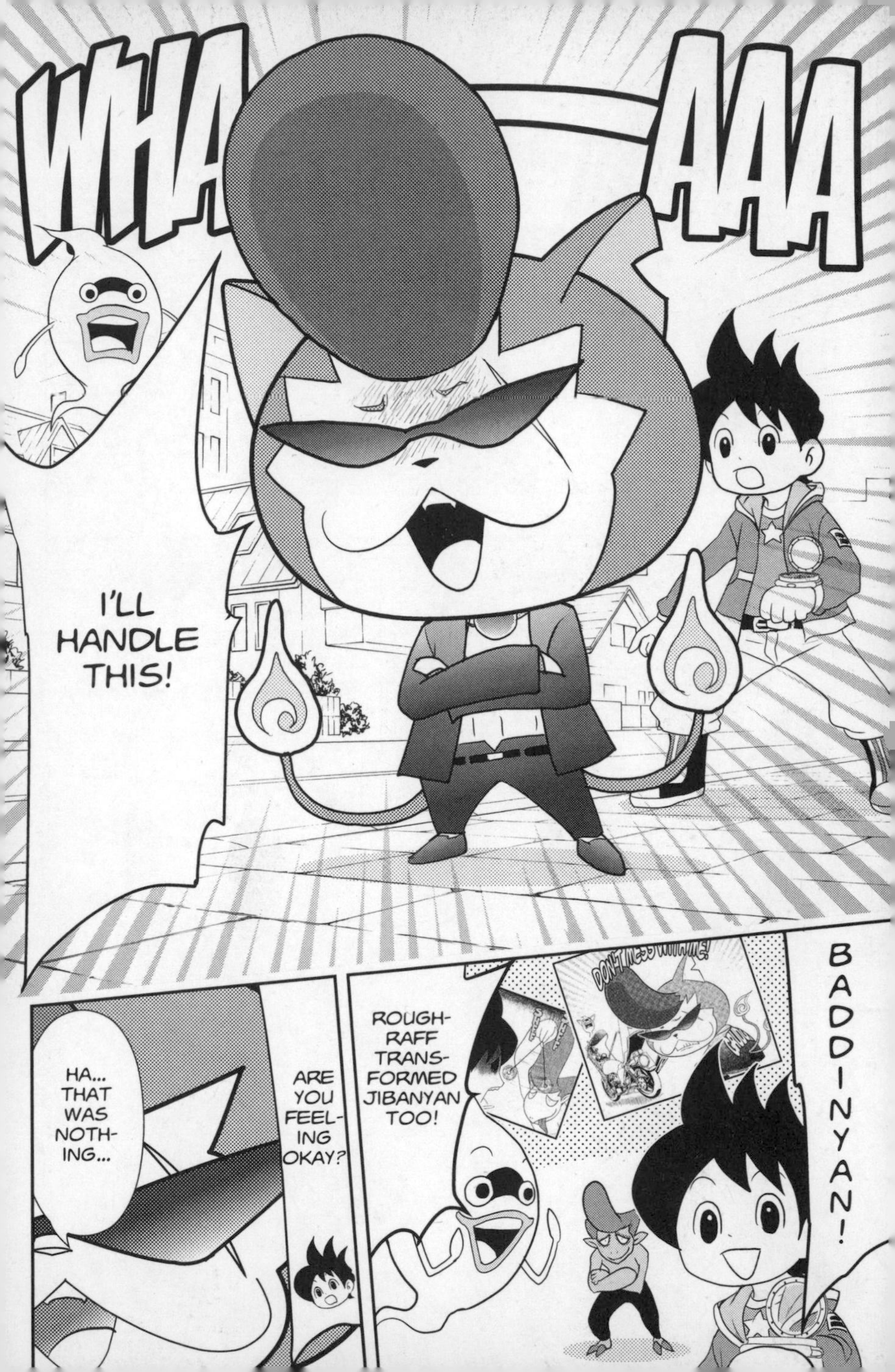

WHAAAAA
I'LL HANDLE THIS!
BADDINYAN!
DON'T MESS WITH ME!
ROUGHRAFF TRANSFORMED JIBANYAN TOO!
ARE YOU FEELING OKAY?
HA... THAT WAS NOTHING...

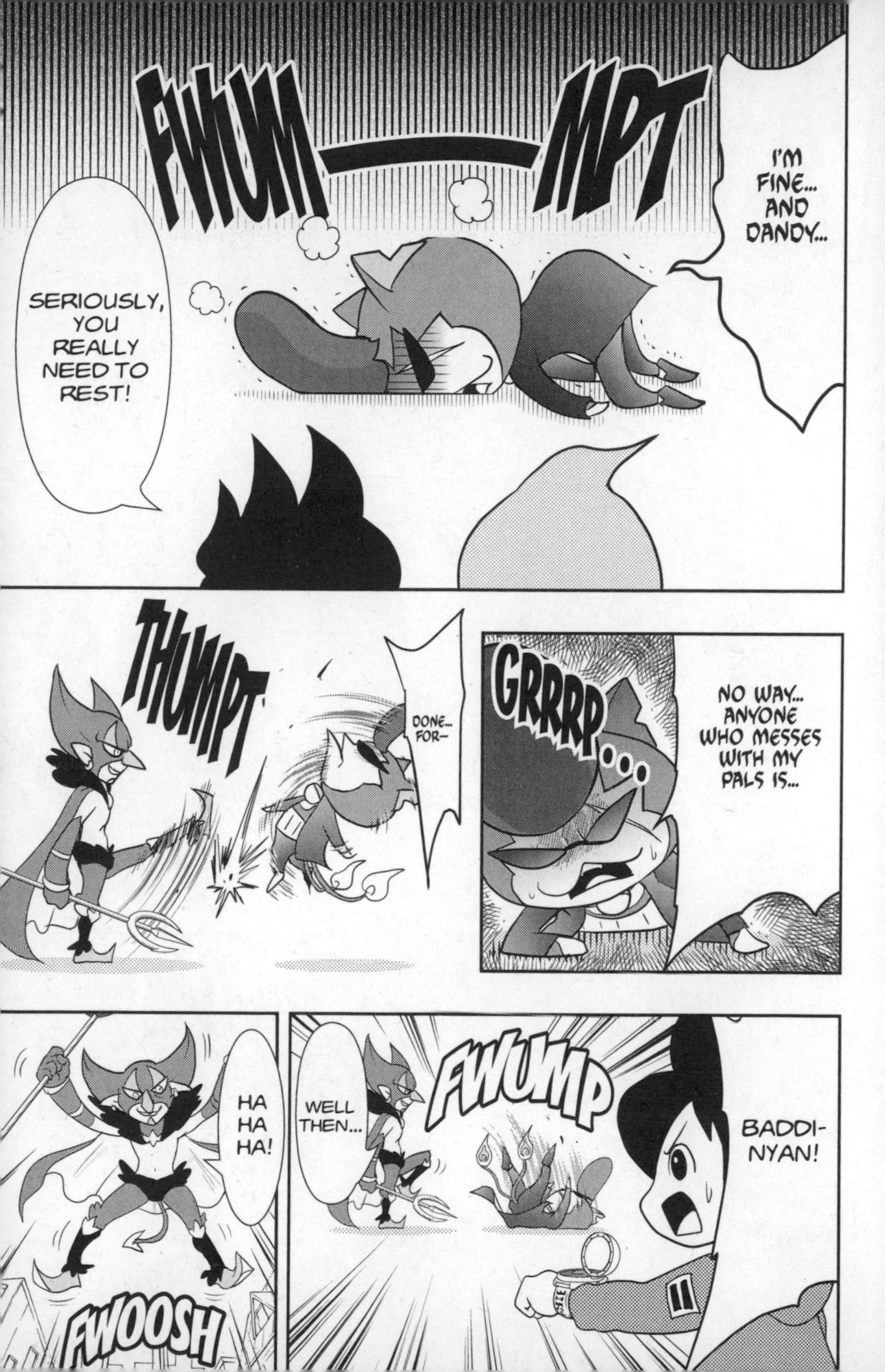
I'M FINE... AND DANDY...
FWUM—MPT
SERIOUSLY, YOU REALLY NEED TO REST!
GRRRP...
NO WAY... ANYONE WHO MESSES WITH MY PALS IS...
DONE... FOR–
THUMPT
BADDI-NYAN!
FWUMP
WELL THEN...
HA HA HA!
FWOOSH

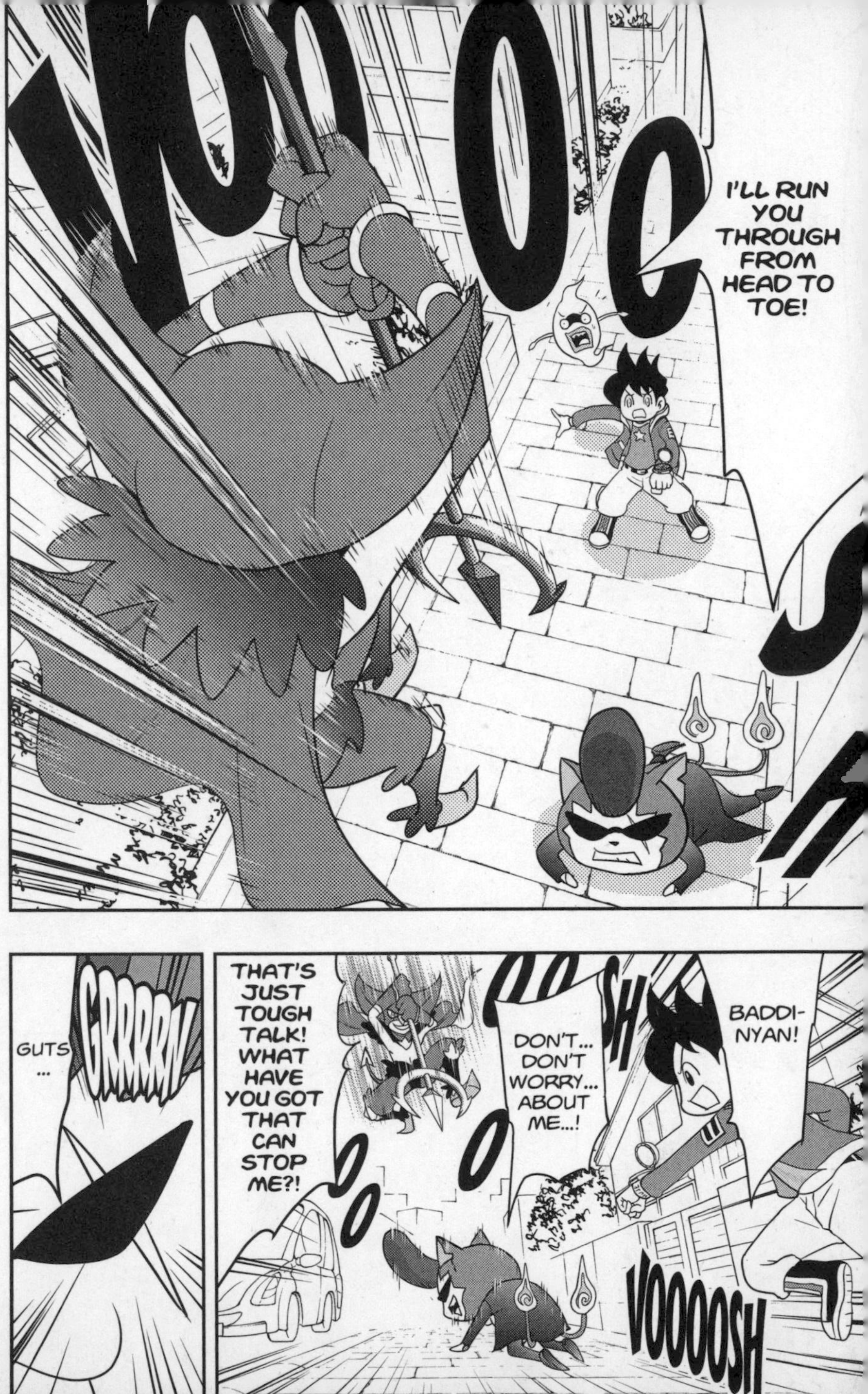
I'LL RUN YOU THROUGH FROM HEAD TO TOE!
BADDI-NYAN!
DON'T... DON'T WORRY... ABOUT ME...!
THAT'S JUST TOUGH TALK! WHAT HAVE YOU GOT THAT CAN STOP ME?!
VOOOOSH
GRRRRN
GUTS ...

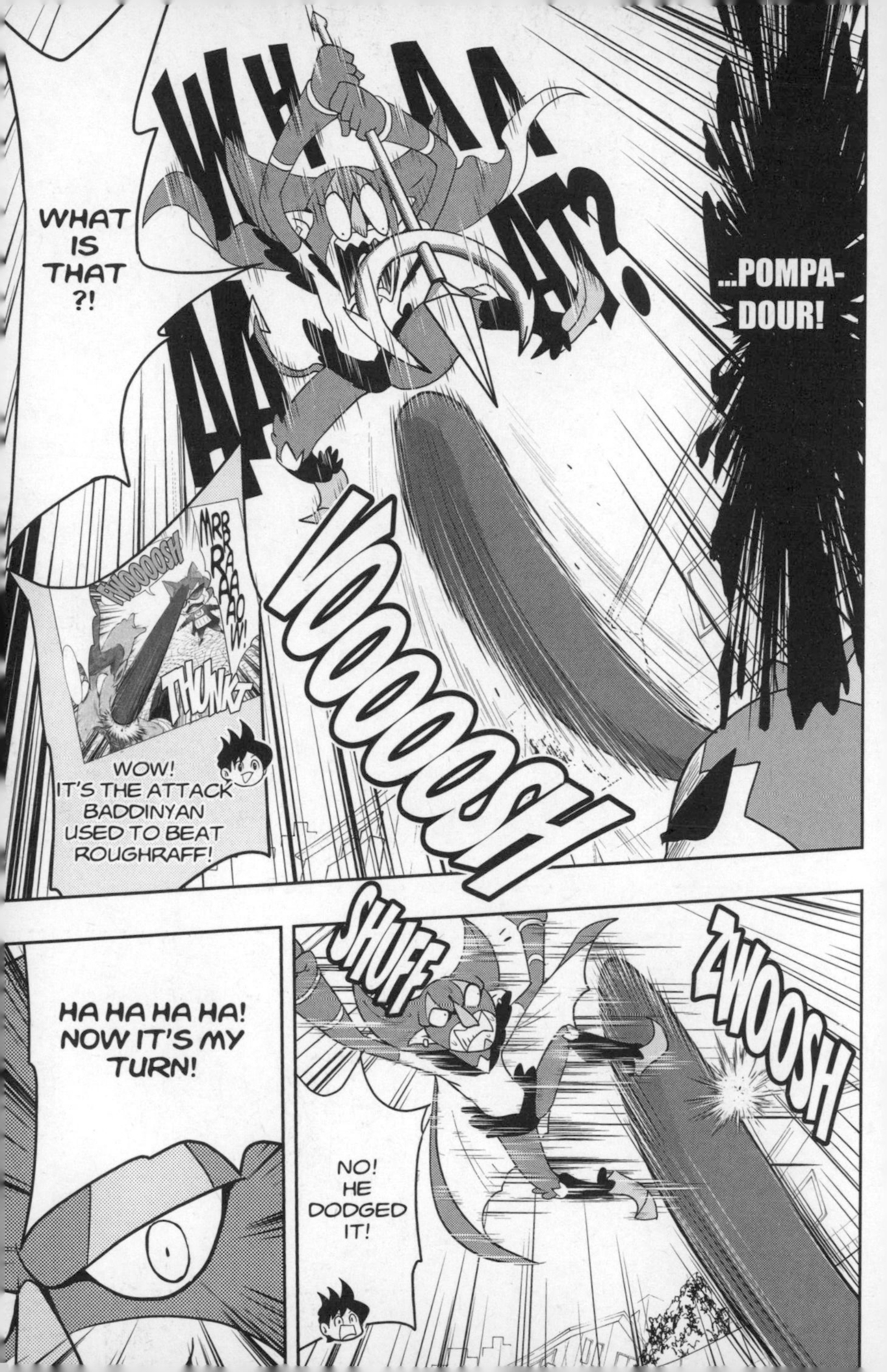
...POMPA-DOUR!
WHAT IS THAT?!
VOOOOOSH
THUNK
WOW! IT'S THE ATTACK BADDINYAN USED TO BEAT ROUGHRAFF!
ZWOOSH
SHUFF
NO! HE DODGED IT!
HA HA HA HA! NOW IT'S MY TURN!

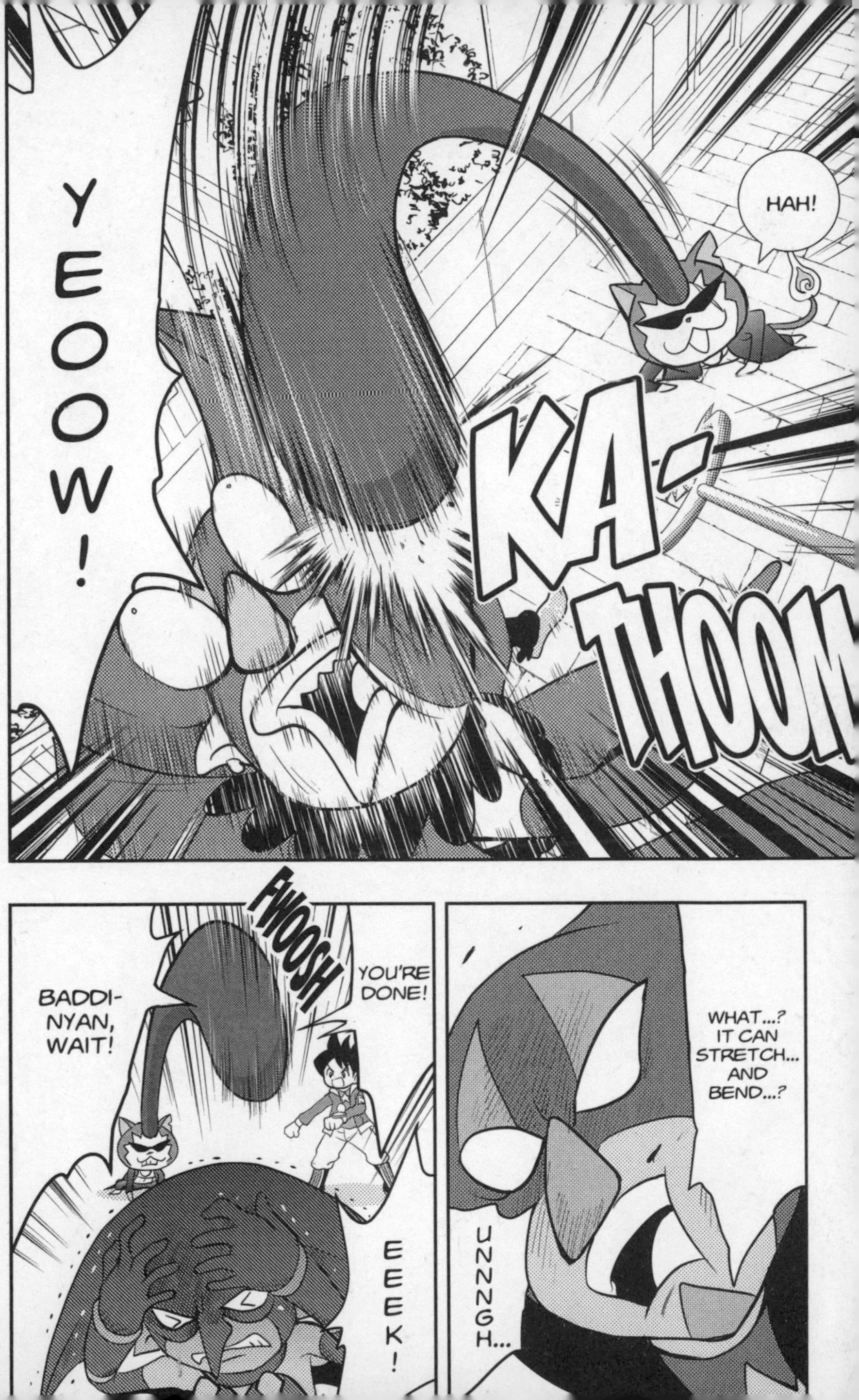
HAH!
KA-THOOM
YEOOW!
WHAT...? IT CAN STRETCH... AND BEND...?
UNNNGH...
FWOOSH
YOU'RE DONE!
BADDI-NYAN, WAIT!
EEEEK!

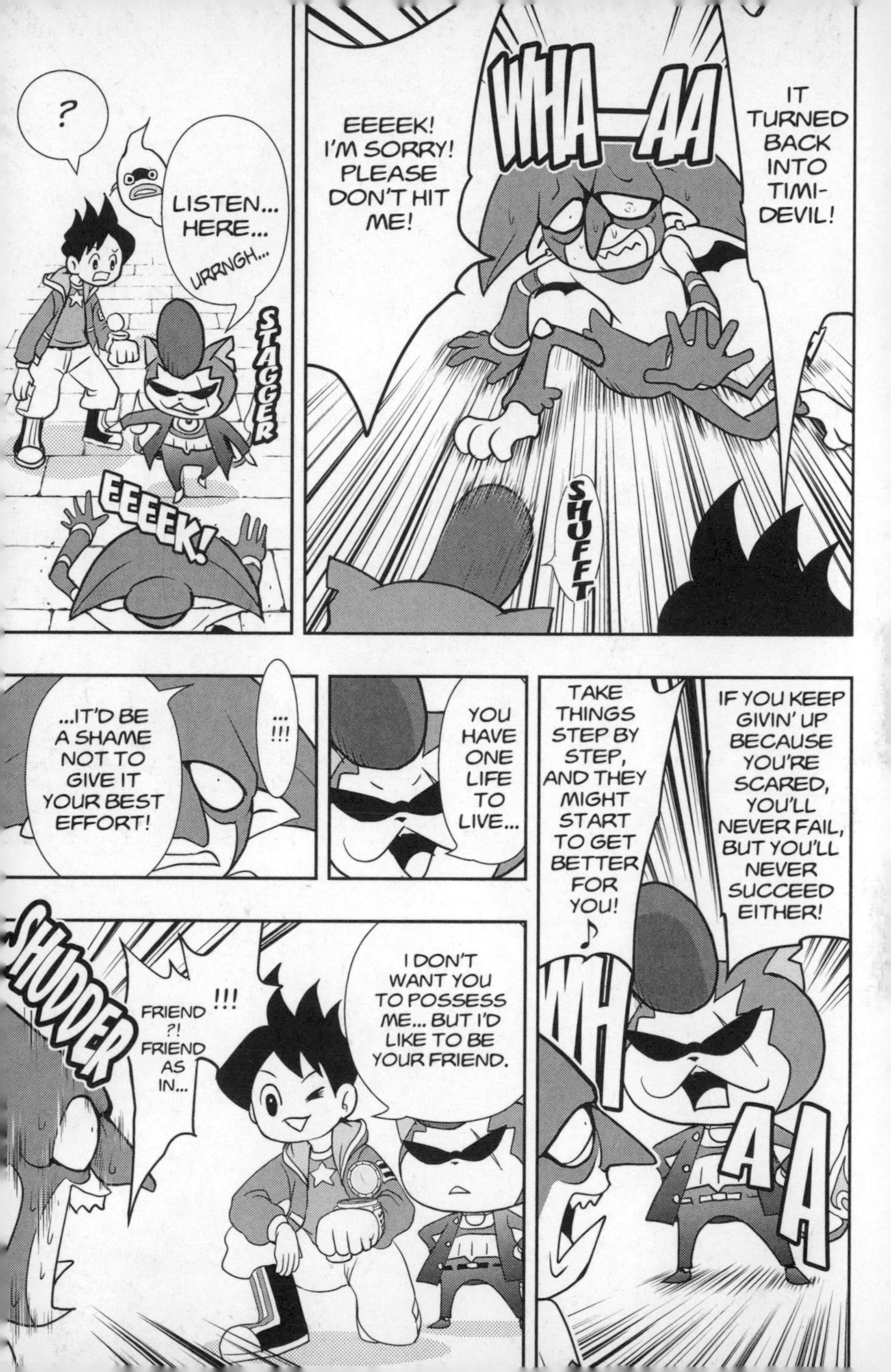
IT TURNED BACK INTO TIMI-DEVIL!
WHA—AA
EEEEK! I'M SORRY! PLEASE DON'T HIT ME!
SHUFFT
?
LISTEN... HERE...
URRNGH...
STAGGER
EEEEK!
IF YOU KEEP GIVIN' UP BECAUSE YOU'RE SCARED, YOU'LL NEVER FAIL, BUT YOU'LL NEVER SUCCEED EITHER!
TAKE THINGS STEP BY STEP, AND THEY MIGHT START TO GET BETTER FOR YOU! ♪
WH
AA
YOU HAVE ONE LIFE TO LIVE...
...IT'D BE A SHAME NOT TO GIVE IT YOUR BEST EFFORT!
... !!!
I DON'T WANT YOU TO POSSESS ME... BUT I'D LIKE TO BE YOUR FRIEND.
!!!
FRIEND?! FRIEND AS IN...
SHUDDER

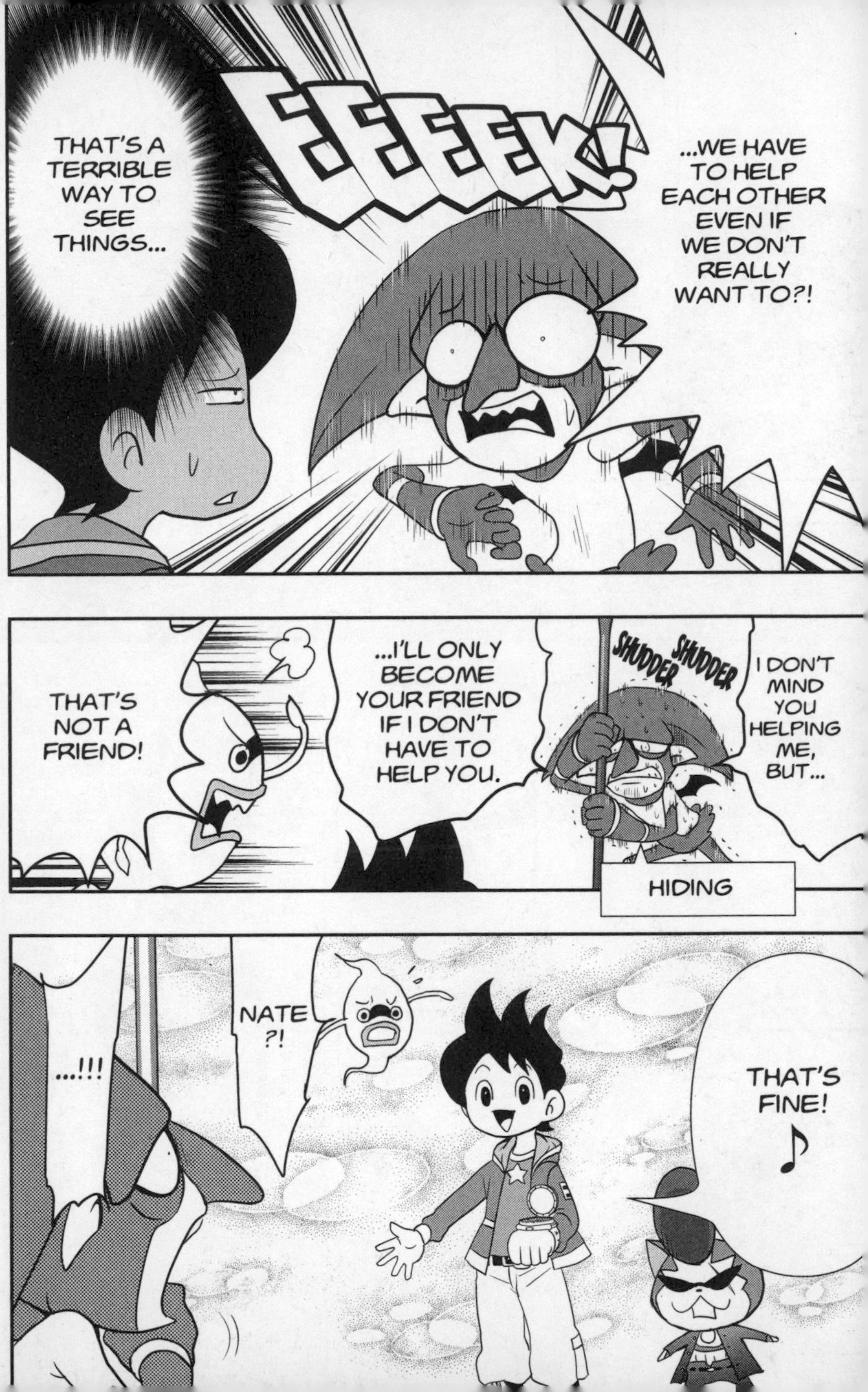
...WE HAVE TO HELP EACH OTHER EVEN IF WE DON'T REALLY WANT TO?!
EEEEK!
THAT'S A TERRIBLE WAY TO SEE THINGS...
I DON'T MIND YOU HELPING ME, BUT...
SHUDDER SHUDDER
HIDING
...I'LL ONLY BECOME YOUR FRIEND IF I DON'T HAVE TO HELP YOU.
THAT'S NOT A FRIEND!
THAT'S FINE! ♪
NATE ?!
...!!!

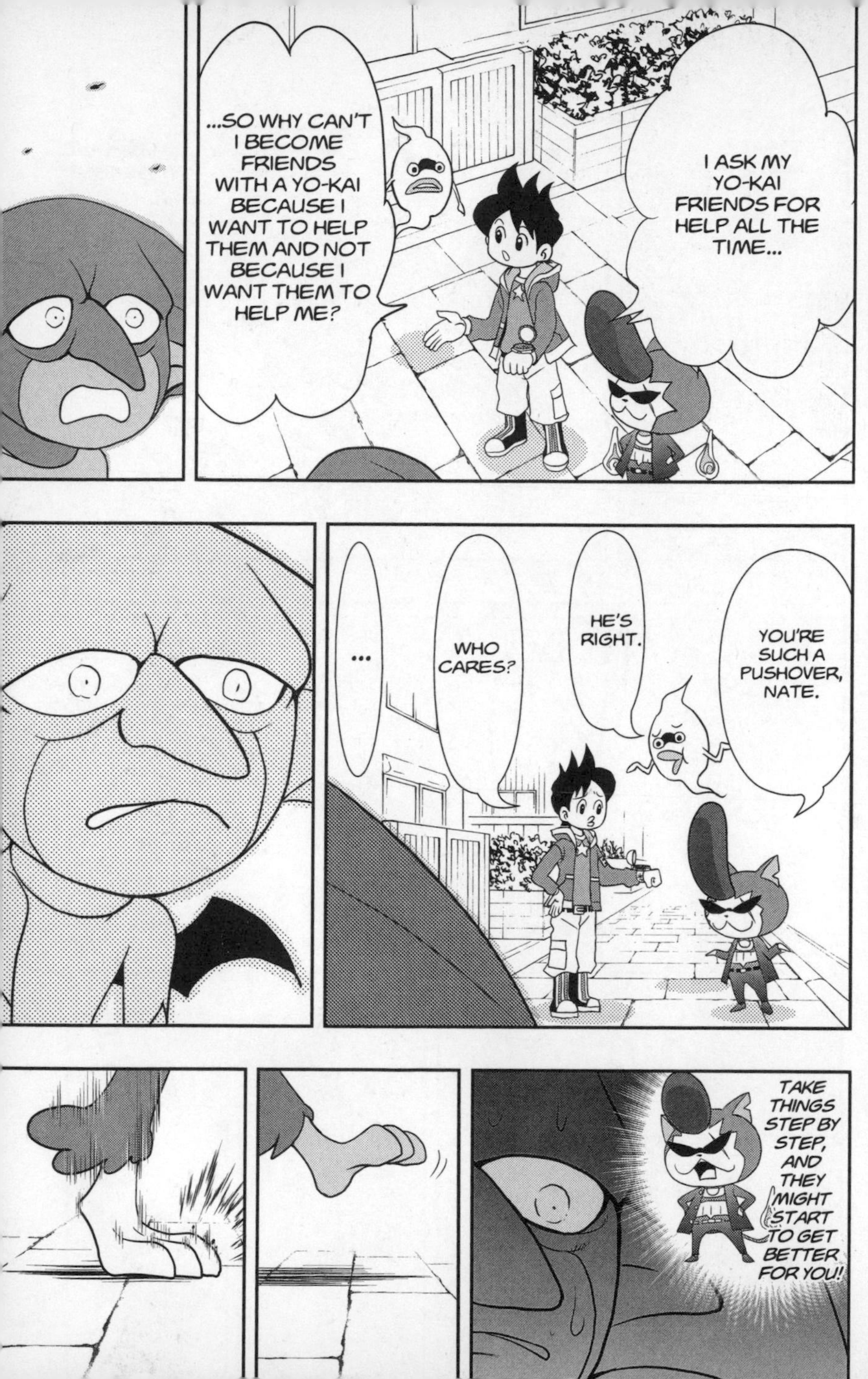
I ASK MY YO-KAI FRIENDS FOR HELP ALL THE TIME...
...SO WHY CAN'T I BECOME FRIENDS WITH A YO-KAI BECAUSE I WANT TO HELP THEM AND NOT BECAUSE I WANT THEM TO HELP ME?
YOU'RE SUCH A PUSHOVER, NATE.
HE'S RIGHT.
WHO CARES?
...
TAKE THINGS STEP BY STEP, AND THEY MIGHT START TO GET BETTER FOR YOU!

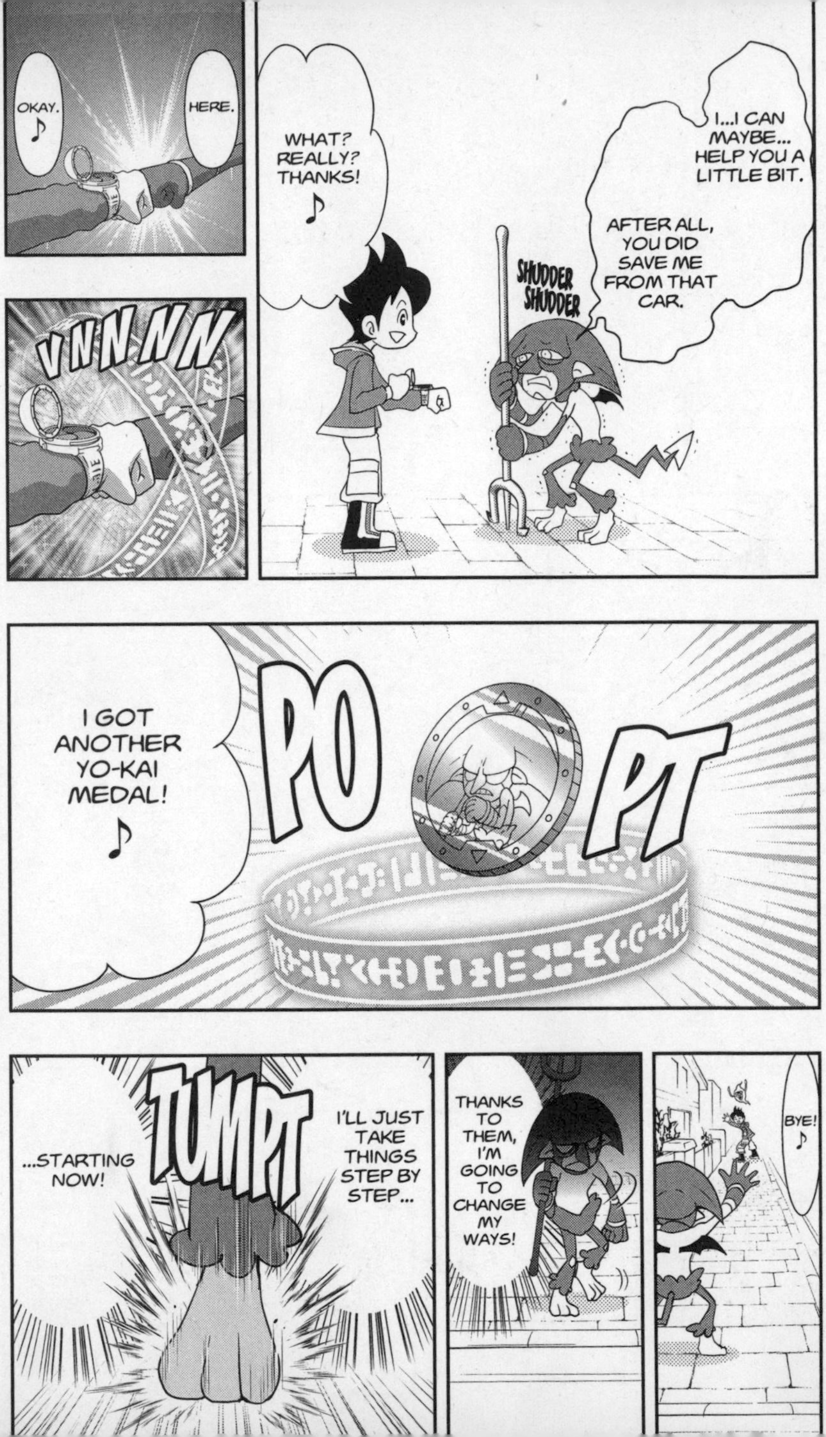
I...I CAN MAYBE... HELP YOU A LITTLE BIT.
AFTER ALL, YOU DID SAVE ME FROM THAT CAR.
SHUDDER SHUDDER
WHAT? REALLY? THANKS! ♪
HERE.
OKAY. ♪
VNNNNN
PO PT
I GOT ANOTHER YO-KAI MEDAL! ♪
BYE! ♪
THANKS TO THEM, I'M GOING TO CHANGE MY WAYS!
I'LL JUST TAKE THINGS STEP BY STEP...
TUMPT
...STARTING NOW!

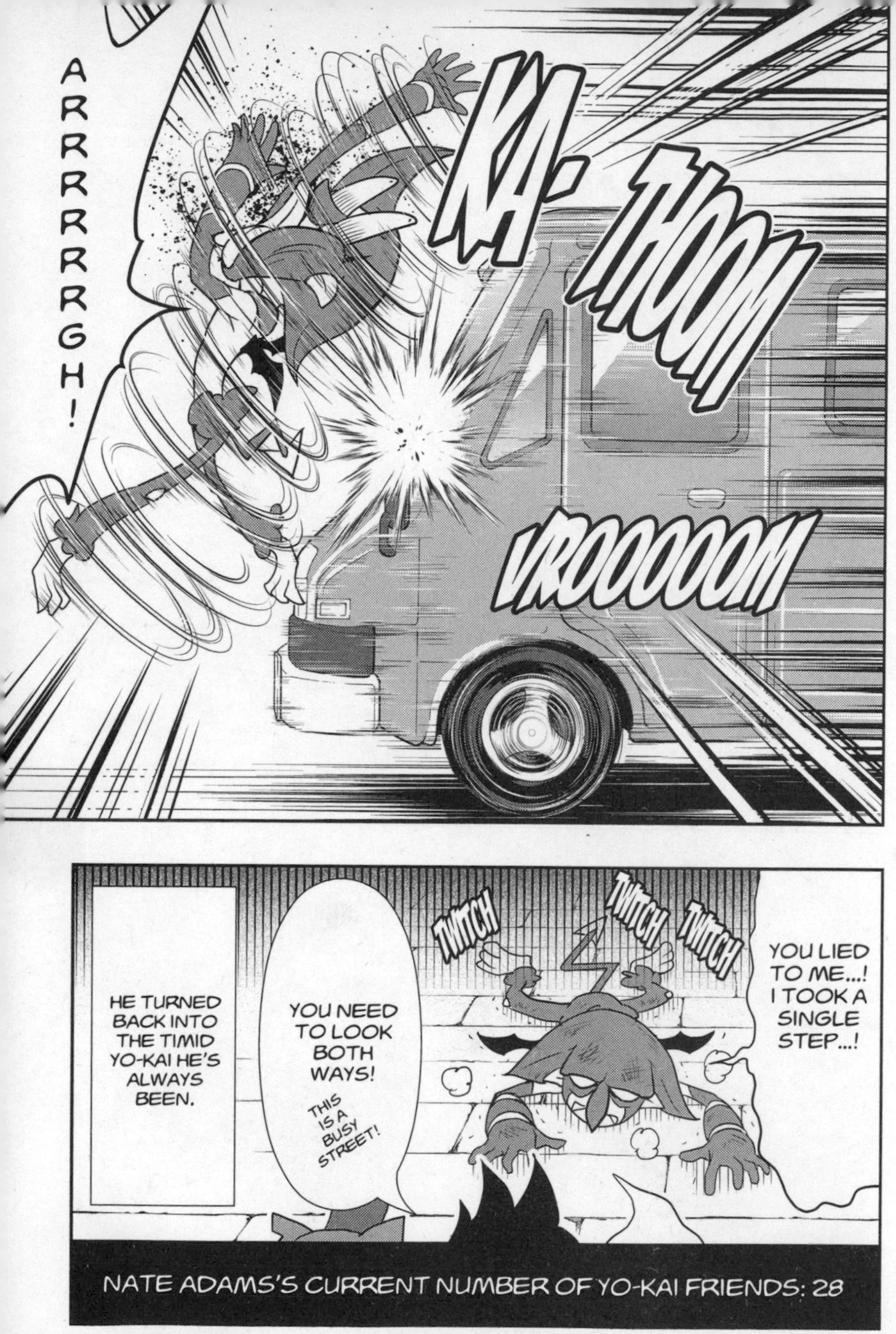
KA- THOOM
VROOOOOM
ARRRRRRGH!
YOU LIED TO ME...! I TOOK A SINGLE STEP...!
TWITCH TWITCH TWITCH
YOU NEED TO LOOK BOTH WAYS!
THIS IS A BUSY STREET!
HE TURNED BACK INTO THE TIMID YO-KAI HE'S ALWAYS BEEN.
NATE ADAMS'S CURRENT NUMBER OF YO-KAI FRIENDS: 28

Chapter 37: THE BEAUTIFUL YO-KAI WHO ABSORBS YOUR VITALITY!

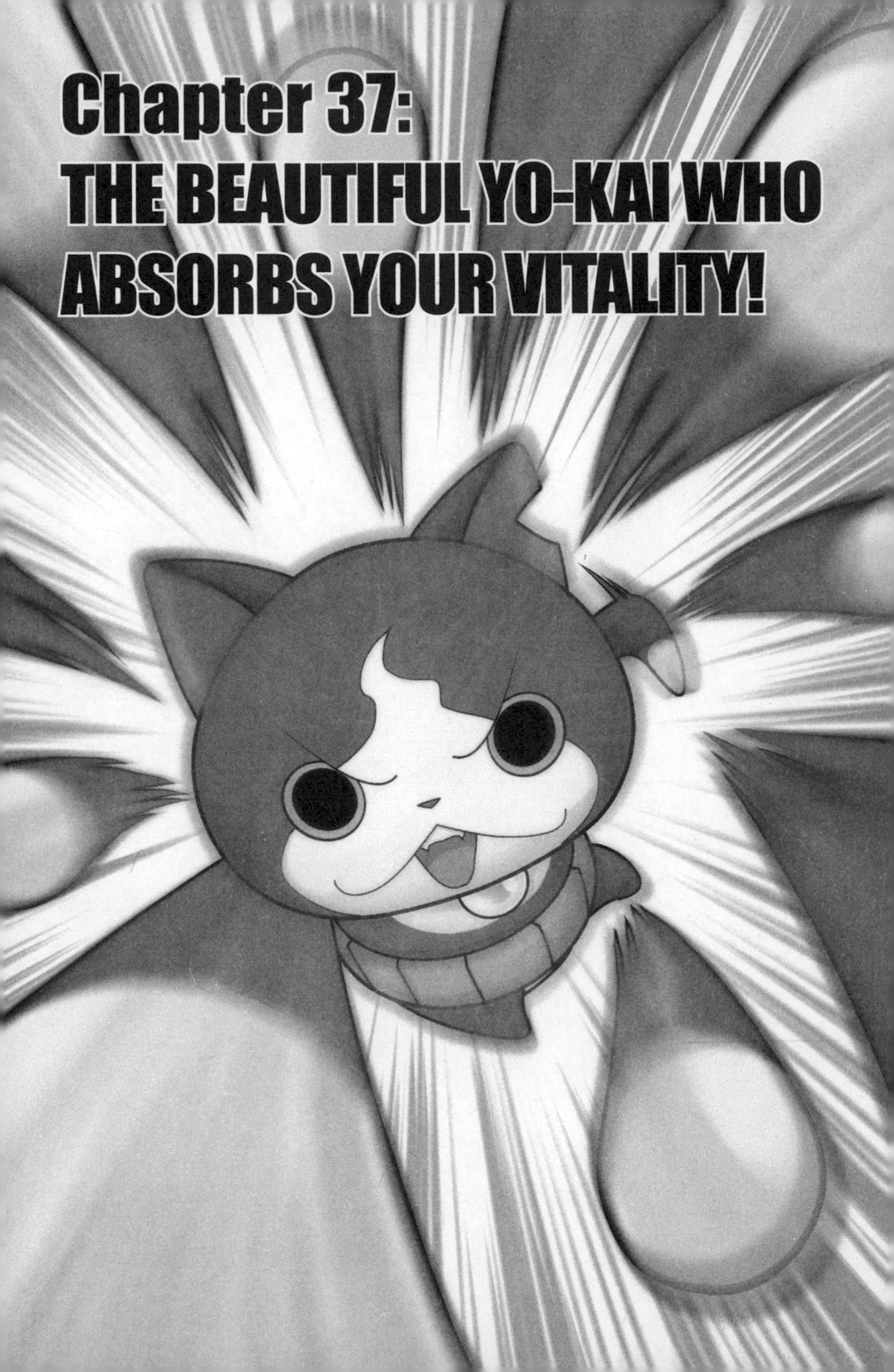

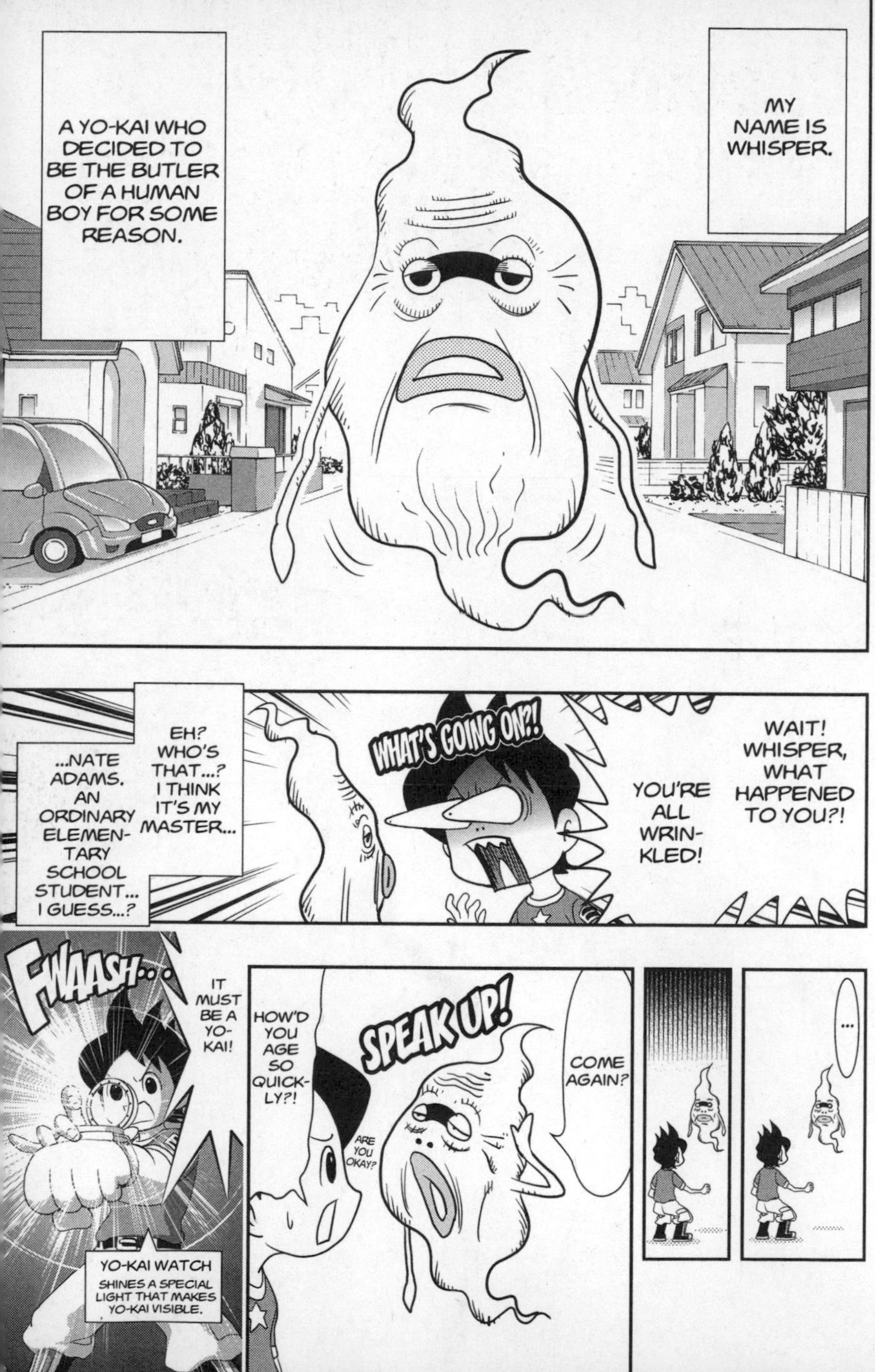
MY NAME IS WHISPER.
A YO-KAI WHO DECIDED TO BE THE BUTLER OF A HUMAN BOY FOR SOME REASON.
WAIT! WHISPER, WHAT HAPPENED TO YOU?!
YOU'RE ALL WRIN-KLED!
WHAT'S GOING ON?!
EH? WHO'S THAT...? I THINK IT'S MY MASTER...
...NATE ADAMS. AN ORDINARY ELEMEN-TARY SCHOOL STUDENT... I GUESS...?
...
COME AGAIN?
SPEAK UP!
HOW'D YOU AGE SO QUICK-LY?!
ARE YOU OKAY?
IT MUST BE A YO-KAI!
FWAASH...
YO-KAI WATCH
SHINES A SPECIAL LIGHT THAT MAKES YO-KAI VISIBLE.

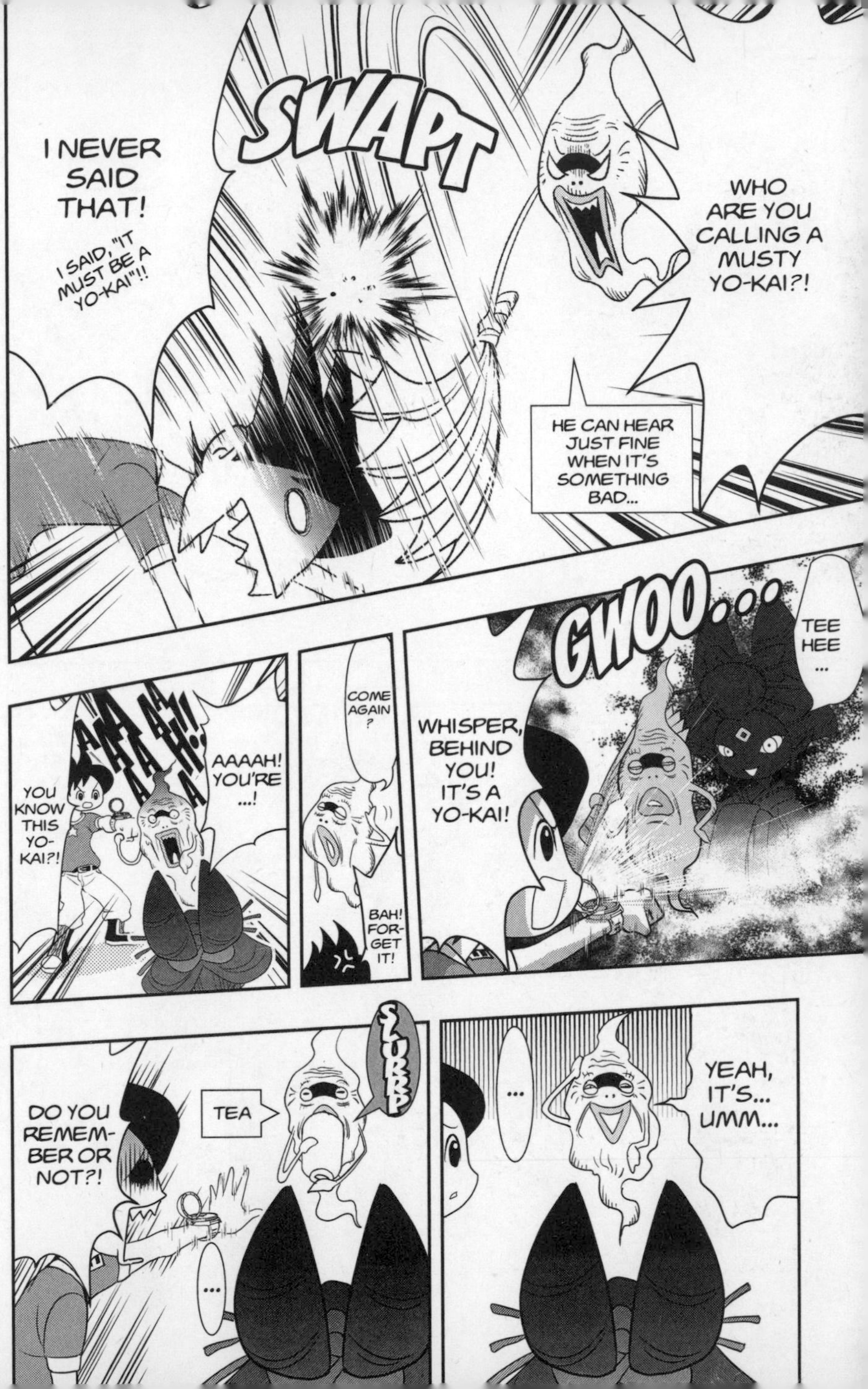

WHO ARE YOU CALLING A MUSTY YO-KAI?!
SWAPT
I NEVER SAID THAT!
I SAID, "IT MUST BE A YO-KAI"!!
HE CAN HEAR JUST FINE WHEN IT'S SOMETHING BAD...
TEE HEE...
GWOO...
WHISPER, BEHIND YOU! IT'S A YO-KAI!
COME AGAIN?
BAH! FOR-GET IT!
AAAAH! YOU'RE ...!
YOU KNOW THIS YO-KAI?!
YEAH, IT'S... UMM...
...
SLURRP
TEA
DO YOU REMEM-BER OR NOT?!
...

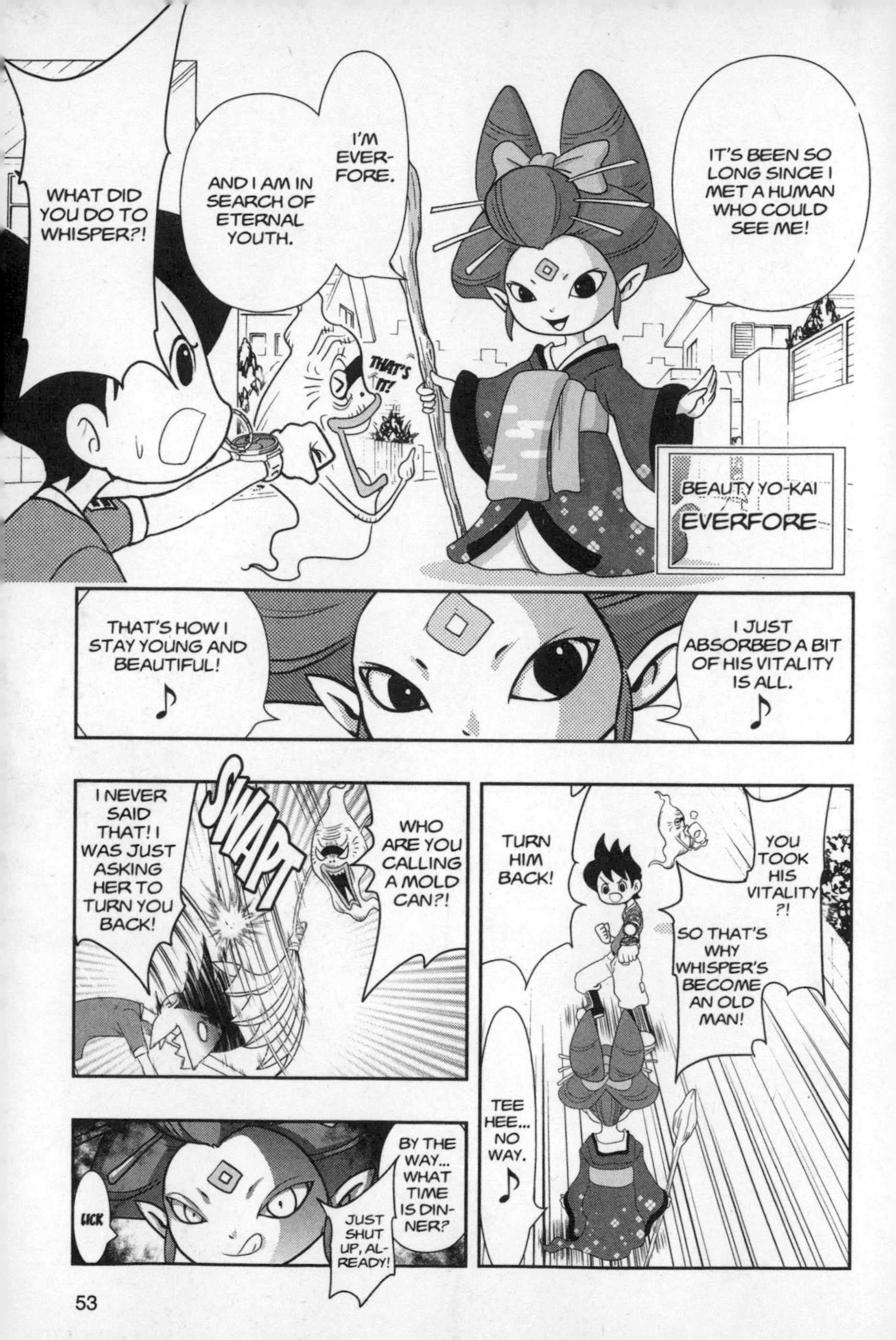
IT'S BEEN SO LONG SINCE I MET A HUMAN WHO COULD SEE ME!
I'M EVER-FORE.
AND I AM IN SEARCH OF ETERNAL YOUTH.
THAT'S IT!
WHAT DID YOU DO TO WHISPER?!
BEAUTY YO-KAI EVERFORE
I JUST ABSORBED A BIT OF HIS VITALITY IS ALL. ♪
THAT'S HOW I STAY YOUNG AND BEAUTIFUL! ♪
YOU TOOK HIS VITALITY?!
SO THAT'S WHY WHISPER'S BECOME AN OLD MAN!
TURN HIM BACK!
TEE HEE... NO WAY. ♪
WHO ARE YOU CALLING A MOLD CAN?!
SWAPT
I NEVER SAID THAT!! I WAS JUST ASKING HER TO TURN YOU BACK!
BY THE WAY... WHAT TIME IS DIN-NER?
JUST SHUT UP, AL-READY!
LICK

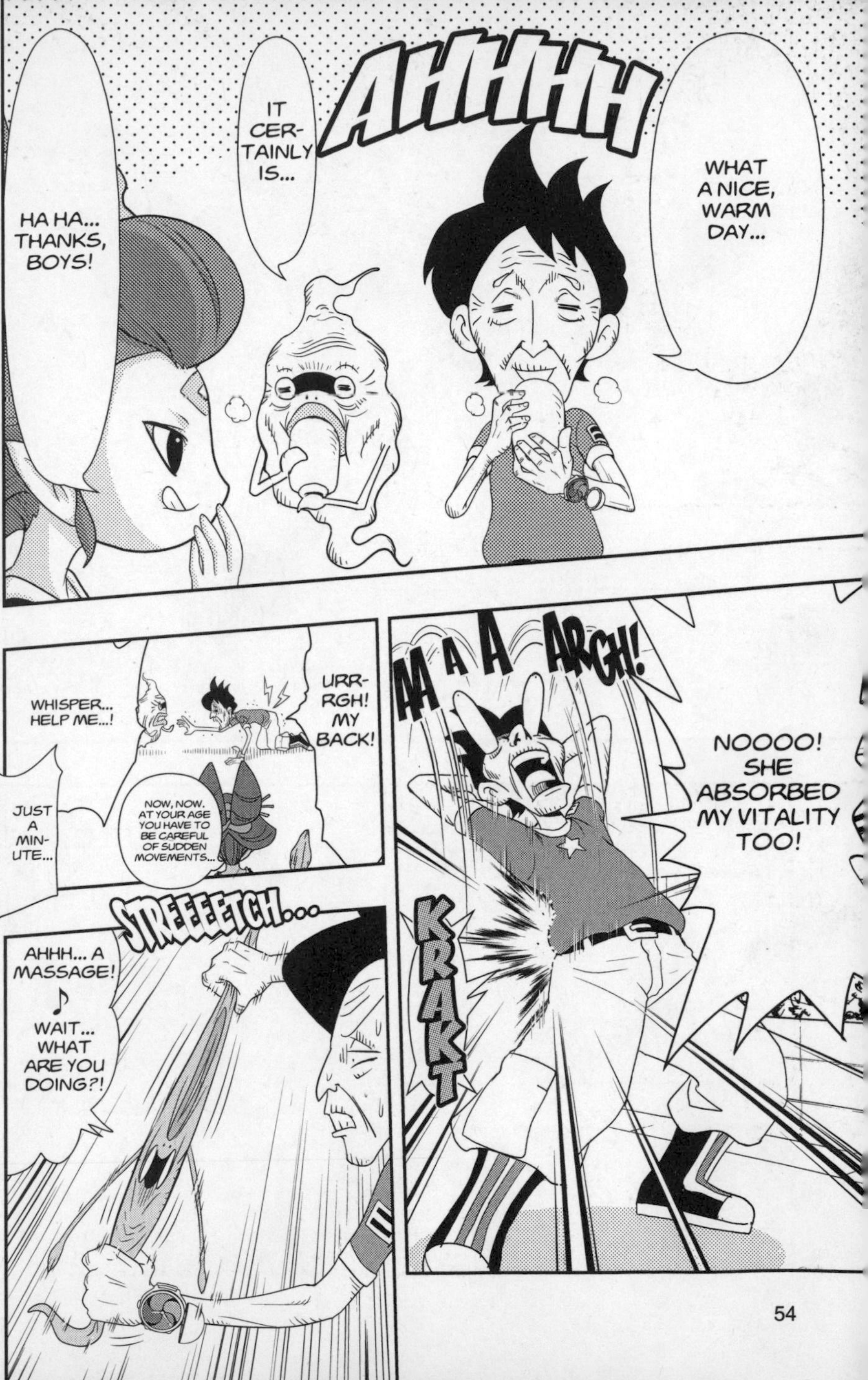
WHAT A NICE, WARM DAY...
AHHHHH
IT CERTAINLY IS...
HA HA... THANKS, BOYS!
AA A A ARGH!
NOOOO! SHE ABSORBED MY VITALITY TOO!
KRAKT
URRRGH! MY BACK!
WHISPER... HELP ME...!
NOW, NOW. AT YOUR AGE YOU HAVE TO BE CAREFUL OF SUDDEN MOVEMENTS...
JUST A MINUTE...
STREEEETCH...
AHHH... A MASSAGE! ♪
WAIT... WHAT ARE YOU DOING?!

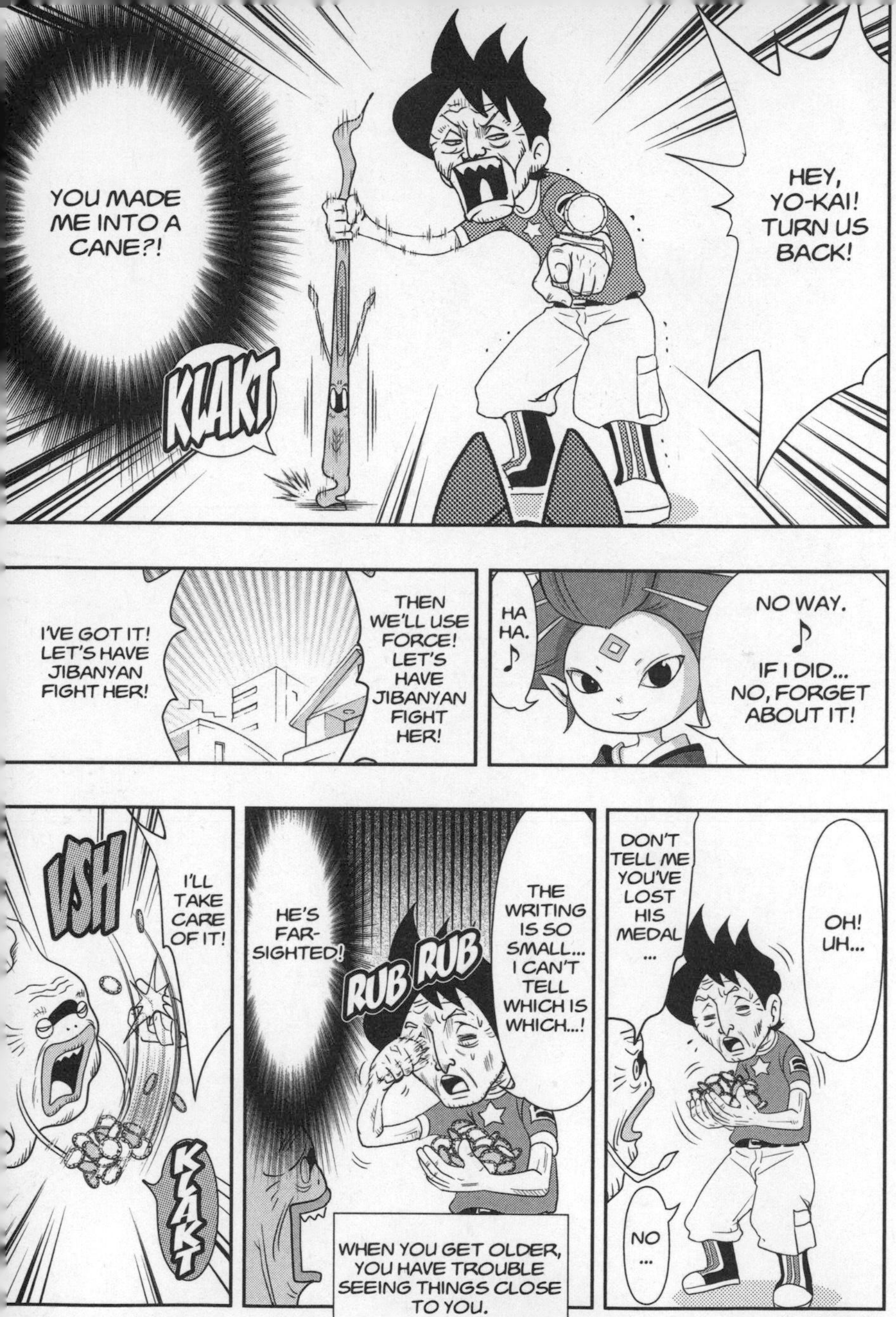
HEY, YO-KAI! TURN US BACK!
YOU MADE ME INTO A CANE?!
KLAKT
NO WAY. ♪
IF I DID... NO, FORGET ABOUT IT!
HA HA. ♪
THEN WE'LL USE FORCE! LET'S HAVE JIBANYAN FIGHT HER!
I'VE GOT IT! LET'S HAVE JIBANYAN FIGHT HER!
OH! UH...
DON'T TELL ME YOU'VE LOST HIS MEDAL ...
NO ...
THE WRITING IS SO SMALL... I CAN'T TELL WHICH IS WHICH...!
HE'S FAR-SIGHTED!
RUB RUB
WHEN YOU GET OLDER, YOU HAVE TROUBLE SEEING THINGS CLOSE TO YOU.
I'LL TAKE CARE OF IT!
VSH
KLAKT

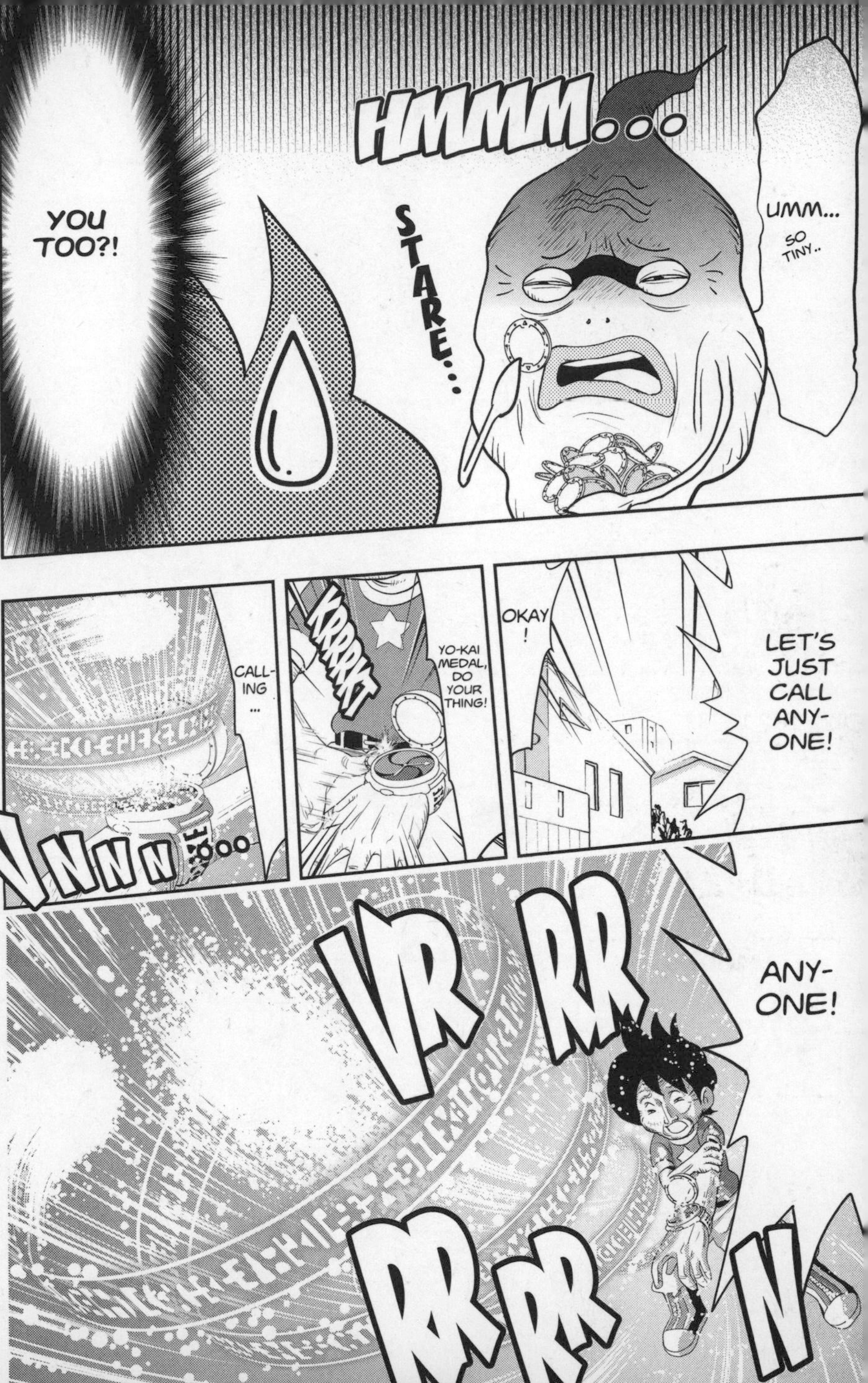
HMMMM...
UMM...
SO TINY..
STARE...
YOU TOO?!
LET'S JUST CALL ANYONE!
OKAY!
YO-KAI MEDAL, DO YOUR THING!
KRRRKT
CALLING...
VNNNN...
ANYONE!
VRRR
RRRRRN

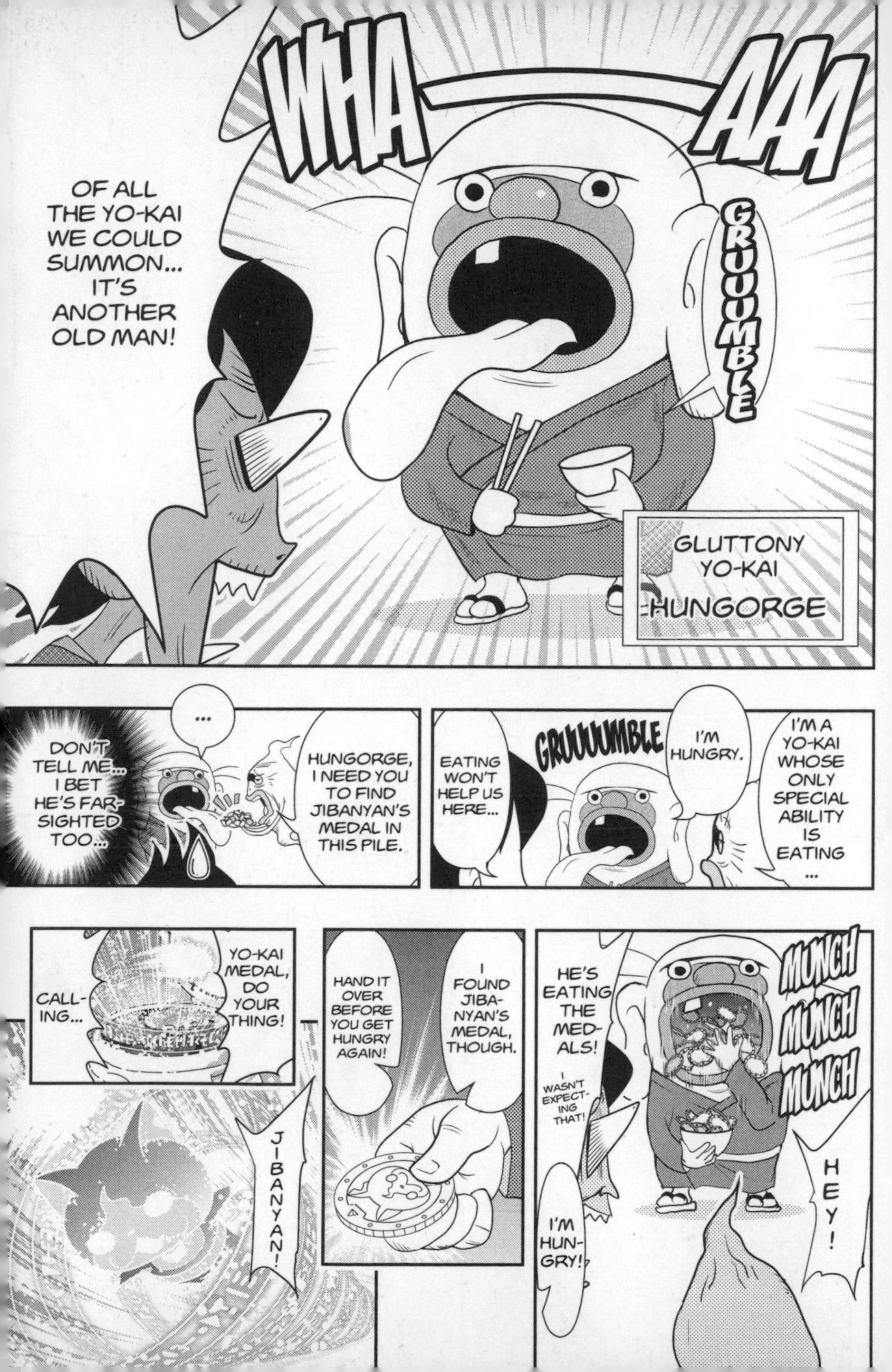
WHA—AAA
GRUUUMBLE
OF ALL THE YO-KAI WE COULD SUMMON... IT'S ANOTHER OLD MAN!
GLUTTONY YO-KAI HUNGORGE
I'M A YO-KAI WHOSE ONLY SPECIAL ABILITY IS EATING...
I'M HUNGRY.
GRUUUUMBLE
EATING WON'T HELP US HERE...
HUNGORGE, I NEED YOU TO FIND JIBANYAN'S MEDAL IN THIS PILE.
...
DON'T TELL ME... I BET HE'S FAR-SIGHTED TOO...
HEY!
MUNCH MUNCH MUNCH
HE'S EATING THE MED-ALS!
I WASN'T EXPECT-ING THAT!
I'M HUN-GRY!
I FOUND JIBA-NYAN'S MEDAL, THOUGH.
HAND IT OVER BEFORE YOU GET HUNGRY AGAIN!
YO-KAI MEDAL, DO YOUR THING!
CALL-ING...
JIBANYAN!

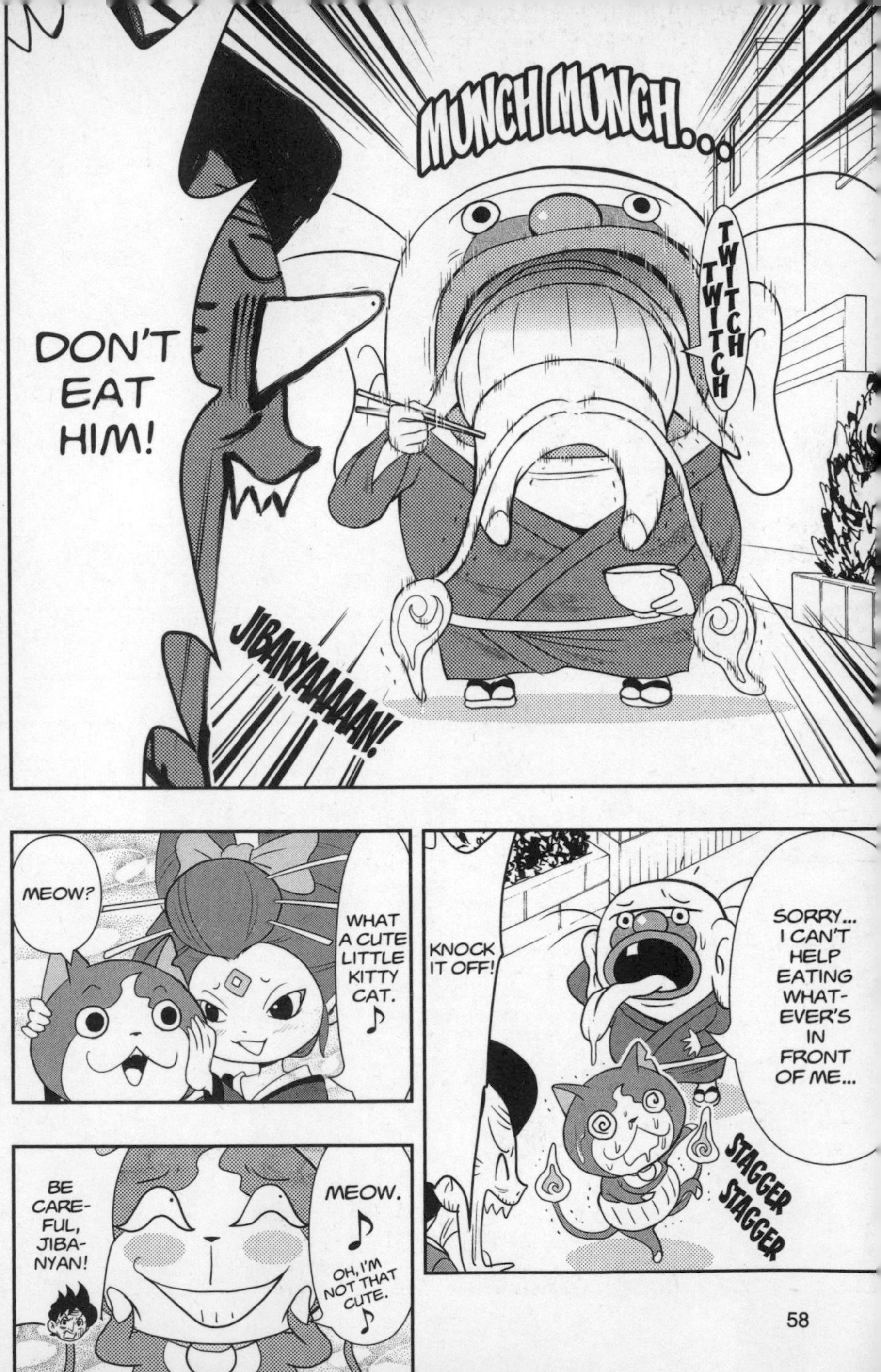
MUNCH MUNCH...
TWITCH TWITCH TWITCH
DON'T EAT HIM!
JIBANYAAAAAAN!
SORRY... I CAN'T HELP EATING WHAT-EVER'S IN FRONT OF ME...
KNOCK IT OFF!
STAGGER STAGGER
WHAT A CUTE LITTLE KITTY CAT. ♪
MEOW?
MEOW. ♪
OH, I'M NOT THAT CUTE. ♪
BE CARE-FUL, JIBA-NYAN!

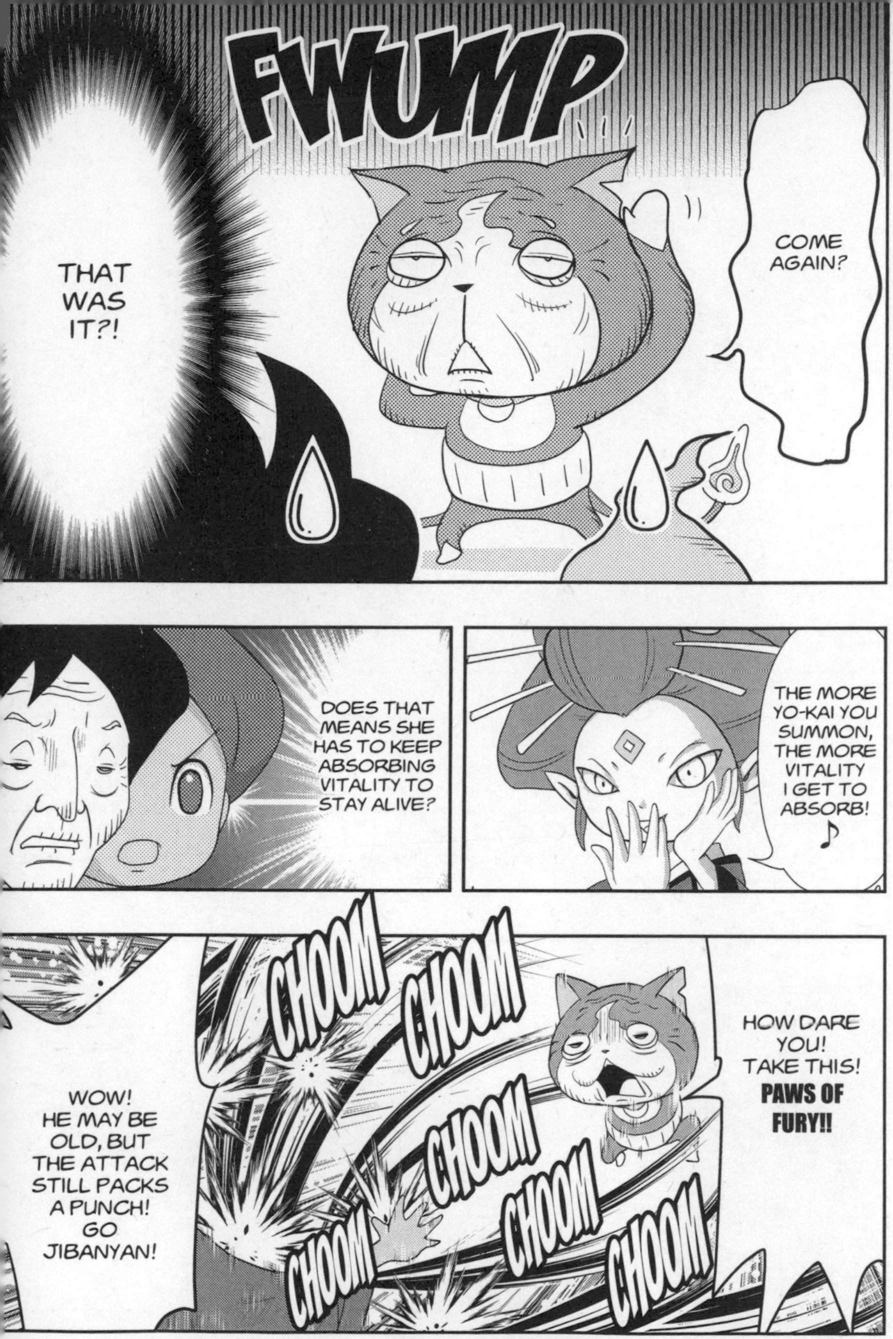
FWUMP
COME AGAIN?
THAT WAS IT?!
THE MORE YO-KAI YOU SUMMON, THE MORE VITALITY I GET TO ABSORB! ♪
DOES THAT MEANS SHE HAS TO KEEP ABSORBING VITALITY TO STAY ALIVE?
HOW DARE YOU! TAKE THIS! PAWS OF FURY!!
CHOOM CHOOM
CHOOM CHOOM CHOOM CHOOM CHOOM
WOW! HE MAY BE OLD, BUT THE ATTACK STILL PACKS A PUNCH! GO JIBANYAN!

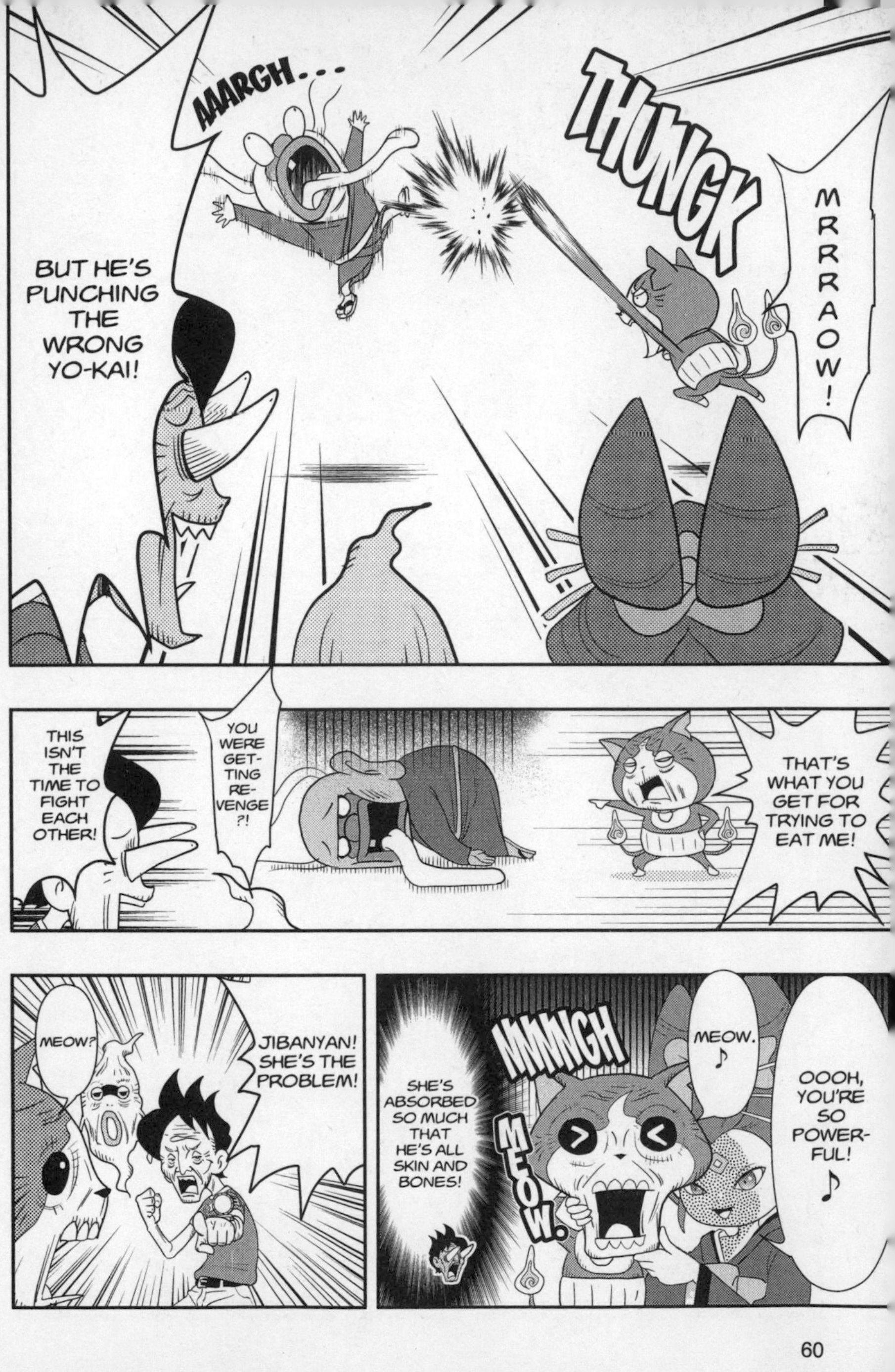
MRRRAOW!
THUNGK
AAARGH...
BUT HE'S PUNCHING THE WRONG YO-KAI!
THAT'S WHAT YOU GET FOR TRYING TO EAT ME!
YOU WERE GET-TING RE-VENGE?!
THIS ISN'T THE TIME TO FIGHT EACH OTHER!
OOOH, YOU'RE SO POWER-FUL! ♪
MEOW. ♪
MMMNGH
SHE'S ABSORBED SO MUCH THAT HE'S ALL SKIN AND BONES!
MEOW. MEOW.
JIBANYAN! SHE'S THE PROBLEM!
MEOW?

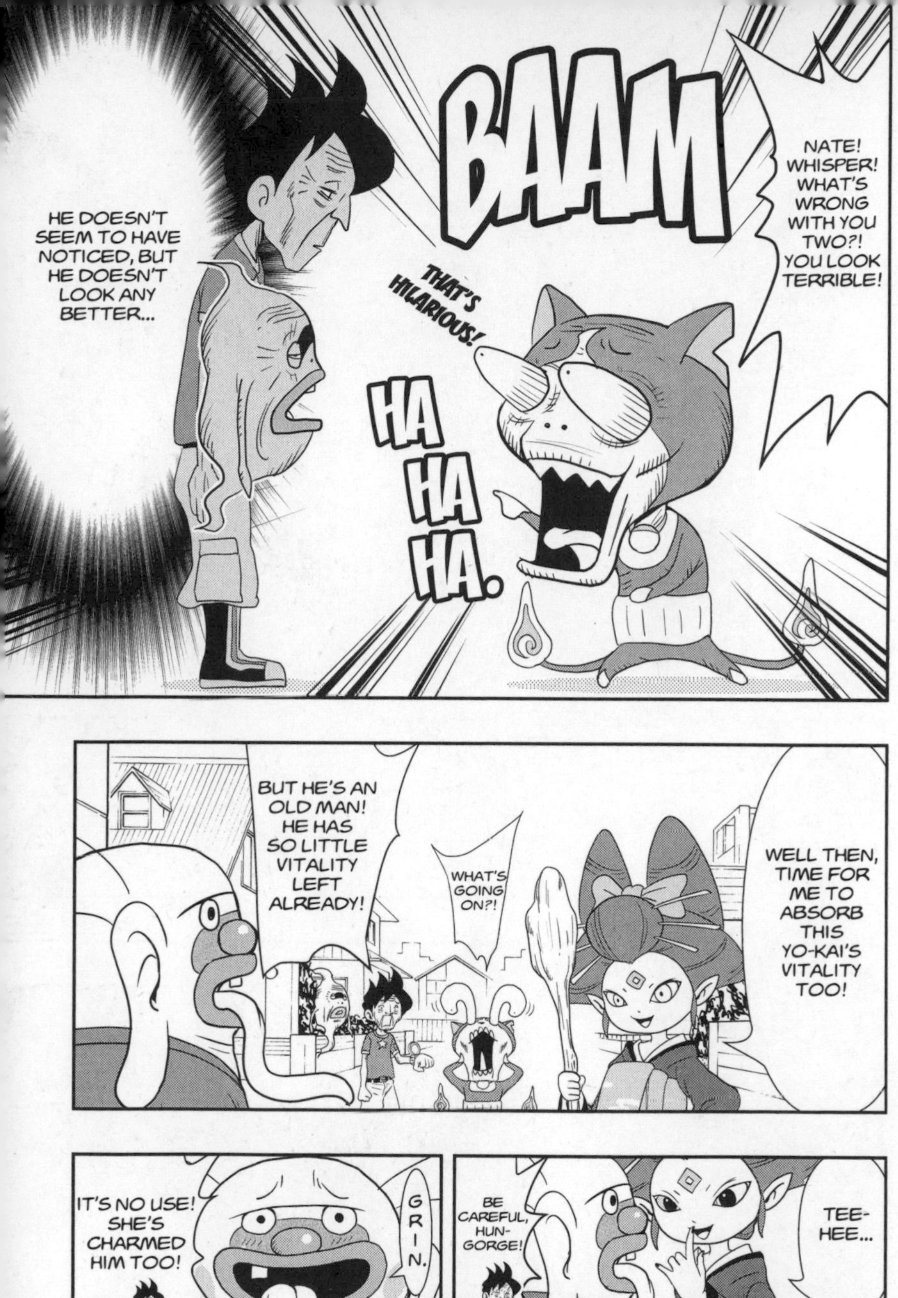
NATE! WHISPER! WHAT'S WRONG WITH YOU TWO?! YOU LOOK TERRIBLE!
BAAM
THAT'S HILARIOUS!
HA HA HA.
HE DOESN'T SEEM TO HAVE NOTICED, BUT HE DOESN'T LOOK ANY BETTER...
WELL THEN, TIME FOR ME TO ABSORB THIS YO-KAI'S VITALITY TOO!
WHAT'S GOING ON?!
BUT HE'S AN OLD MAN! HE HAS SO LITTLE VITALITY LEFT ALREADY!
TEE-HEE...
BE CAREFUL, HUN-GORGE!
GRIN.
IT'S NO USE! SHE'S CHARMED HIM TOO!

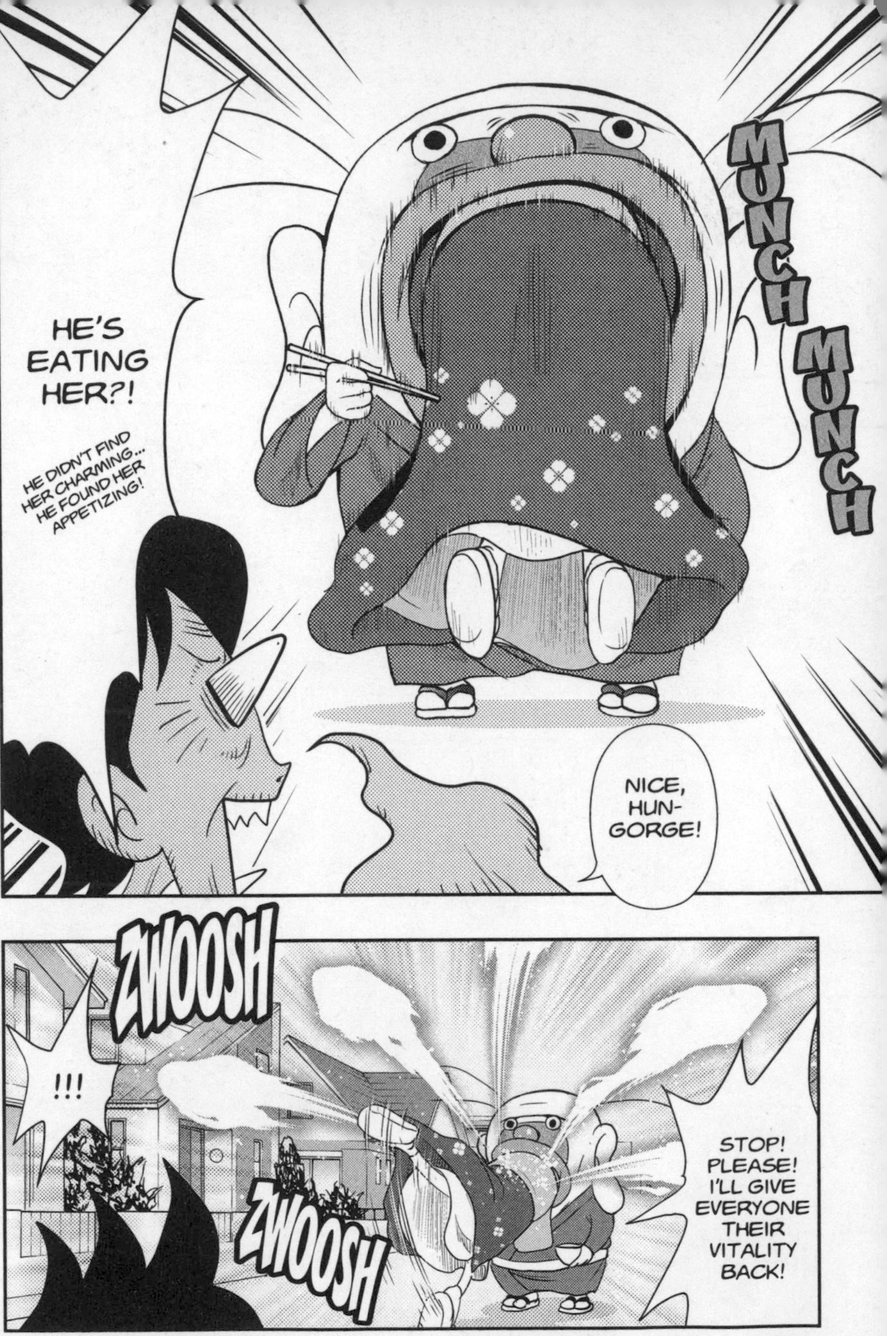
MUNCH MUNCH
HE'S EATING HER?!
HE DIDN'T FIND HER CHARMING... HE FOUND HER APPETIZING!
NICE, HUN-GORGE!
STOP! PLEASE! I'LL GIVE EVERYONE THEIR VITALITY BACK!
ZWOOSH
!!!
ZWOOSH

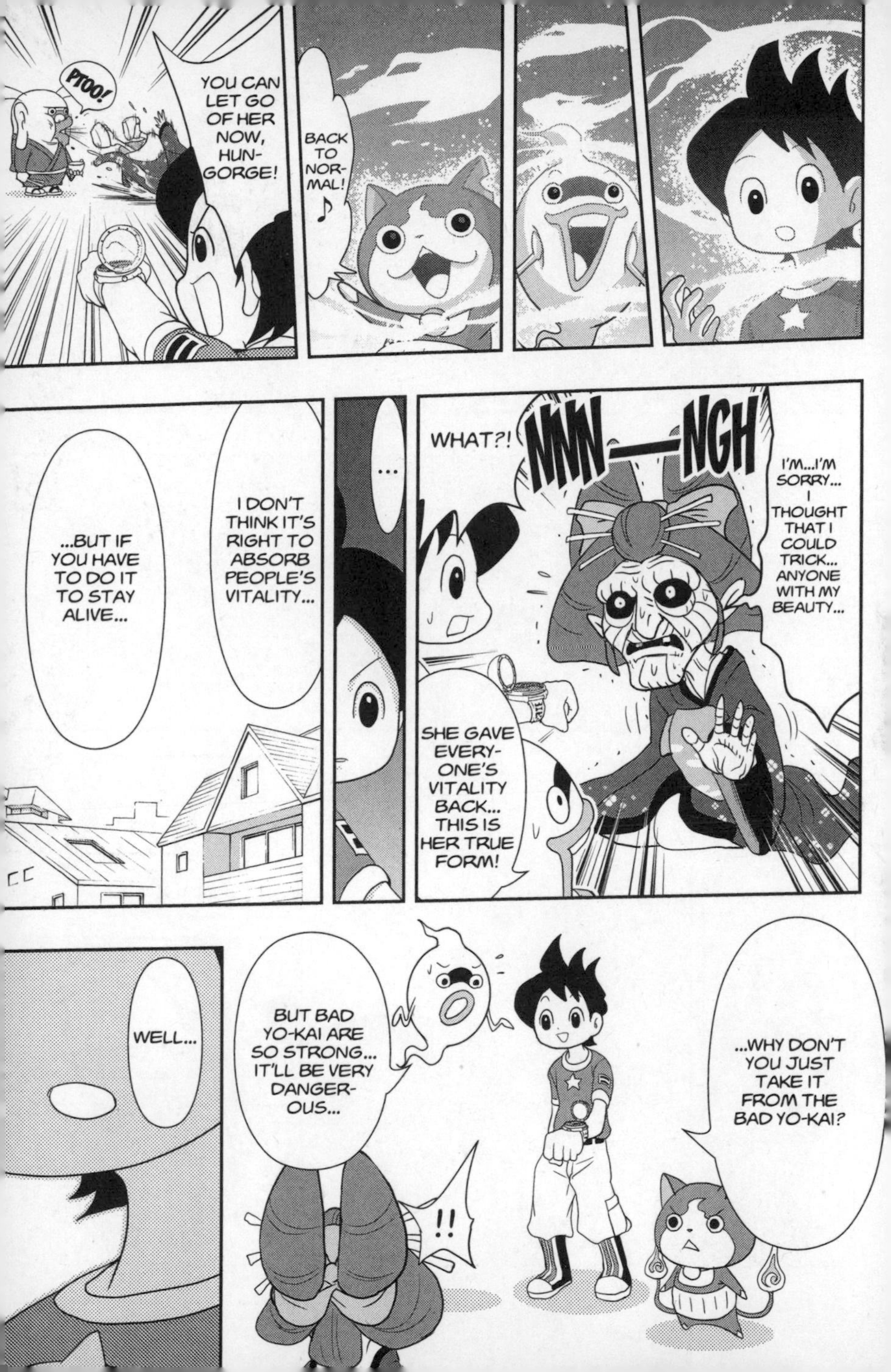
BACK TO NORMAL! ♪
YOU CAN LET GO OF HER NOW, HUN-GORGE!
PTOO!
NNNN—NGH
I'M...I'M SORRY... I THOUGHT THAT I COULD TRICK... ANYONE WITH MY BEAUTY...
WHAT?!
SHE GAVE EVERY-ONE'S VITALITY BACK... THIS IS HER TRUE FORM!
...
I DON'T THINK IT'S RIGHT TO ABSORB PEOPLE'S VITALITY...
...BUT IF YOU HAVE TO DO IT TO STAY ALIVE...
...WHY DON'T YOU JUST TAKE IT FROM THE BAD YO-KAI?
BUT BAD YO-KAI ARE SO STRONG... IT'LL BE VERY DANGER-OUS...
!!
WELL...

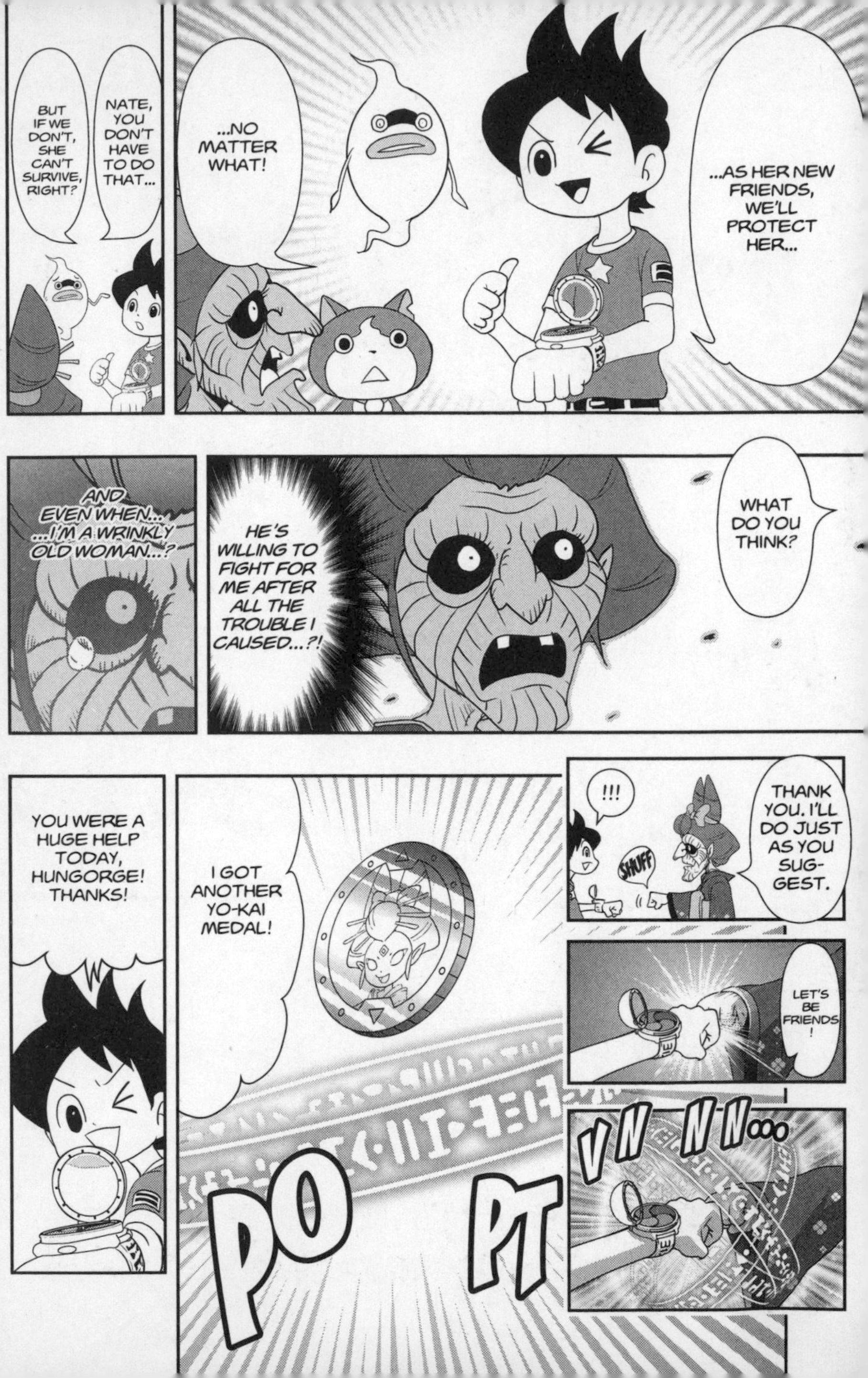
...AS HER NEW FRIENDS, WE'LL PROTECT HER...
...NO MATTER WHAT!
NATE, YOU DON'T HAVE TO DO THAT...
BUT IF WE DON'T, SHE CAN'T SURVIVE, RIGHT?
WHAT DO YOU THINK?
HE'S WILLING TO FIGHT FOR ME AFTER ALL THE TROUBLE I CAUSED...?!
AND EVEN WHEN... ...I'M A WRINKLY OLD WOMAN...?
THANK YOU. I'LL DO JUST AS YOU SUG-GEST.
!!!
SHUFF
LET'S BE FRIENDS!
VN NN NN...
PO
PT
I GOT ANOTHER YO-KAI MEDAL!
YOU WERE A HUGE HELP TODAY, HUNGORGE! THANKS!

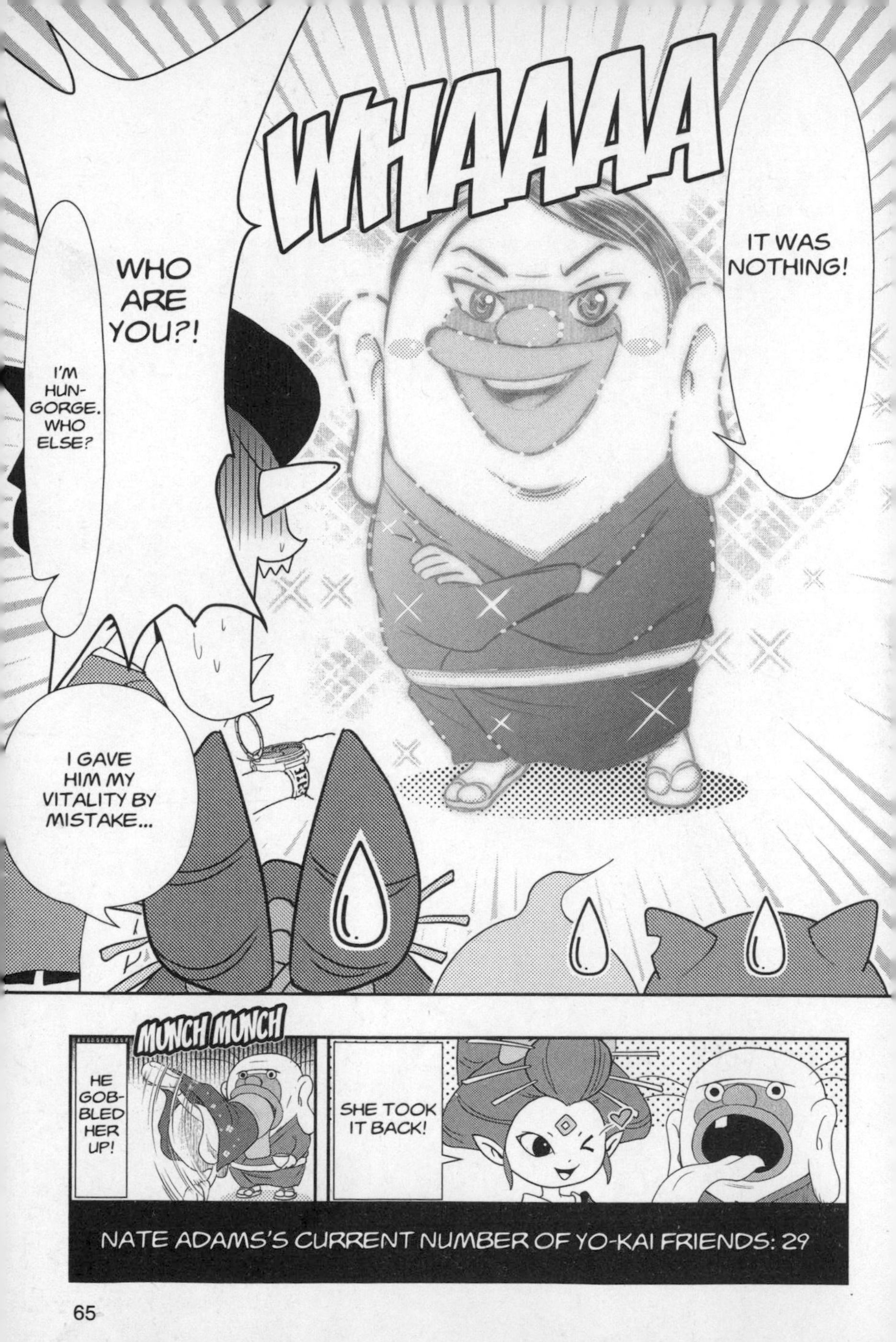
WHAAAA
IT WAS NOTHING!
WHO ARE YOU?!
I'M HUN-GORGE. WHO ELSE?
I GAVE HIM MY VITALITY BY MISTAKE...
SHE TOOK IT BACK!
MUNCH MUNCH
HE GOB-BLED HER UP!
NATE ADAMS'S CURRENT NUMBER OF YO-KAI FRIENDS: 29

CHAPTER 38: INTRODUCING... THE CLASSIC YO-KAI!!

FEATURING UMBRELLA YO-KAI PALLYSOL

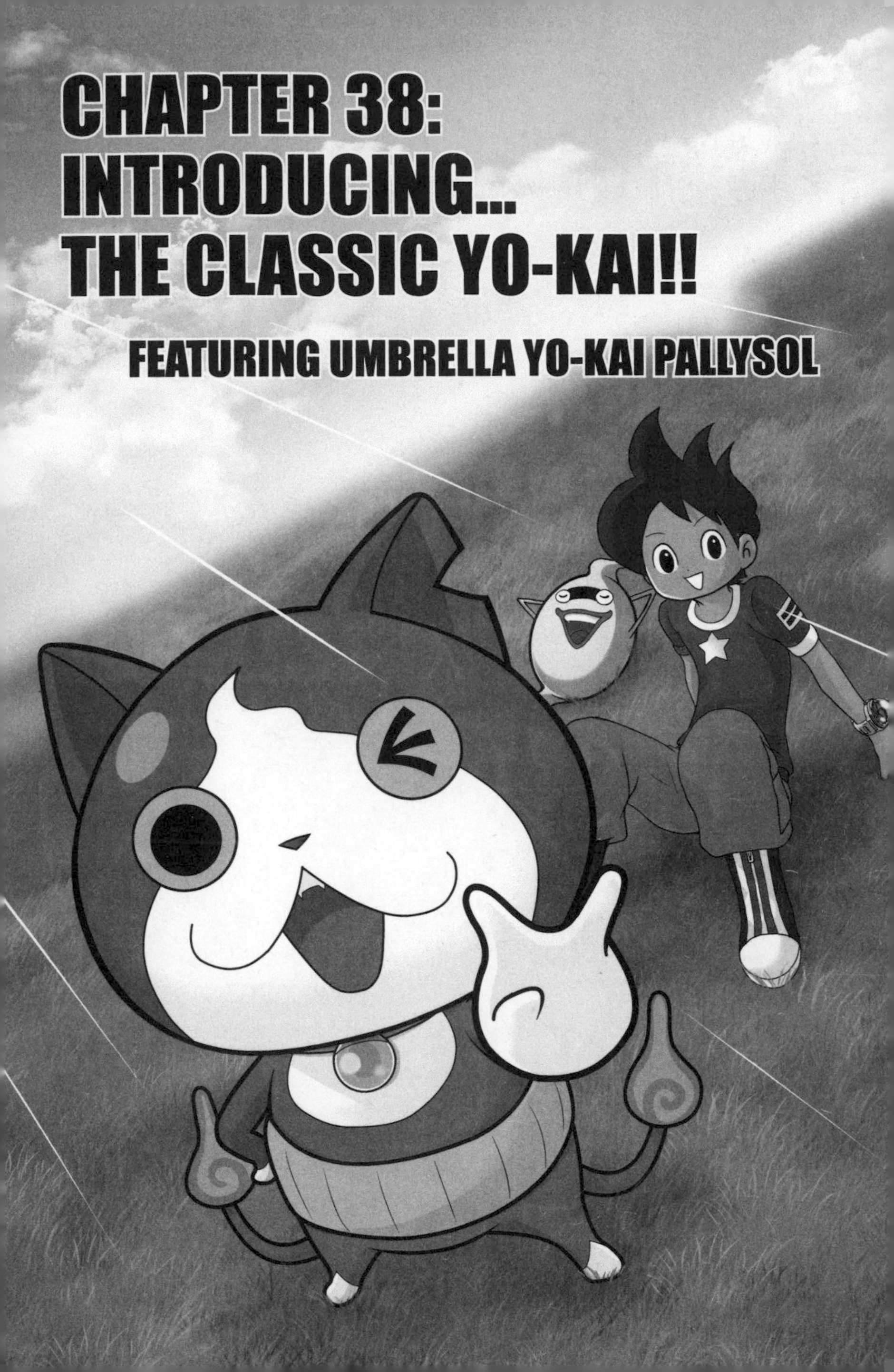

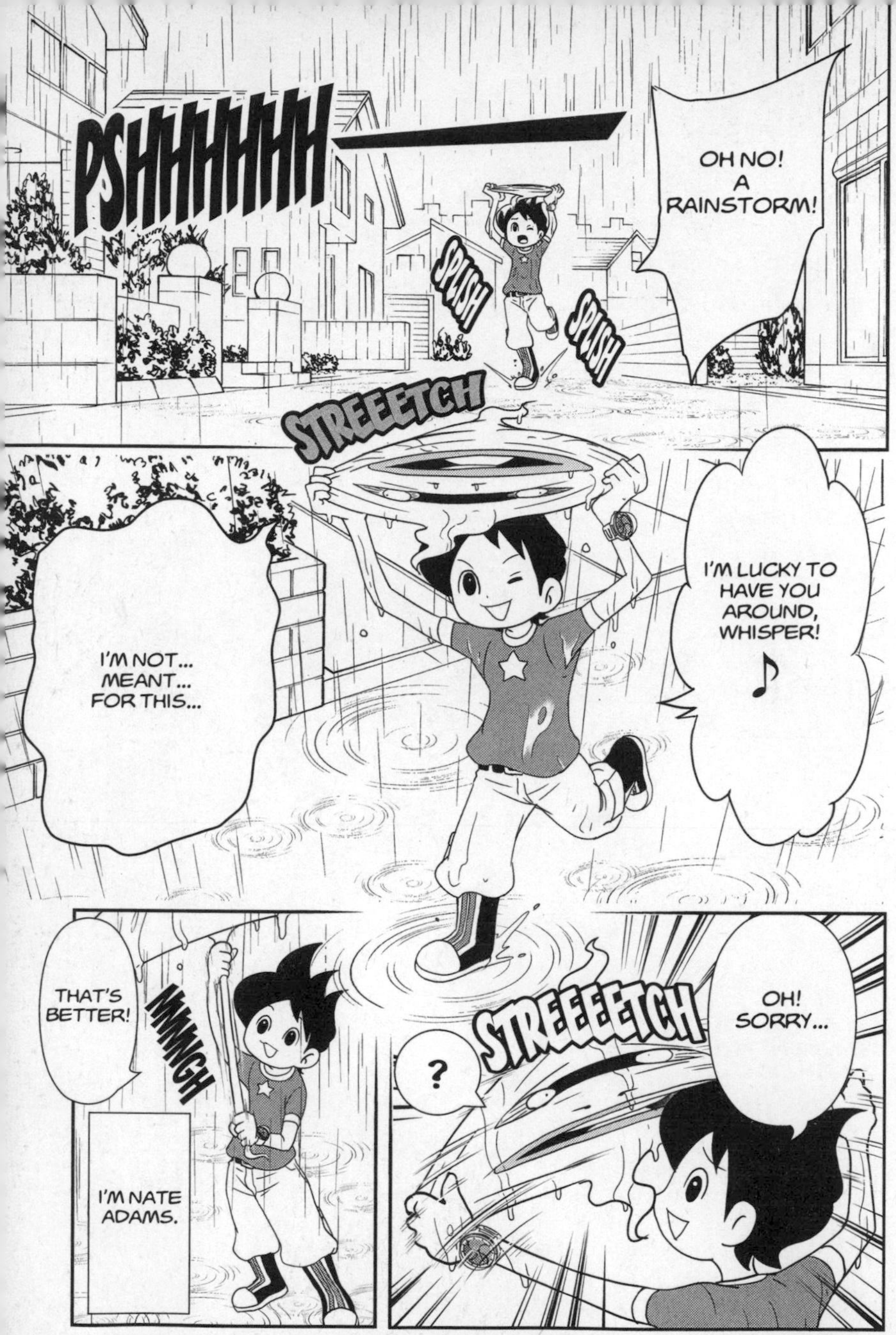
PSHHHHHH
OH NO! A RAINSTORM!
SPLISH
SPLISH
STREEETCH
I'M LUCKY TO HAVE YOU AROUND, WHISPER! ♪
I'M NOT... MEANT... FOR THIS...
OH! SORRY...
STREEEETCH
?
THAT'S BETTER!
MMMNGH
I'M NATE ADAMS.

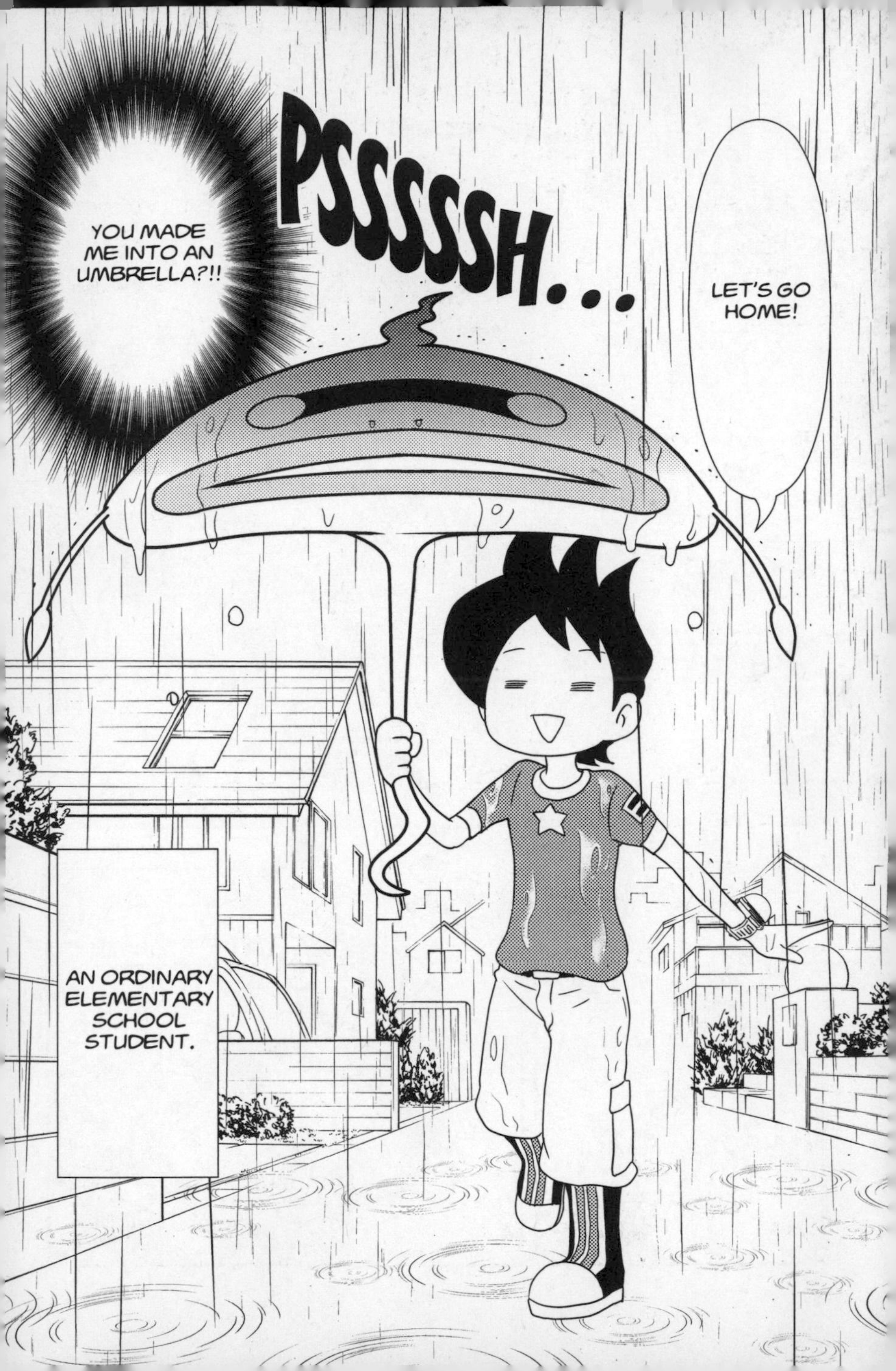
LET'S GO HOME!
PSSSSSH...
YOU MADE ME INTO AN UMBRELLA?!!
AN ORDINARY ELEMENTARY SCHOOL STUDENT.

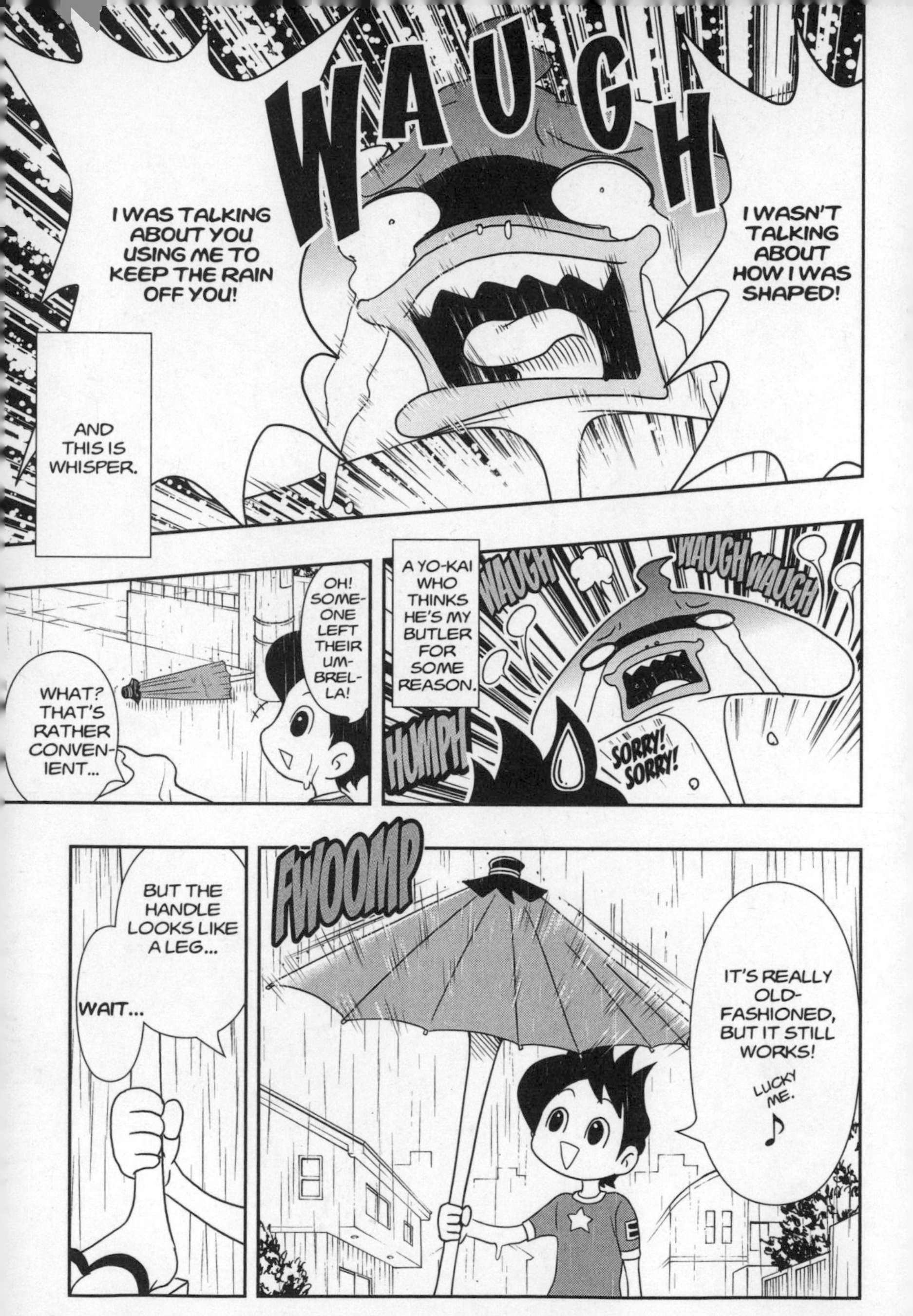
WAUGH
I WASN'T TALKING ABOUT HOW I WAS SHAPED!
I WAS TALKING ABOUT YOU USING ME TO KEEP THE RAIN OFF YOU!
AND THIS IS WHISPER.
A YO-KAI WHO THINKS HE'S MY BUTLER FOR SOME REASON.
WAUGH WAUGH
WAUGH
SORRY! SORRY!
HUMPH
OH! SOME-ONE LEFT THEIR UM-BREL-LA!
WHAT? THAT'S RATHER CONVEN-IENT...
FWOOMP
IT'S REALLY OLD-FASHIONED, BUT IT STILL WORKS!
LUCKY ME. ♪
BUT THE HANDLE LOOKS LIKE A LEG...
WAIT...

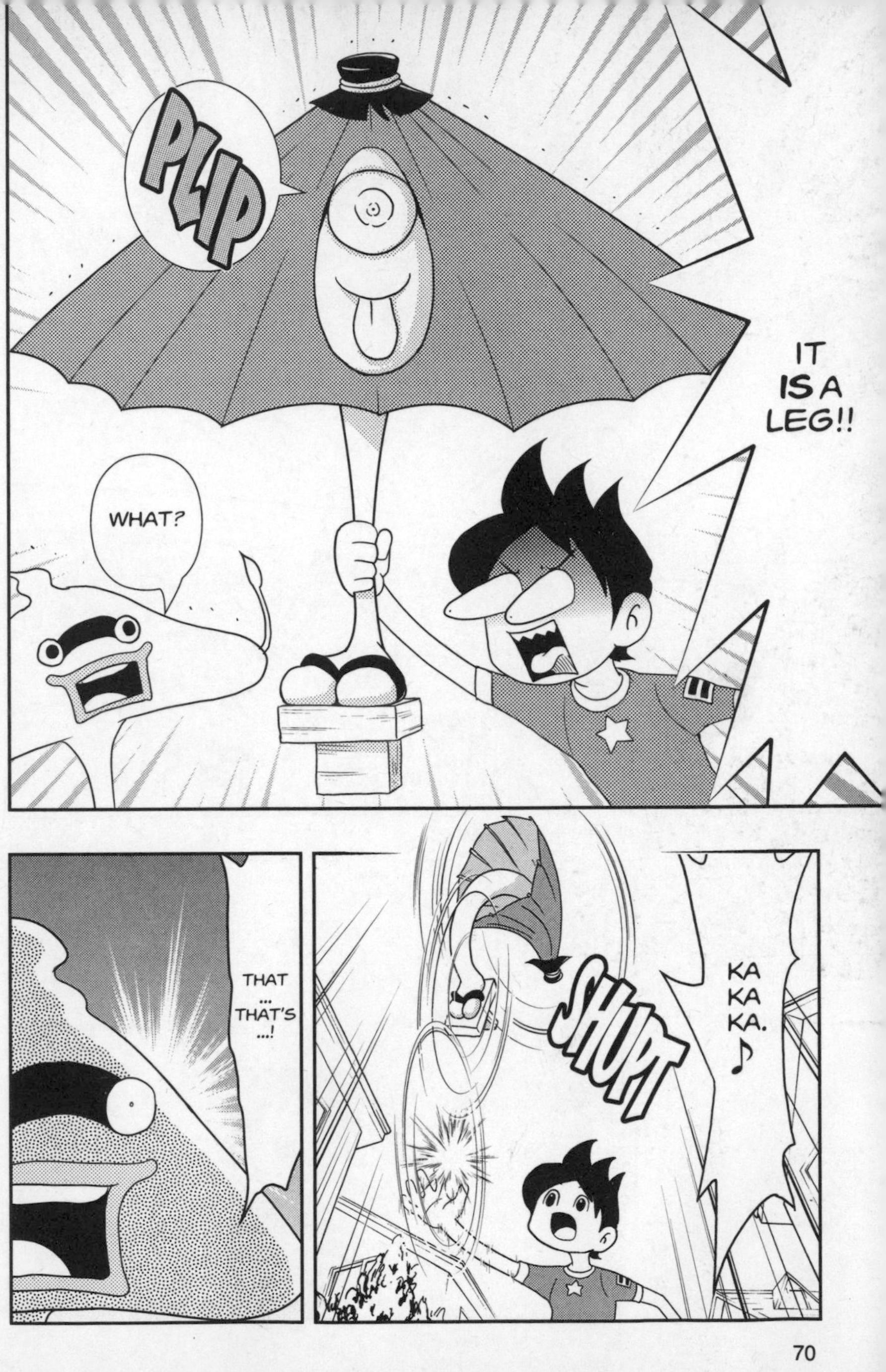
IT IS A LEG!!
PLIP
WHAT?
KA KA KA. ♪
SHUPT
THAT ... THAT'S ...!

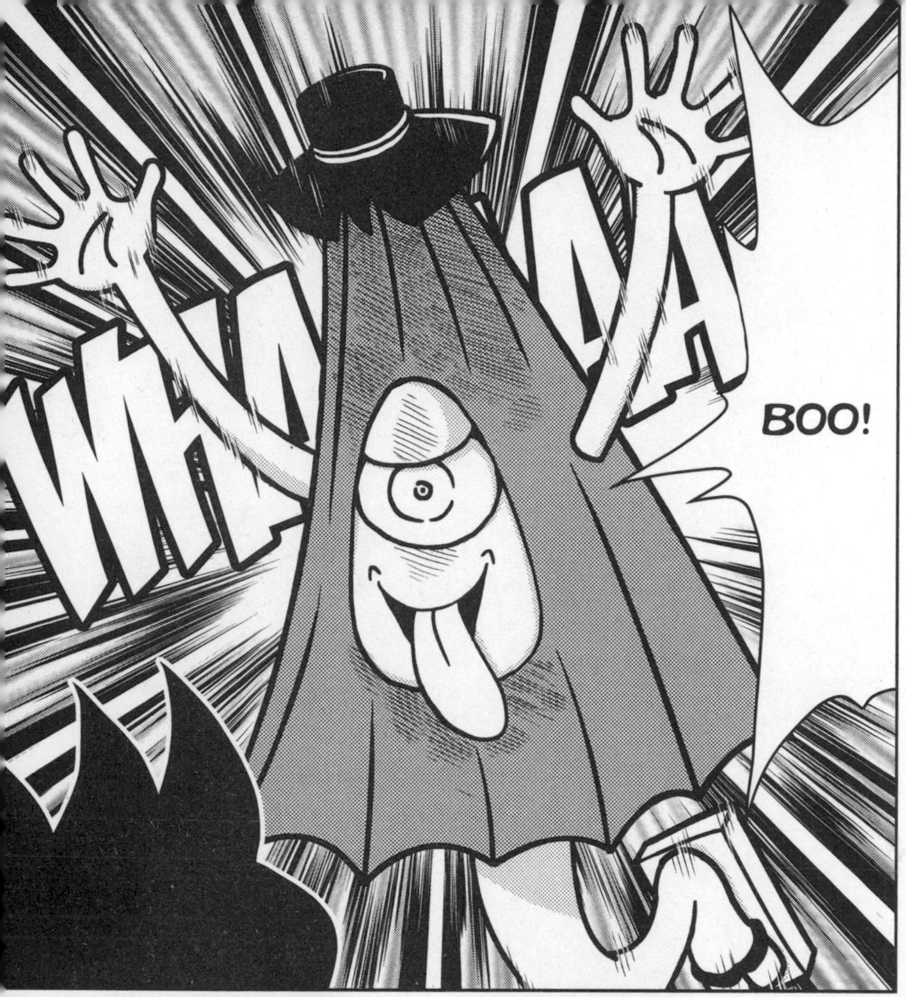
WHA
DA
BOO!

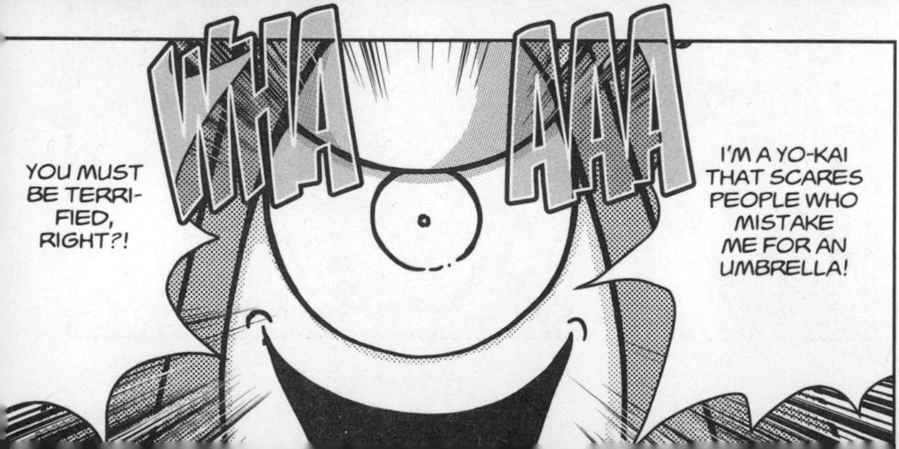
WHA
AAA
I'M A YO-KAI THAT SCARES PEOPLE WHO MISTAKE ME FOR AN UMBRELLA!
YOU MUST BE TERRI-FIED, RIGHT?!

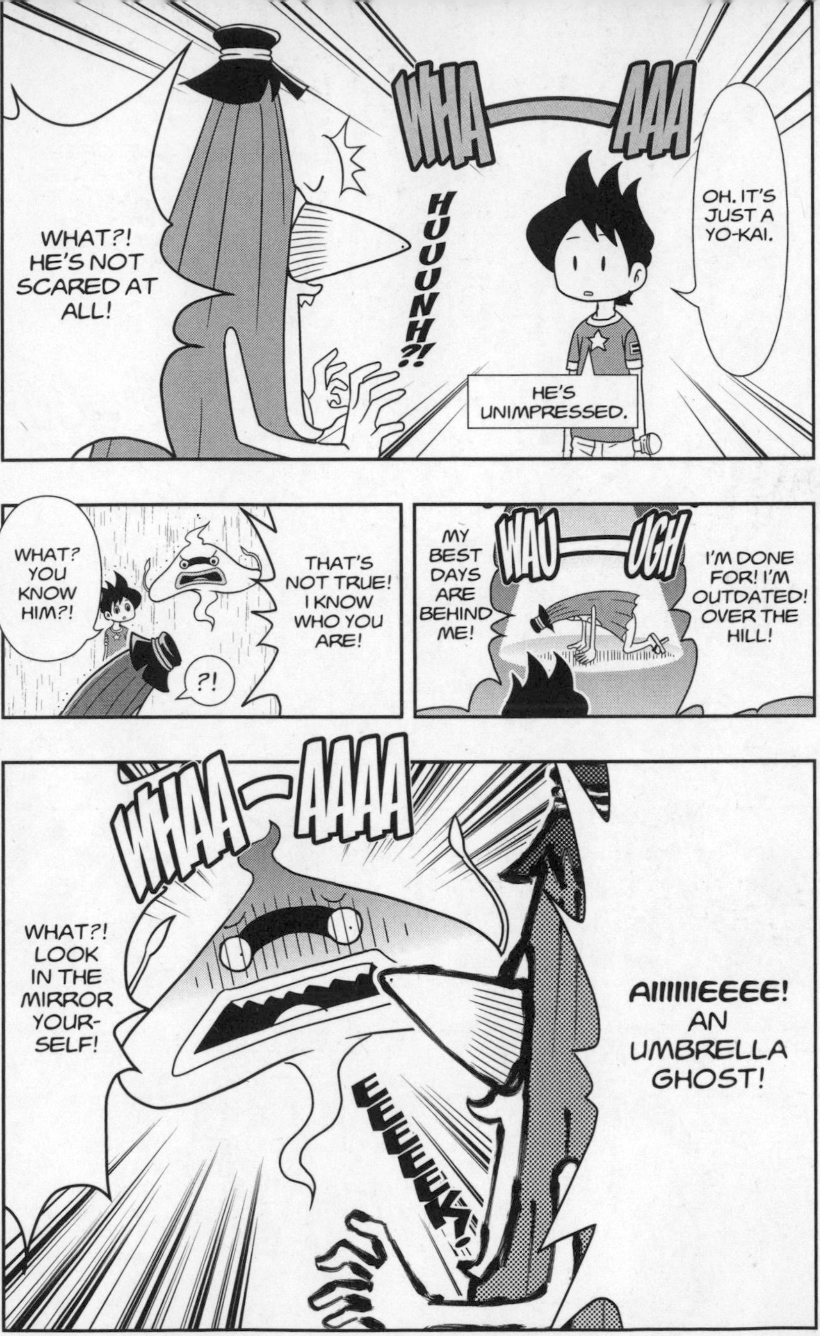
OH. IT'S JUST A YO-KAI.
WHA—AAA
HUUUUNH?!
HE'S UNIMPRESSED.
WHAT?! HE'S NOT SCARED AT ALL!
I'M DONE FOR! I'M OUTDATED! OVER THE HILL!
WAU—UGH
MY BEST DAYS ARE BEHIND ME!
THAT'S NOT TRUE! I KNOW WHO YOU ARE!
WHAT? YOU KNOW HIM?!
?!
WHAA—AAAA
AIIIIIEEEE! AN UMBRELLA GHOST!
WHAT?! LOOK IN THE MIRROR YOURSELF!
EEEEEK?!

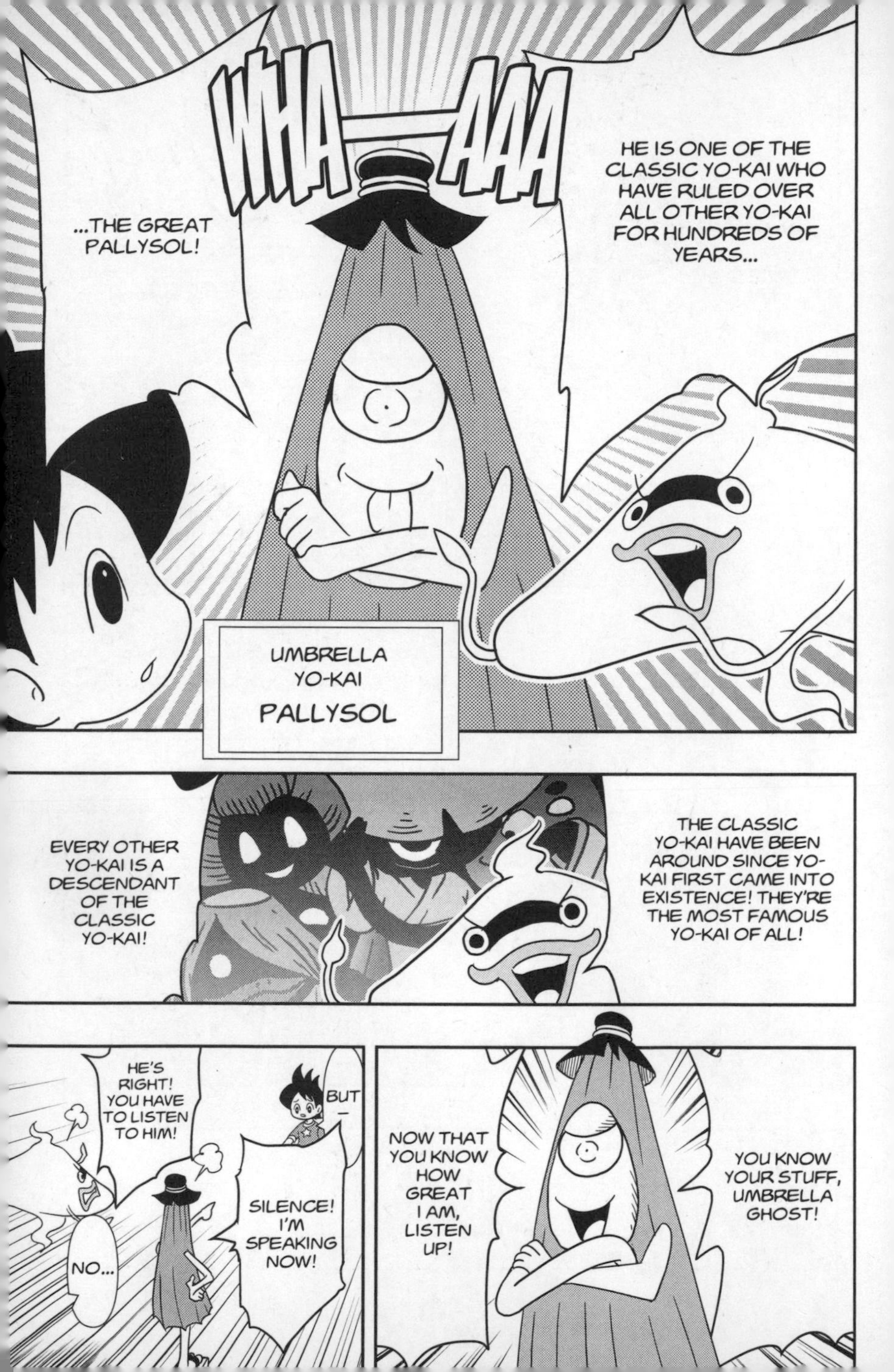
HE IS ONE OF THE CLASSIC YO-KAI WHO HAVE RULED OVER ALL OTHER YO-KAI FOR HUNDREDS OF YEARS...
WHA—AAA
...THE GREAT PALLYSOL!
UMBRELLA YO-KAI
PALLYSOL
THE CLASSIC YO-KAI HAVE BEEN AROUND SINCE YO-KAI FIRST CAME INTO EXISTENCE! THEY'RE THE MOST FAMOUS YO-KAI OF ALL!
EVERY OTHER YO-KAI IS A DESCENDANT OF THE CLASSIC YO-KAI!
YOU KNOW YOUR STUFF, UMBRELLA GHOST!
NOW THAT YOU KNOW HOW GREAT I AM, LISTEN UP!
BUT—
SILENCE! I'M SPEAKING NOW!
HE'S RIGHT! YOU HAVE TO LISTEN TO HIM!
NO...

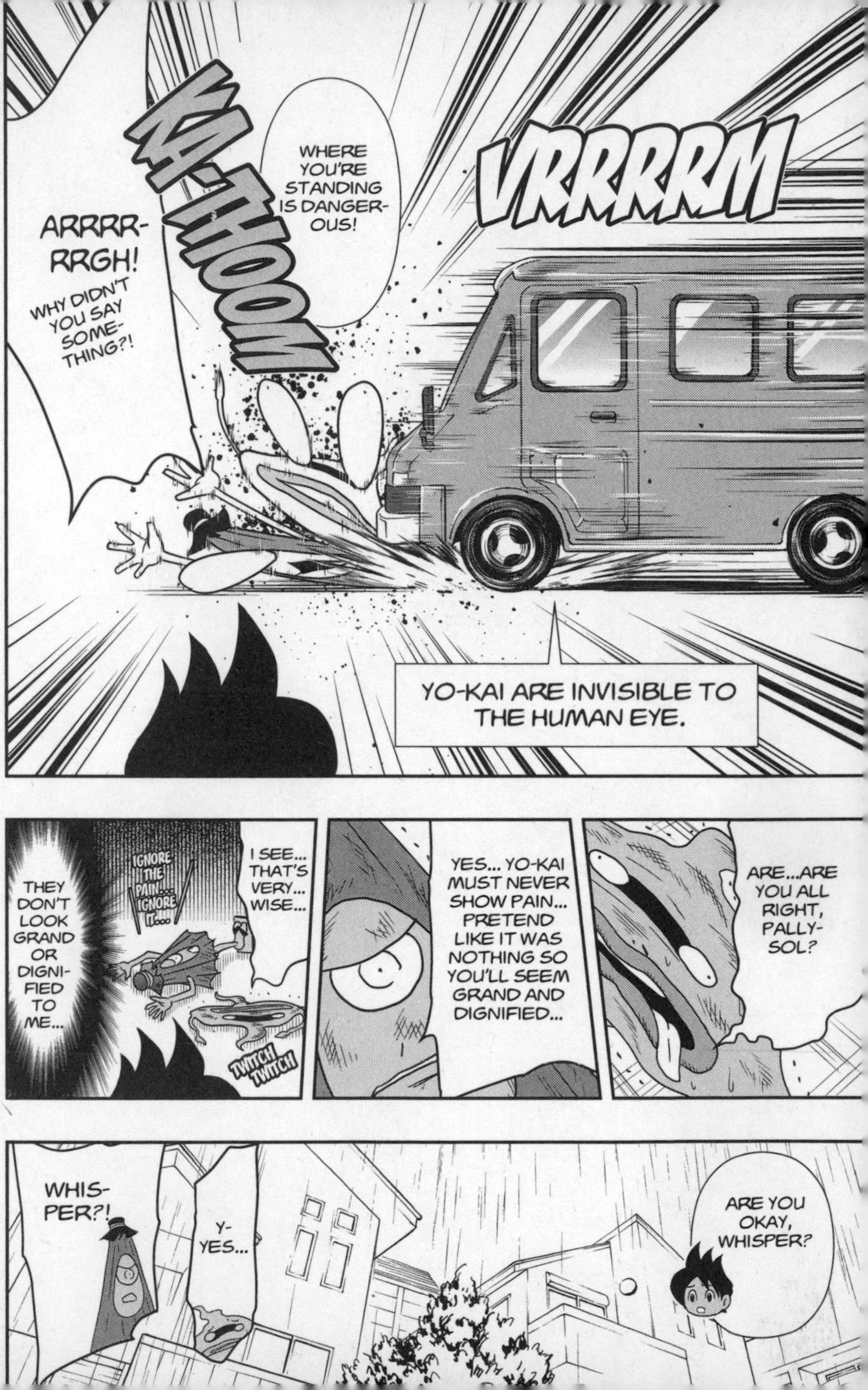
VRRRRM
WHERE YOU'RE STANDING IS DANGER-OUS!
KA-THOOOM
ARRRR-RRGH!
WHY DIDN'T YOU SAY SOME-THING?!
YO-KAI ARE INVISIBLE TO THE HUMAN EYE.
ARE...ARE YOU ALL RIGHT, PALLY-SOL?
YES... YO-KAI MUST NEVER SHOW PAIN... PRETEND LIKE IT WAS NOTHING SO YOU'LL SEEM GRAND AND DIGNIFIED...
I SEE... THAT'S VERY... WISE...
IGNORE THE PAIN... IGNORE IT...
THEY DON'T LOOK GRAND OR DIGNI-FIED TO ME...
TWITCH TWITCH
ARE YOU OKAY, WHISPER?
Y-YES...
WHIS-PER?!

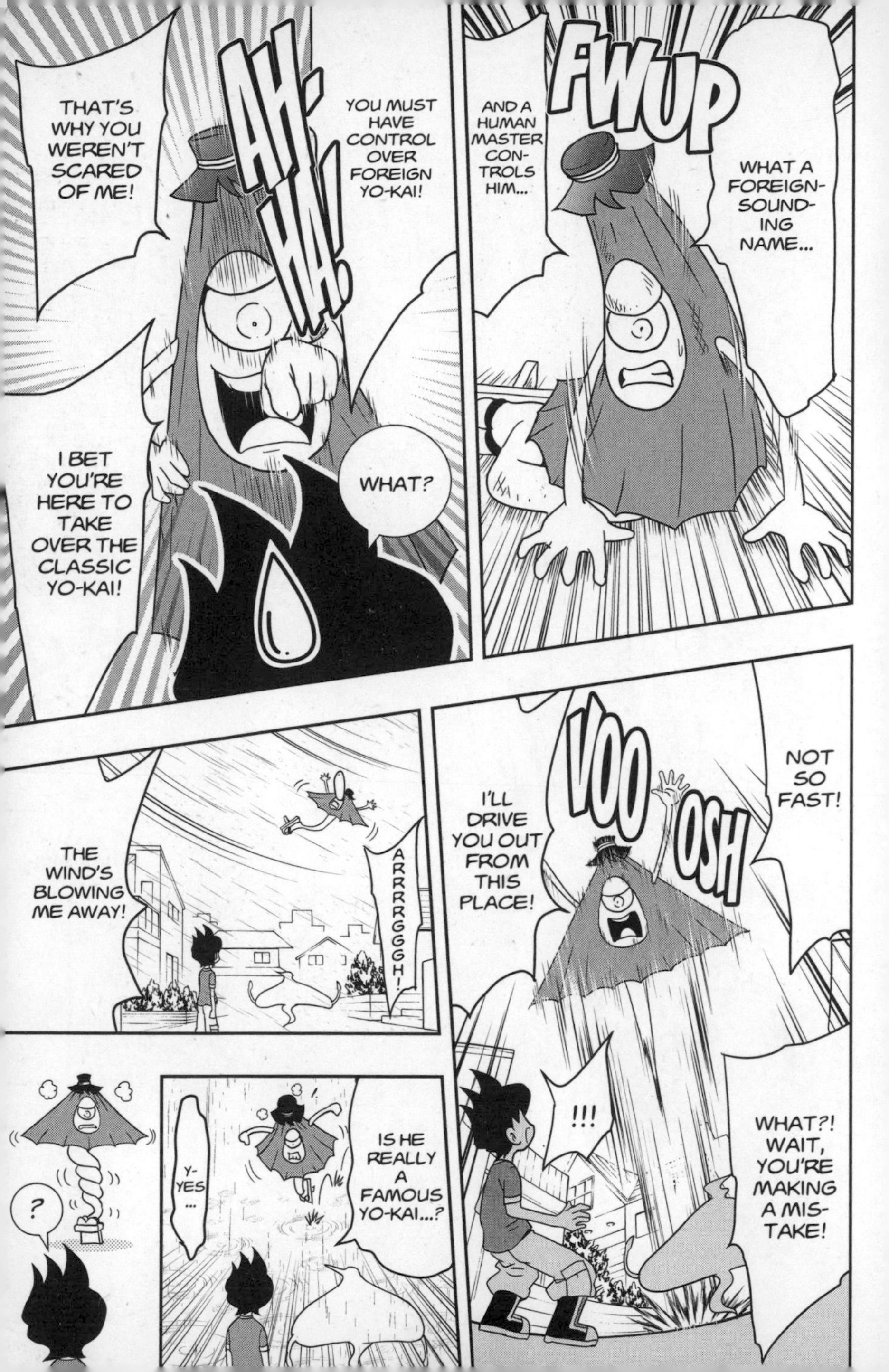
WHAT A FOREIGN-SOUNDING NAME...
FWUP
AND A HUMAN MASTER CONTROLS HIM...
YOU MUST HAVE CONTROL OVER FOREIGN YO-KAI!
AH-HA!
THAT'S WHY YOU WEREN'T SCARED OF ME!
WHAT?
I BET YOU'RE HERE TO TAKE OVER THE CLASSIC YO-KAI!
NOT SO FAST!
VOOOSH
I'LL DRIVE YOU OUT FROM THIS PLACE!
!!!
WHAT?! WAIT, YOU'RE MAKING A MISTAKE!
ARRRRGGGH!
THE WIND'S BLOWING ME AWAY!
IS HE REALLY A FAMOUS YO-KAI...?
!
Y-YES...
?

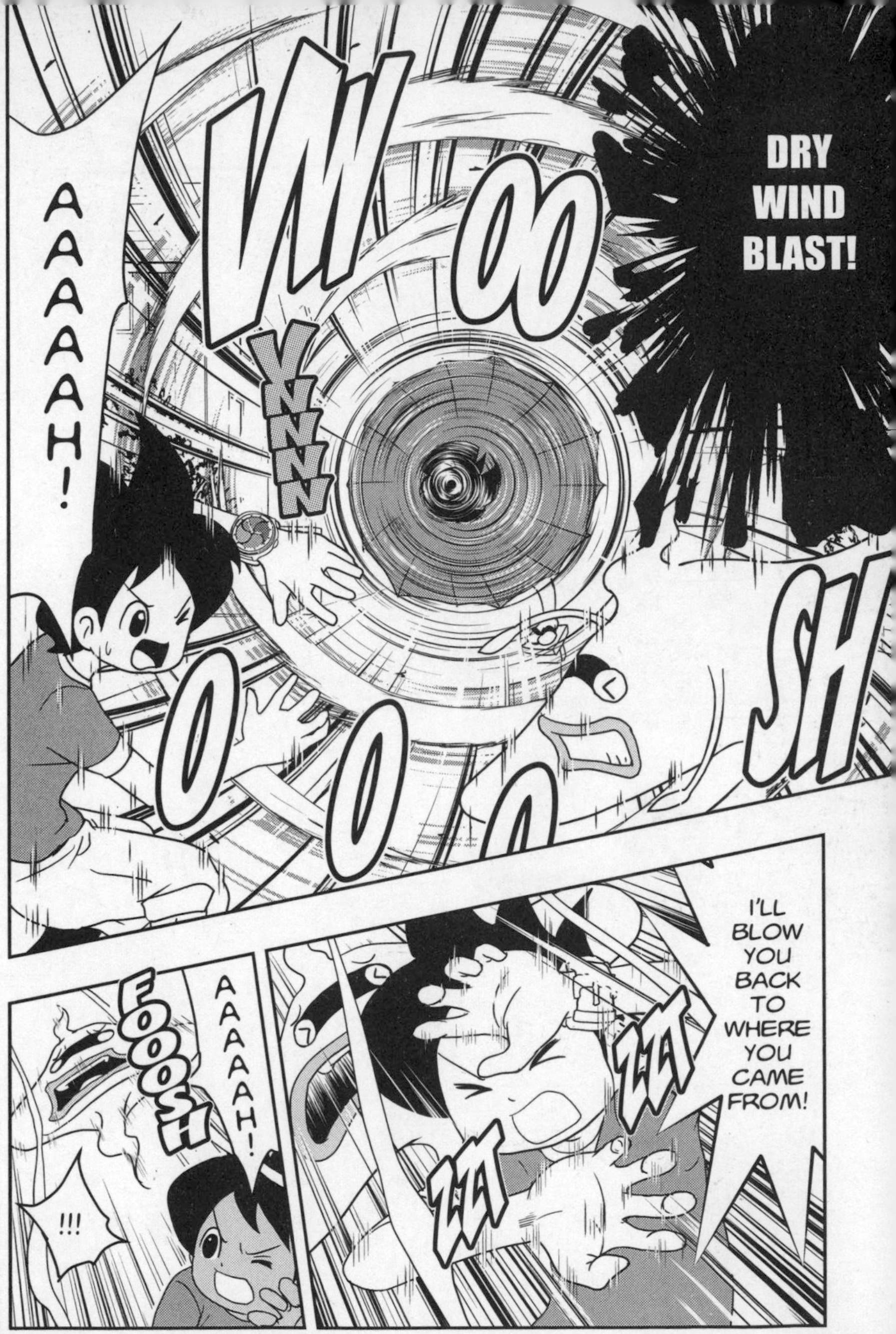
DRY WIND BLAST!
VW
OO
VNNN
AAAAAAH!
OOO
SH
I'LL BLOW YOU BACK TO WHERE YOU CAME FROM!
ZZT
ZZT
FOOOSH
AAAAAAH!
!!!

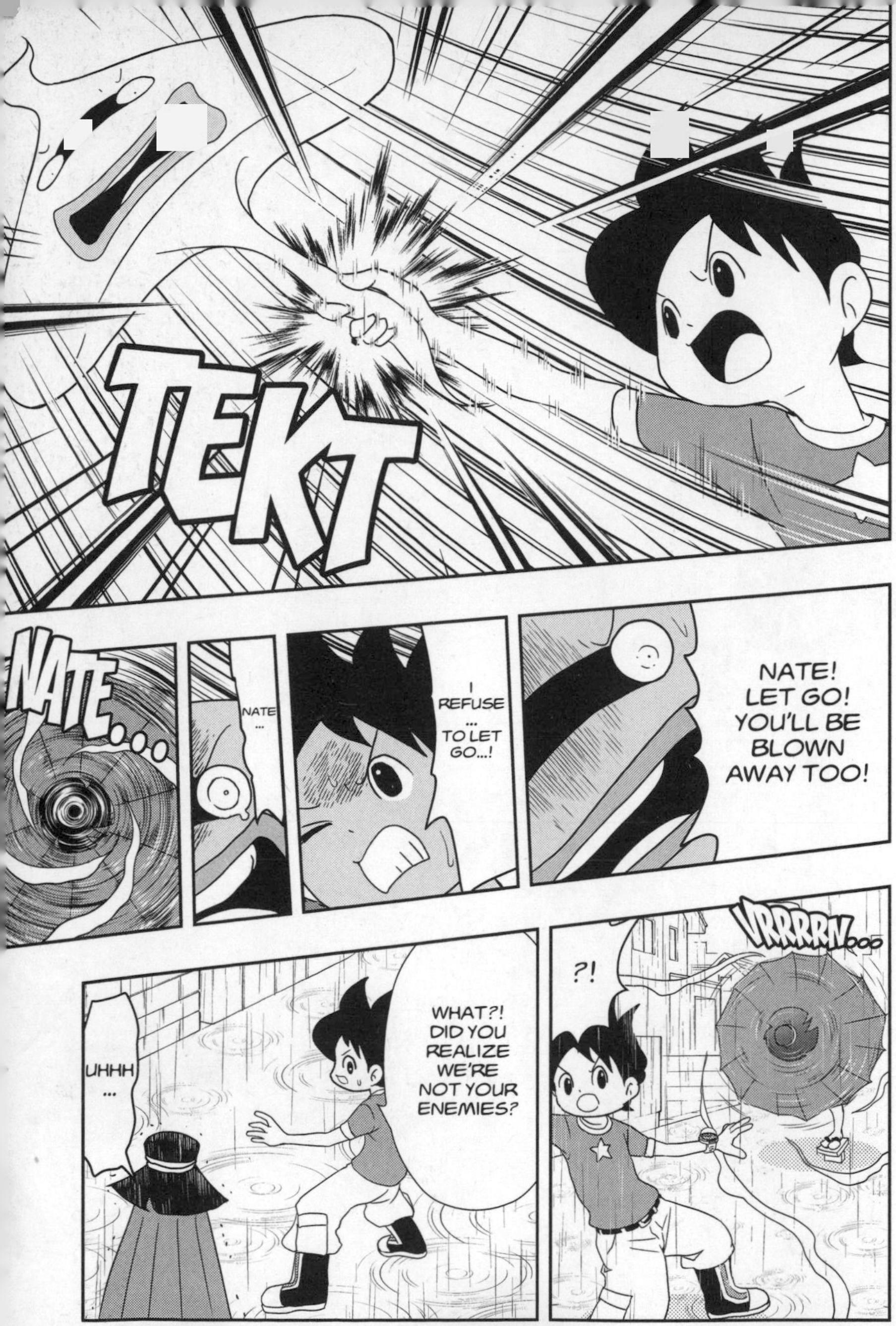
TEKT
NATE! LET GO! YOU'LL BE BLOWN AWAY TOO!
I REFUSE ... TO LET GO...!
NATE ...
NATE...
VRRRRN...
?!
WHAT?! DID YOU REALIZE WE'RE NOT YOUR ENEMIES?
UHHH ...

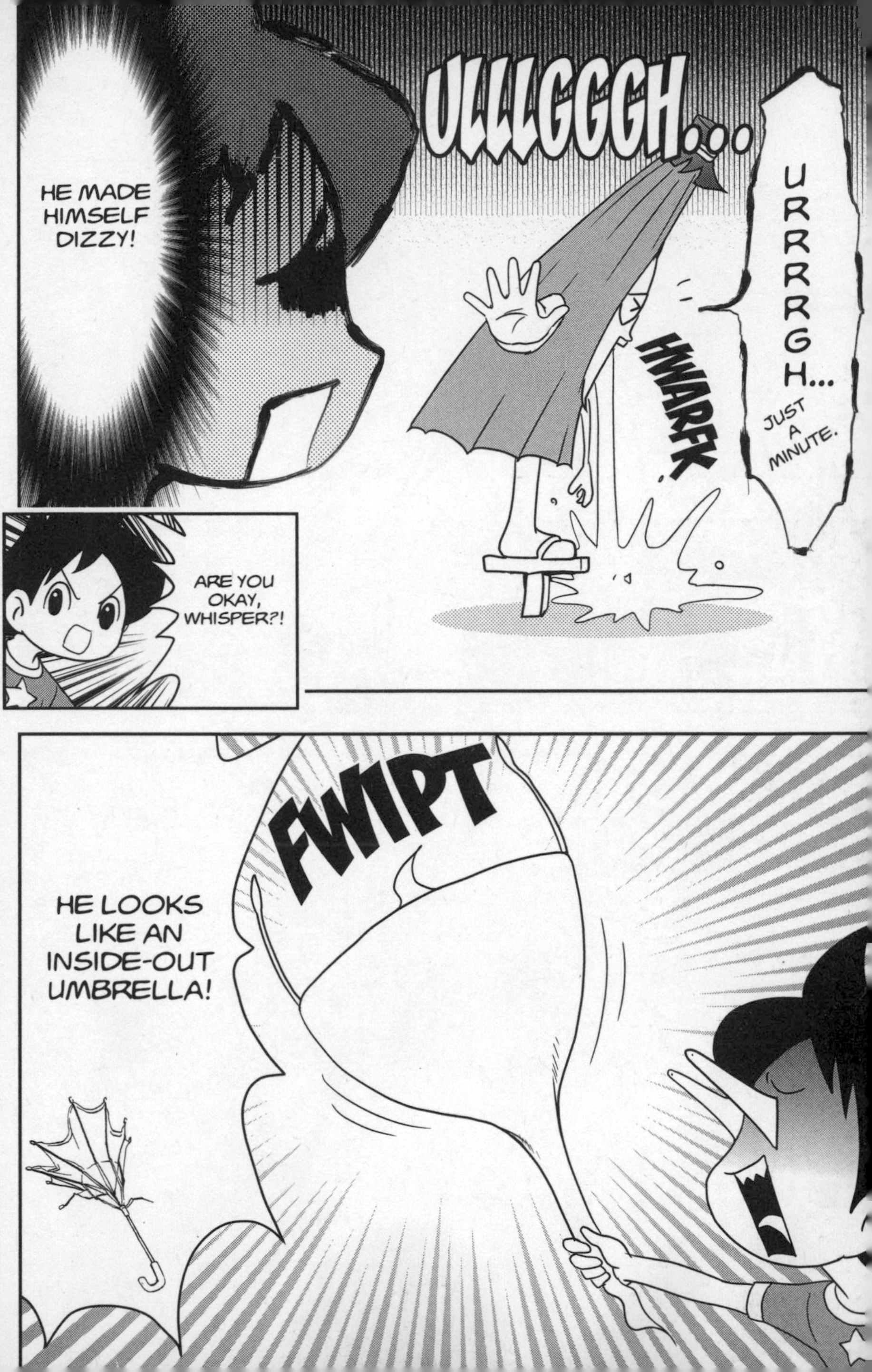
ULLLGGGH...
URRRRGH... JUST A MINUTE.
HWARFK
HE MADE HIMSELF DIZZY!
ARE YOU OKAY, WHISPER?!
FWIPT
HE LOOKS LIKE AN INSIDE-OUT UMBRELLA!

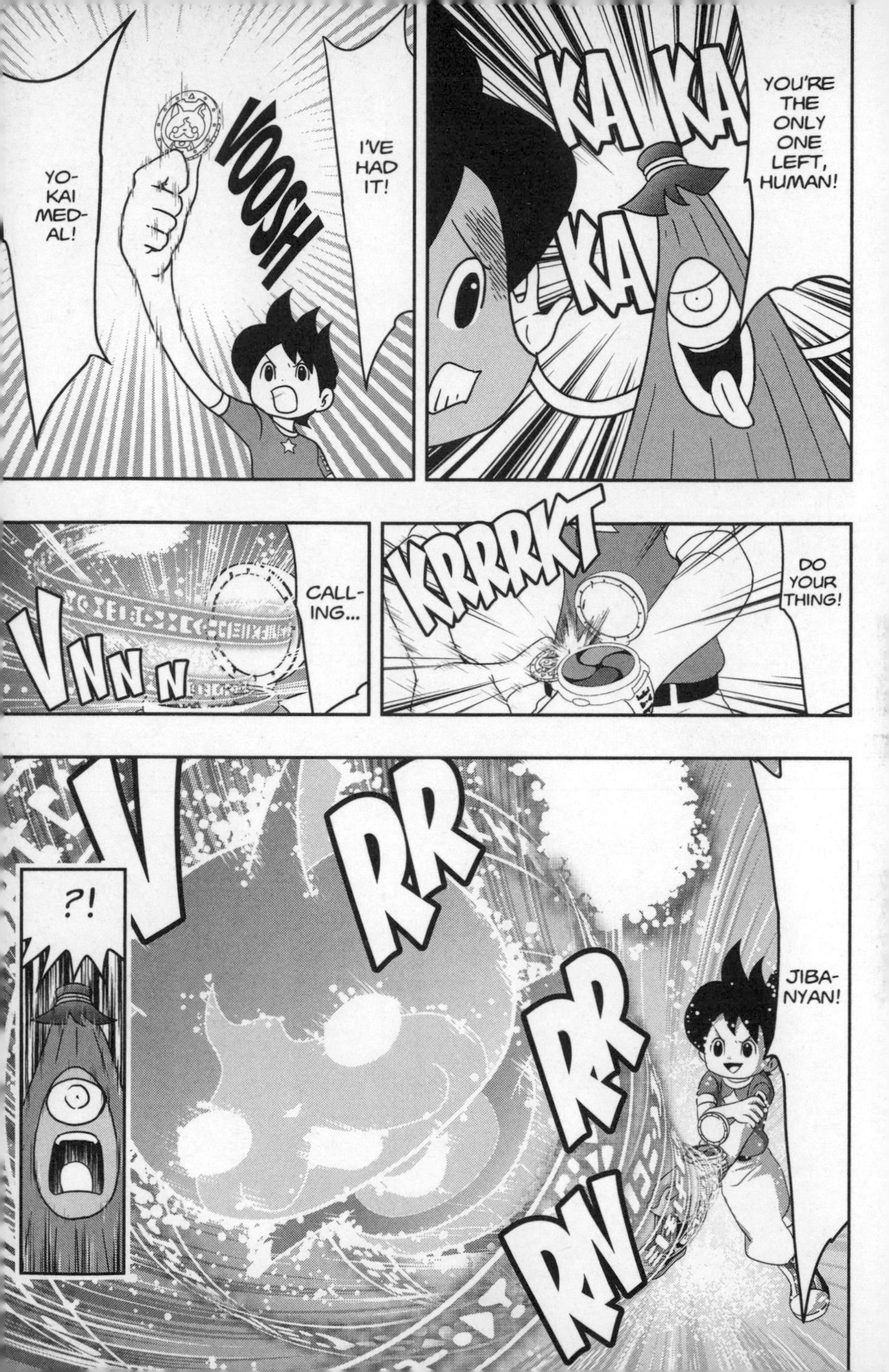

KA KA
YOU'RE THE ONLY ONE LEFT, HUMAN!
KA
I'VE HAD IT!
VOOSH
YO-KAI MED-AL!
DO YOUR THING!
KRRRKT
CALL-ING...
VNNN N
JIBA-NYAN!
V RR RR RN
?!

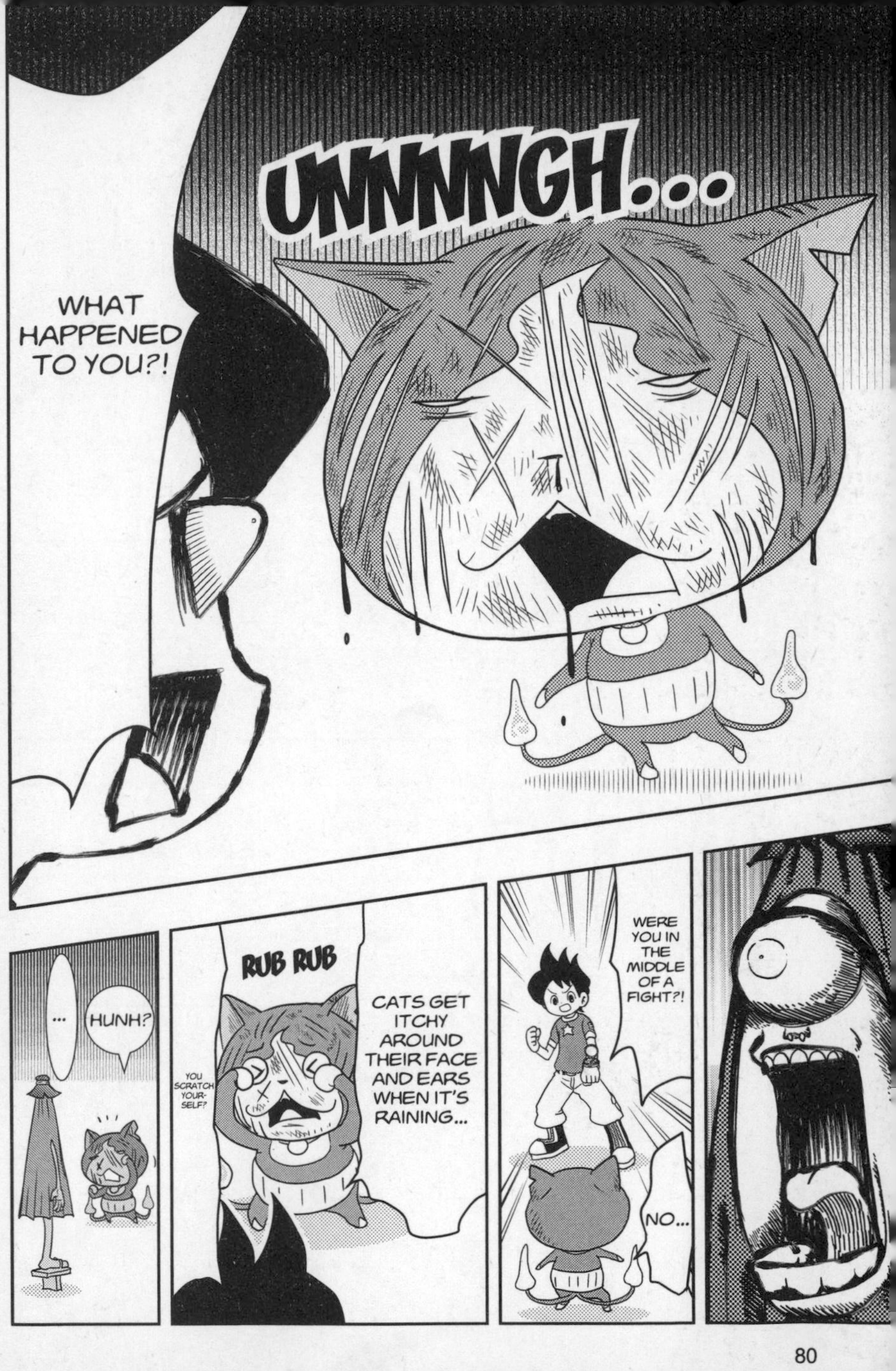
UNNNNGH...
WHAT HAPPENED TO YOU?!
WERE YOU IN THE MIDDLE OF A FIGHT?!
NO...
CATS GET ITCHY AROUND THEIR FACE AND EARS WHEN IT'S RAINING...
RUB RUB
YOU SCRATCH YOUR-SELF?
HUNH?
...

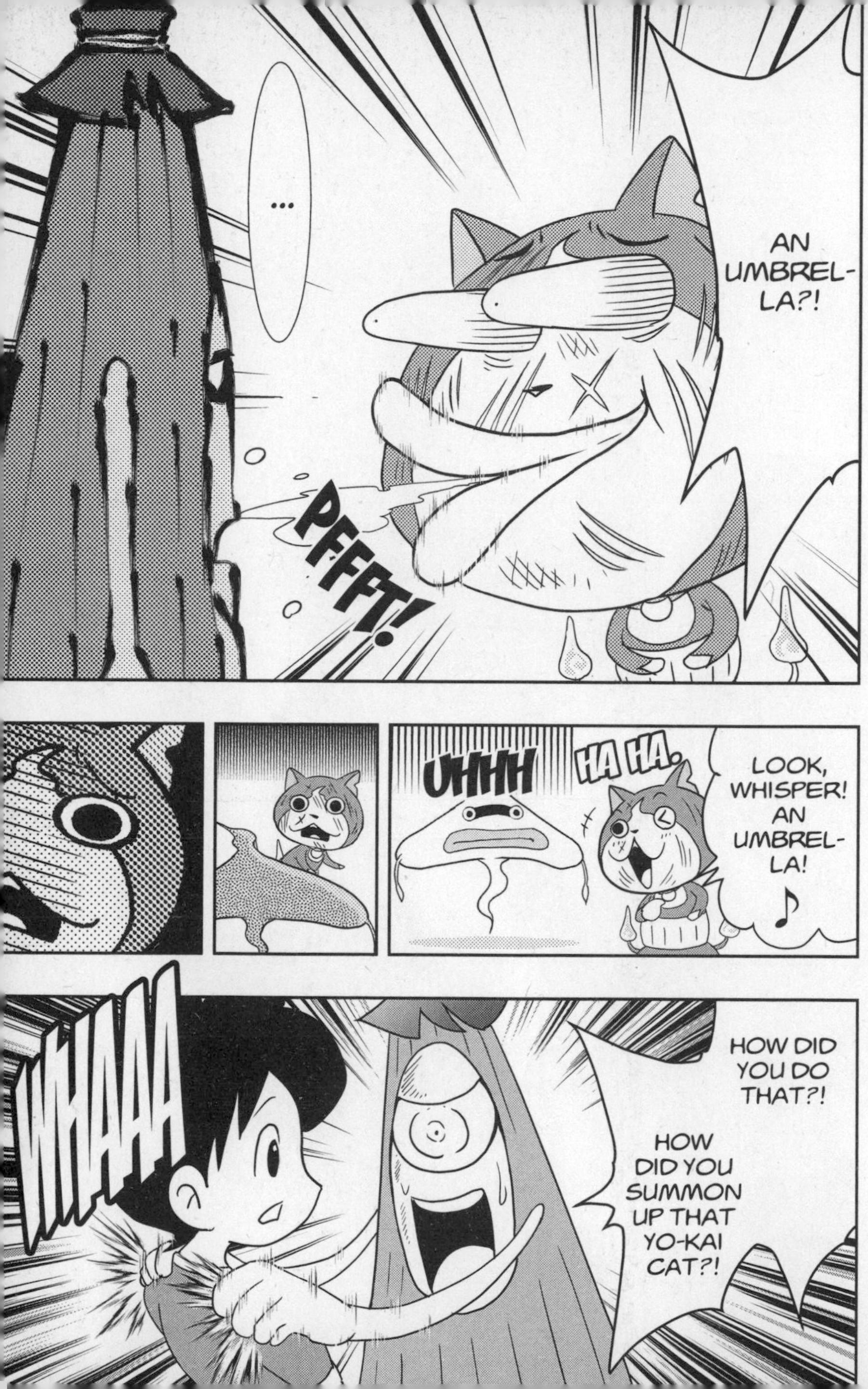
AN UMBREL-LA?!
...
PFFFT!
LOOK, WHISPER! AN UMBREL-LA!
♪
HA HA.
UHHH
HOW DID YOU DO THAT?!
HOW DID YOU SUMMON UP THAT YO-KAI CAT?!
WHAAA

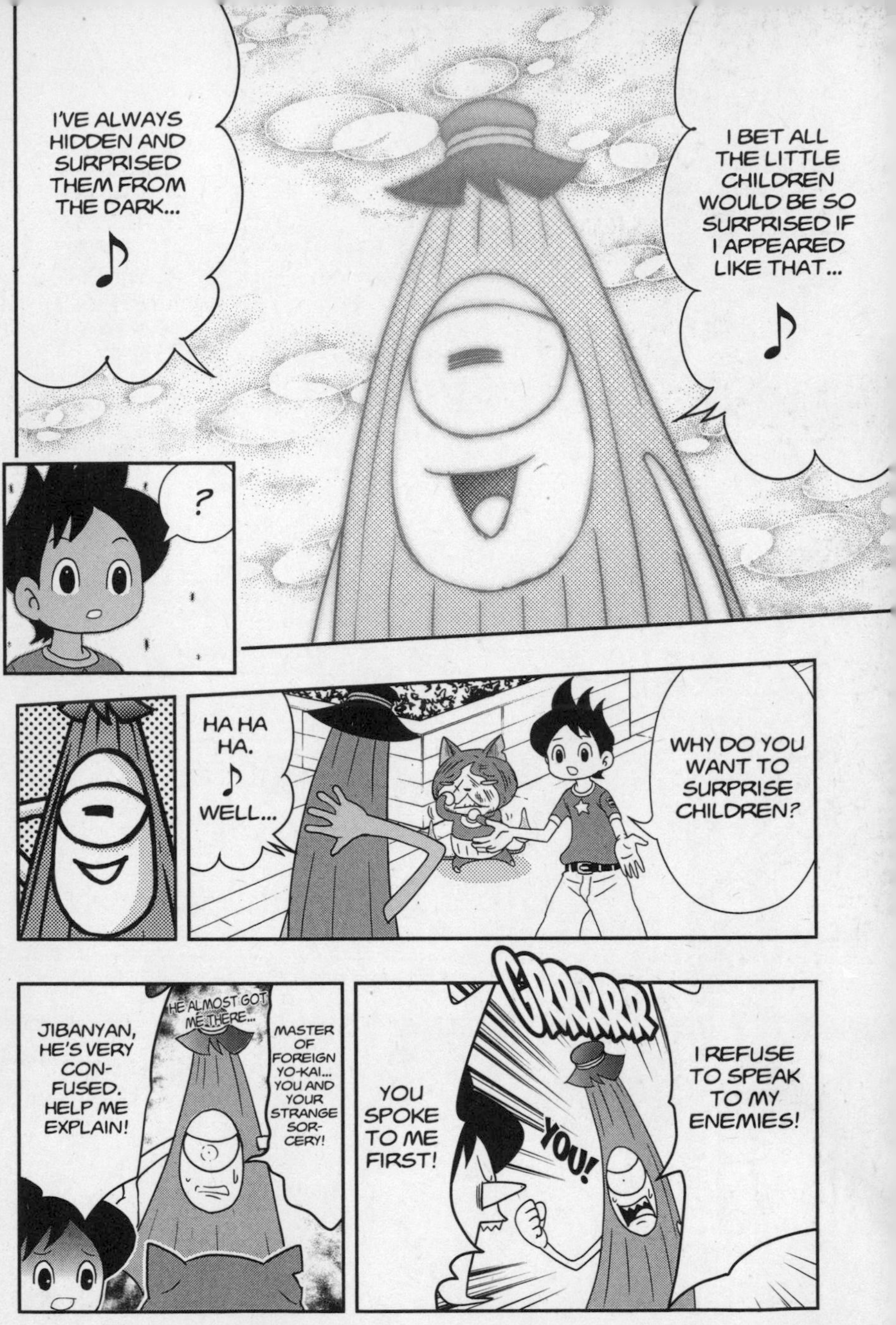
I BET ALL THE LITTLE CHILDREN WOULD BE SO SURPRISED IF I APPEARED LIKE THAT... ♪
I'VE ALWAYS HIDDEN AND SURPRISED THEM FROM THE DARK... ♪
?
WHY DO YOU WANT TO SURPRISE CHILDREN?
HA HA HA. ♪ WELL...
GRRRRR
I REFUSE TO SPEAK TO MY ENEMIES!
YOU!
YOU SPOKE TO ME FIRST!
MASTER OF FOREIGN YO-KAI... YOU AND YOUR STRANGE SOR-CERY!
HE ALMOST GOT ME THERE...
JIBANYAN, HE'S VERY CON-FUSED. HELP ME EXPLAIN!

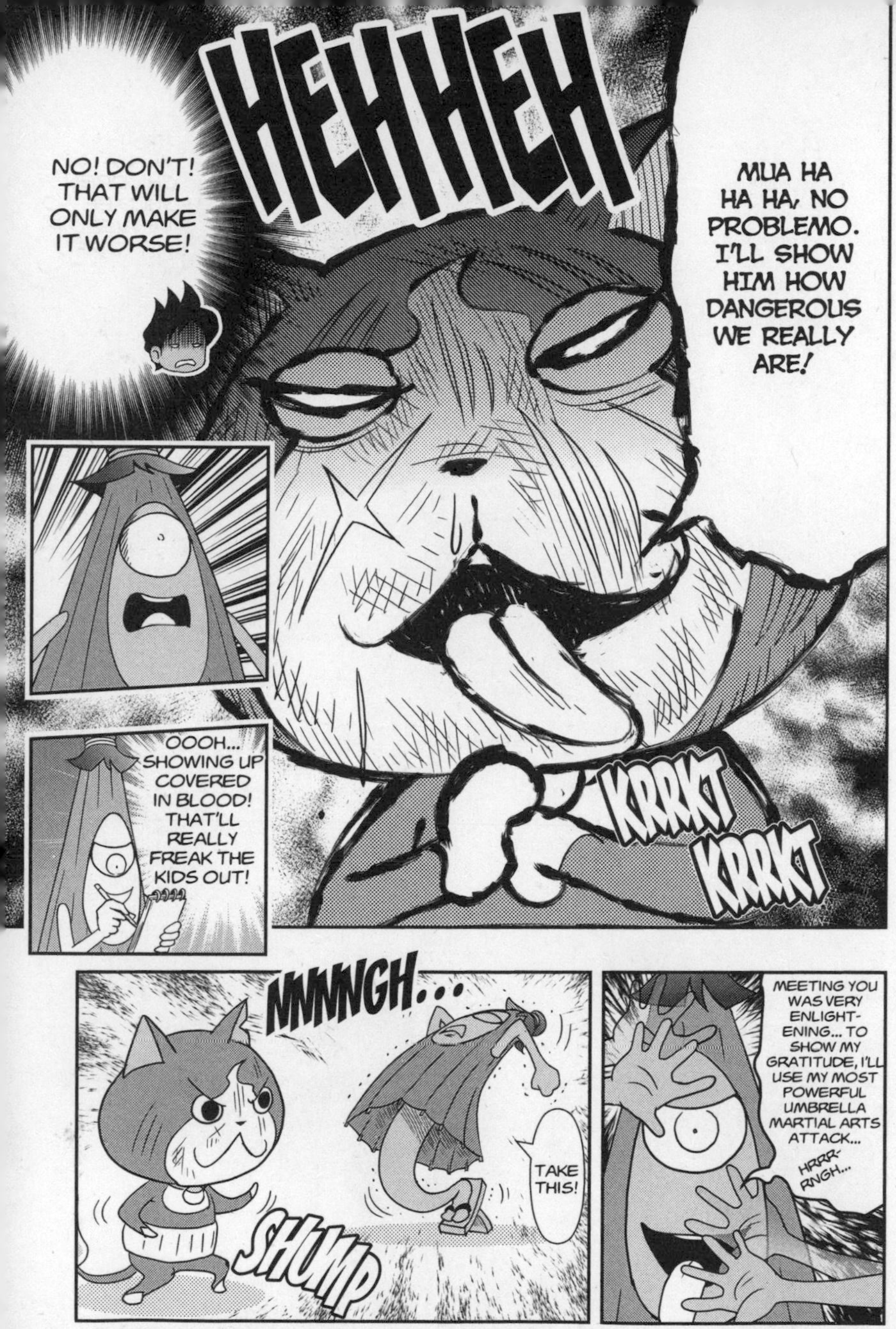
MUA HA HA HA, NO PROBLEMO. I'LL SHOW HIM HOW DANGEROUS WE REALLY ARE!
HEHHEH
NO! DON'T! THAT WILL ONLY MAKE IT WORSE!
KRRKT KRRKT
OOOH... SHOWING UP COVERED IN BLOOD! THAT'LL REALLY FREAK THE KIDS OUT!
MEETING YOU WAS VERY ENLIGHT-ENING... TO SHOW MY GRATITUDE, I'LL USE MY MOST POWERFUL UMBRELLA MARTIAL ARTS ATTACK...
HRRR-RNGH...
NNNNGH...
TAKE THIS!
SHUMP

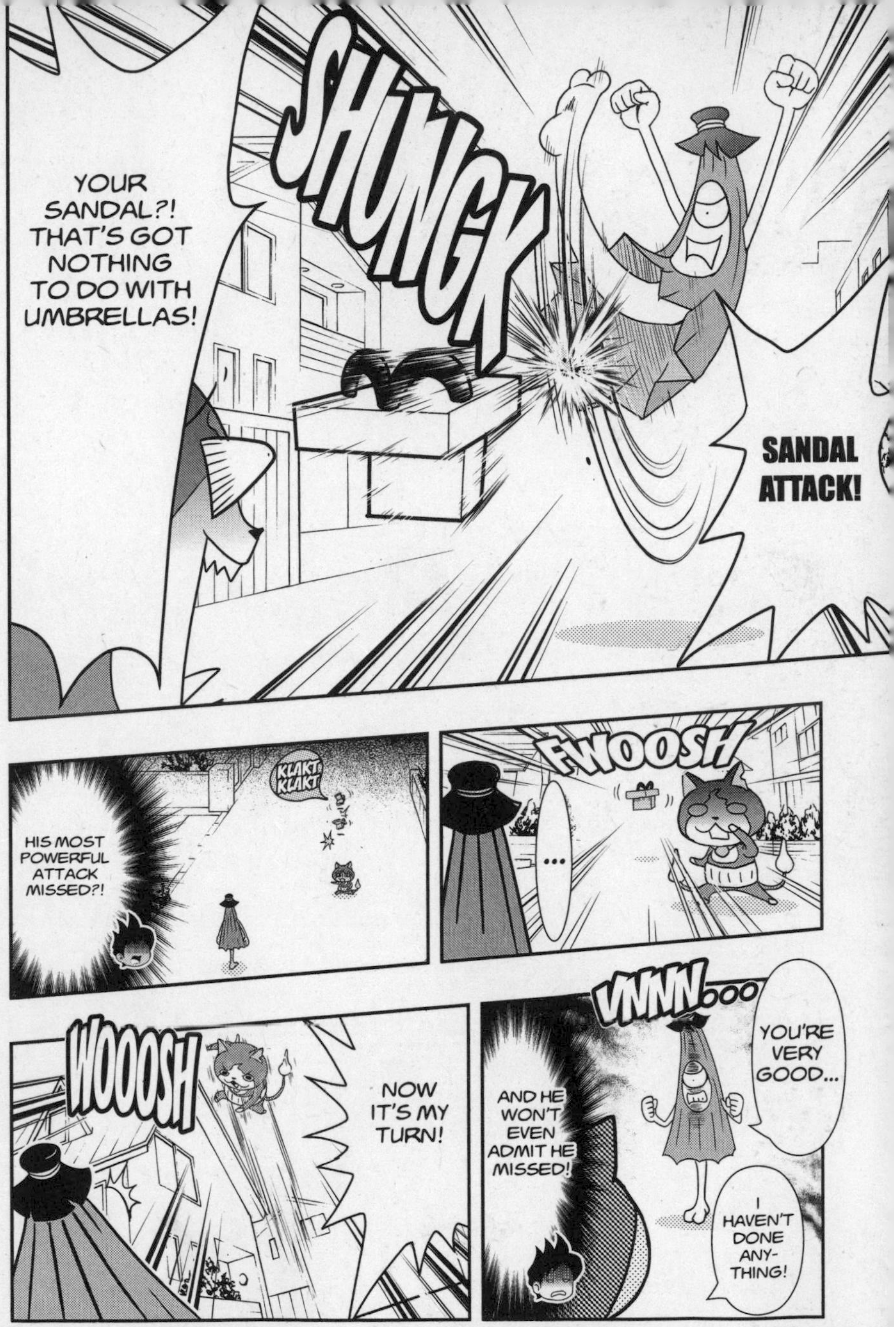

SHUNGK
SANDAL ATTACK!
YOUR SANDAL?! THAT'S GOT NOTHING TO DO WITH UMBRELLAS!
FWOOSH
...
KLAKT KLAKT
HIS MOST POWERFUL ATTACK MISSED?!
VNNNooo
YOU'RE VERY GOOD...
I HAVEN'T DONE ANY-THING!
AND HE WON'T EVEN ADMIT HE MISSED!
WOOOSH
NOW IT'S MY TURN!

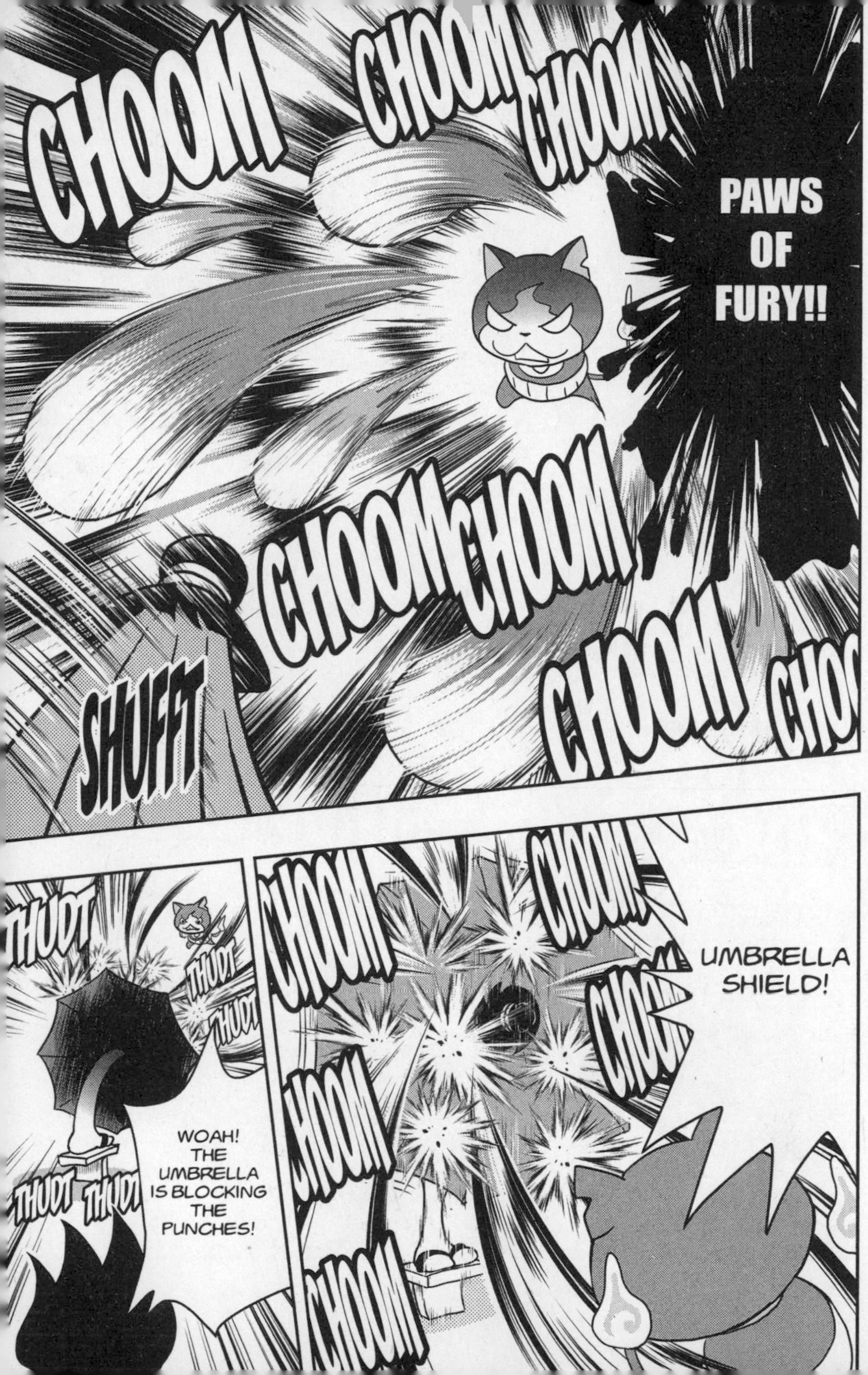
PAWS OF FURY!!
CHOOM
CHOOM
CHOOM
CHOOM
CHOOM
CHOOM
CHOO
SHUFFT
UMBRELLA SHIELD!
CHOOM
CHOO
CHOOM
HOOM
CHOOM
THUDT
THUDT
THUDT
WOAH! THE UMBRELLA IS BLOCKING THE PUNCHES!
THUDT
THUDT

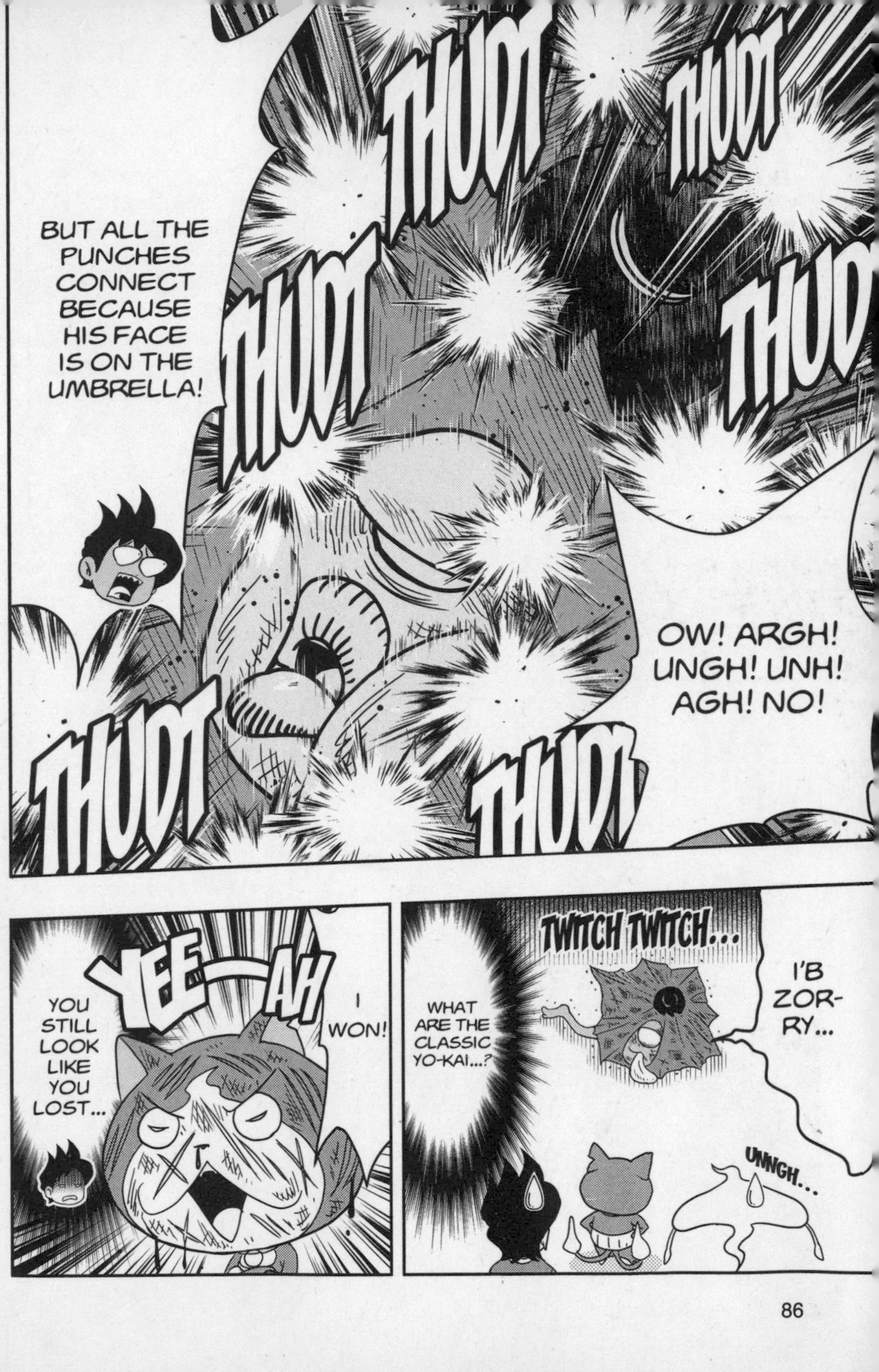
THUDT
THUDT
THUDT
THUD
OW! ARGH! UNGH! UNH! AGH! NO!
THUDT
BUT ALL THE PUNCHES CONNECT BECAUSE HIS FACE IS ON THE UMBRELLA!
THUDT
THUDT
TWITCH TWITCH...
I'B ZORRY...
WHAT ARE THE CLASSIC YO-KAI...?
UNNGH...
YEE—AH
I WON!
YOU STILL LOOK LIKE YOU LOST...

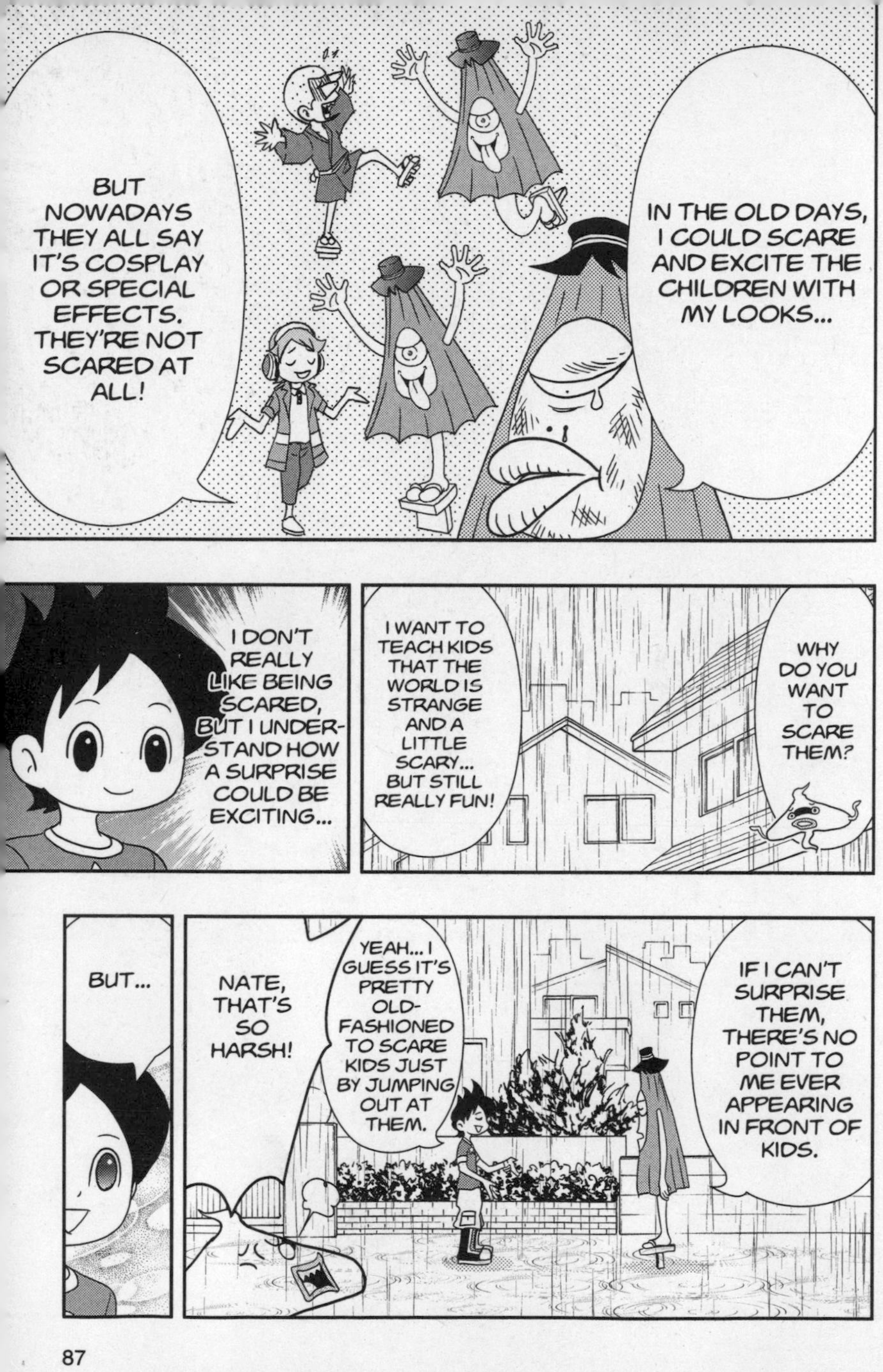
IN THE OLD DAYS, I COULD SCARE AND EXCITE THE CHILDREN WITH MY LOOKS...
BUT NOWADAYS THEY ALL SAY IT'S COSPLAY OR SPECIAL EFFECTS. THEY'RE NOT SCARED AT ALL!
WHY DO YOU WANT TO SCARE THEM?
I WANT TO TEACH KIDS THAT THE WORLD IS STRANGE AND A LITTLE SCARY... BUT STILL REALLY FUN!
I DON'T REALLY LIKE BEING SCARED, BUT I UNDER-STAND HOW A SURPRISE COULD BE EXCITING...
IF I CAN'T SURPRISE THEM, THERE'S NO POINT TO ME EVER APPEARING IN FRONT OF KIDS.
YEAH... I GUESS IT'S PRETTY OLD-FASHIONED TO SCARE KIDS JUST BY JUMPING OUT AT THEM.
NATE, THAT'S SO HARSH!
BUT...

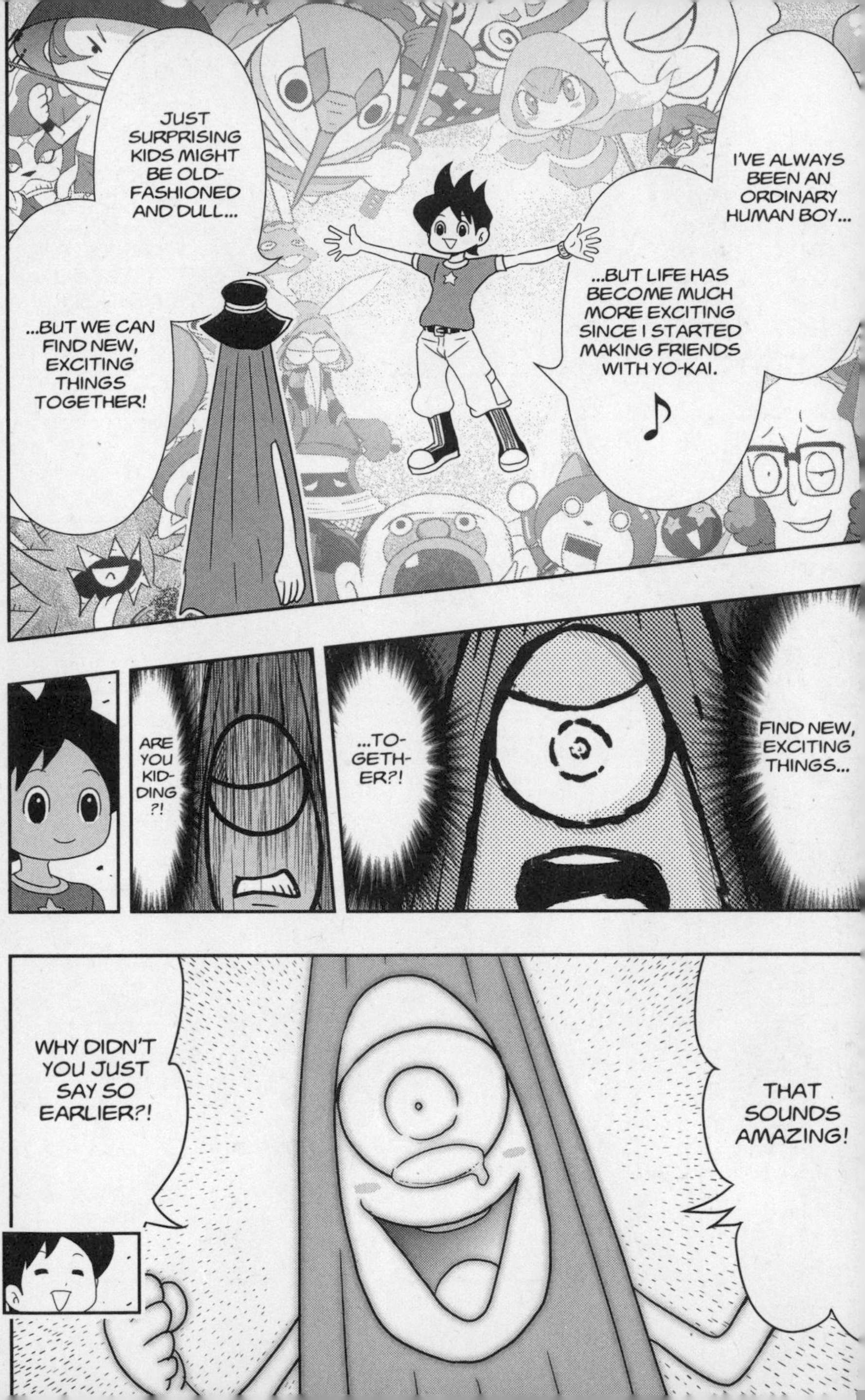
I'VE ALWAYS BEEN AN ORDINARY HUMAN BOY...
...BUT LIFE HAS BECOME MUCH MORE EXCITING SINCE I STARTED MAKING FRIENDS WITH YO-KAI. ♪
JUST SURPRISING KIDS MIGHT BE OLD-FASHIONED AND DULL...
...BUT WE CAN FIND NEW, EXCITING THINGS TOGETHER!
FIND NEW, EXCITING THINGS...
...TO-GETH-ER?!
ARE YOU KID-DING?!
THAT SOUNDS AMAZING!
WHY DIDN'T YOU JUST SAY SO EARLIER?!

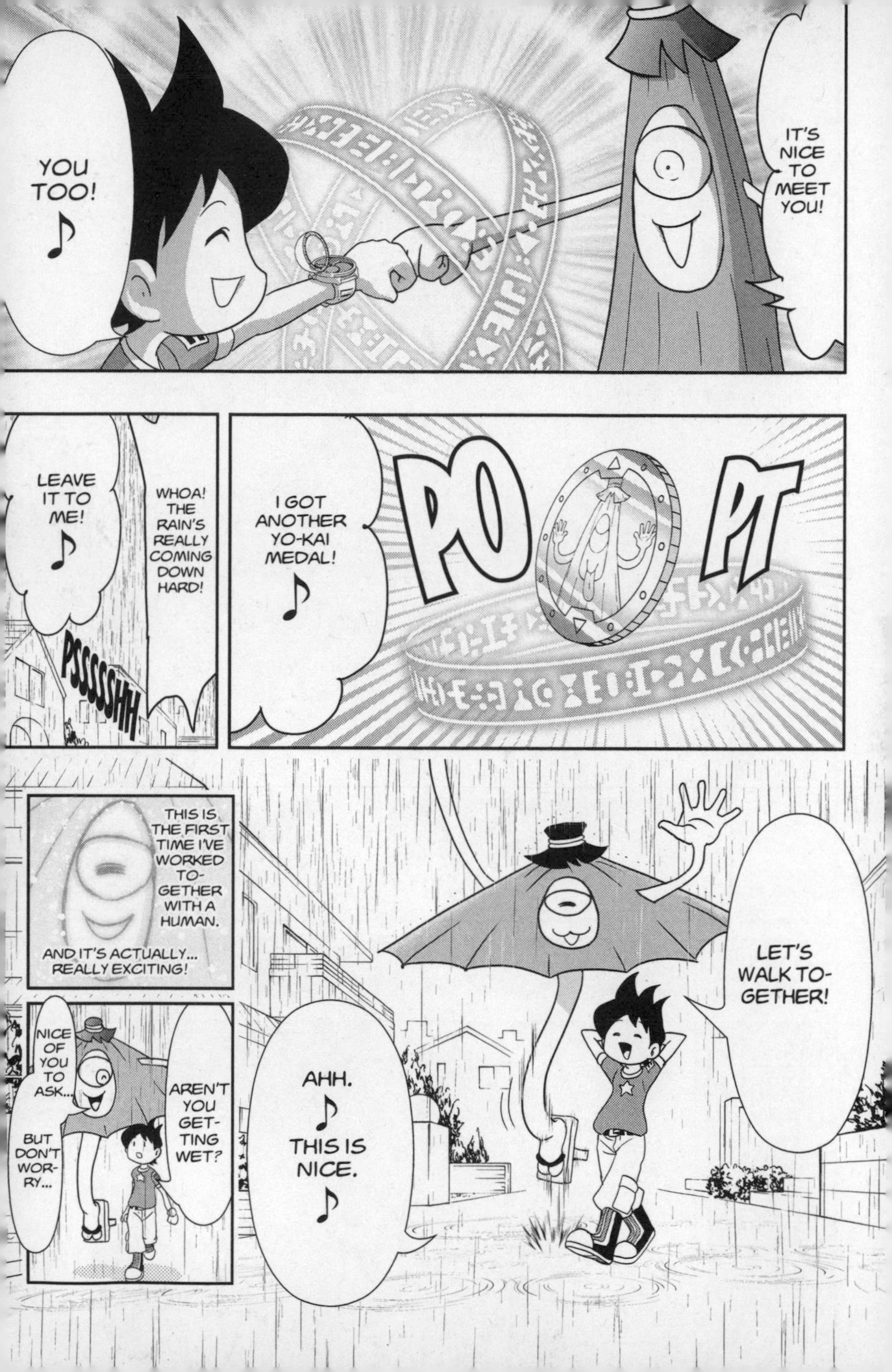
IT'S NICE TO MEET YOU!
YOU TOO! ♪
I GOT ANOTHER YO-KAI MEDAL! ♪
PO
PT
WHOA! THE RAIN'S REALLY COMING DOWN HARD!
LEAVE IT TO ME! ♪
PSSSSSHH
LET'S WALK TO-GETHER!
AHH. ♪ THIS IS NICE. ♪
THIS IS THE FIRST TIME I'VE WORKED TO-GETHER WITH A HUMAN.
AND IT'S ACTUALLY... REALLY EXCITING!
AREN'T YOU GET-TING WET?
NICE OF YOU TO ASK...
BUT DON'T WOR-RY...

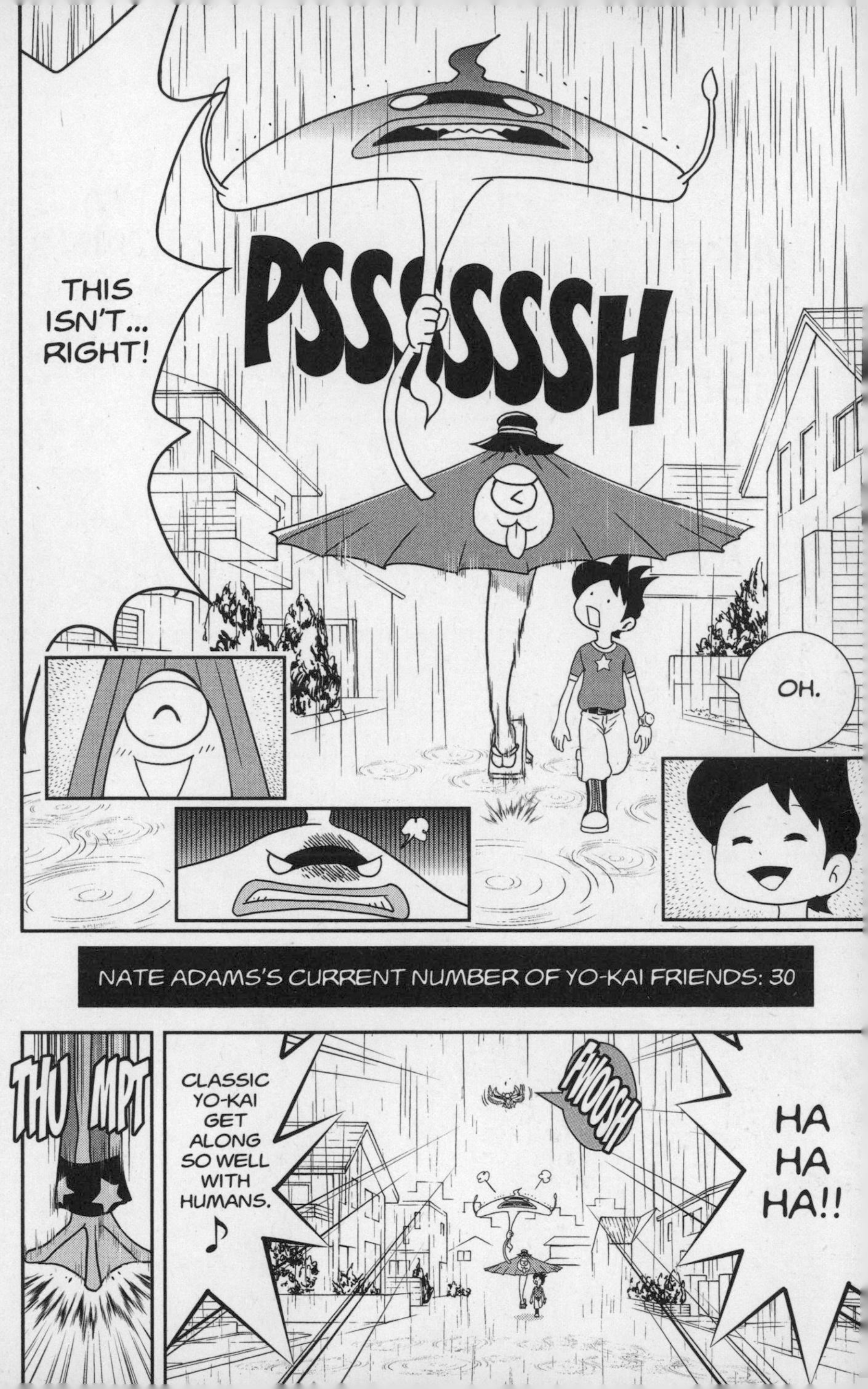
PSSSSSH
THIS ISN'T... RIGHT!
OH.
NATE ADAMS'S CURRENT NUMBER OF YO-KAI FRIENDS: 30
HA HA HA!!
FWOOSH
CLASSIC YO-KAI GET ALONG SO WELL WITH HUMANS. ♪
THUMPT

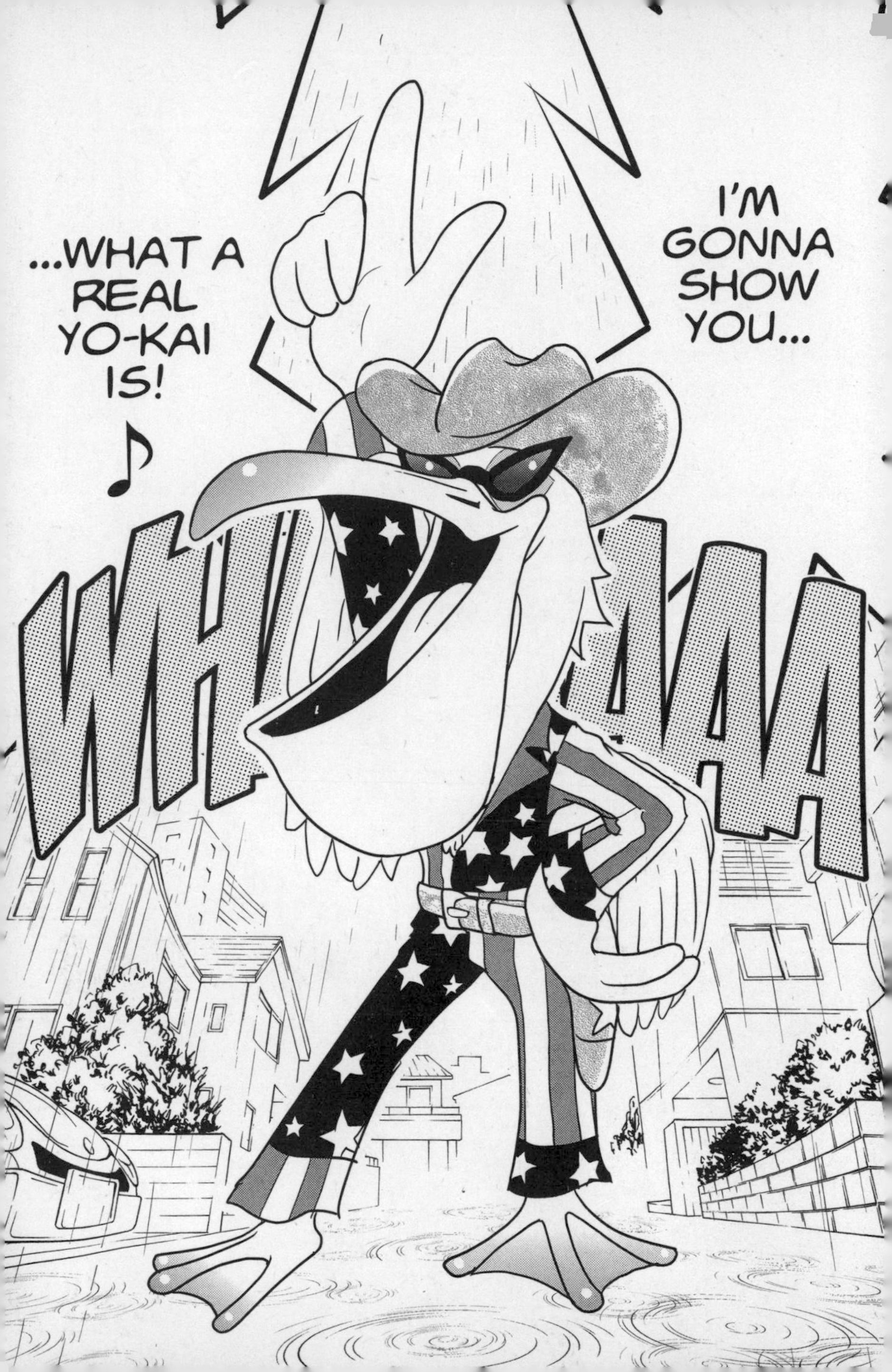
I'M GONNA SHOW YOU...
...WHAT A REAL YO-KAI IS! ♪
WH AAA

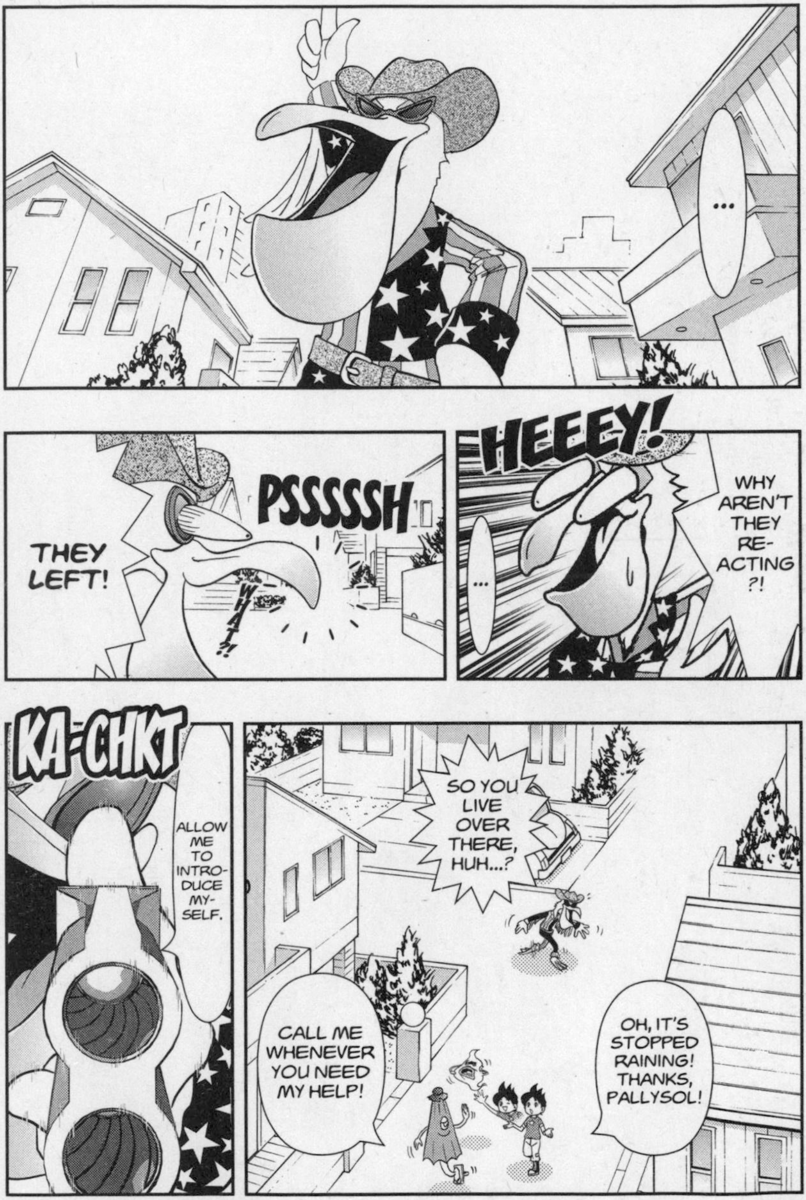
...
HEEEY!
WHY AREN'T THEY RE-ACTING?!
...
PSSSSSH
WHAT?!
THEY LEFT!
SO YOU LIVE OVER THERE, HUH...?
OH, IT'S STOPPED RAINING! THANKS, PALLYSOL!
CALL ME WHENEVER YOU NEED MY HELP!
KA-CHKT
ALLOW ME TO INTRO-DUCE MY-SELF.

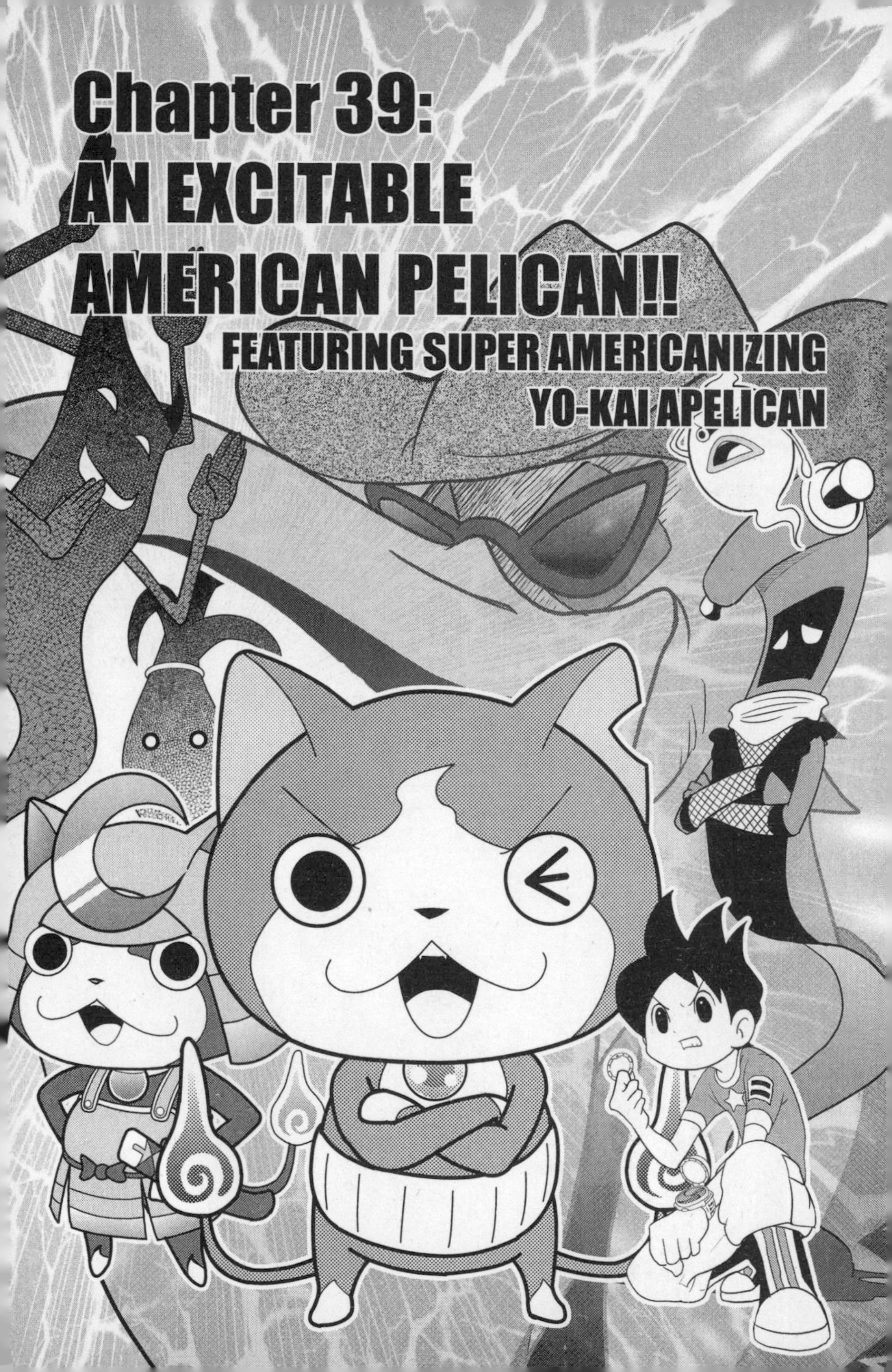
Chapter 39:
AN EXCITABLE
AMERICAN PELICAN!!
FEATURING SUPER AMERICANIZING
YO-KAI APELICAN

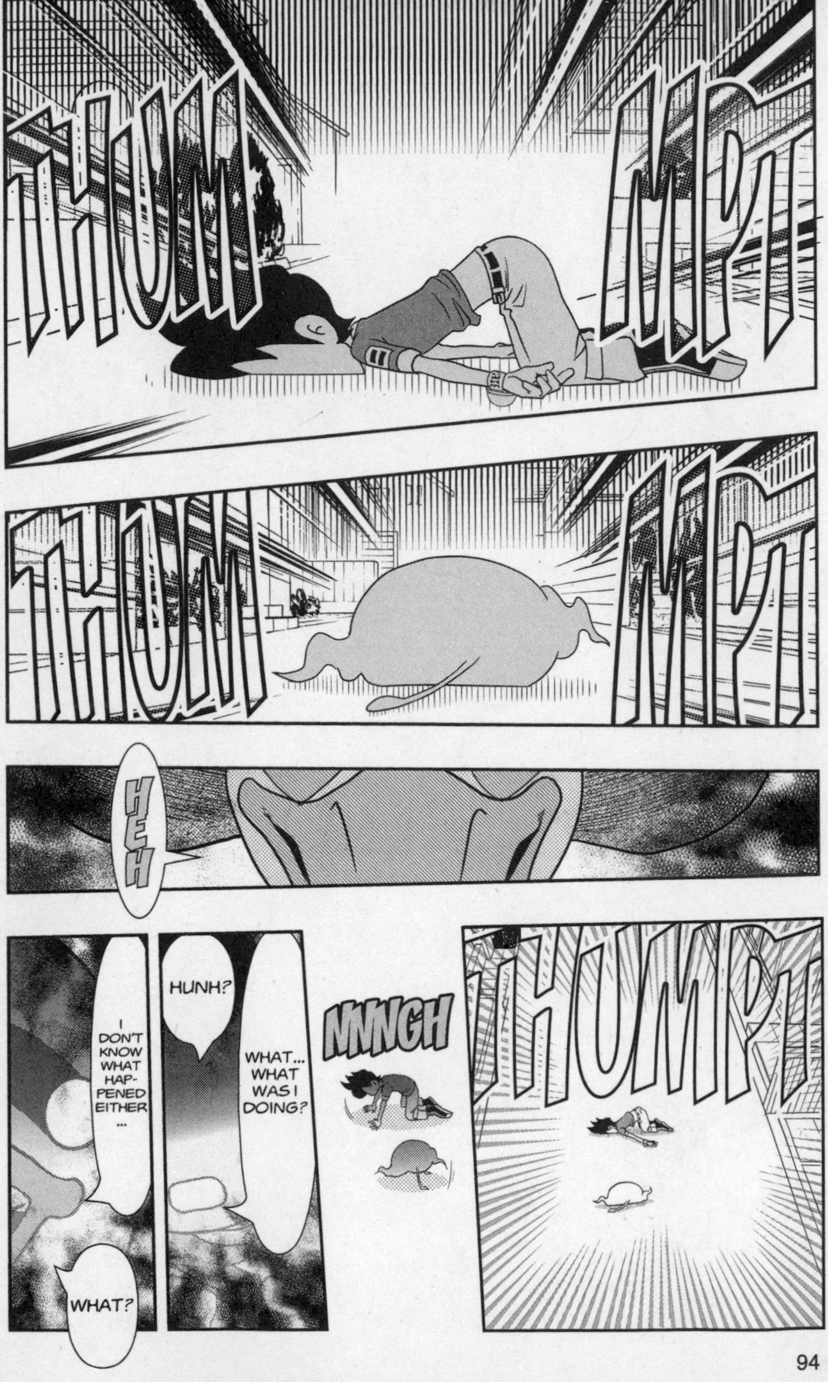
THUMMPH!
THUMMPH!
HEH
THUMPH!
NNNGH
WHAT... WHAT WAS I DOING?
HUNH?
I DON'T KNOW WHAT HAP-PENED EITHER...
WHAT?

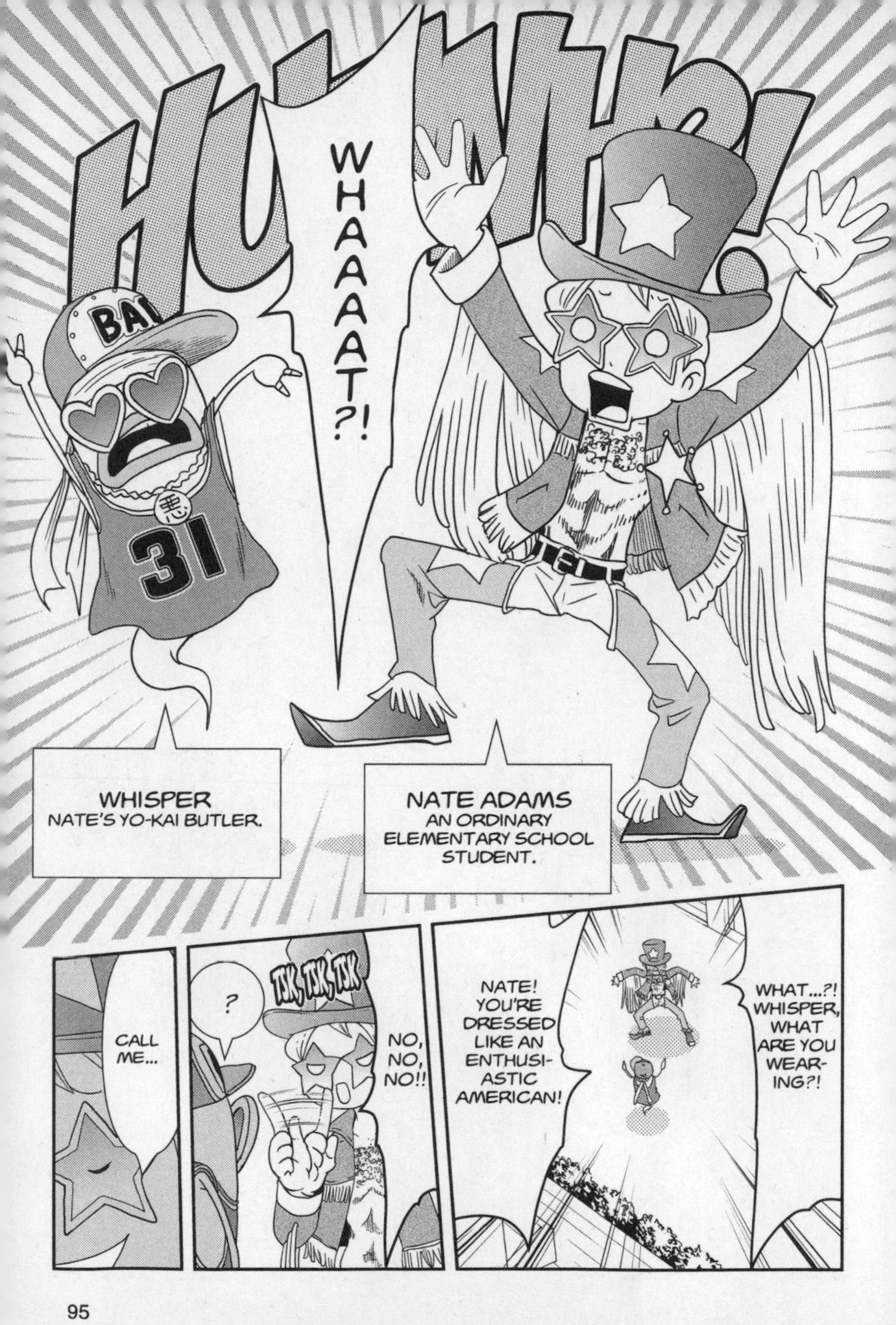
WHAAAAAT?!
NATE ADAMS
AN ORDINARY ELEMENTARY SCHOOL STUDENT.
WHISPER
NATE'S YO-KAI BUTLER.
WHAT...?! WHISPER, WHAT ARE YOU WEAR-ING?!
NATE! YOU'RE DRESSED LIKE AN ENTHUSI-ASTIC AMERICAN!
NO, NO, NO!!
TSK, TSK, TSK
?
CALL ME...

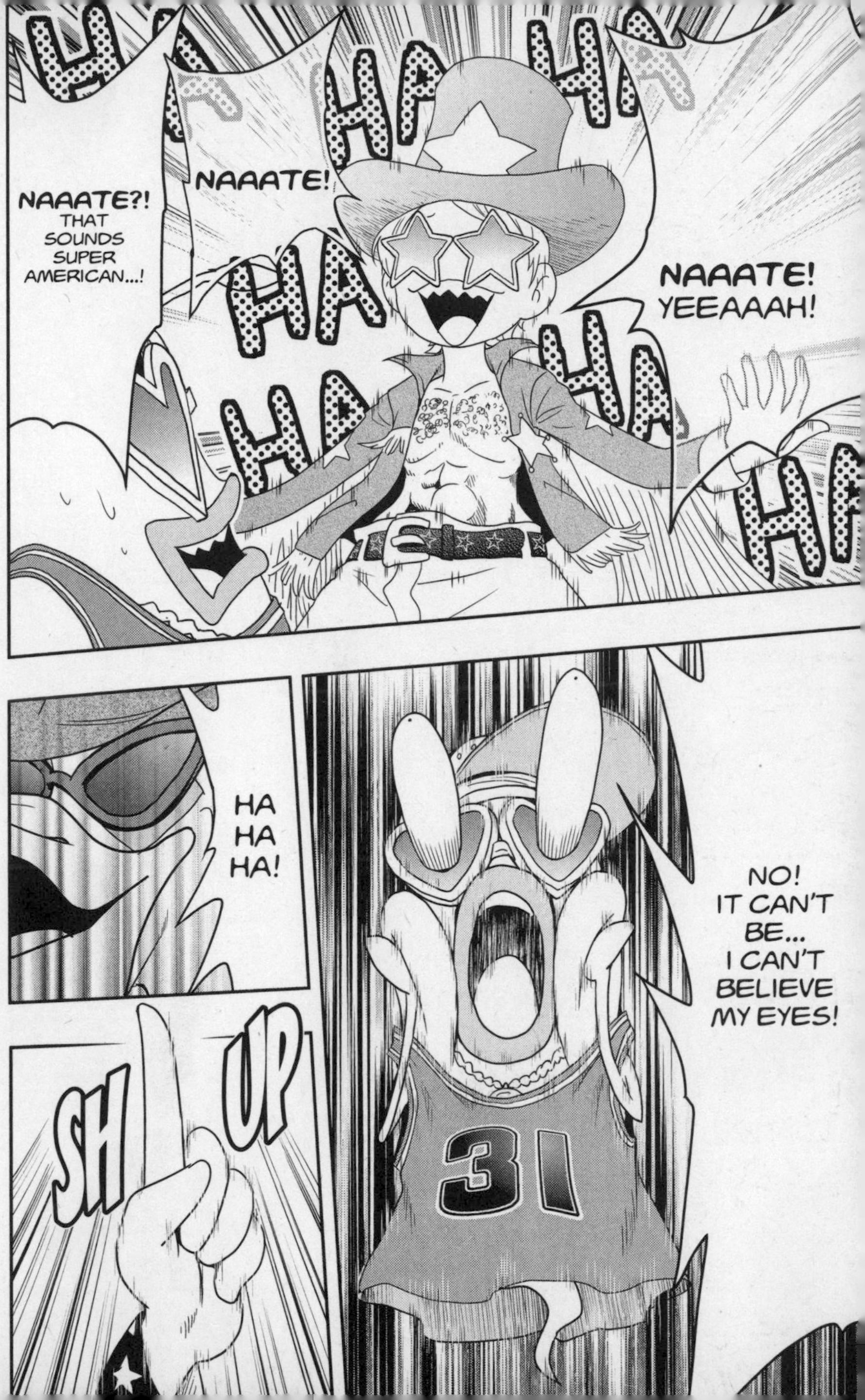
HA HA HA
NAAATE! YEEEAAAH!
NAAATE!
NAAATE?! THAT SOUNDS SUPER AMERICAN...!
HA HA HA
NO! IT CAN'T BE... I CAN'T BELIEVE MY EYES!
HA HA HA!
SH UP

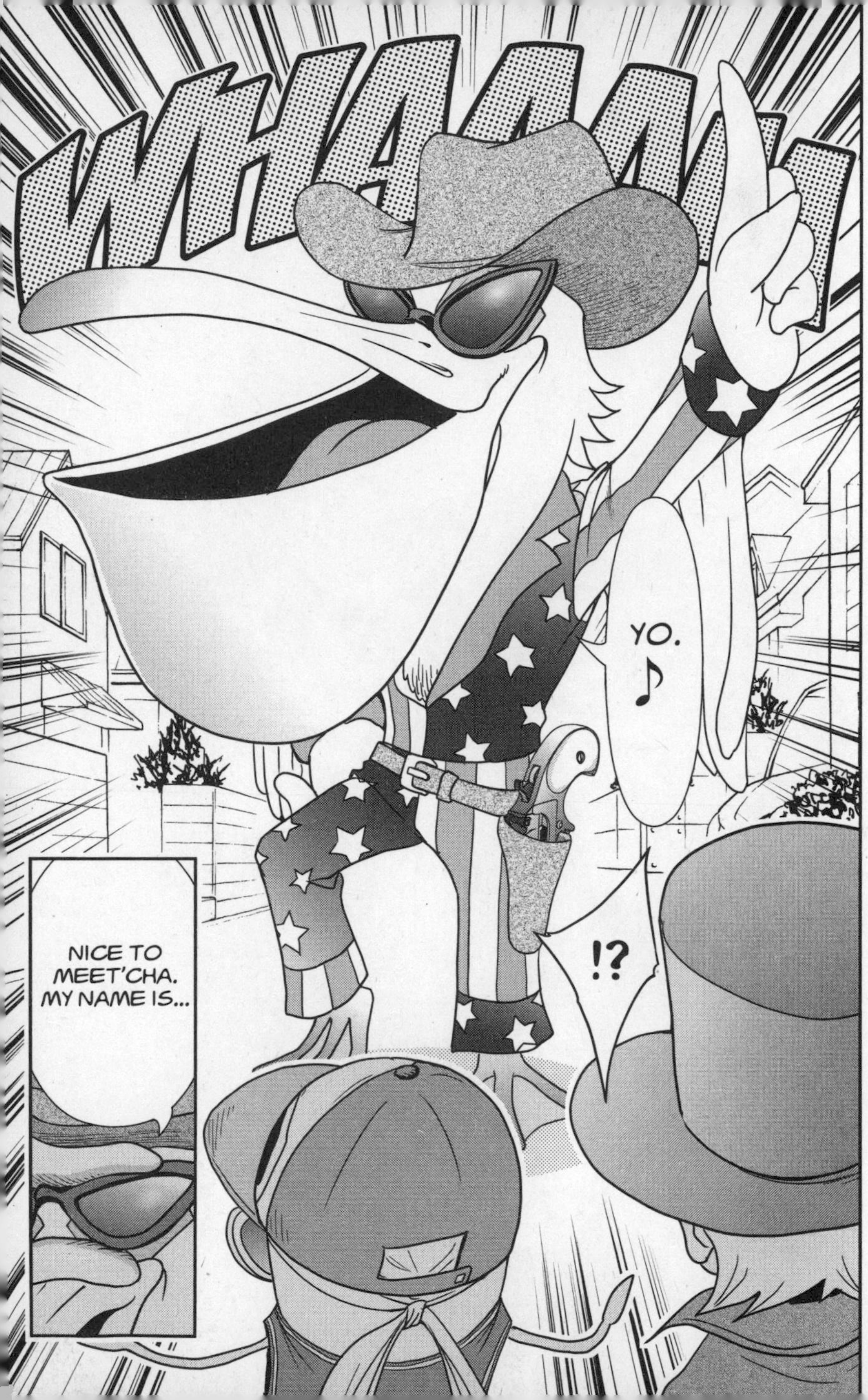
YO. ♪
!?
NICE TO MEET'CHA. MY NAME IS...

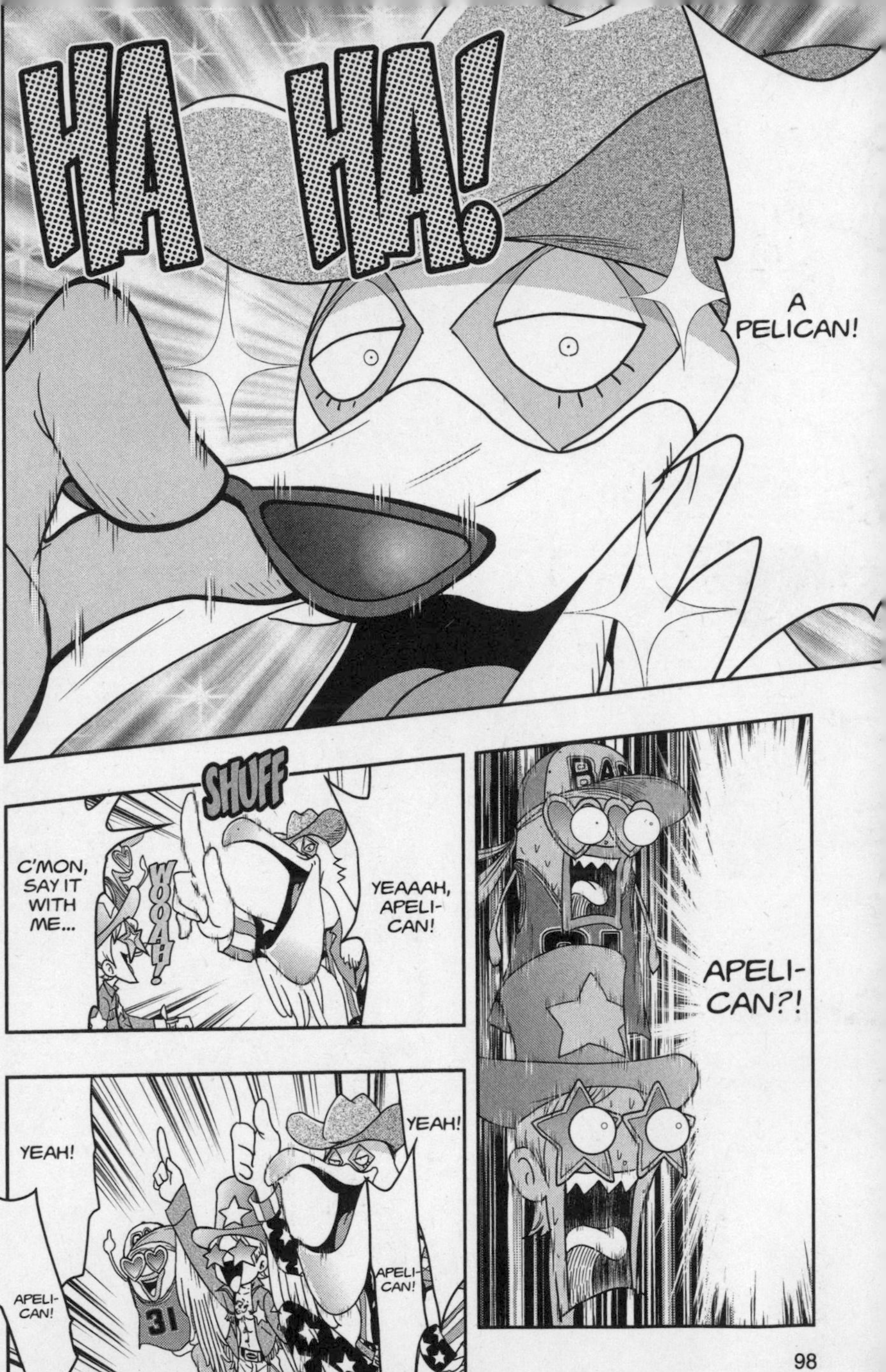
HA HA!
A PELICAN!
APELI-CAN?!
SHUFF
YEAAAH, APELI-CAN!
C'MON, SAY IT WITH ME...
YEAH!
YEAH!
APELI-CAN!
APELI-CAN!

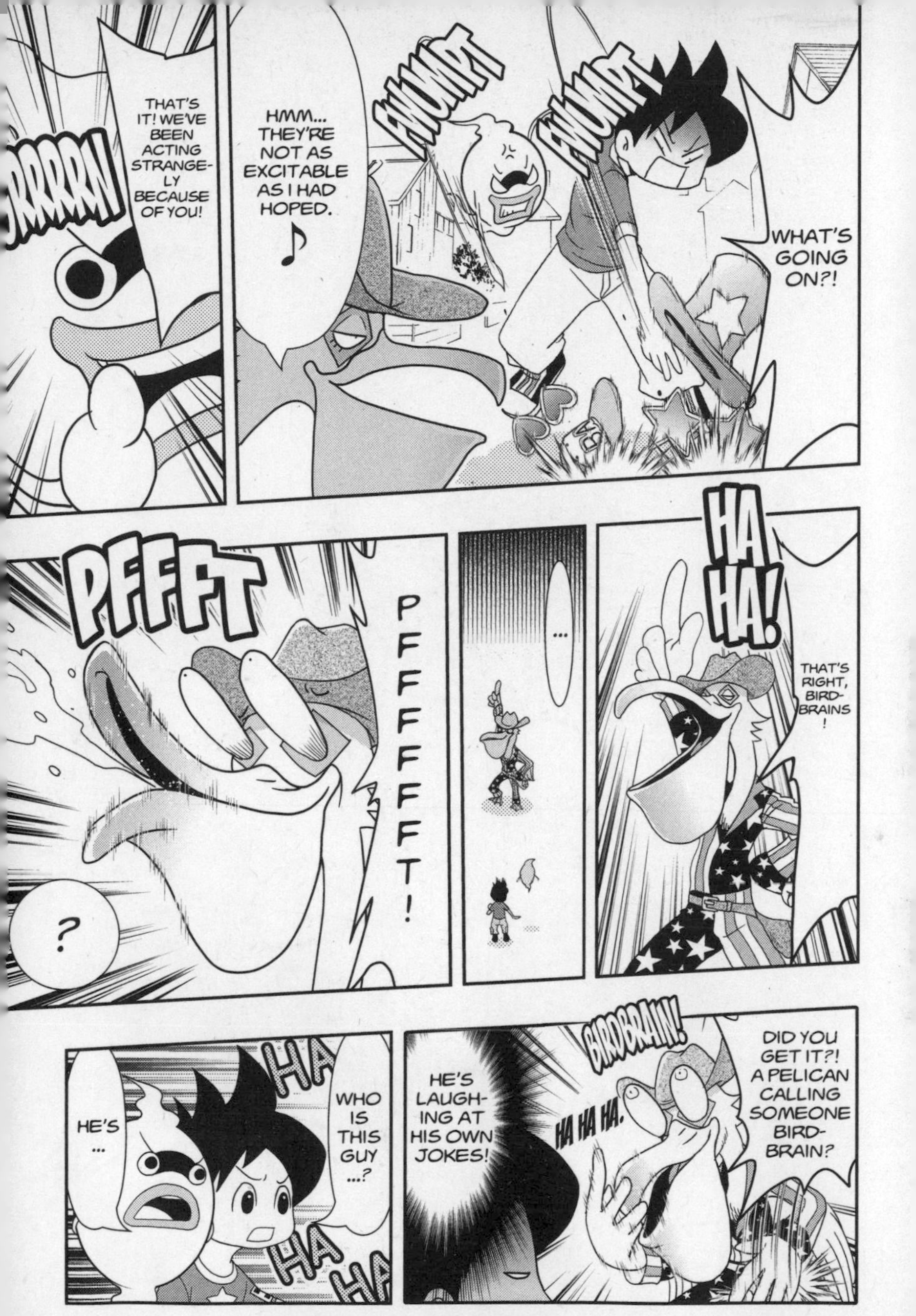
FWUMPT
FWUMPT
WHAT'S GOING ON?!
HMM... THEY'RE NOT AS EXCITABLE AS I HAD HOPED. ♪
RRRRN
THAT'S IT! WE'VE BEEN ACTING STRANGE-LY BECAUSE OF YOU!
HA HA!
THAT'S RIGHT, BIRD-BRAINS!
...
PFFFT
PFFFFFFFT!
?
BIRDBRAIN!
DID YOU GET IT?! A PELICAN CALLING SOMEONE BIRD-BRAIN?
HA HA HA.
HE'S LAUGH-ING AT HIS OWN JOKES!
HA
WHO IS THIS GUY ...?
HE'S ...
HA HA

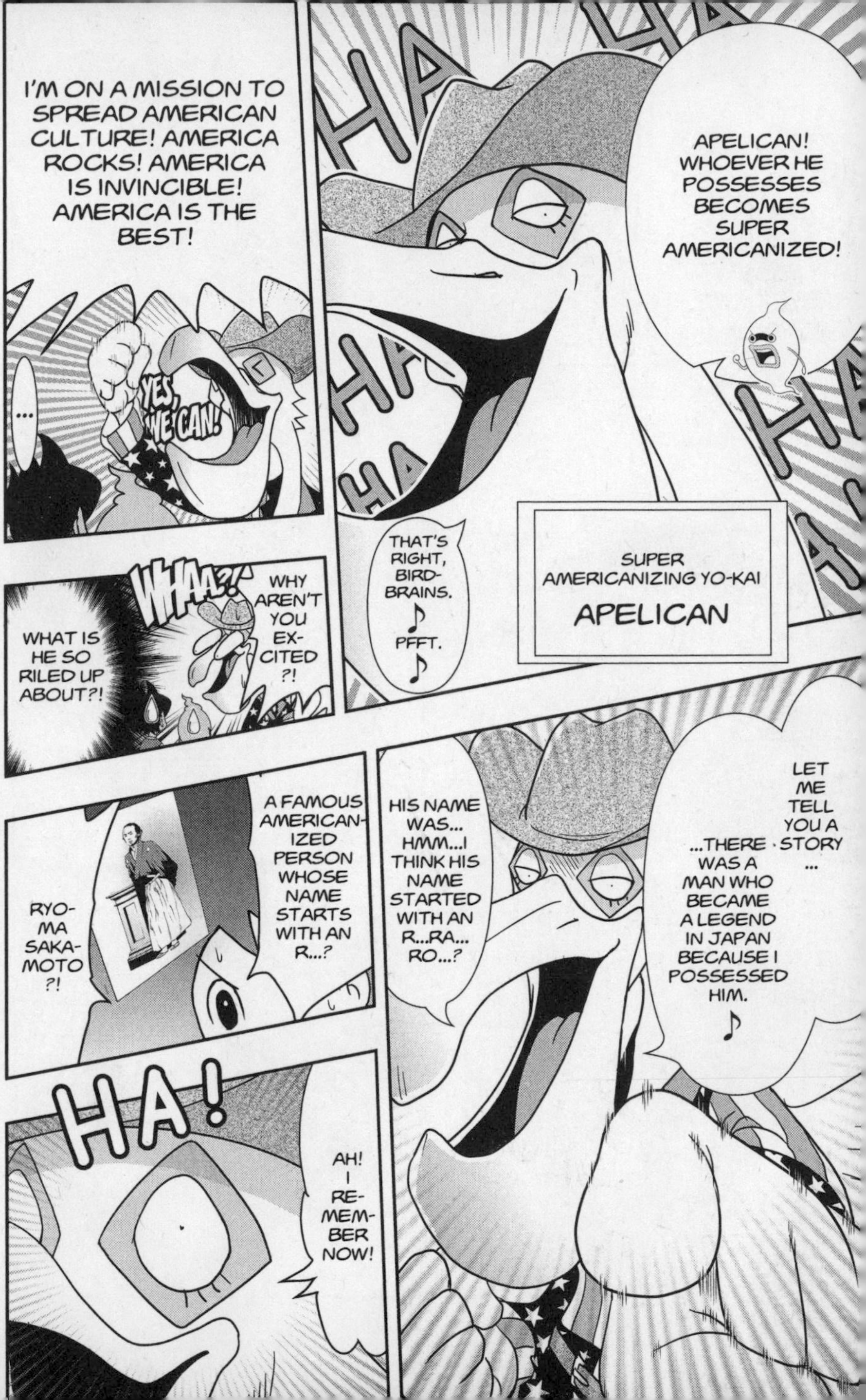
HA HA HA
APELICAN! WHOEVER HE POSSESSES BECOMES SUPER AMERICANIZED!
HA HA HA
SUPER AMERICANIZING YO-KAI
APELICAN
THAT'S RIGHT, BIRD-BRAINS. ♪ PFFT. ♪
I'M ON A MISSION TO SPREAD AMERICAN CULTURE! AMERICA ROCKS! AMERICA IS INVINCIBLE! AMERICA IS THE BEST!
YES, WE CAN!
...
WHY AREN'T YOU EXCITED?!
WHAAA?!
WHAT IS HE SO RILED UP ABOUT?!
LET ME TELL YOU A STORY...
...THERE WAS A MAN WHO BECAME A LEGEND IN JAPAN BECAUSE I POSSESSED HIM. ♪
HIS NAME WAS... HMM...I THINK HIS NAME STARTED WITH AN R...RA... RO...?
A FAMOUS AMERICANIZED PERSON WHOSE NAME STARTS WITH AN R...?
RYOMA SAKAMOTO?!
HA!
AH! I REMEMBER NOW!

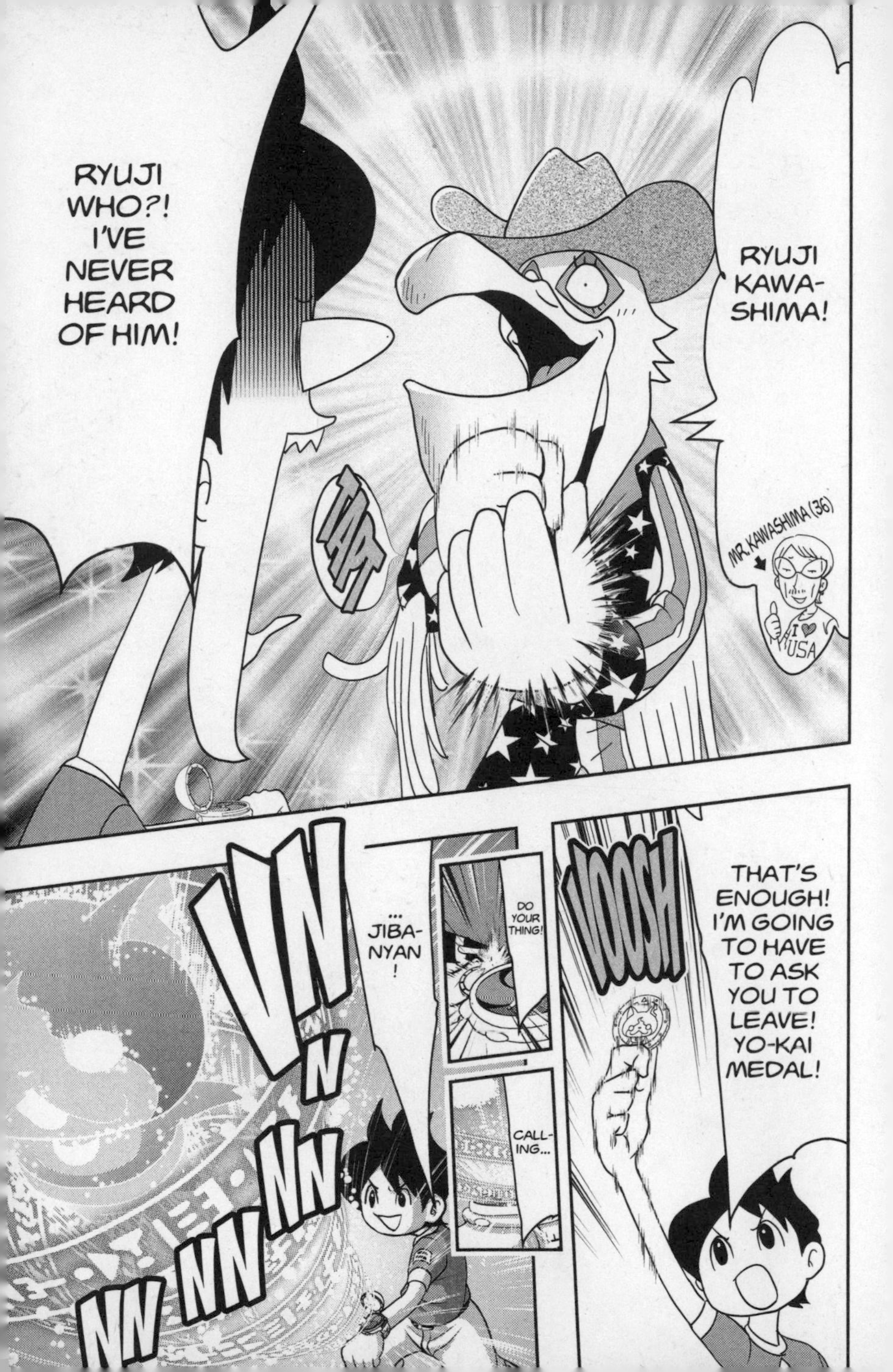
RYUJI KAWA-SHIMA!
MR. KAWASHIMA (36)
I ♥ USA
TAP!
RYUJI WHO?! I'VE NEVER HEARD OF HIM!
THAT'S ENOUGH! I'M GOING TO HAVE TO ASK YOU TO LEAVE! YO-KAI MEDAL!
VOOSH
DO YOUR THING!
CALL-ING...
... JIBA-NYAN!
VINNNNNNNNNN

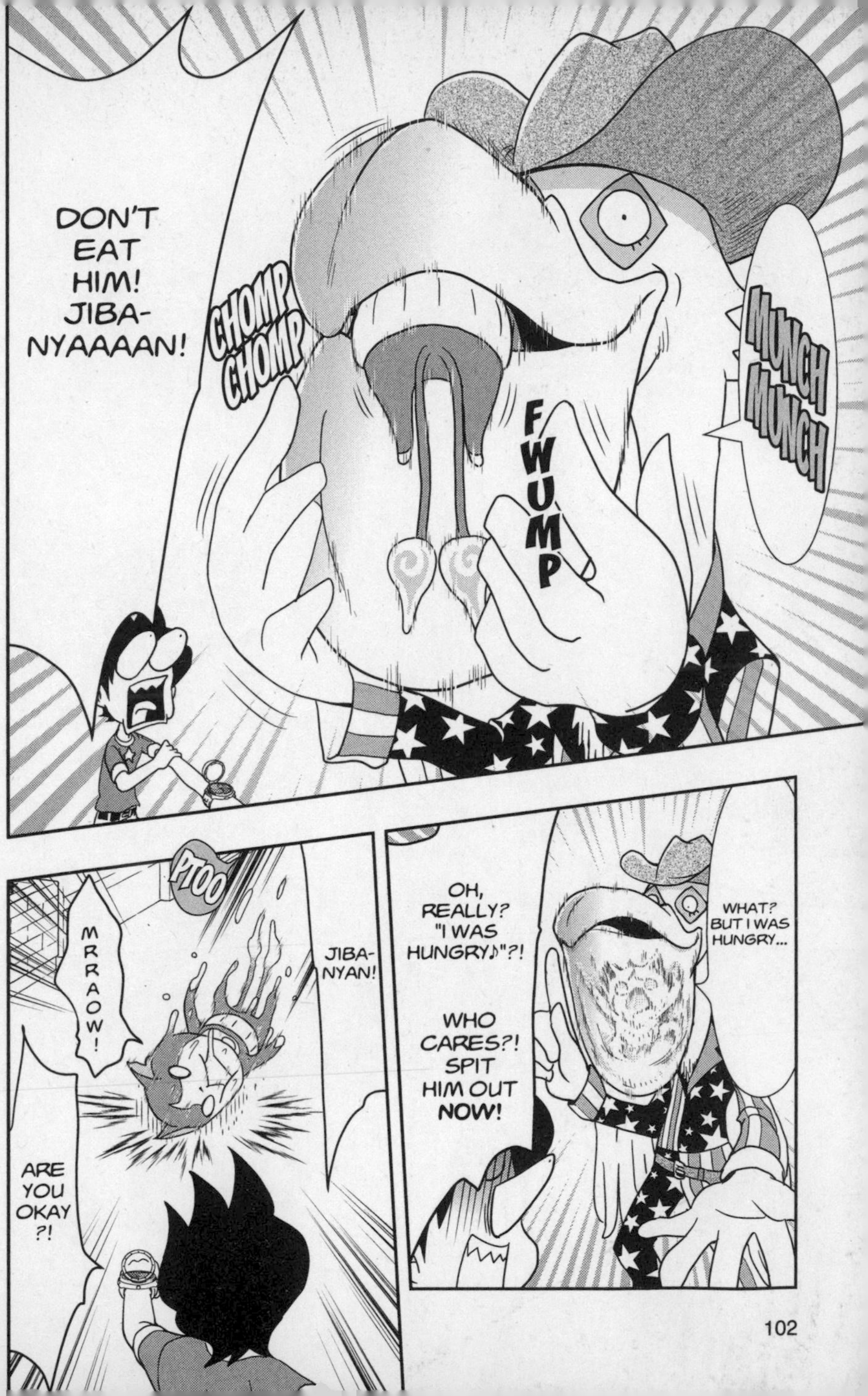
MUNCH MUNCH
FWUMP
CHOMP CHOMP
DON'T EAT HIM! JIBA-NYAAAAN!
WHAT? BUT I WAS HUNGRY...
OH, REALLY? "I WAS HUNGRY♪"?!
WHO CARES?! SPIT HIM OUT NOW!
PTOO
JIBA-NYAN!
MRRAOW!
ARE YOU OKAY?!

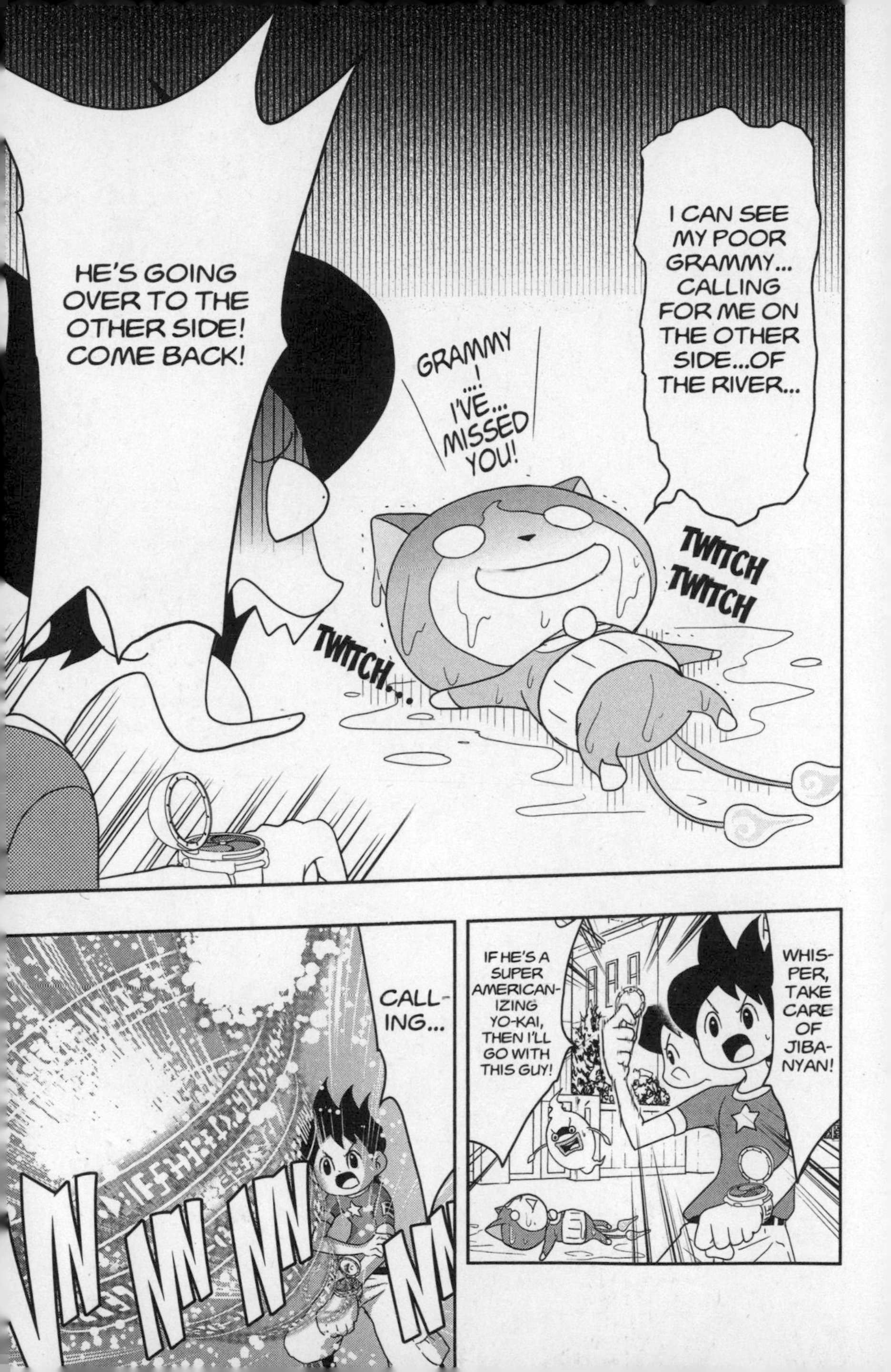
I CAN SEE MY POOR GRAMMY... CALLING FOR ME ON THE OTHER SIDE...OF THE RIVER...
GRAMMY...! I'VE... MISSED YOU!
HE'S GOING OVER TO THE OTHER SIDE! COME BACK!
TWITCH TWITCH
TWITCH...
WHISPER, TAKE CARE OF JIBANYAN!
IF HE'S A SUPER AMERICANIZING YO-KAI, THEN I'LL GO WITH THIS GUY!
CALLING...
NNNNNN

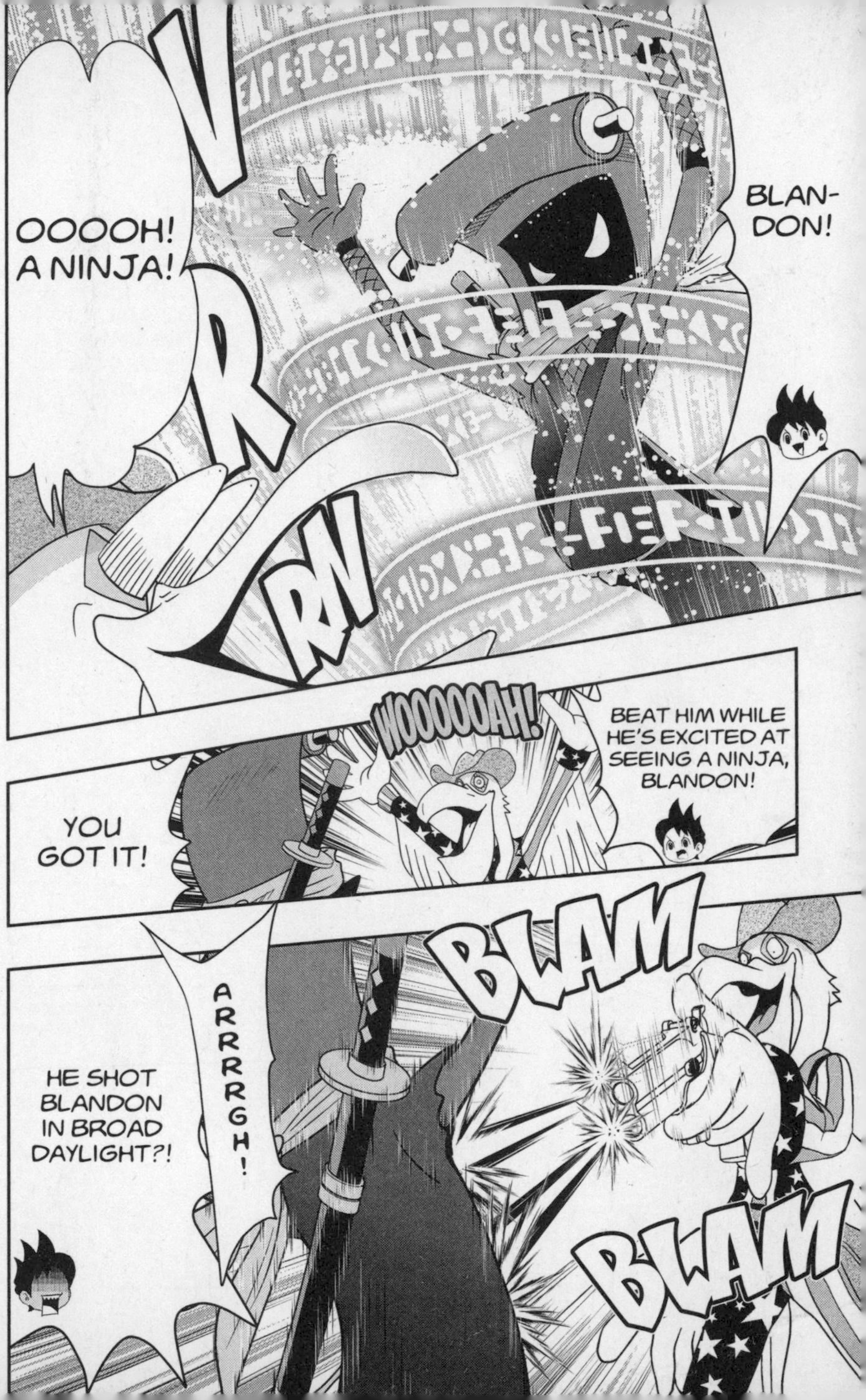
BLAN-DON!
VRRN
OOOOH! A NINJA!
WOOOOOAH!
BEAT HIM WHILE HE'S EXCITED AT SEEING A NINJA, BLANDON!
YOU GOT IT!
BLAM
BLAM
ARRRRGH!
HE SHOT BLANDON IN BROAD DAYLIGHT?!

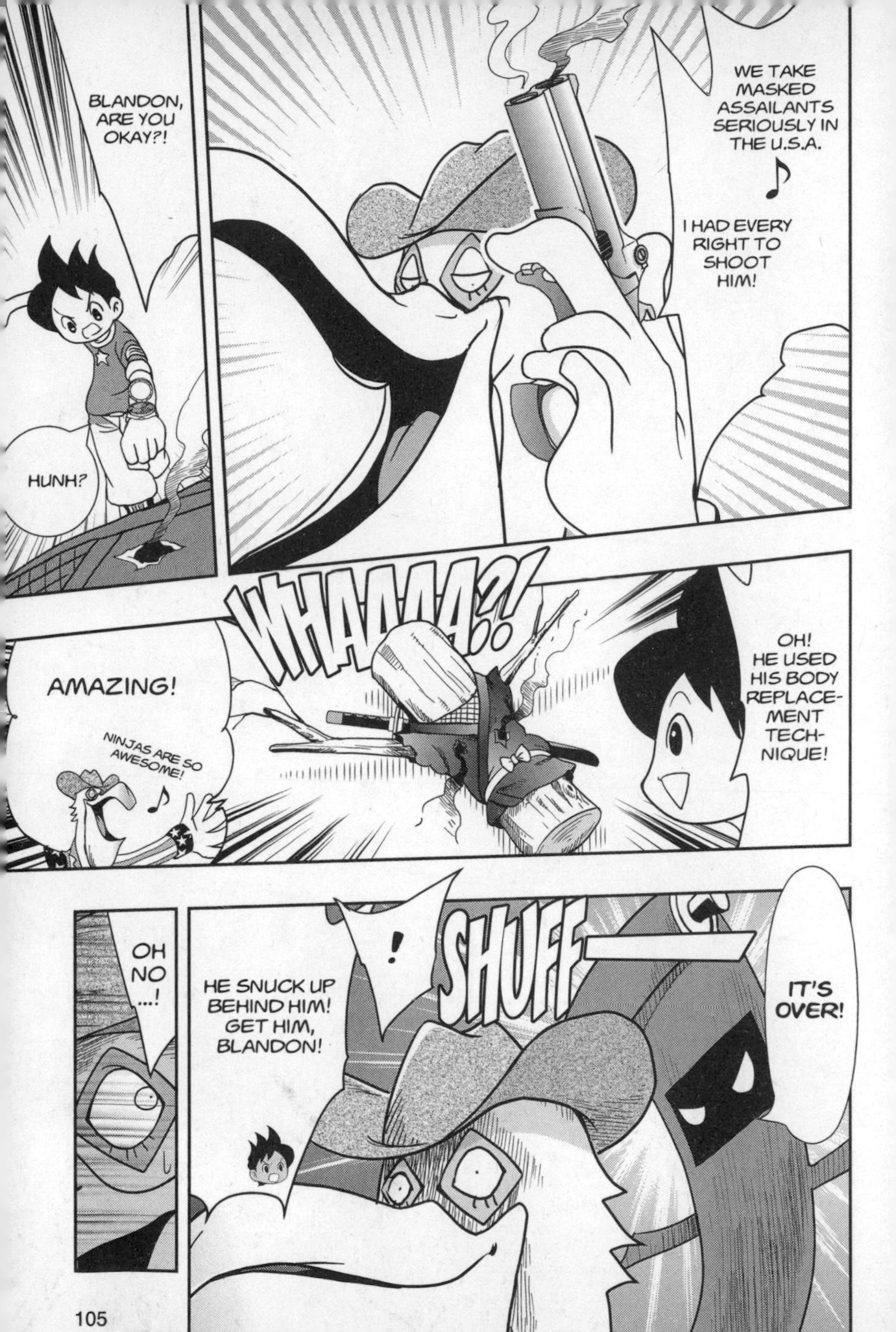
WE TAKE MASKED ASSAILANTS SERIOUSLY IN THE U.S.A. ♪
I HAD EVERY RIGHT TO SHOOT HIM!
BLANDON, ARE YOU OKAY?!
HUNH?
OH! HE USED HIS BODY REPLACEMENT-MENT TECH-NIQUE!
WHAAAA?!
AMAZING!
NINJAS ARE SO AWESOME! ♪
IT'S OVER!
SHUFF—
!
HE SNUCK UP BEHIND HIM! GET HIM, BLANDON!
OH NO ...!

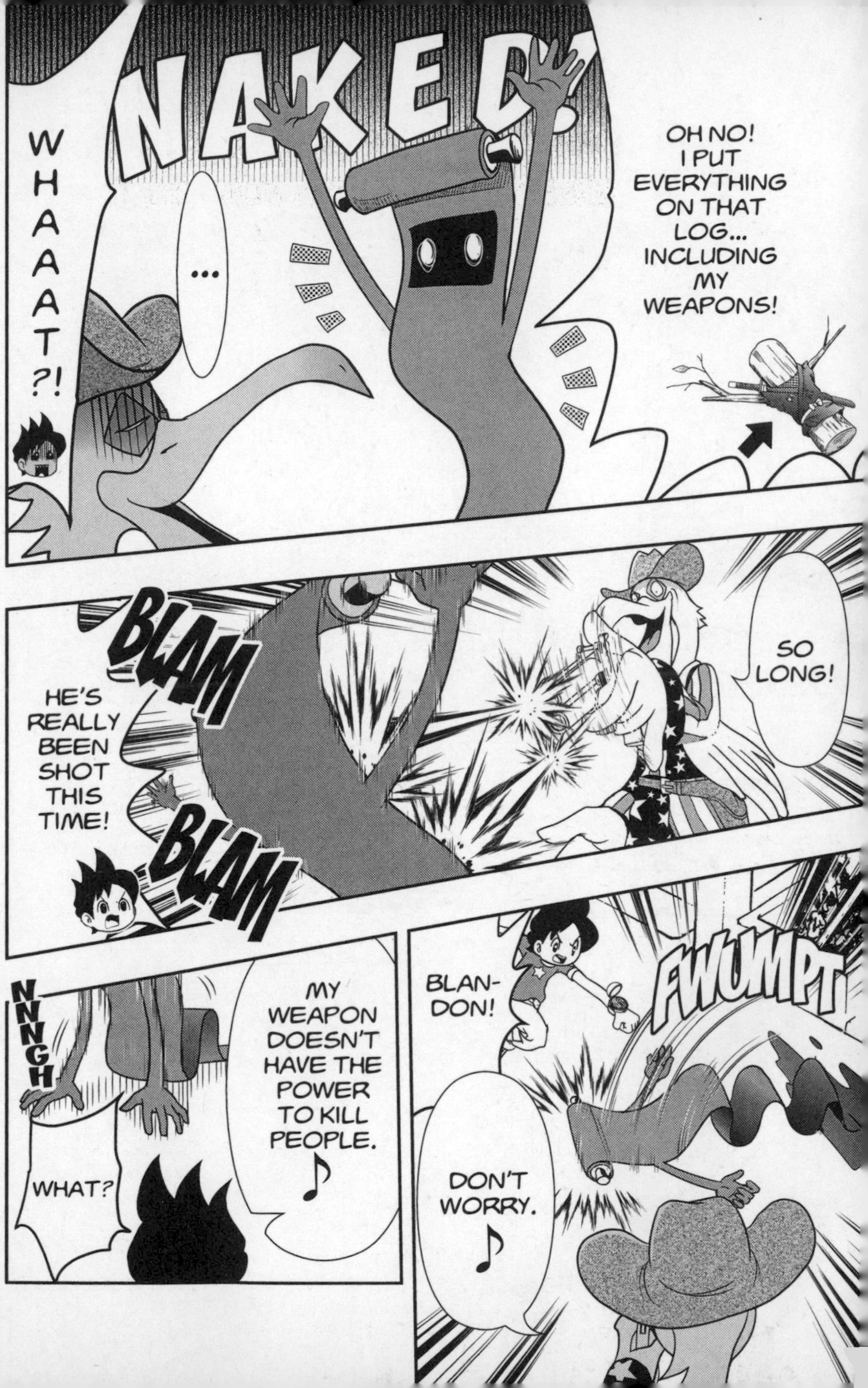
NAKED!
OH NO! I PUT EVERYTHING ON THAT LOG... INCLUDING MY WEAPONS!
...
WHAAAAT?!
SO LONG!
BLAM
BLAM
HE'S REALLY BEEN SHOT THIS TIME!
BLAN-DON!
FWUMPT
DON'T WORRY. ♪
MY WEAPON DOESN'T HAVE THE POWER TO KILL PEOPLE. ♪
NNNGH
WHAT?

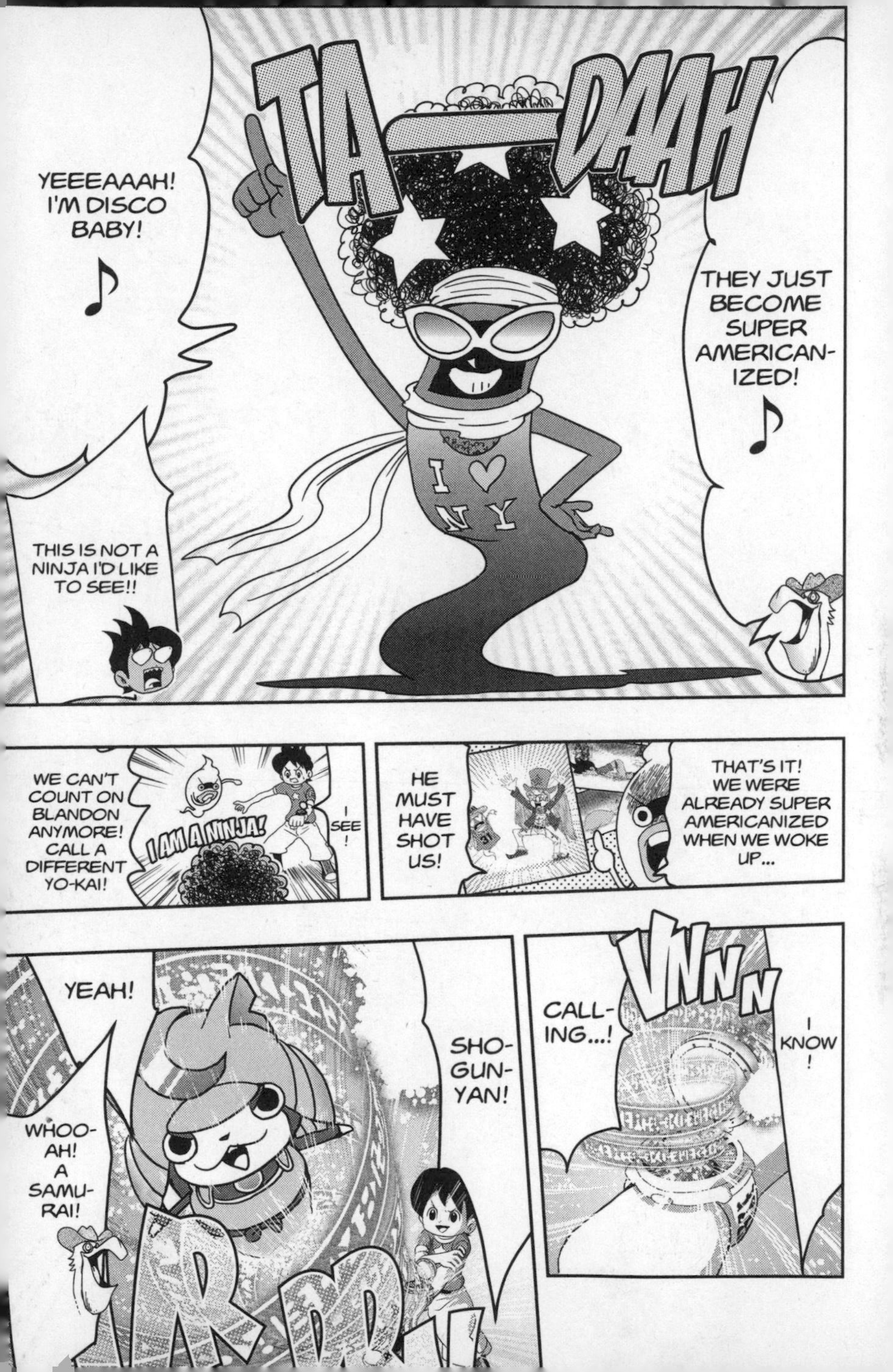
TA—DAAH
THEY JUST BECOME SUPER AMERICAN-IZED! ♪
YEEEAAAH! I'M DISCO BABY! ♪
THIS IS NOT A NINJA I'D LIKE TO SEE!!
THAT'S IT! WE WERE ALREADY SUPER AMERICANIZED WHEN WE WOKE UP...
HE MUST HAVE SHOT US!
I SEE!
I AM A NINJA!
WE CAN'T COUNT ON BLANDON ANYMORE! CALL A DIFFERENT YO-KAI!
I KNOW!
VNNNN
CALLING...!
SHO-GUN-YAN!
YEAH!
WHOO-AH! A SAMU-RAI!

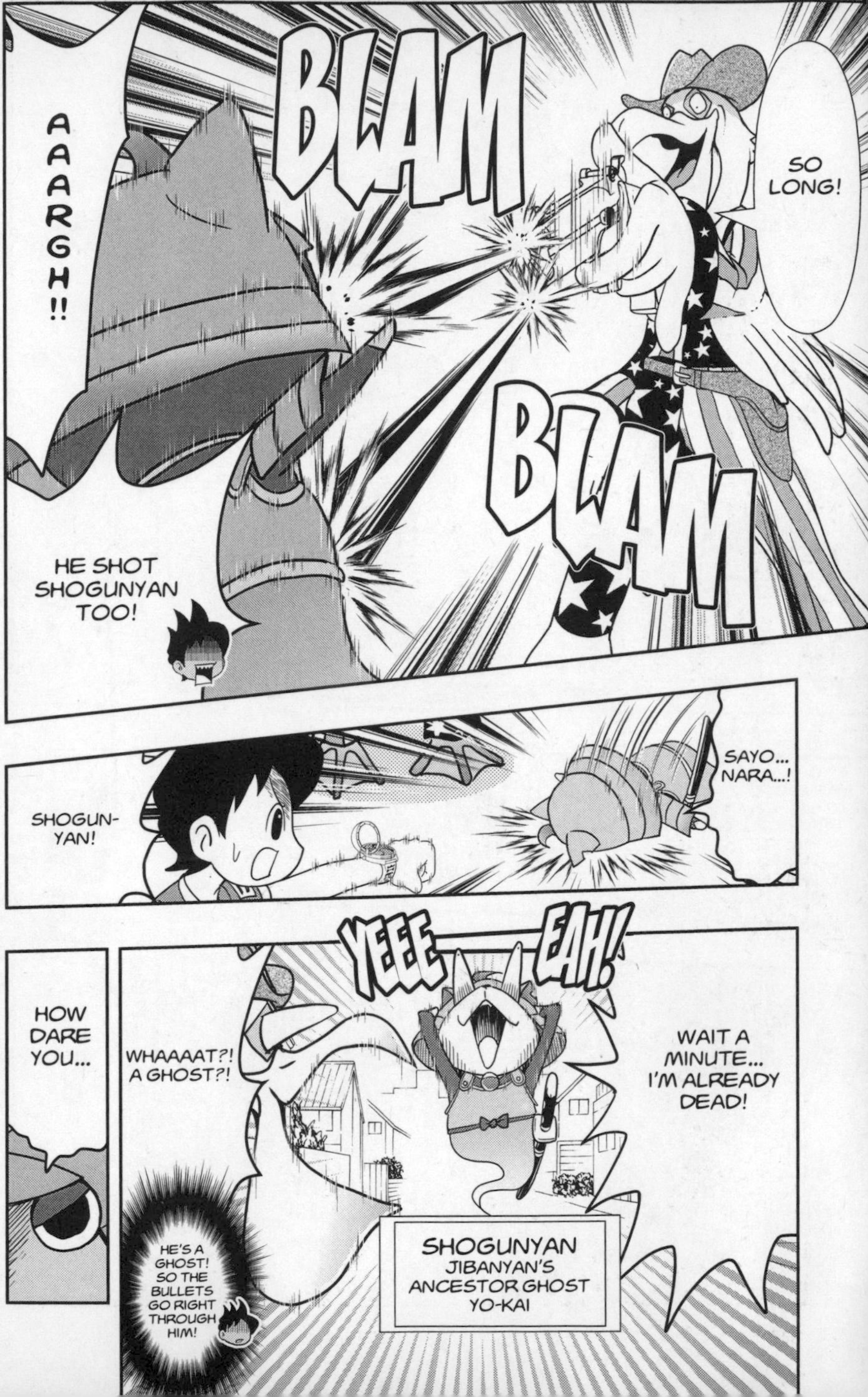
SO LONG!
BLAM
BLAM
AAAARGH!!
HE SHOT SHOGUNYAN TOO!
SAYO... NARA...!
SHOGUN-YAN!
YEEE—EAH!
WAIT A MINUTE... I'M ALREADY DEAD!
WHAAAAT?! A GHOST?!
SHOGUNYAN
JIBANYAN'S ANCESTOR GHOST YO-KAI
HE'S A GHOST! SO THE BULLETS GO RIGHT THROUGH HIM!
HOW DARE YOU...

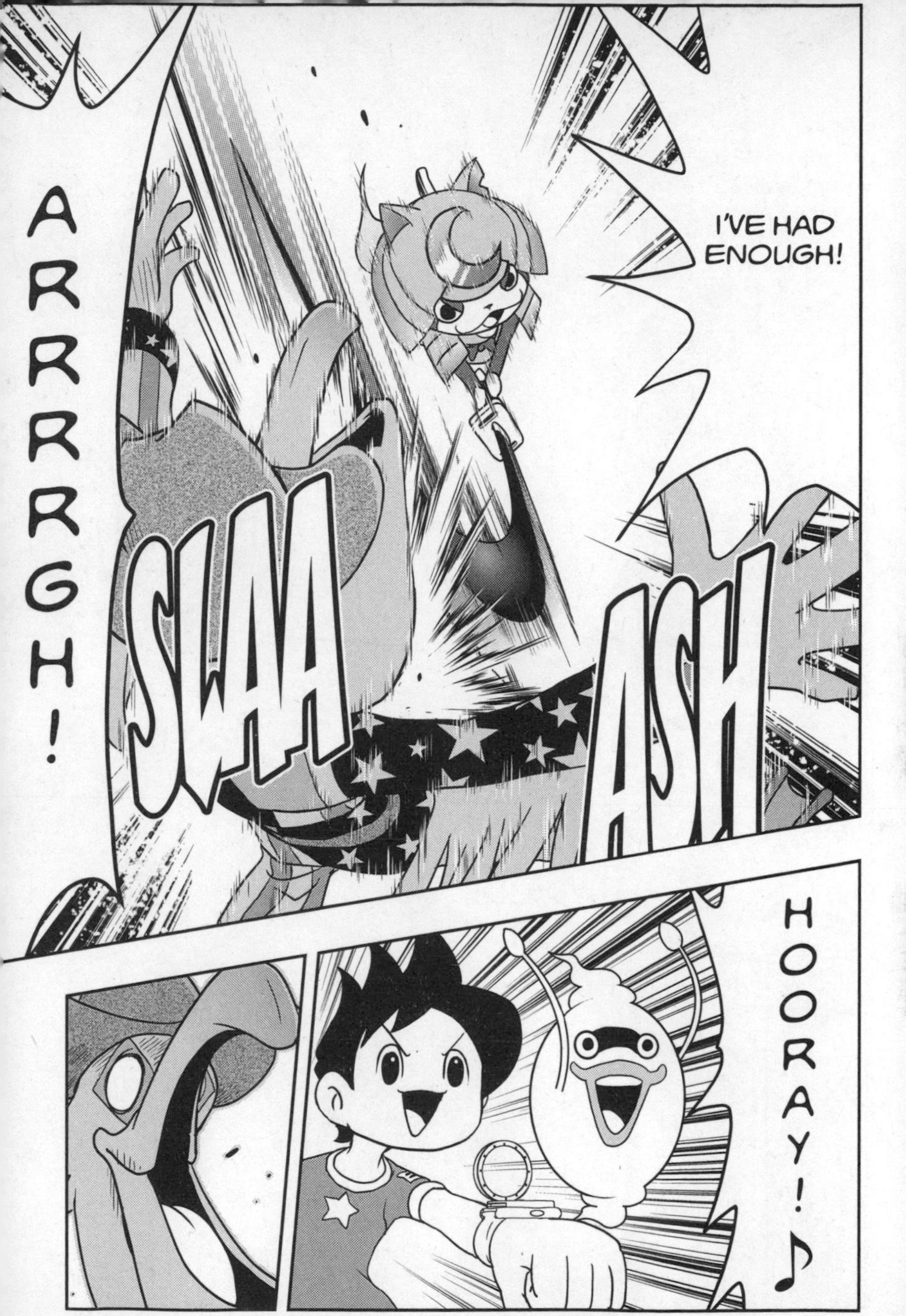
I'VE HAD ENOUGH!
SWAAASH
ARRRRGH!
HOORAY!♪

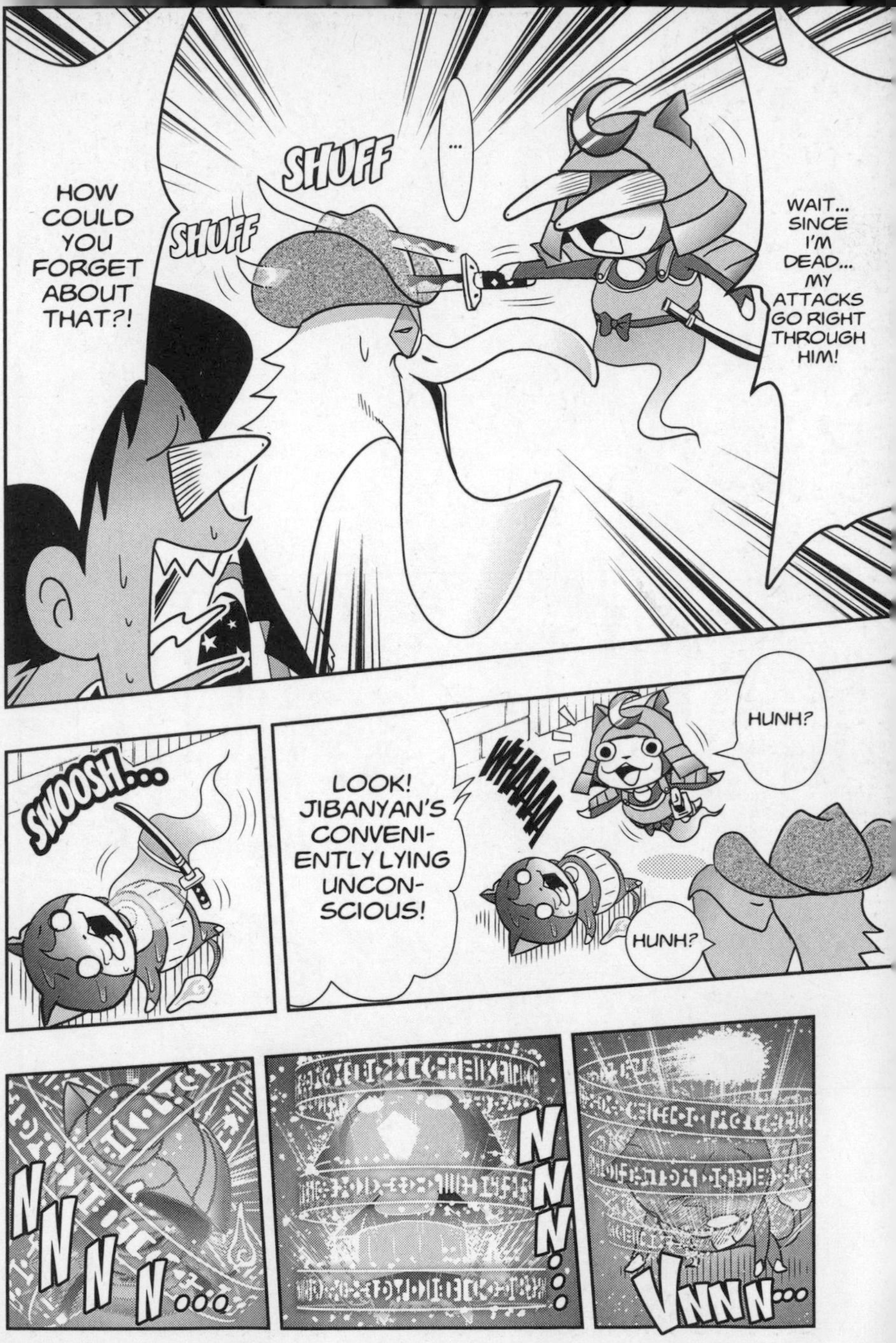

...
WAIT... SINCE I'M DEAD... MY ATTACKS GO RIGHT THROUGH HIM!
SHUFF
SHUFF
HOW COULD YOU FORGET ABOUT THAT?!
HUNH?
WHAAAA
LOOK! JIBANYAN'S CONVENI-ENTLY LYING UNCON-SCIOUS!
HUNH?
SWOOSH...
VNNN...
NNN...
NNNN...

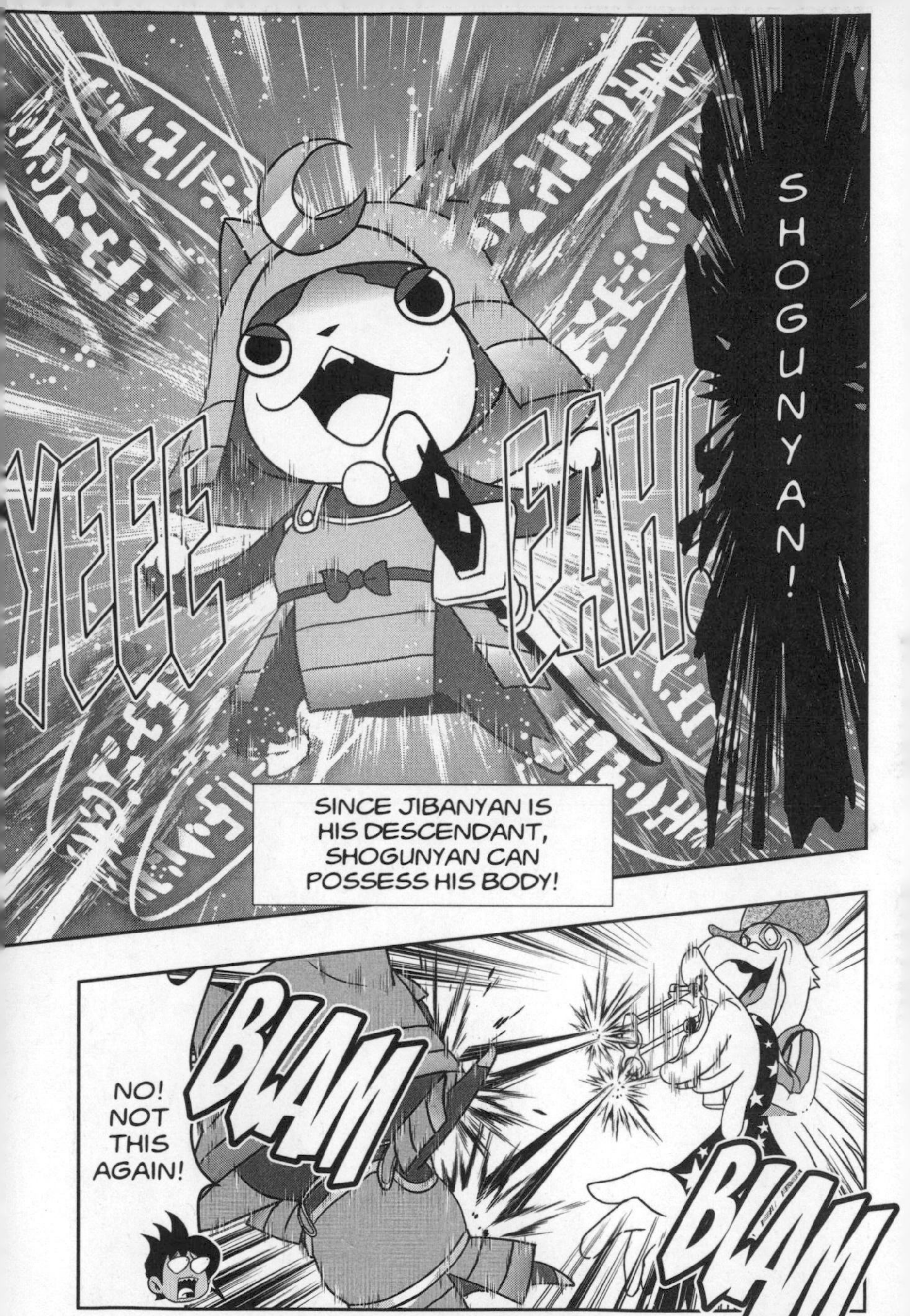
SHOGUNYAN!
YEEEEEAAH!
SINCE JIBANYAN IS HIS DESCENDANT, SHOGUNYAN CAN POSSESS HIS BODY!
BLAM
NO! NOT THIS AGAIN!
BLAM

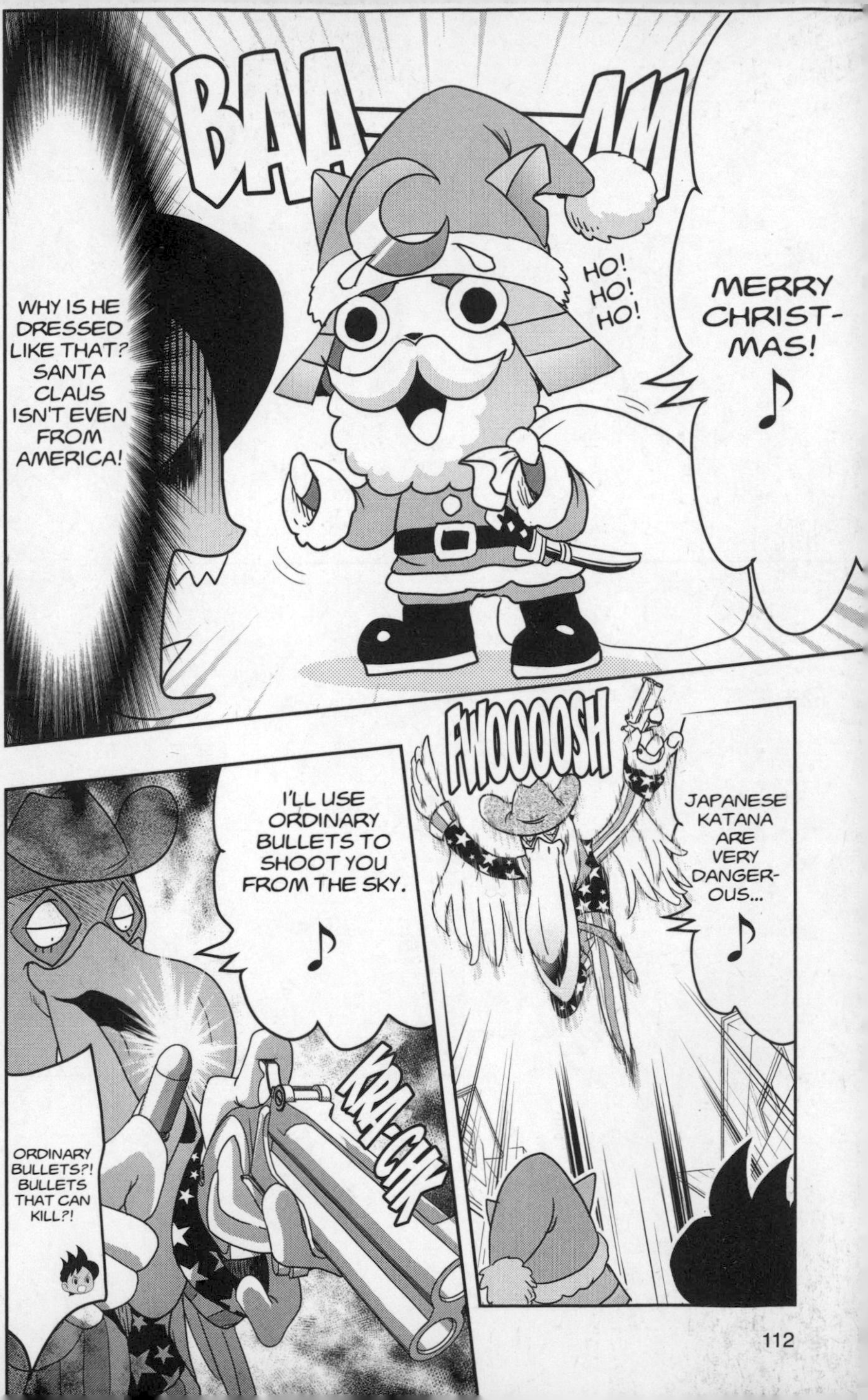
BAA AM
HO! HO! HO!
MERRY CHRIST-MAS! ♪
WHY IS HE DRESSED LIKE THAT? SANTA CLAUS ISN'T EVEN FROM AMERICA!
FWOOOOSH
JAPANESE KATANA ARE VERY DANGER-OUS... ♪
I'LL USE ORDINARY BULLETS TO SHOOT YOU FROM THE SKY. ♪
KRA-CHK
ORDINARY BULLETS?! BULLETS THAT CAN KILL?!

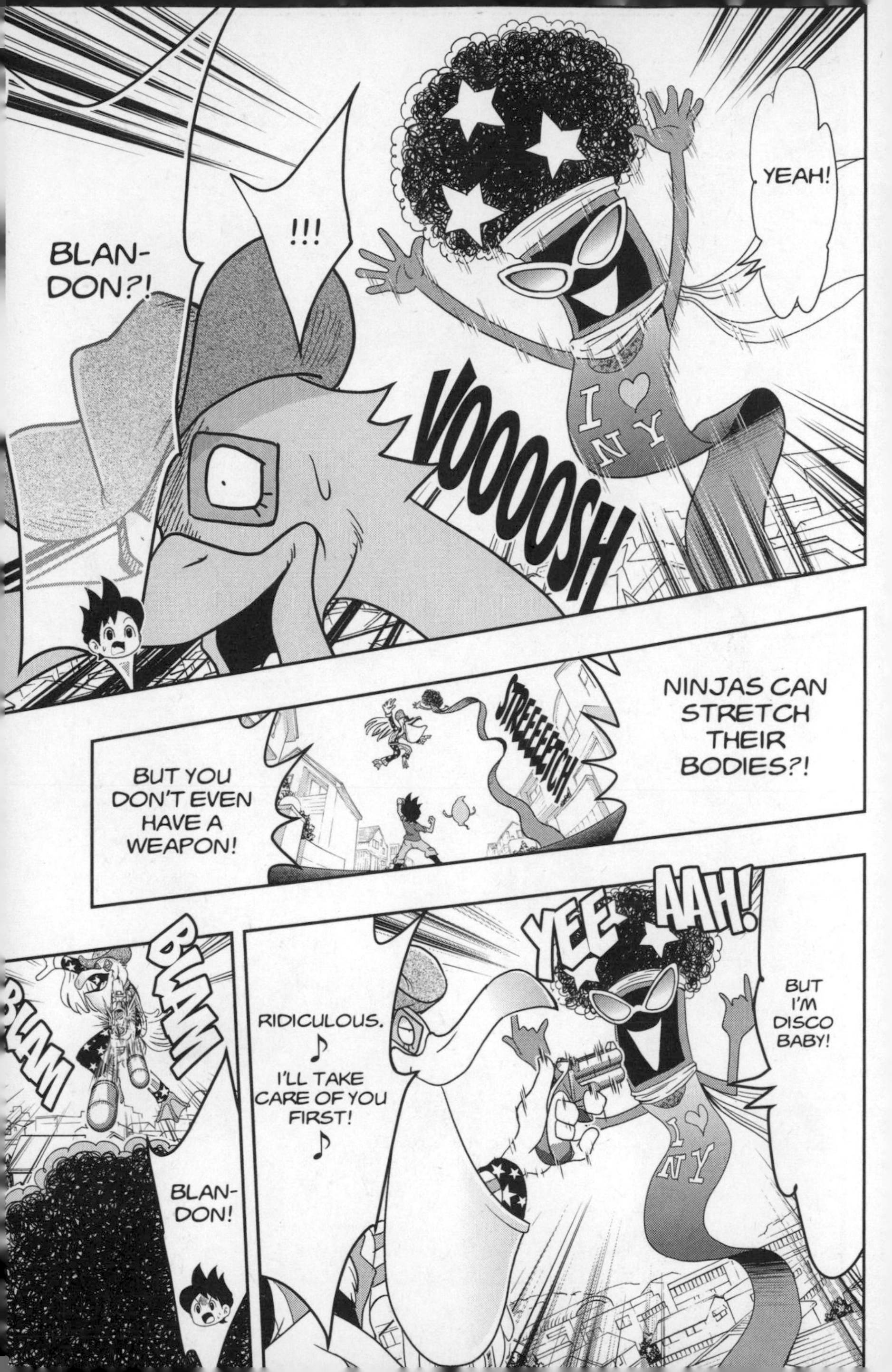
YEAH!
!!!
BLAN-DON?!
VOOOOOSH
NINJAS CAN STRETCH THEIR BODIES?!
STREEEETCH
BUT YOU DON'T EVEN HAVE A WEAPON!
YEE-AAH!
BUT I'M DISCO BABY!
RIDICULOUS. ♪
I'LL TAKE CARE OF YOU FIRST! ♪
BLAM
BLAM
BLAN-DON!

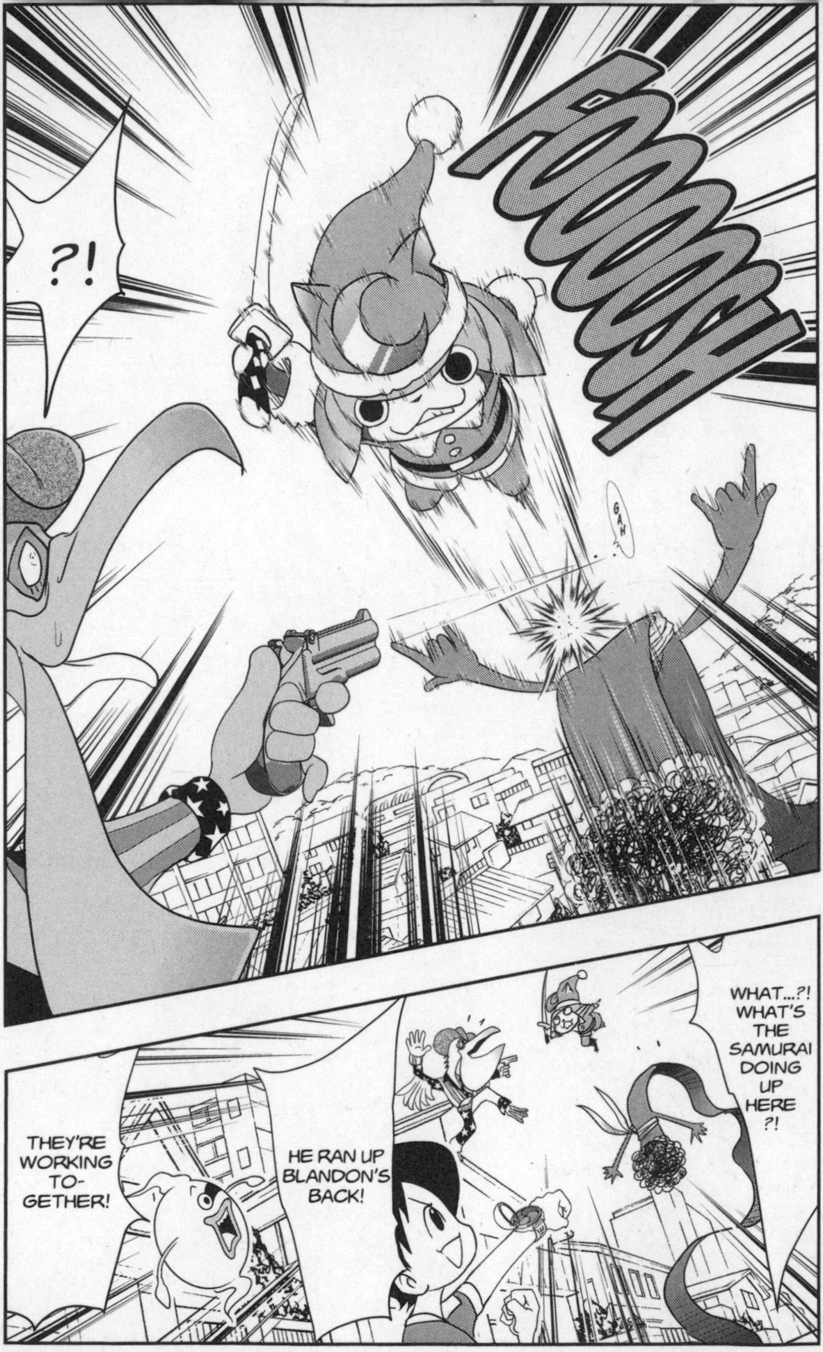
FOOOSH
?!
GAH
WHAT...?! WHAT'S THE SAMURAI DOING UP HERE ?!
HE RAN UP BLANDON'S BACK!
THEY'RE WORKING TO-GETHER!

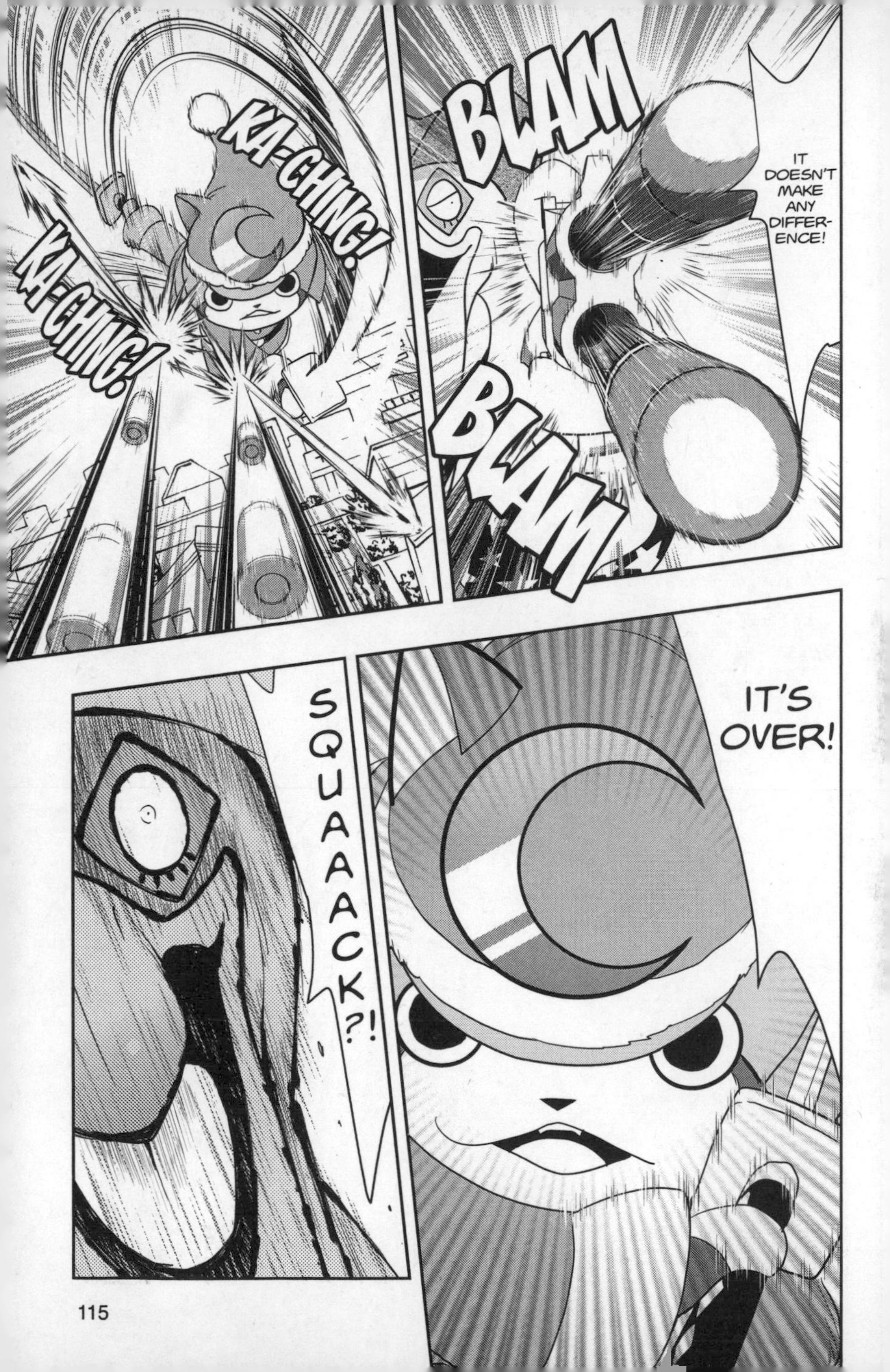
BLAM
BLAM
IT DOESN'T MAKE ANY DIFFERENCE!
KA-CHING!
KA-CHING!
IT'S OVER!
SQUAAAACK?!

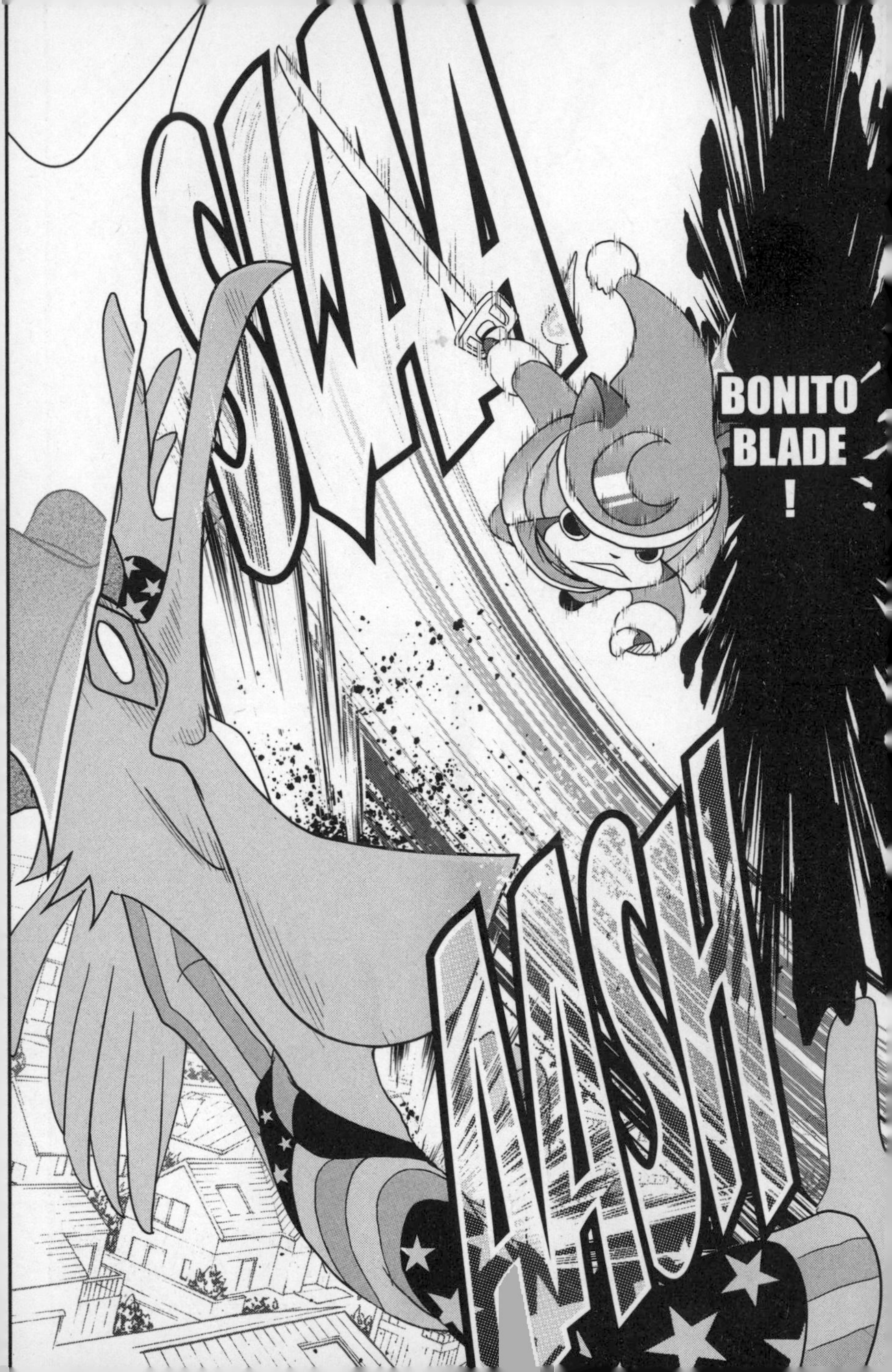
BONITO BLADE !

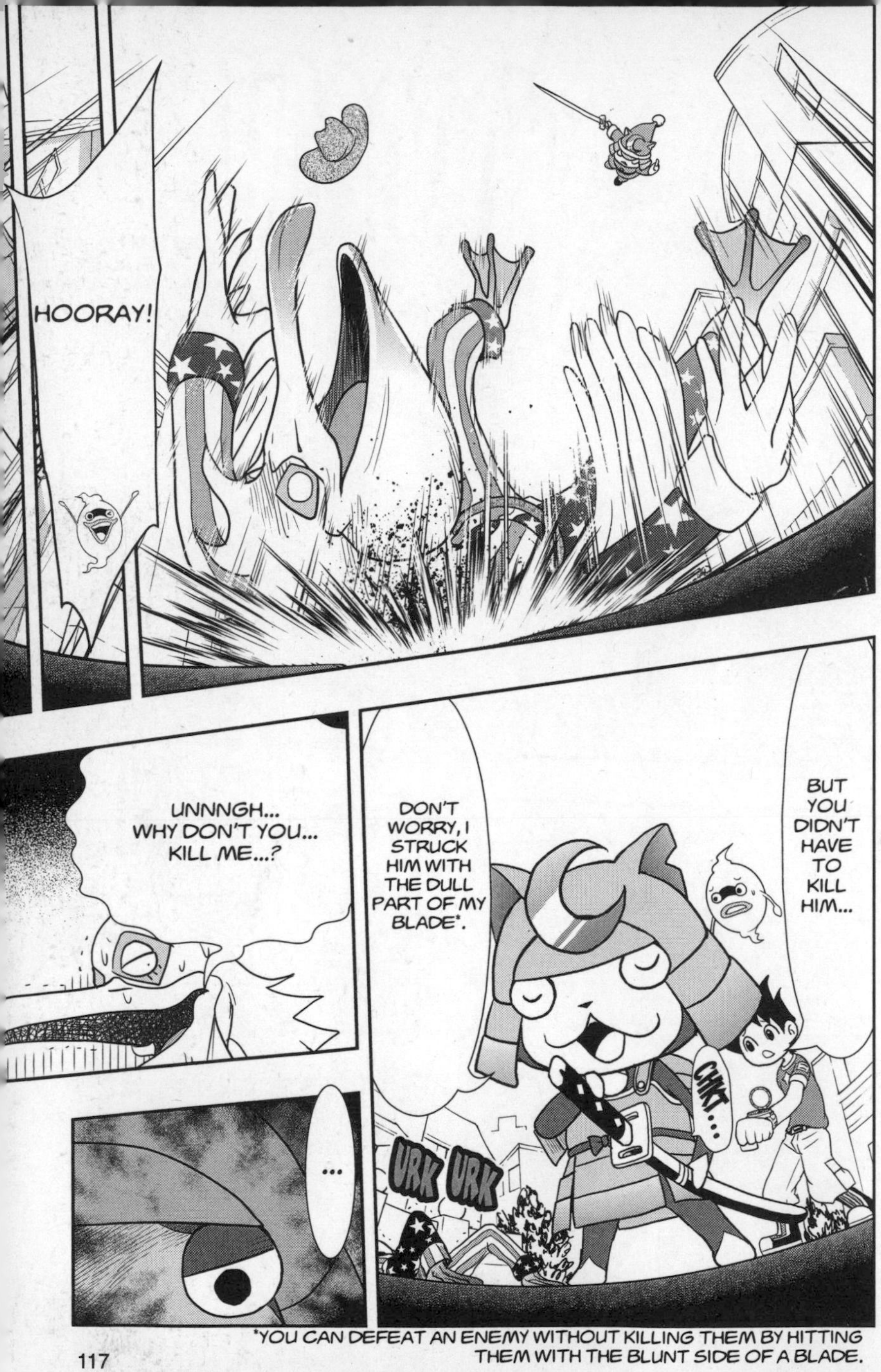
HOORAY!
BUT YOU DIDN'T HAVE TO KILL HIM...
DON'T WORRY, I STRUCK HIM WITH THE DULL PART OF MY BLADE*.
CHKT...
URK URK
UNNNGH... WHY DON'T YOU... KILL ME...?
...

*YOU CAN DEFEAT AN ENEMY WITHOUT KILLING THEM BY HITTING THEM WITH THE BLUNT SIDE OF A BLADE.

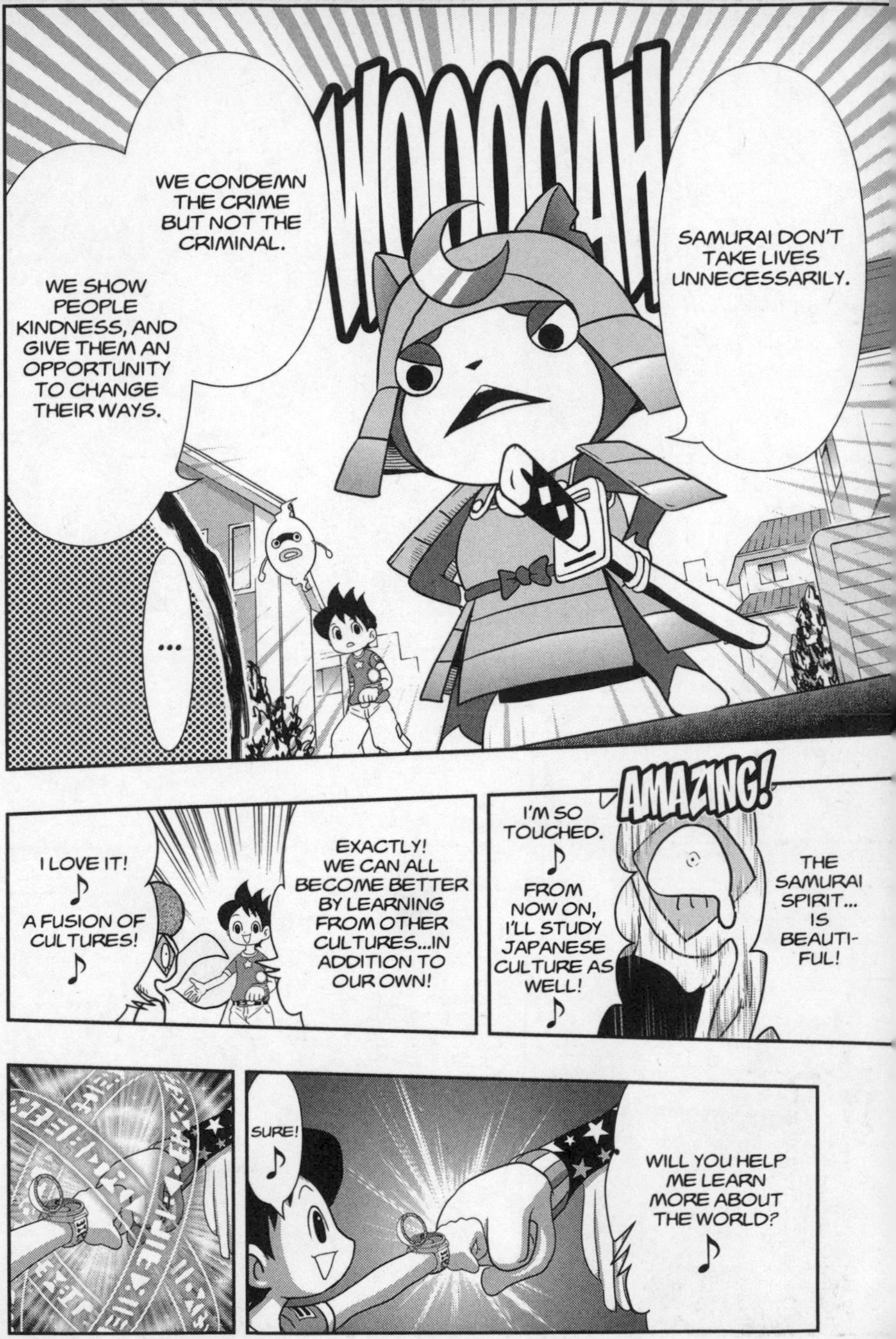
SAMURAI DON'T TAKE LIVES UNNECESSARILY.
WOOOOAH
WE CONDEMN THE CRIME BUT NOT THE CRIMINAL.
WE SHOW PEOPLE KINDNESS, AND GIVE THEM AN OPPORTUNITY TO CHANGE THEIR WAYS.
...
THE SAMURAI SPIRIT... IS BEAUTI-FUL!
AMAZING!
I'M SO TOUCHED. ♪
FROM NOW ON, I'LL STUDY JAPANESE CULTURE AS WELL! ♪
EXACTLY! WE CAN ALL BECOME BETTER BY LEARNING FROM OTHER CULTURES...IN ADDITION TO OUR OWN!
I LOVE IT! ♪
A FUSION OF CULTURES! ♪
WILL YOU HELP ME LEARN MORE ABOUT THE WORLD? ♪
SURE! ♪

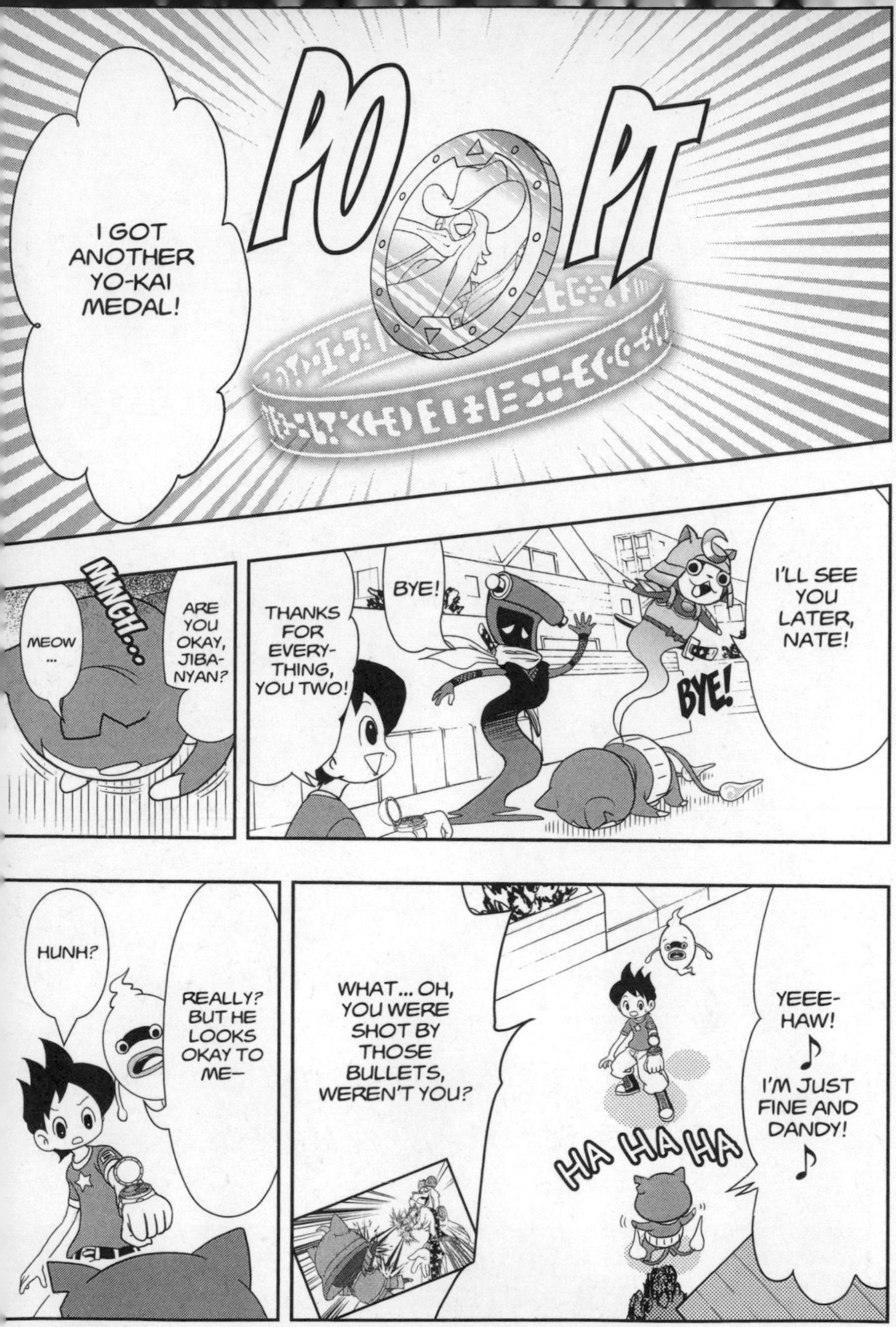
PO PIT
I GOT ANOTHER YO-KAI MEDAL!
I'LL SEE YOU LATER, NATE!
BYE!
BYE!
THANKS FOR EVERY-THING, YOU TWO!
ARE YOU OKAY, JIBA-NYAN?
MNNGH...
MEOW ...
YEEE-HAW! ♪ I'M JUST FINE AND DANDY! ♪
HA HA HA
WHAT... OH, YOU WERE SHOT BY THOSE BULLETS, WEREN'T YOU?
REALLY? BUT HE LOOKS OKAY TO ME—
HUNH?

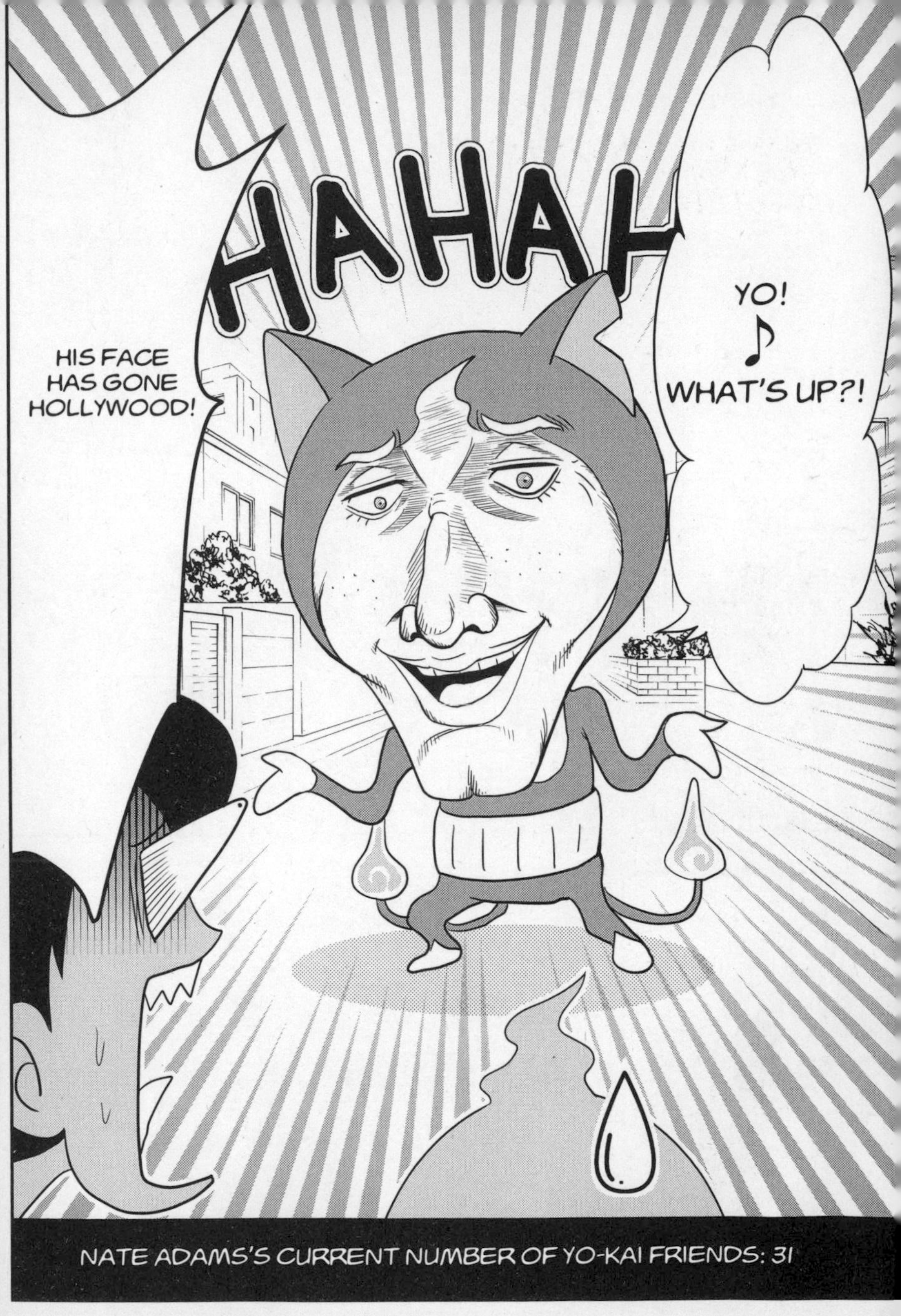
YO! ♪ WHAT'S UP?!
HAHAH
HIS FACE HAS GONE HOLLYWOOD!
NATE ADAMS'S CURRENT NUMBER OF YO-KAI FRIENDS: 31

C'MON!

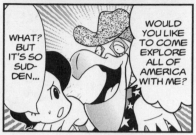

WOULD YOU LIKE TO COME EXPLORE ALL OF AMERICA WITH ME?
WHAT? BUT IT'S SO SUD-DEN...
TSK TSK TSK...
NO, NO! THERE'S NO-THING TO WORRY ABOUT!
WHAT SHOULD I DO...
HEY-HEY-HEY!
C'MON! C'MON!
C'MON! C'MON!
YOU'RE PRETTY PUSHY... HAVE YOU BEEN BACK RECENT-LY?
PFFFT
YEAH! I JUST FLEW IN THIS MORN-ING!
GET IT?! I'M A PELICAN!
I DON'T GET IT...

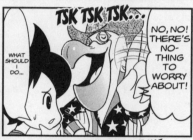

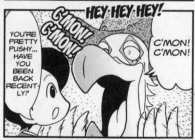

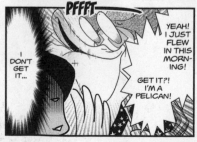

Chapter 40: BEWARE THE PRANKSTER!

FEATURING PRANKSTER YO-KAI BOYCLOPS

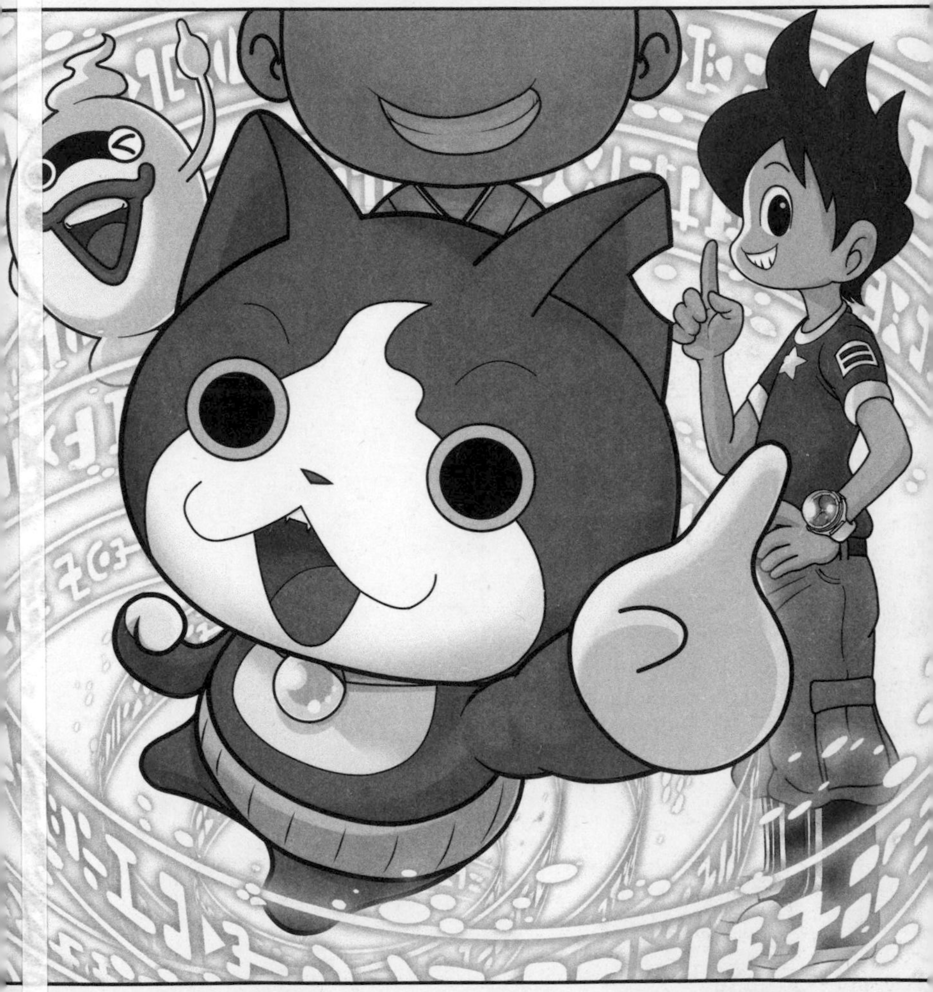

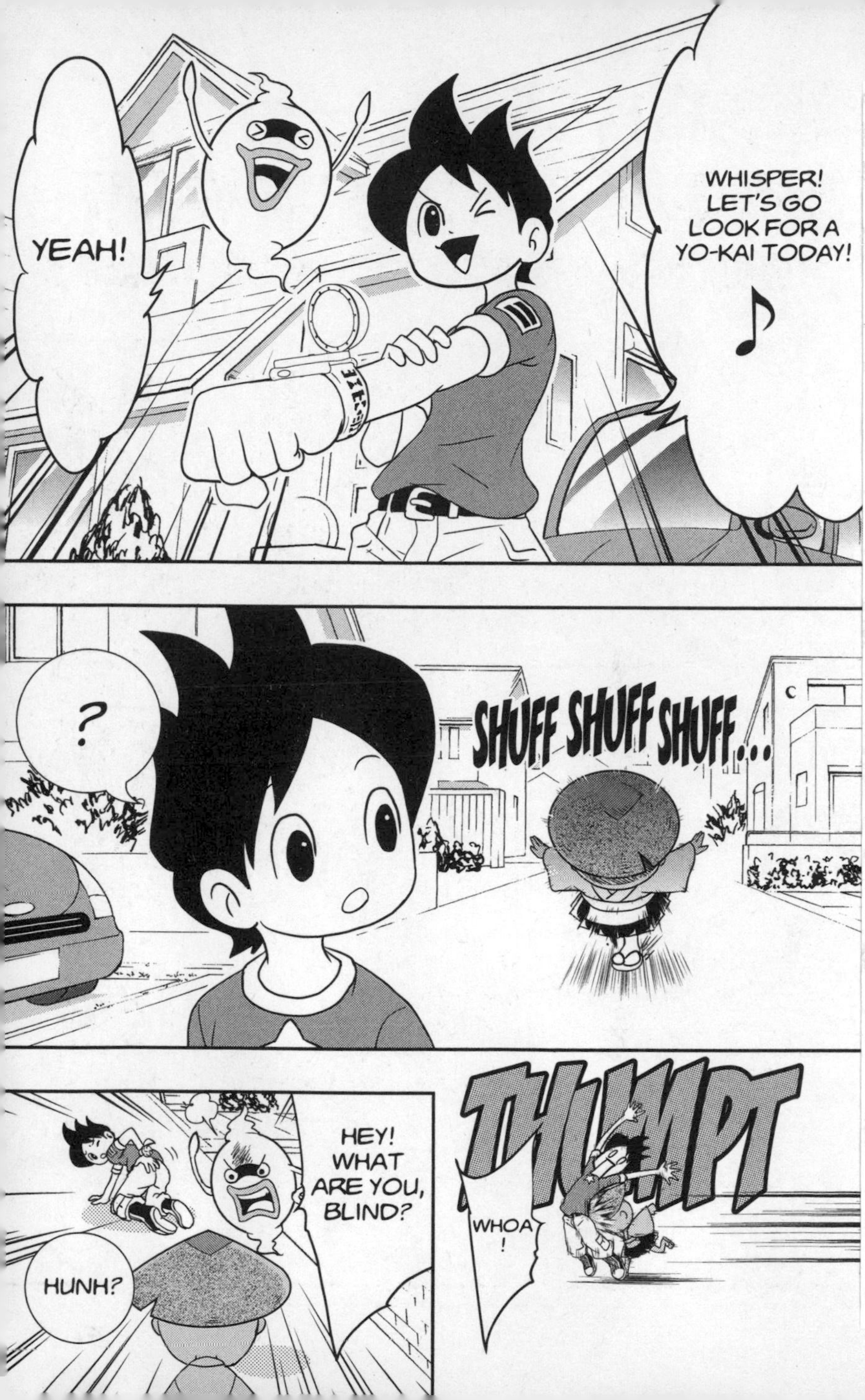
WHISPER! LET'S GO LOOK FOR A YO-KAI TODAY! ♪
YEAH!
SHUFF SHUFF SHUFF...
?
THUMPT
WHOA!
HEY! WHAT ARE YOU, BLIND?
HUNH?

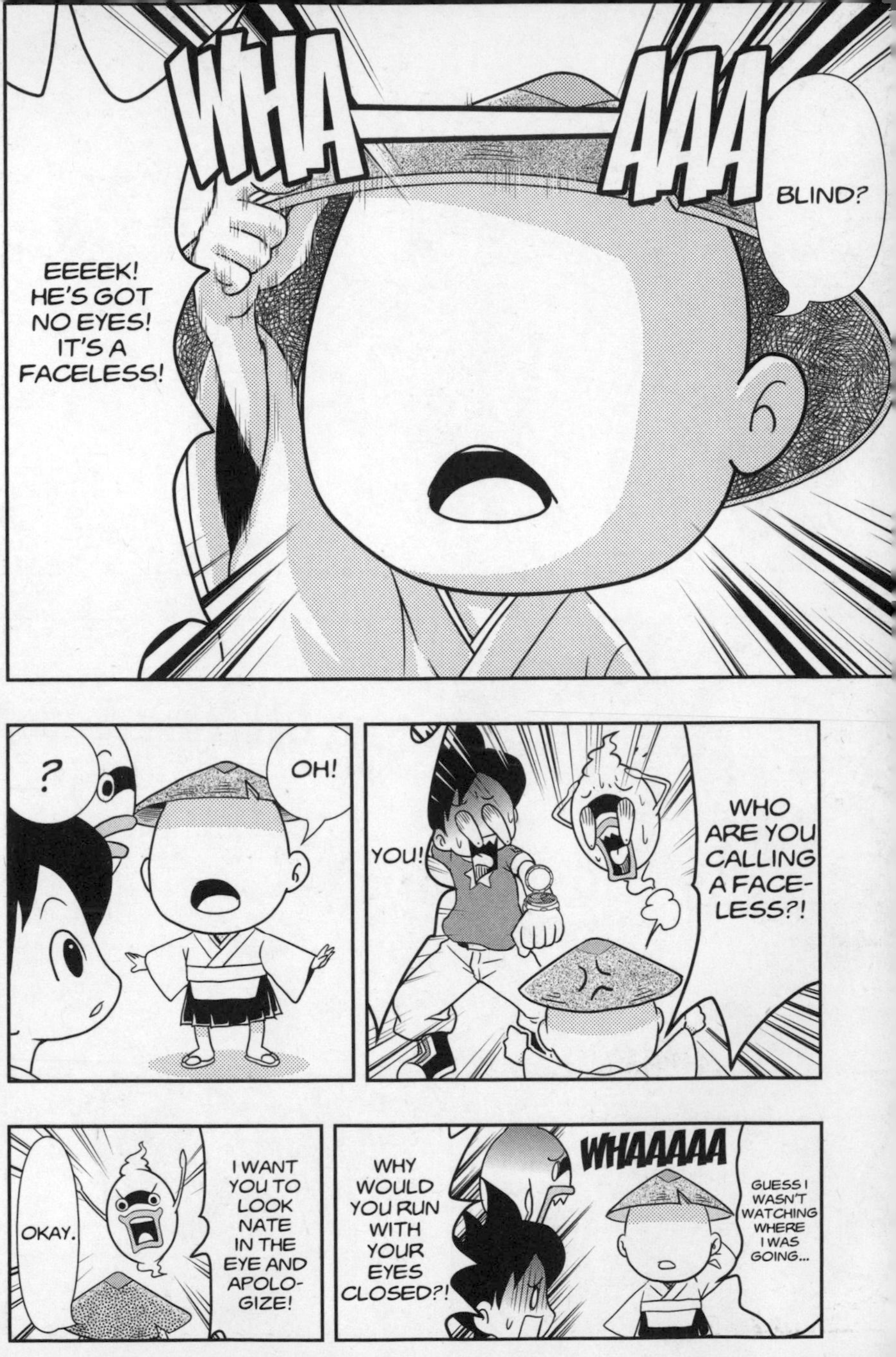
WHAAAA
BLIND?
EEEEK! HE'S GOT NO EYES! IT'S A FACELESS!
WHO ARE YOU CALLING A FACELESS?!
YOU!
OH!
?
GUESS I WASN'T WATCHING WHERE I WAS GOING...
WHAAAAA
WHY WOULD YOU RUN WITH YOUR EYES CLOSED?!
I WANT YOU TO LOOK NATE IN THE EYE AND APOLOGIZE!
OKAY.

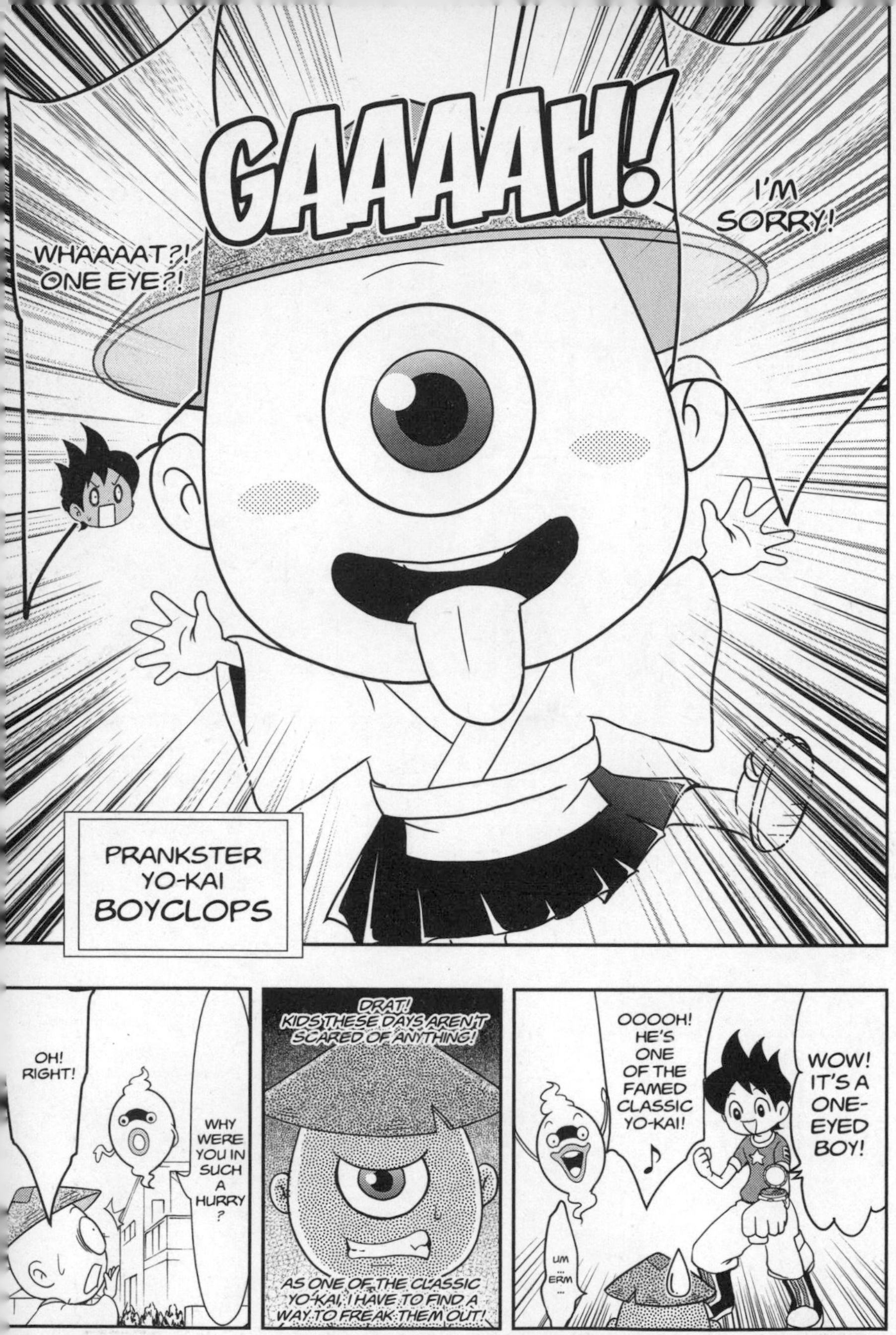
GAAAAH!
I'M SORRY!
WHAAAAT?! ONE EYE?!
PRANKSTER YO-KAI BOYCLOPS
WOW! IT'S A ONE-EYED BOY!
OOOOH! HE'S ONE OF THE FAMED CLASSIC YO-KAI! ♪
UM ... ERM ...
DRAT! KIDS THESE DAYS AREN'T SCARED OF ANYTHING!
AS ONE OF THE CLASSIC YO-KAI, I HAVE TO FIND A WAY TO FREAK THEM OUT!
WHY WERE YOU IN SUCH A HURRY?
OH! RIGHT!

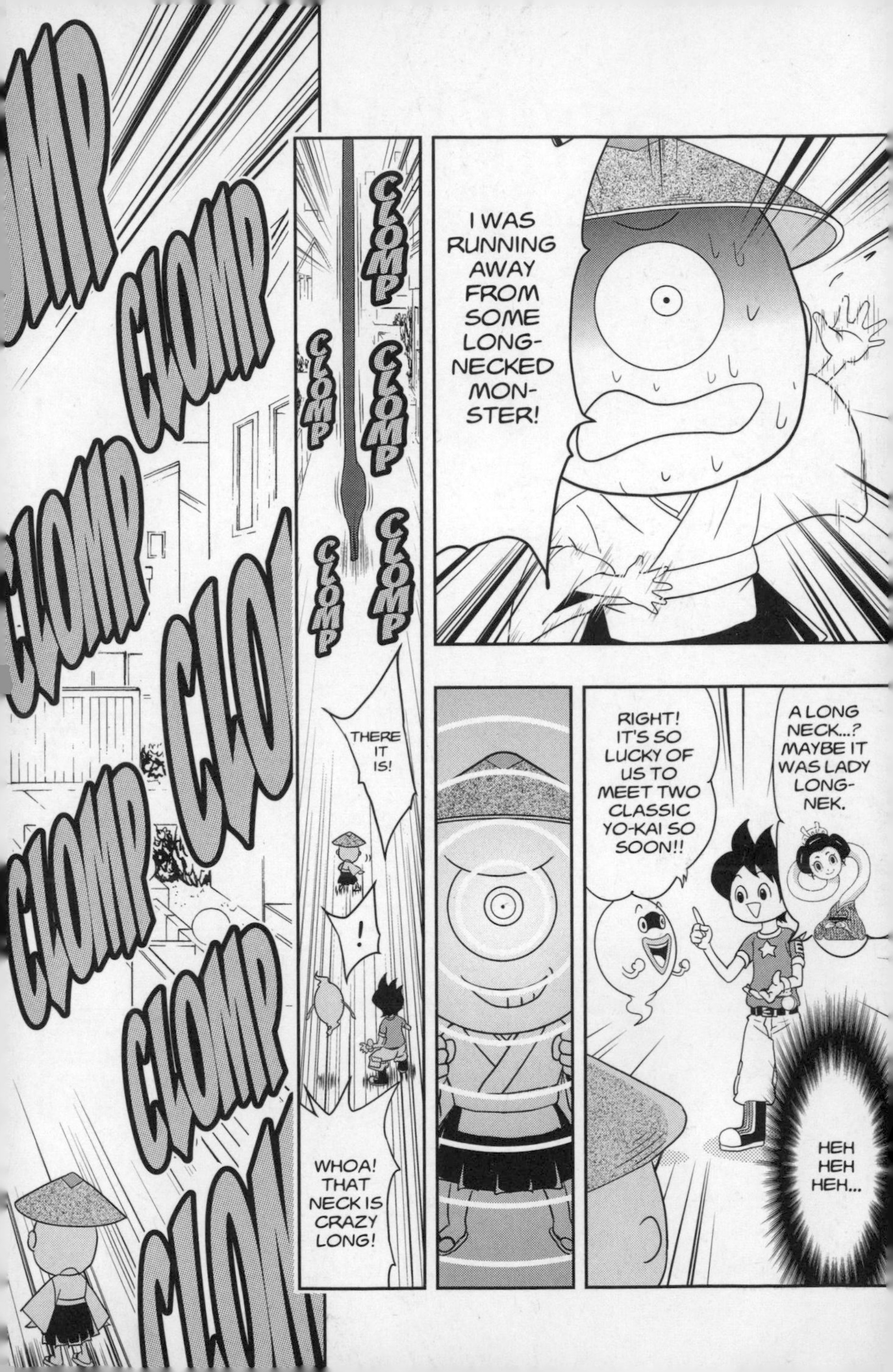
I WAS RUNNING AWAY FROM SOME LONG-NECKED MON-STER!
A LONG NECK...? MAYBE IT WAS LADY LONG-NEK.
RIGHT! IT'S SO LUCKY OF US TO MEET TWO CLASSIC YO-KAI SO SOON!!
HEH HEH HEH...
CLOMP
CLOMP
CLOMP
CLOMP
CLOMP
THERE IT IS!
!
WHOA! THAT NECK IS CRAZY LONG!
CLOMP
CLOMP
CLOMP
CLOMP
CLOMP

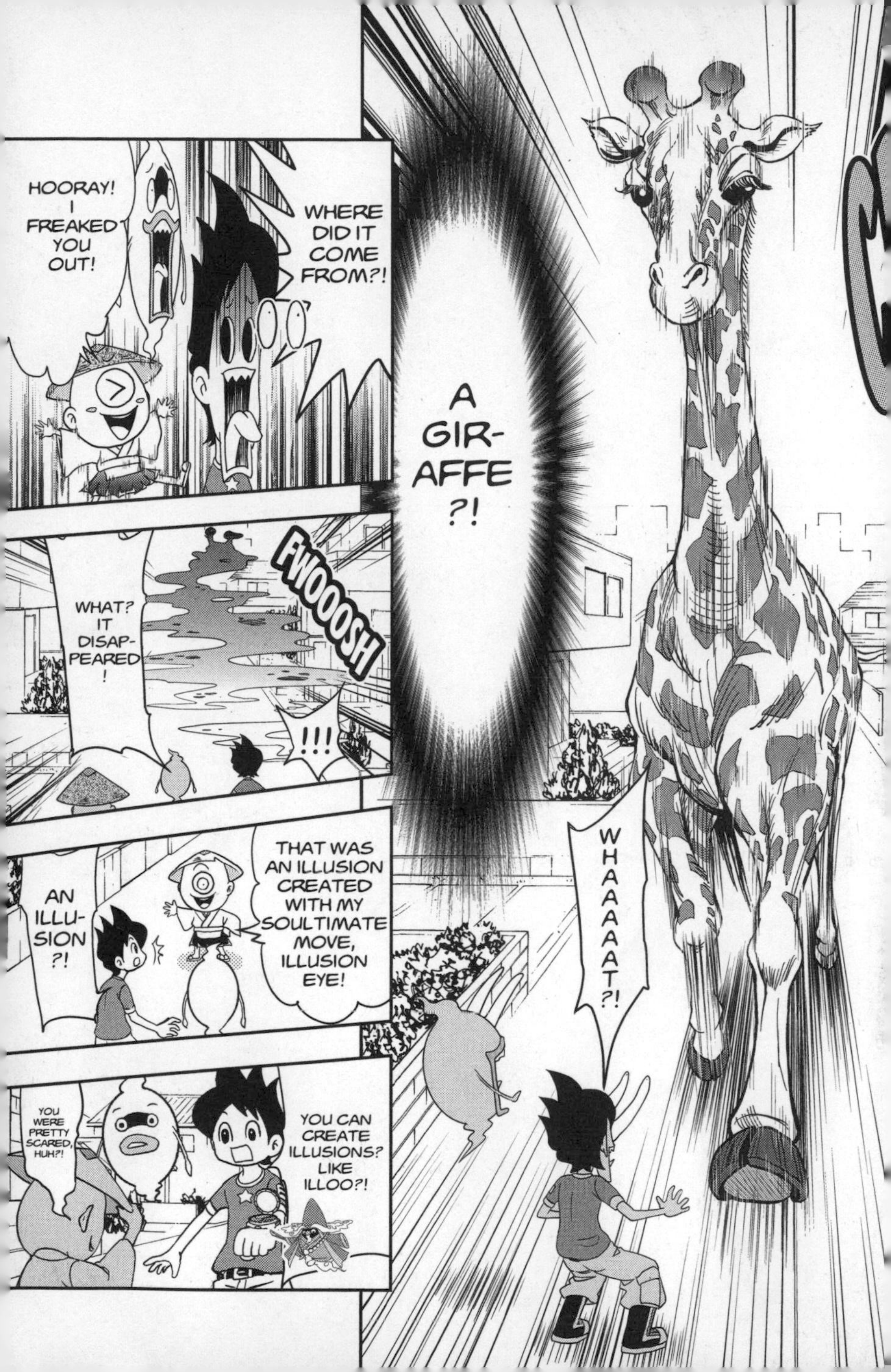
A GIR-AFFE?!
WHAAAAAAT?!
WHERE DID IT COME FROM?!
HOORAY! I FREAKED YOU OUT!
FWOOOSH
WHAT? IT DISAP-PEARED!
!!!
THAT WAS AN ILLUSION CREATED WITH MY SOULTIMATE MOVE, ILLUSION EYE!
AN ILLU-SION?!
YOU CAN CREATE ILLUSIONS? LIKE ILLOO?!
YOU WERE PRETTY SCARED, HUH?!

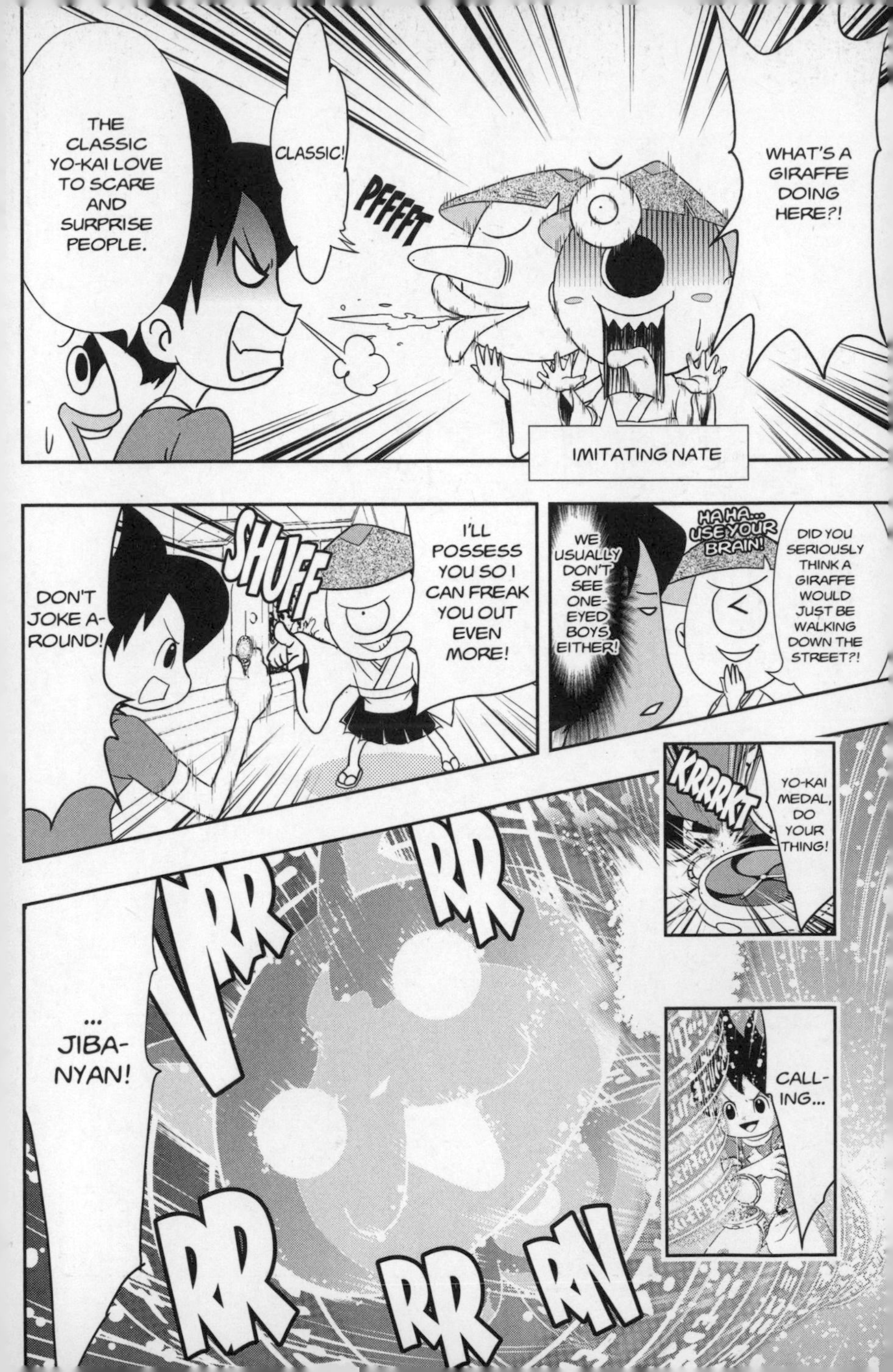
WHAT'S A GIRAFFE DOING HERE?!
IMITATING NATE
PFFFFT
CLASSIC!
THE CLASSIC YO-KAI LOVE TO SCARE AND SURPRISE PEOPLE.
DID YOU SERIOUSLY THINK A GIRAFFE WOULD JUST BE WALKING DOWN THE STREET?!
HA HA... USE YOUR BRAIN!
WE USUALLY DON'T SEE ONE-EYED BOYS EITHER!
I'LL POSSESS YOU SO I CAN FREAK YOU OUT EVEN MORE!
SHUFF
DON'T JOKE A-ROUND!
KRRRKT
YO-KAI MEDAL, DO YOUR THING!
CALL-ING...
VRR
RR
... JIBA-NYAN!
RR
RR
RRV

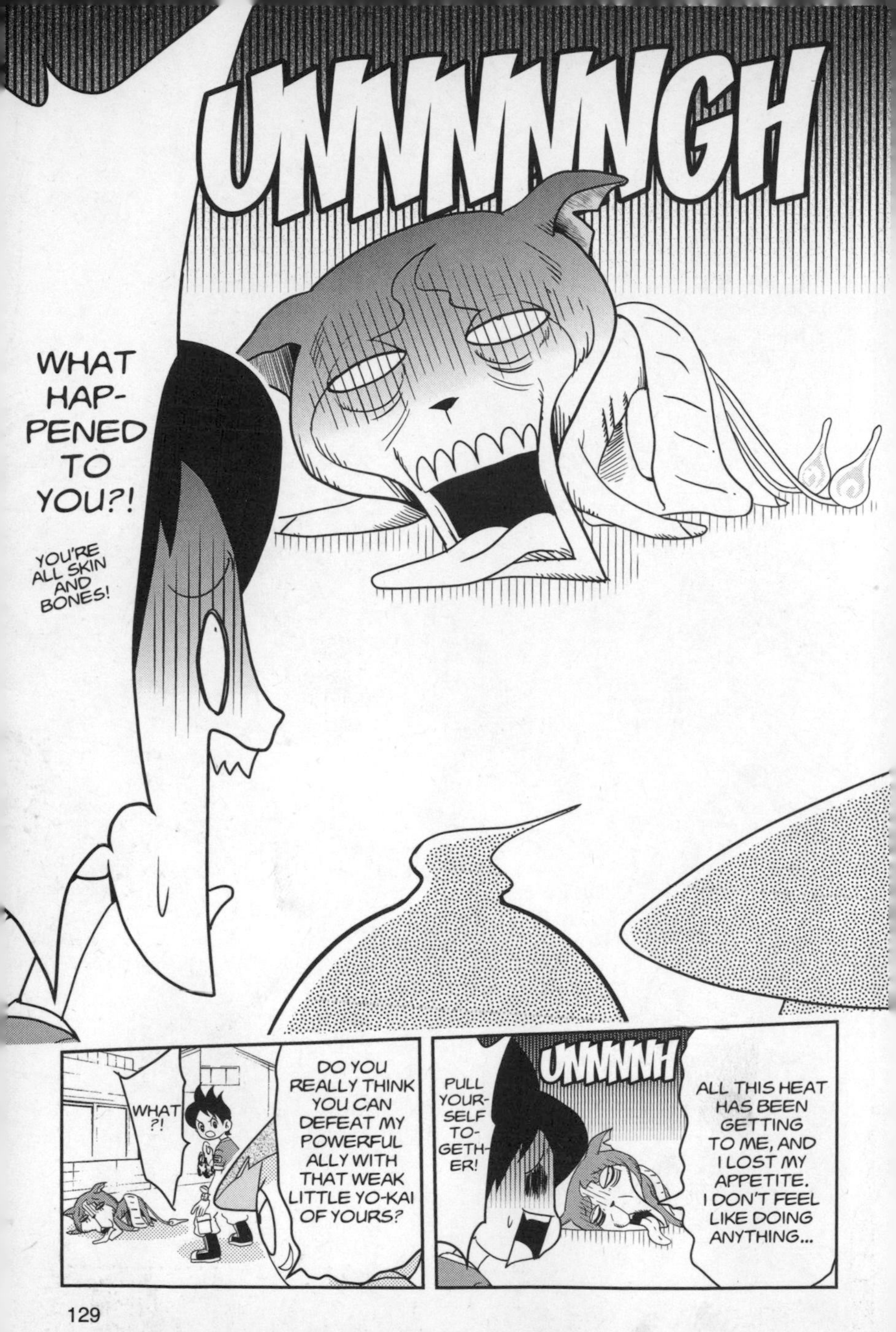

UNNNNNGH
WHAT HAP-PENED TO YOU?!
YOU'RE ALL SKIN AND BONES!
UNNNNH
ALL THIS HEAT HAS BEEN GETTING TO ME, AND I LOST MY APPETITE. I DON'T FEEL LIKE DOING ANYTHING...
PULL YOUR-SELF TO-GETH-ER!
DO YOU REALLY THINK YOU CAN DEFEAT MY POWERFUL ALLY WITH THAT WEAK LITTLE YO-KAI OF YOURS?
WHAT?!

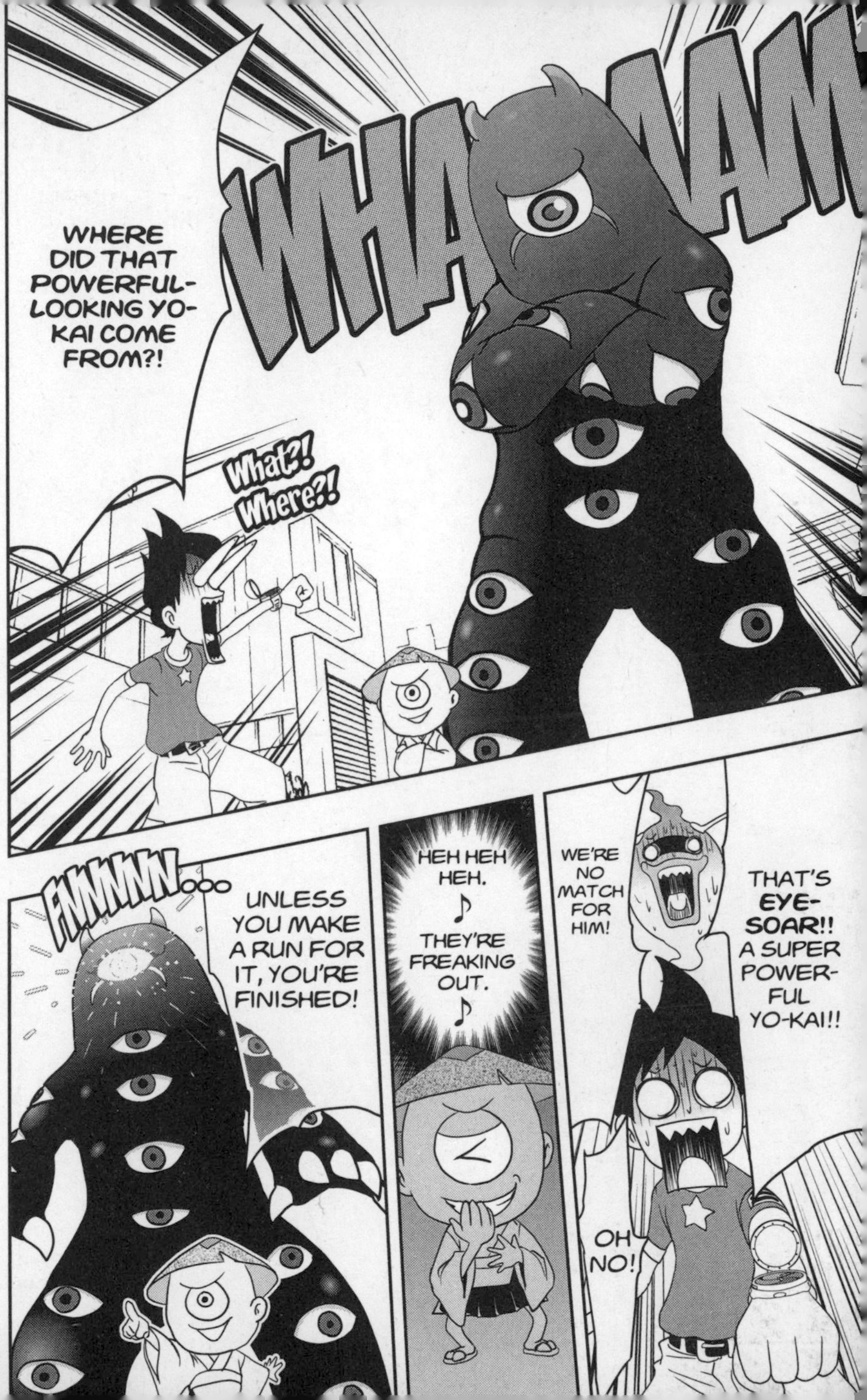
WHERE DID THAT POWERFUL-LOOKING YO-KAI COME FROM?!
What?! Where?!
THAT'S **EYE-SOAR**!! A SUPER POWERFUL YO-KAI!!
WE'RE NO MATCH FOR HIM!
OH NO!
HEH HEH HEH. ♪
THEY'RE FREAKING OUT. ♪
UNLESS YOU MAKE A RUN FOR IT, YOU'RE FINISHED!

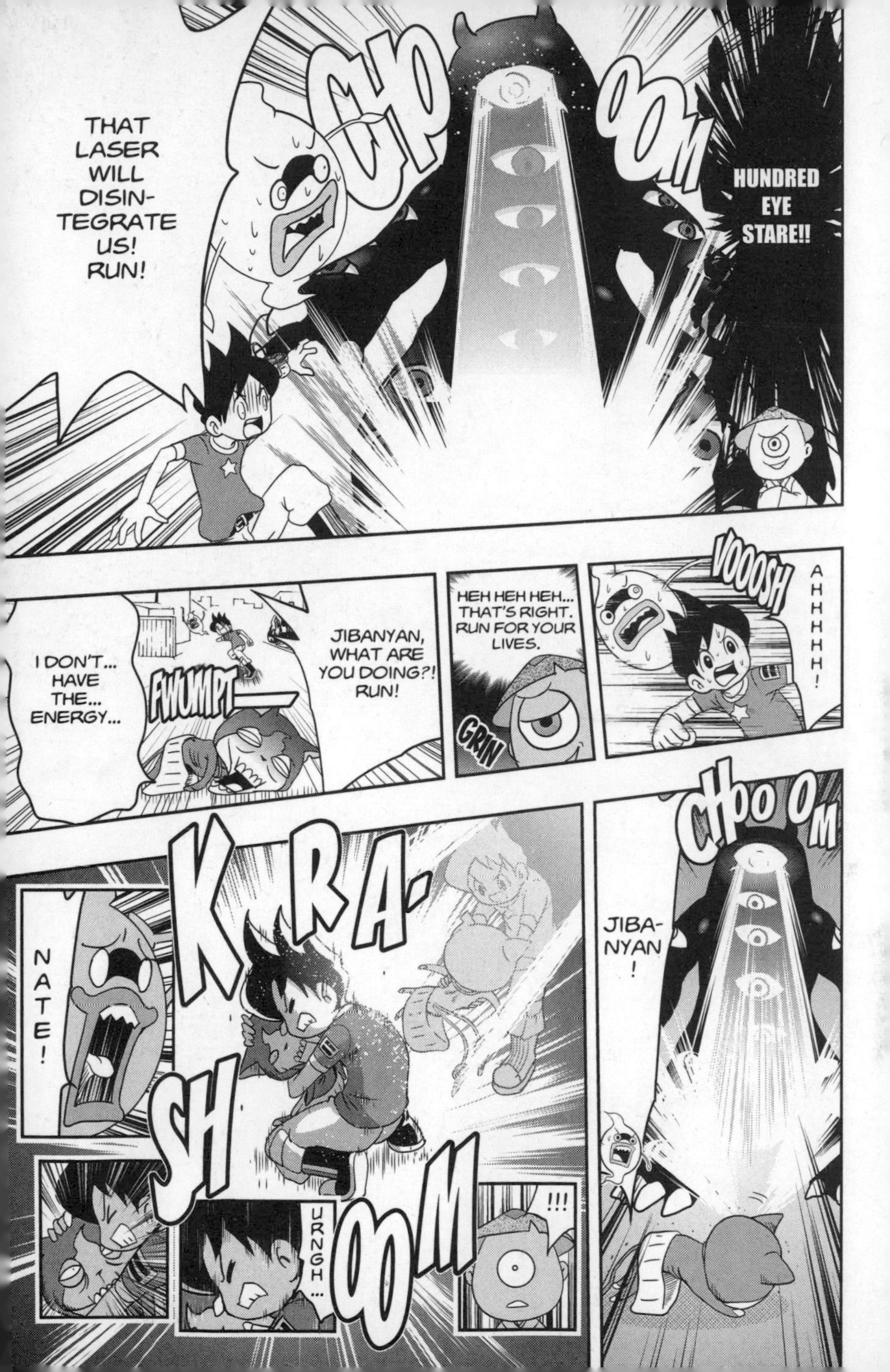
CHOOOOM
HUNDRED EYE STARE!!
THAT LASER WILL DISINTEGRATE US! RUN!
VOOOSH
AHHHHHH!
HEH HEH HEH... THAT'S RIGHT. RUN FOR YOUR LIVES.
GRIN
JIBANYAN, WHAT ARE YOU DOING?! RUN!
FWUMPT
I DON'T... HAVE THE... ENERGY...
CHOOOM
JIBANYAN!
KRA-SHOOOM
NATE!
!!!
URNGH...

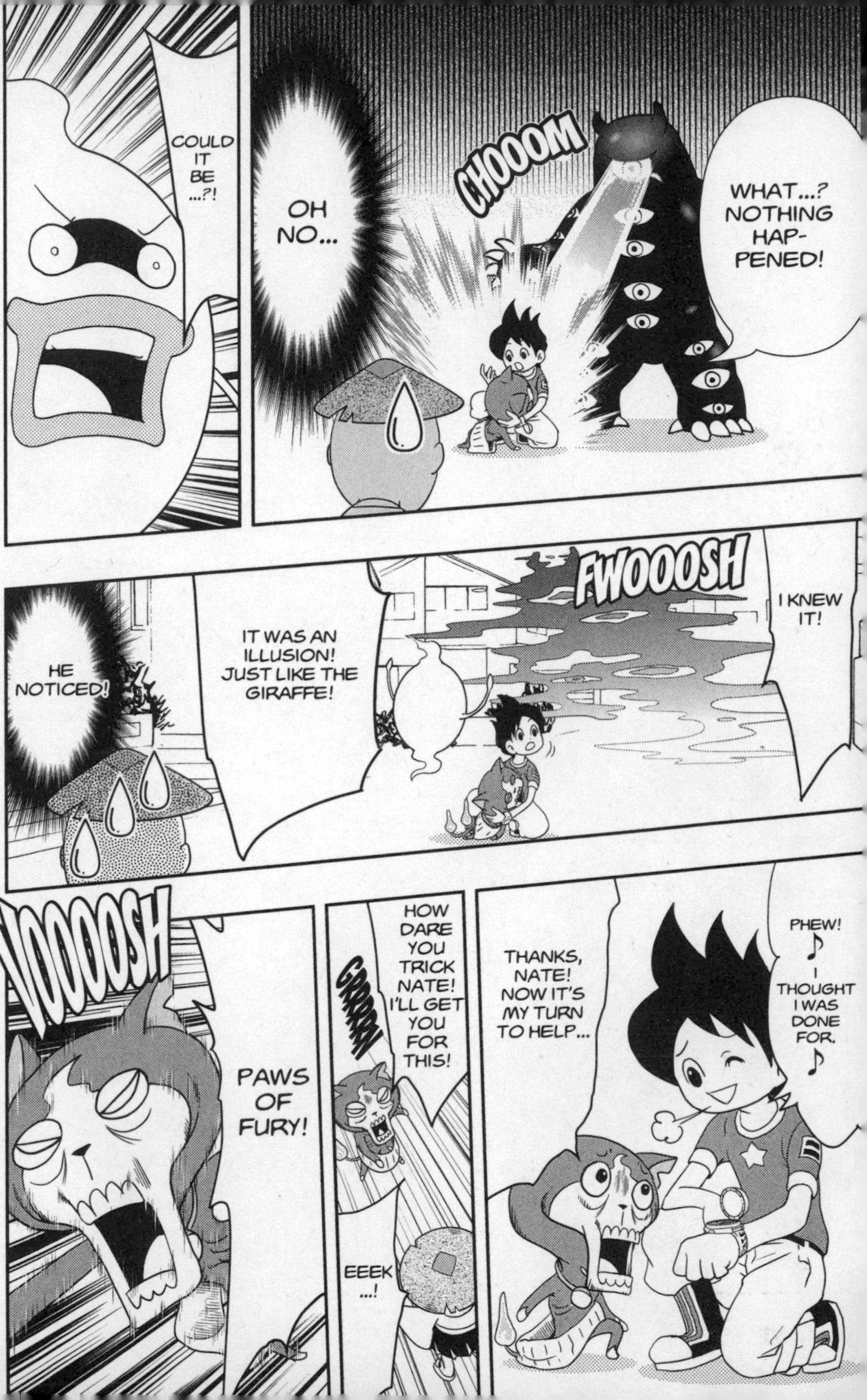
CHOOOM
WHAT...? NOTHING HAP-PENED!
OH NO...
COULD IT BE ...?!
I KNEW IT!
FWOOOSH
IT WAS AN ILLUSION! JUST LIKE THE GIRAFFE!
HE NOTICED!
PHEW! ♪ I THOUGHT I WAS DONE FOR. ♪
THANKS, NATE! NOW IT'S MY TURN TO HELP...
HOW DARE YOU TRICK NATE! I'LL GET YOU FOR THIS!
EEEK ...!
VOOOOSH
PAWS OF FURY!

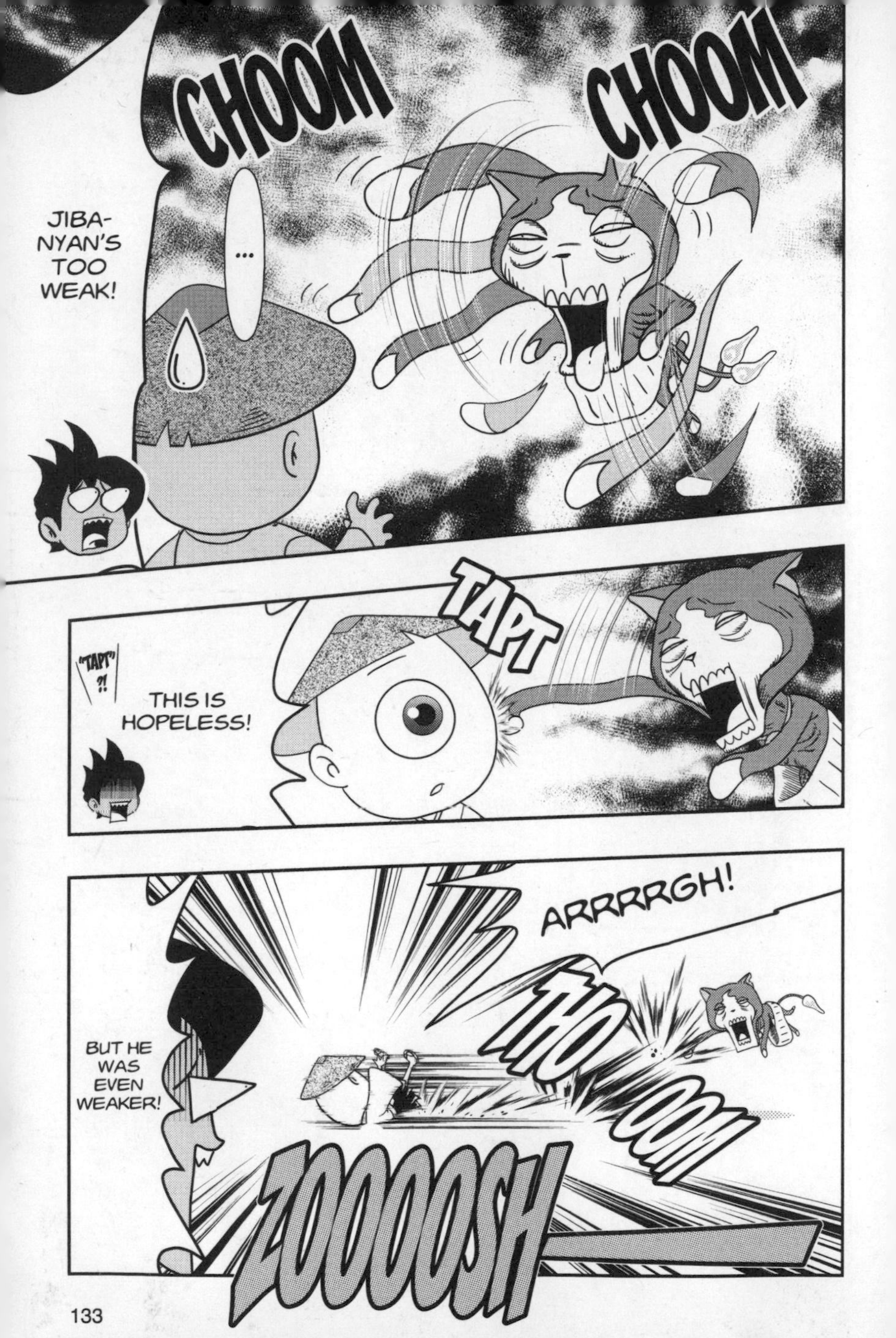
CHOOM
CHOOM
...
JIBA-NYAN'S TOO WEAK!
TAPT
"TAPT" ?!
THIS IS HOPELESS!
ARRRRGH!
THOOOOM
BUT HE WAS EVEN WEAKER!
ZOOOOSH

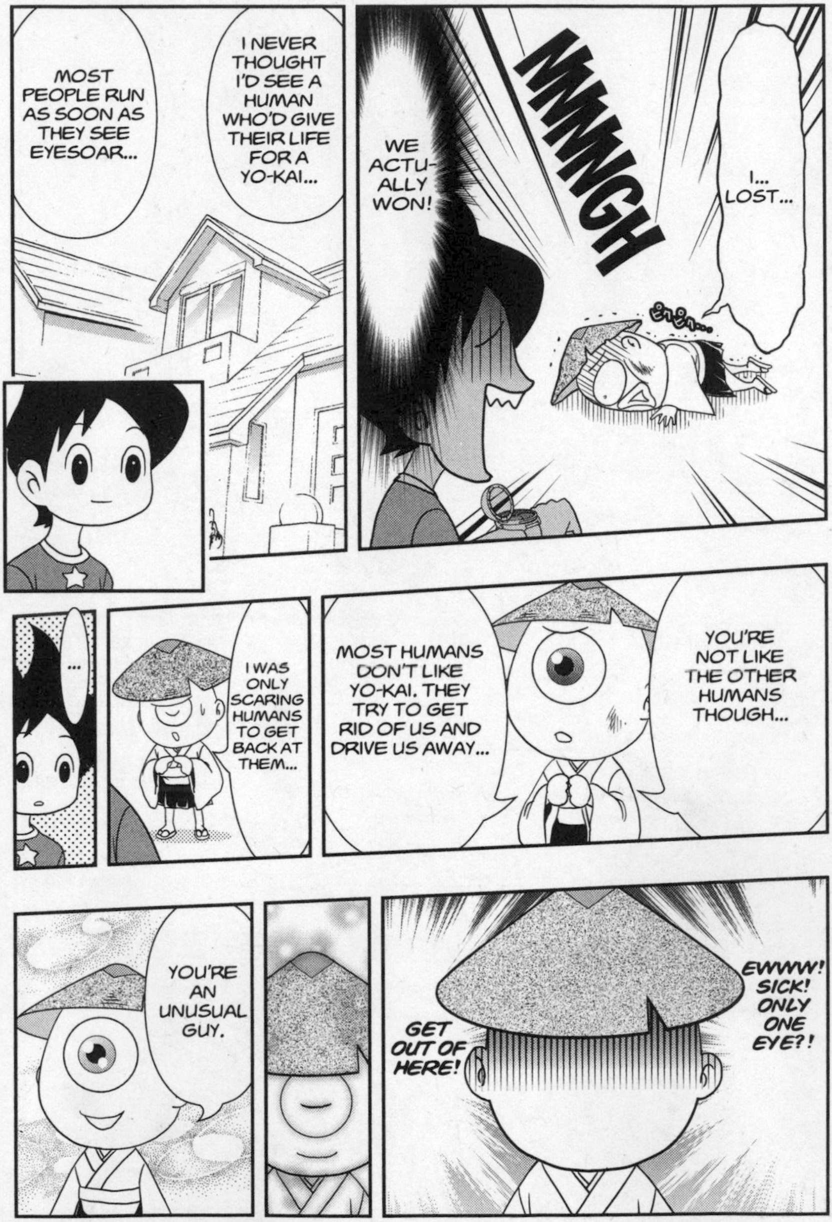

I... LOST...
MMMNGH
WE ACTU- ALLY WON!
I NEVER THOUGHT I'D SEE A HUMAN WHO'D GIVE THEIR LIFE FOR A YO-KAI...
MOST PEOPLE RUN AS SOON AS THEY SEE EYESOAR...
YOU'RE NOT LIKE THE OTHER HUMANS THOUGH...
MOST HUMANS DON'T LIKE YO-KAI. THEY TRY TO GET RID OF US AND DRIVE US AWAY...
I WAS ONLY SCARING HUMANS TO GET BACK AT THEM...
...
EWWW! SICK! ONLY ONE EYE?!
GET OUT OF HERE!
YOU'RE AN UNUSUAL GUY.

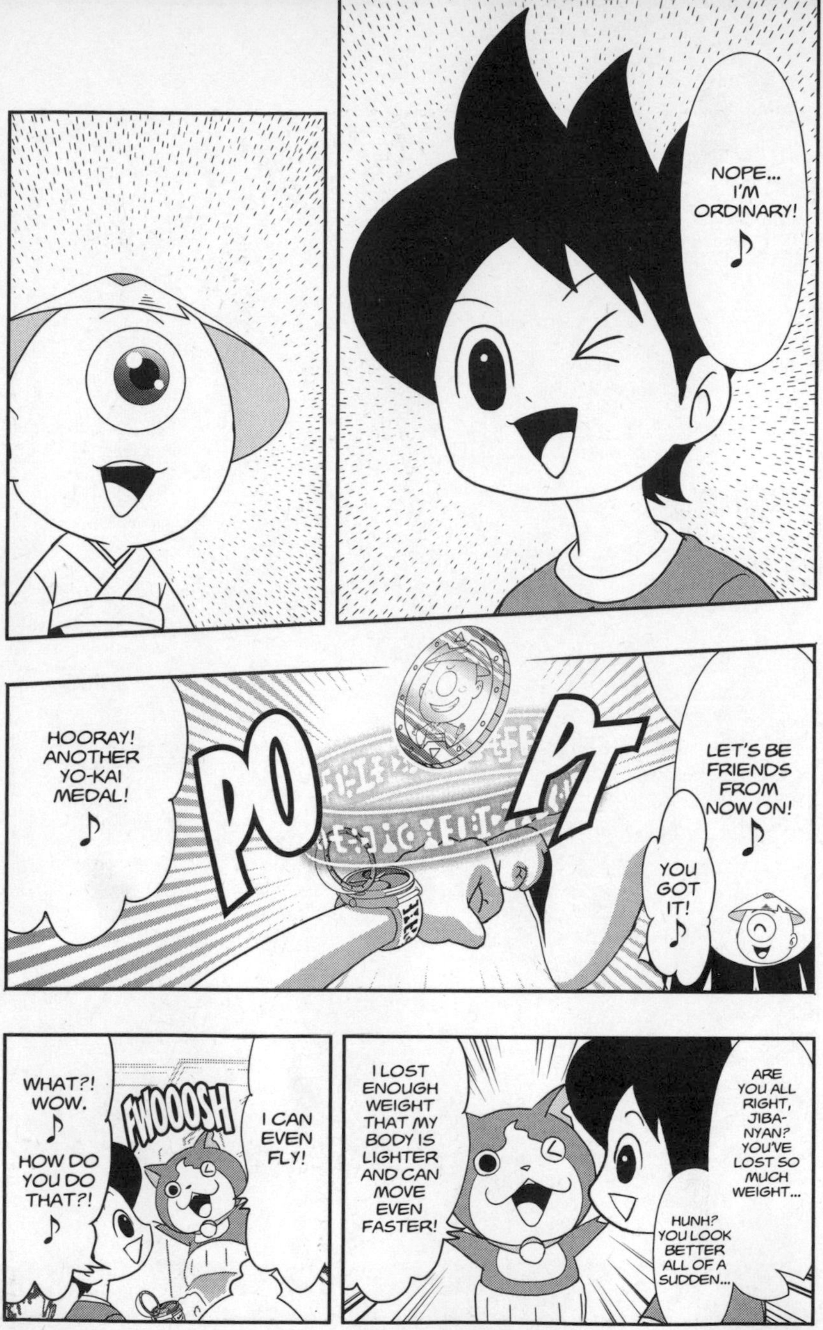
NOPE... I'M ORDINARY! ♪
LET'S BE FRIENDS FROM NOW ON! ♪
YOU GOT IT! ♪
PO PT
HOORAY! ANOTHER YO-KAI MEDAL! ♪
ARE YOU ALL RIGHT, JIBA-NYAN? YOU'VE LOST SO MUCH WEIGHT...
HUNH? YOU LOOK BETTER ALL OF A SUDDEN...
I LOST ENOUGH WEIGHT THAT MY BODY IS LIGHTER AND CAN MOVE EVEN FASTER!
I CAN EVEN FLY!
FWOOOSH
WHAT?! WOW. ♪
HOW DO YOU DO THAT?! ♪

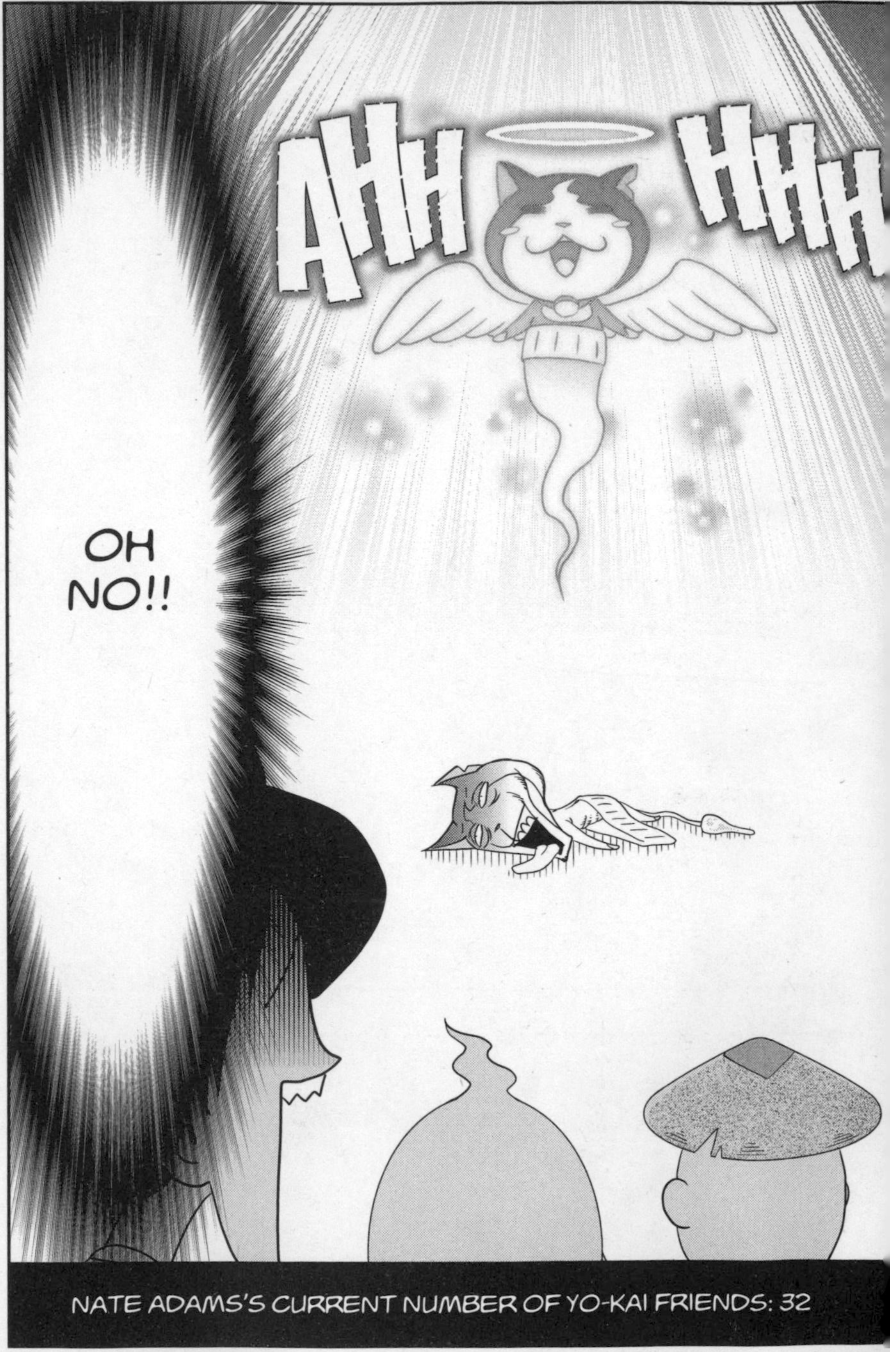
AHH HHHH
OH NO!!
NATE ADAMS'S CURRENT NUMBER OF YO-KAI FRIENDS: 32

YO-KAI WATCH 5

THE RETURN OF BOYCLOPS

YOU'RE SUCH A BIG HELP ON RAINY DAYS, PALLYSOL.
PSSSSSH
SHUFF
THUMPT
WHOA!
OOPS, SORRY.
BOOOO!
...
AHHHH!
IT'S ME.
OH! IT'S YOU, NATE.
AIIIIIIE! IT'S A ONE-EYED MON-STER!
YOU'VE ONLY GOT ONE EYE TOO!

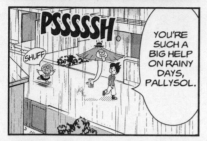

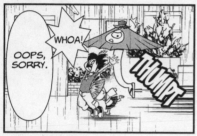

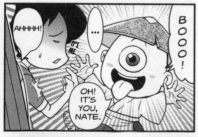

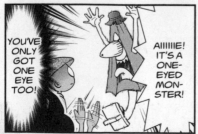

Chapter 41:
A PEACEFUL WORLD... WITHOUT EMOTION?!

FEATURING EXPRESSIONLESS YO-KAI FAYSOFF

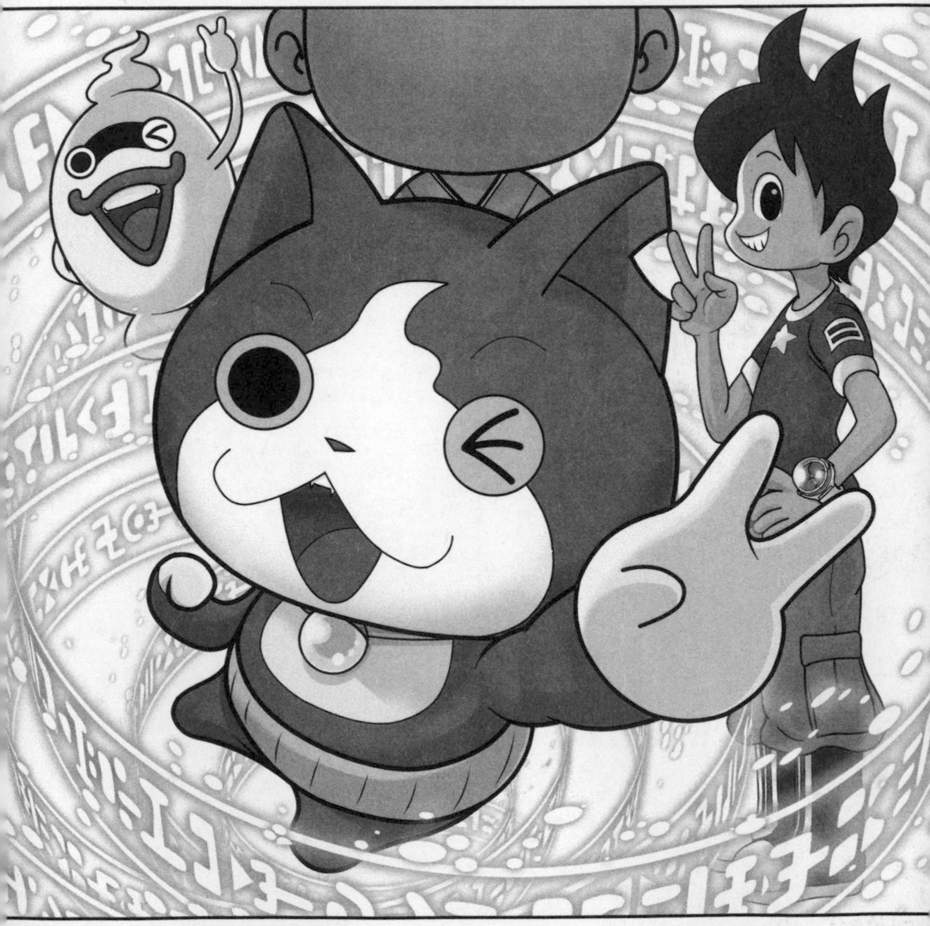

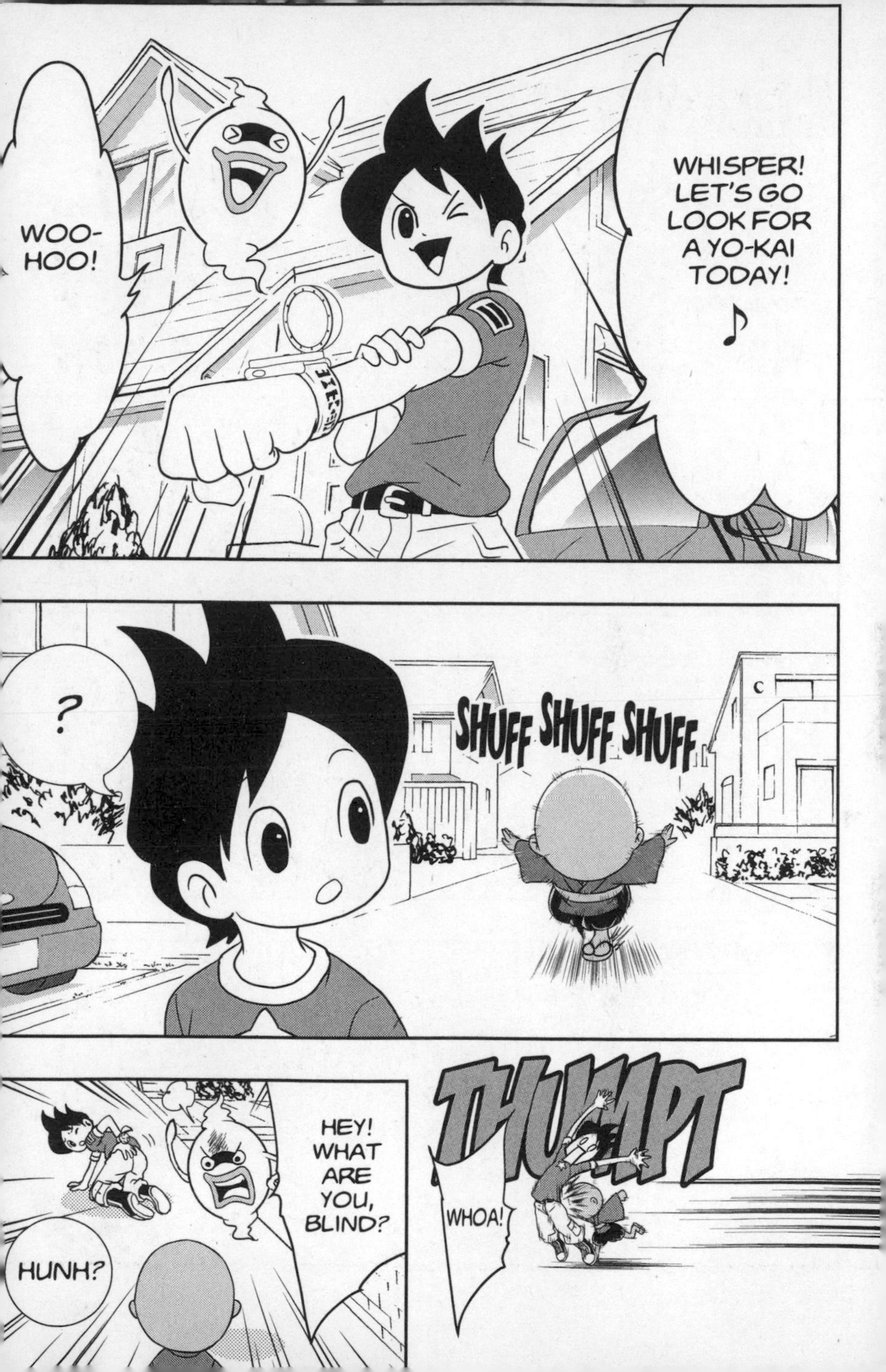
WHISPER! LET'S GO LOOK FOR A YO-KAI TODAY! ♪
WOO-HOO!
SHUFF SHUFF SHUFF
?
THUMPT
WHOA!
HEY! WHAT ARE YOU, BLIND?
HUNH?

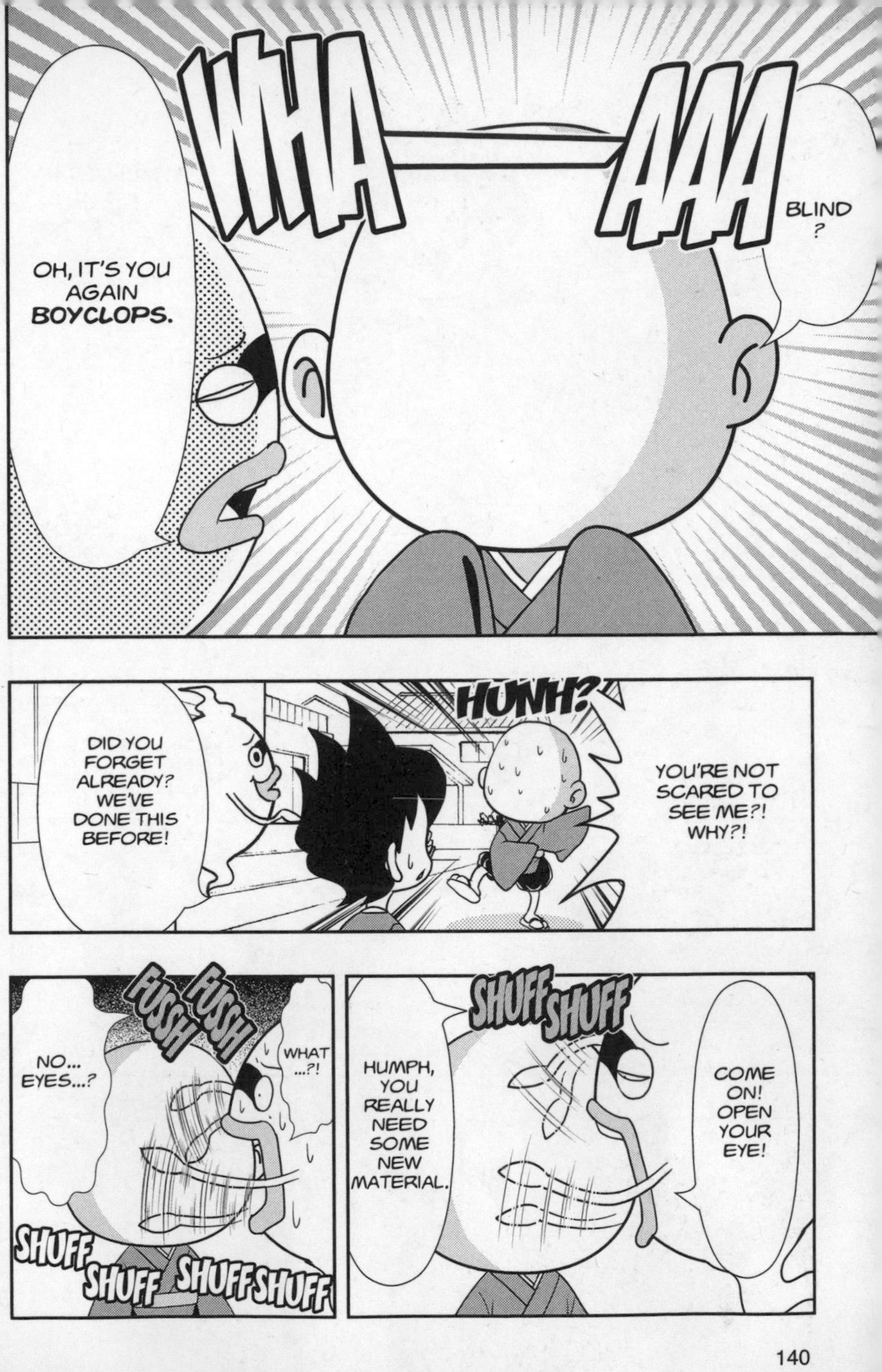

BLIND ?
WHAAAA
OH, IT'S YOU AGAIN BOYCLOPS.
YOU'RE NOT SCARED TO SEE ME?! WHY?!
HUNH?
DID YOU FORGET ALREADY? WE'VE DONE THIS BEFORE!
COME ON! OPEN YOUR EYE!
SHUFF SHUFF
HUMPH, YOU REALLY NEED SOME NEW MATERIAL.
WHAT ...?!
FUSSH FUSSH
NO... EYES...?
SHUFF SHUFF SHUFF SHUFF

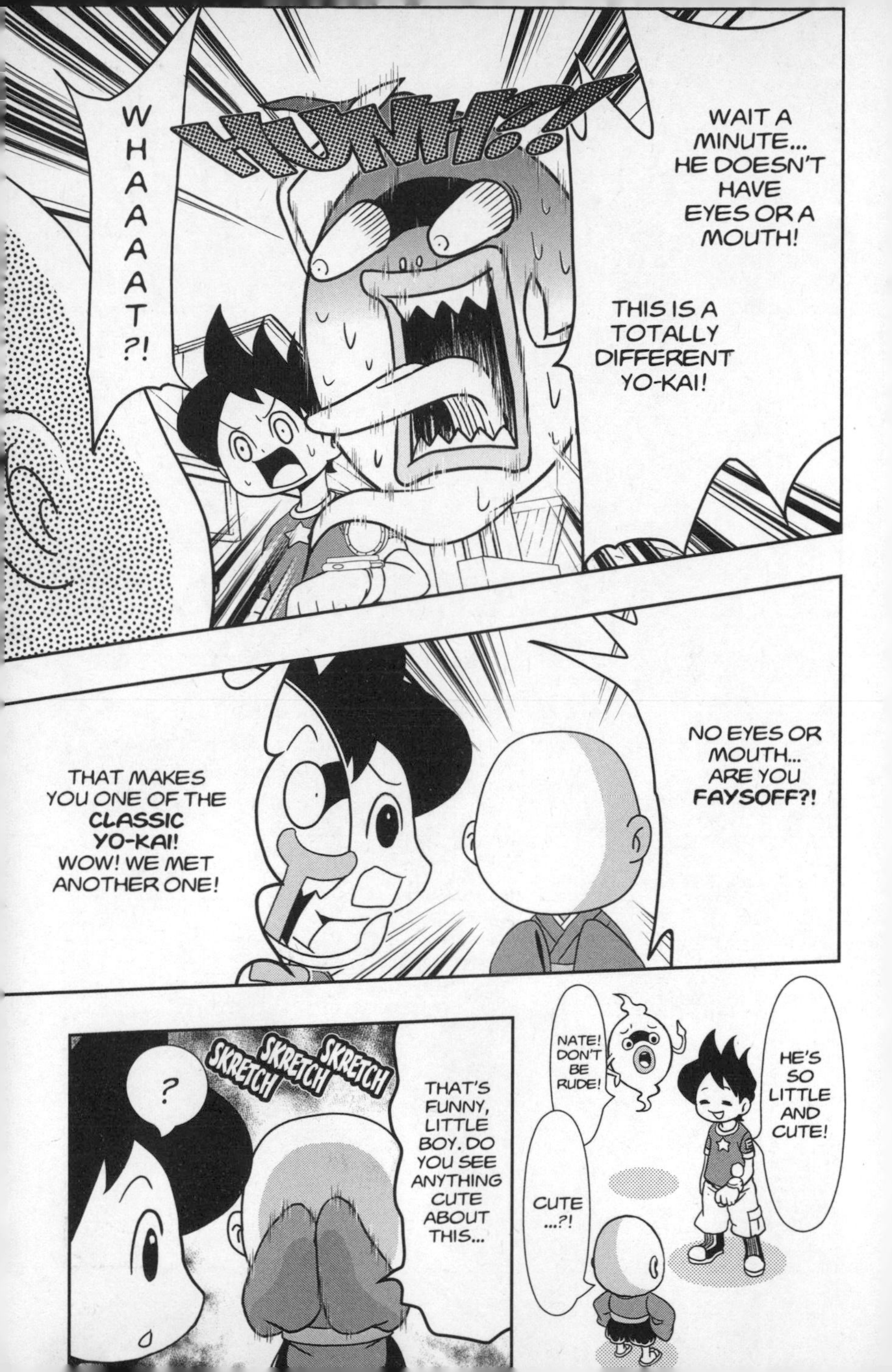
WAIT A MINUTE... HE DOESN'T HAVE EYES OR A MOUTH!
THIS IS A TOTALLY DIFFERENT YO-KAI!
WHAAAAAT?!
NO EYES OR MOUTH... ARE YOU **FAYSOFF?!**
THAT MAKES YOU ONE OF THE **CLASSIC YO-KAI!** WOW! WE MET ANOTHER ONE!
HE'S SO LITTLE AND CUTE!
NATE! DON'T BE RUDE!
CUTE ...?!
THAT'S FUNNY, LITTLE BOY. DO YOU SEE ANYTHING CUTE ABOUT THIS...
SKRETCH
SKRETCH
SKRETCH
?

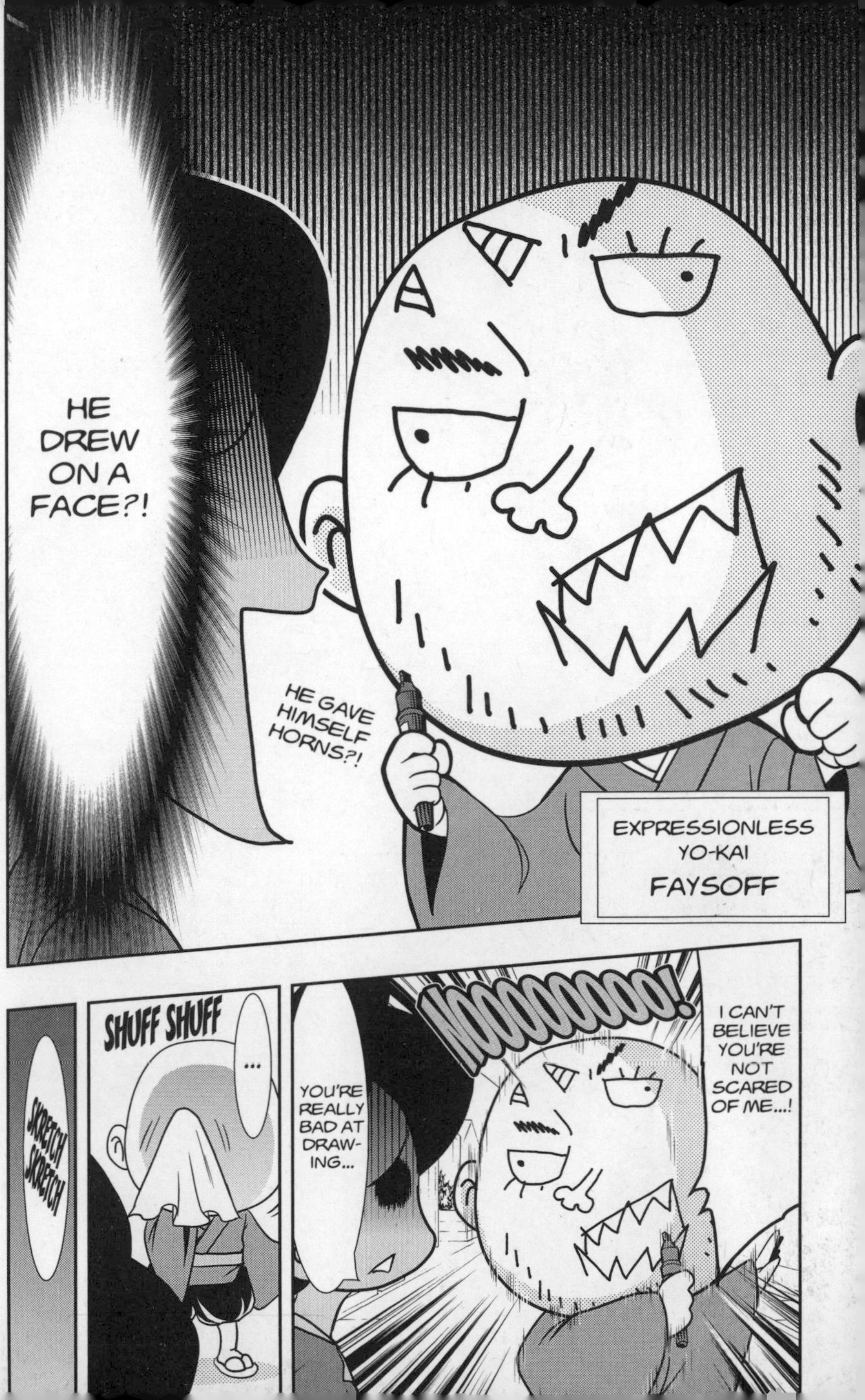

HE DREW ON A FACE?!
HE GAVE HIMSELF HORNS?!
EXPRESSIONLESS YO-KAI FAYSOFF
NOOOOOOOO!
I CAN'T BELIEVE YOU'RE NOT SCARED OF ME...!
YOU'RE REALLY BAD AT DRAW-ING...
SHUFF SHUFF
...
SKRETCH SKRETCH

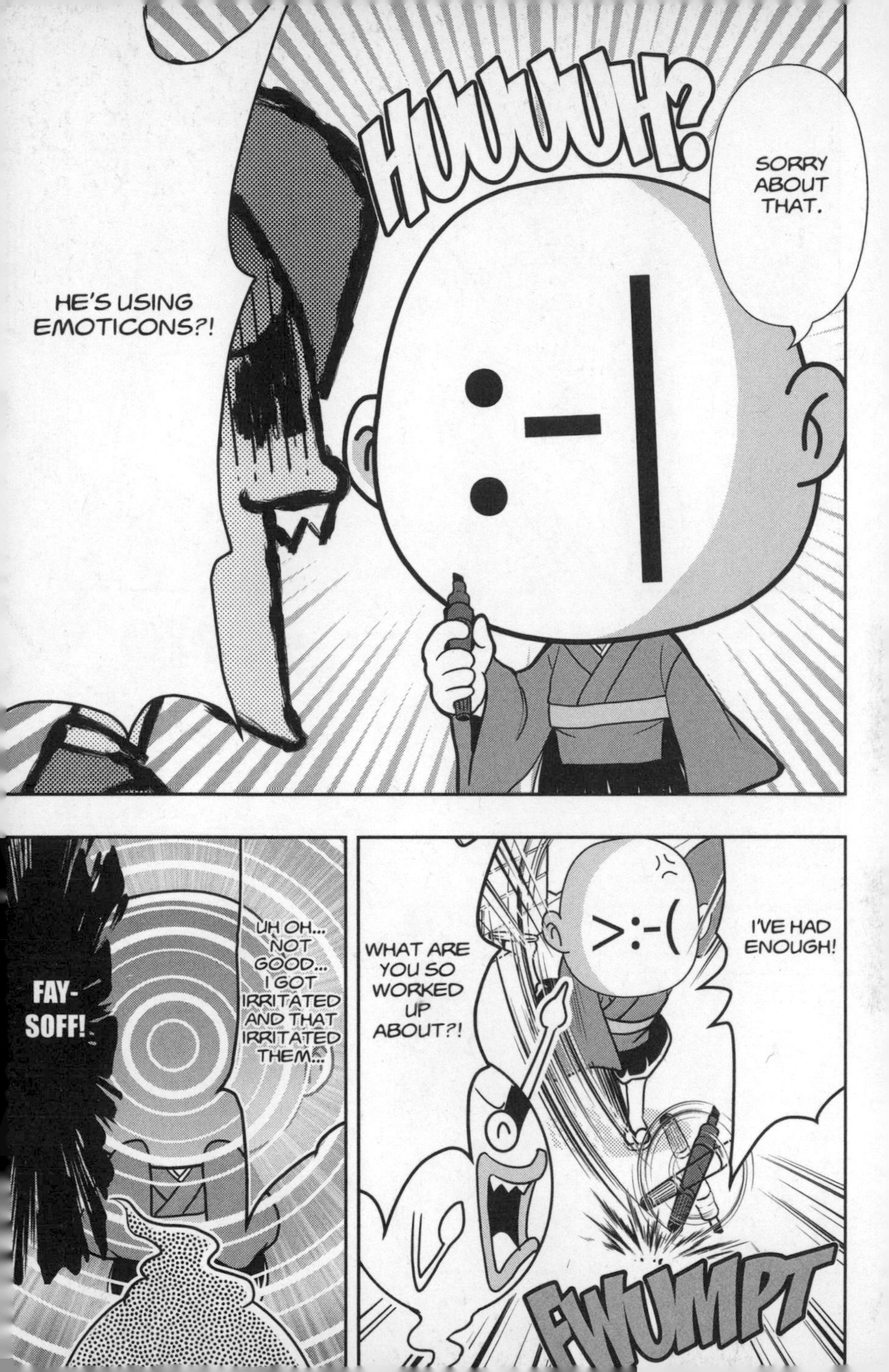
SORRY ABOUT THAT.
HUUUUUH?!
HE'S USING EMOTICONS?!
I'VE HAD ENOUGH!
WHAT ARE YOU SO WORKED UP ABOUT?!
FWUMPT
UH OH... NOT GOOD... I GOT IRRITATED AND THAT IRRITATED THEM...
FAY-SOFF!

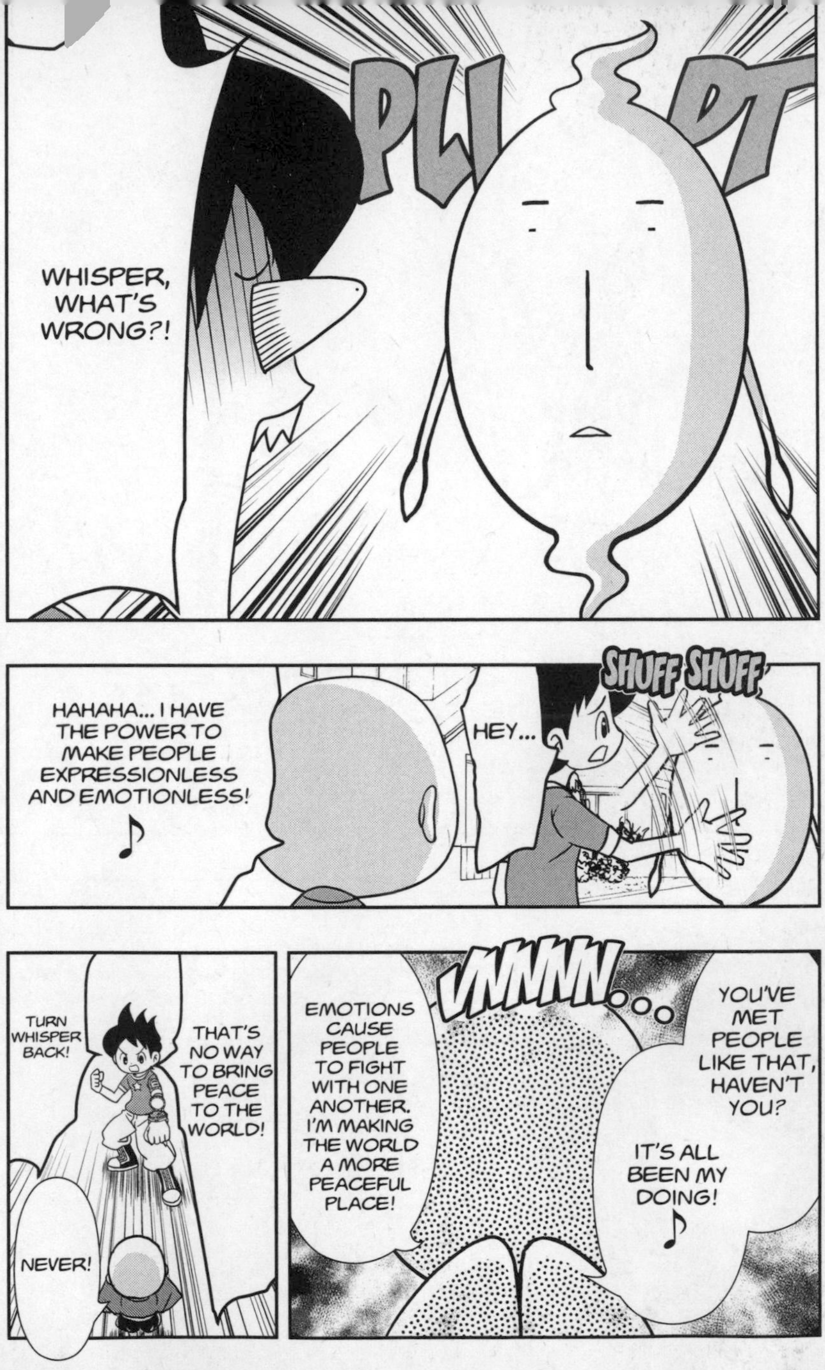
PLI
PT
WHISPER, WHAT'S WRONG?!
SHUFF SHUFF
HEY...
HAHAHA... I HAVE THE POWER TO MAKE PEOPLE EXPRESSIONLESS AND EMOTIONLESS! ♪
VNNNN...
YOU'VE MET PEOPLE LIKE THAT, HAVEN'T YOU?
IT'S ALL BEEN MY DOING! ♪
EMOTIONS CAUSE PEOPLE TO FIGHT WITH ONE ANOTHER. I'M MAKING THE WORLD A MORE PEACEFUL PLACE!
THAT'S NO WAY TO BRING PEACE TO THE WORLD!
TURN WHISPER BACK!
NEVER!

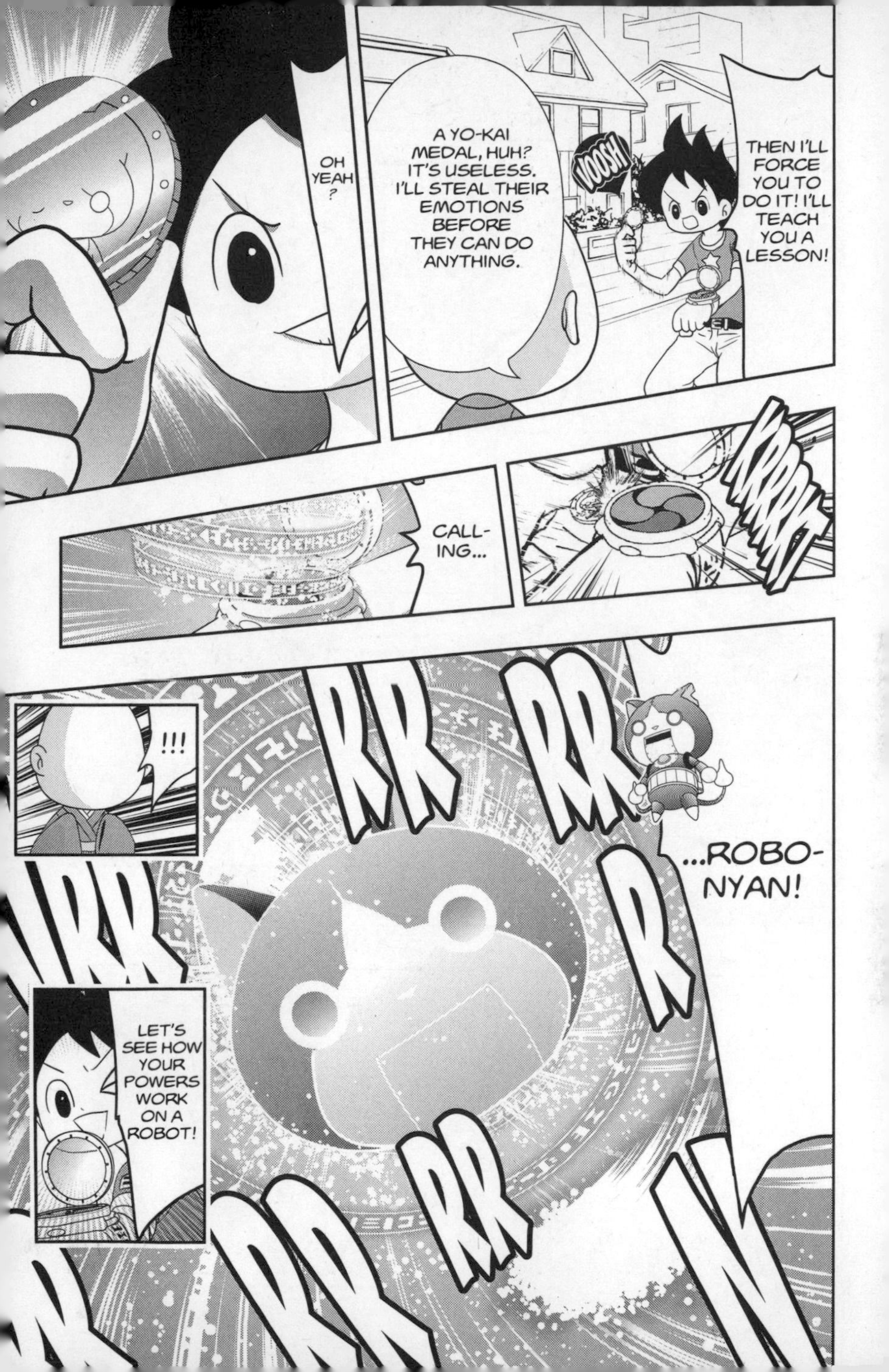
THEN I'LL FORCE YOU TO DO IT! I'LL TEACH YOU A LESSON!
VOOSH
A YO-KAI MEDAL, HUH? IT'S USELESS. I'LL STEAL THEIR EMOTIONS BEFORE THEY CAN DO ANYTHING.
OH YEAH?
KRRRK
CALLING...
...ROBO-NYAN!
!!!
LET'S SEE HOW YOUR POWERS WORK ON A ROBOT!

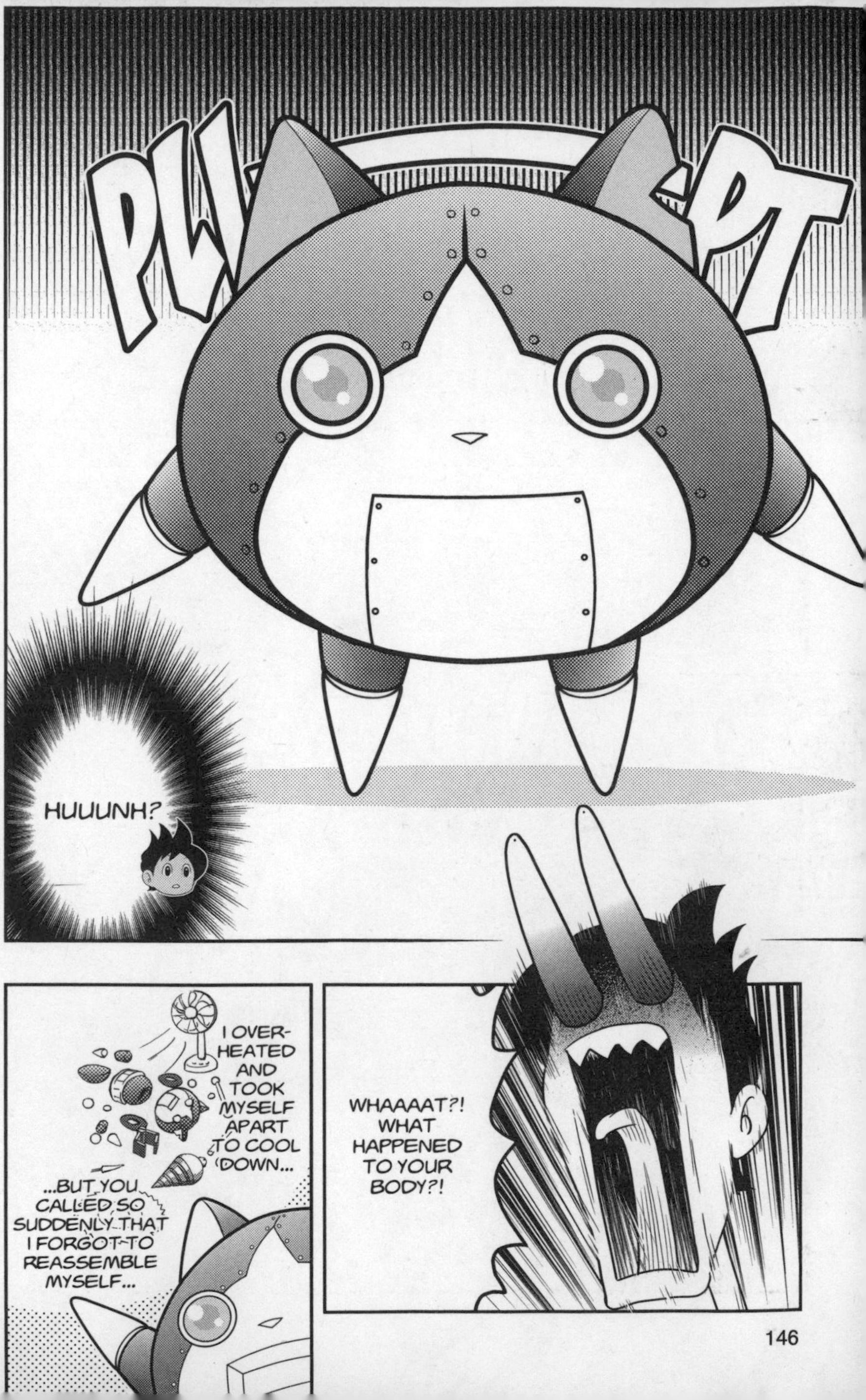
HUUUNH?
WHAAAAT?! WHAT HAPPENED TO YOUR BODY?!
I OVERHEATED AND TOOK MYSELF APART TO COOL DOWN...
...BUT YOU CALLED SO SUDDENLY THAT I FORGOT TO REASSEMBLE MYSELF...

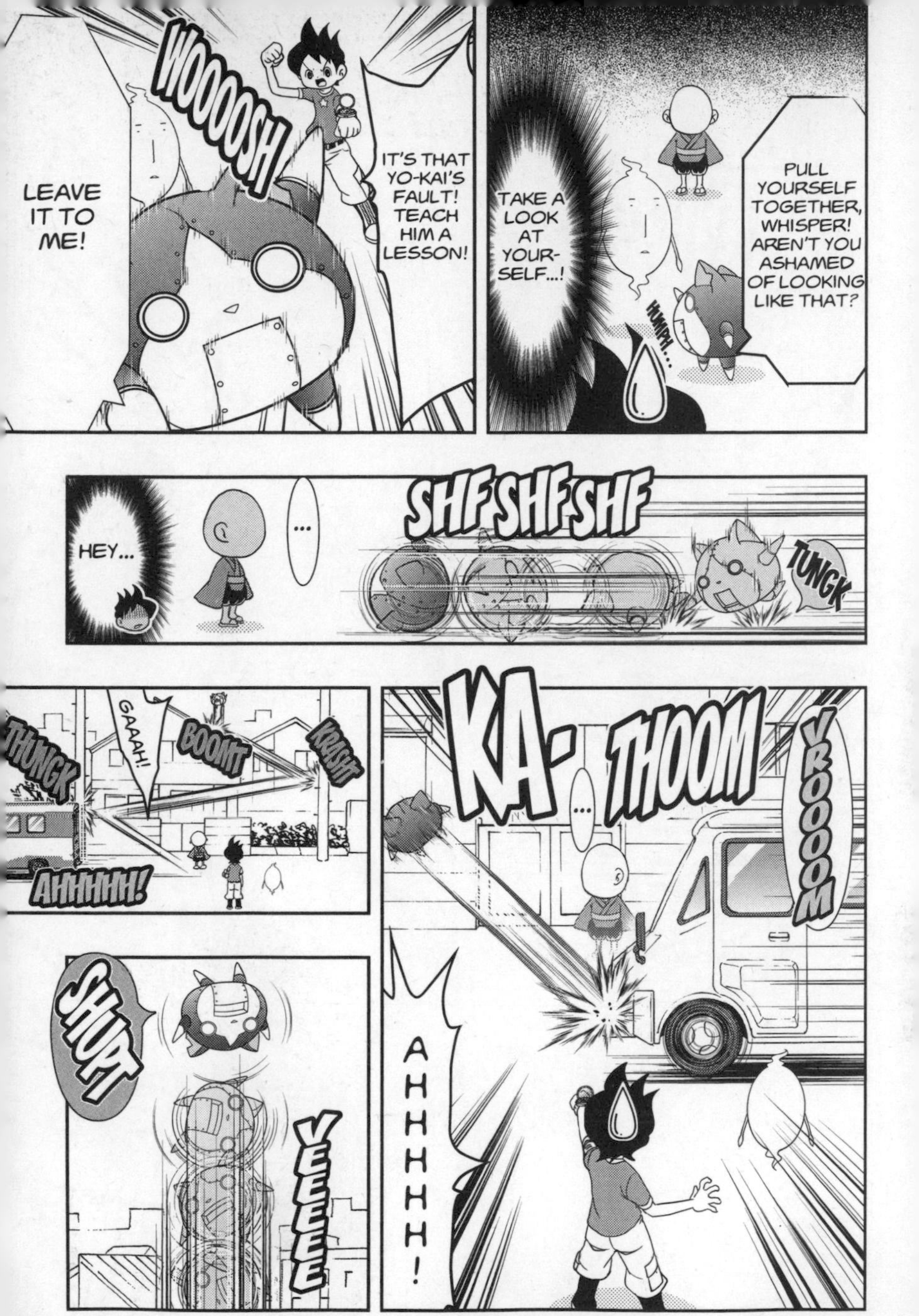
PULL YOURSELF TOGETHER, WHISPER! AREN'T YOU ASHAMED OF LOOKING LIKE THAT?
HUMPH...
TAKE A LOOK AT YOURSELF...!
IT'S THAT YO-KAI'S FAULT! TEACH HIM A LESSON!
WOOOOSH
LEAVE IT TO ME!
TUNGK
SHF SHF SHF
...
HEY...
VROOOOOM
KA-THOOM
...
AHHHHHH!
KRASH
BOOMT
GAAAH!
THUNGK
AHHHHHH!
VEEEEE
SHUPT!

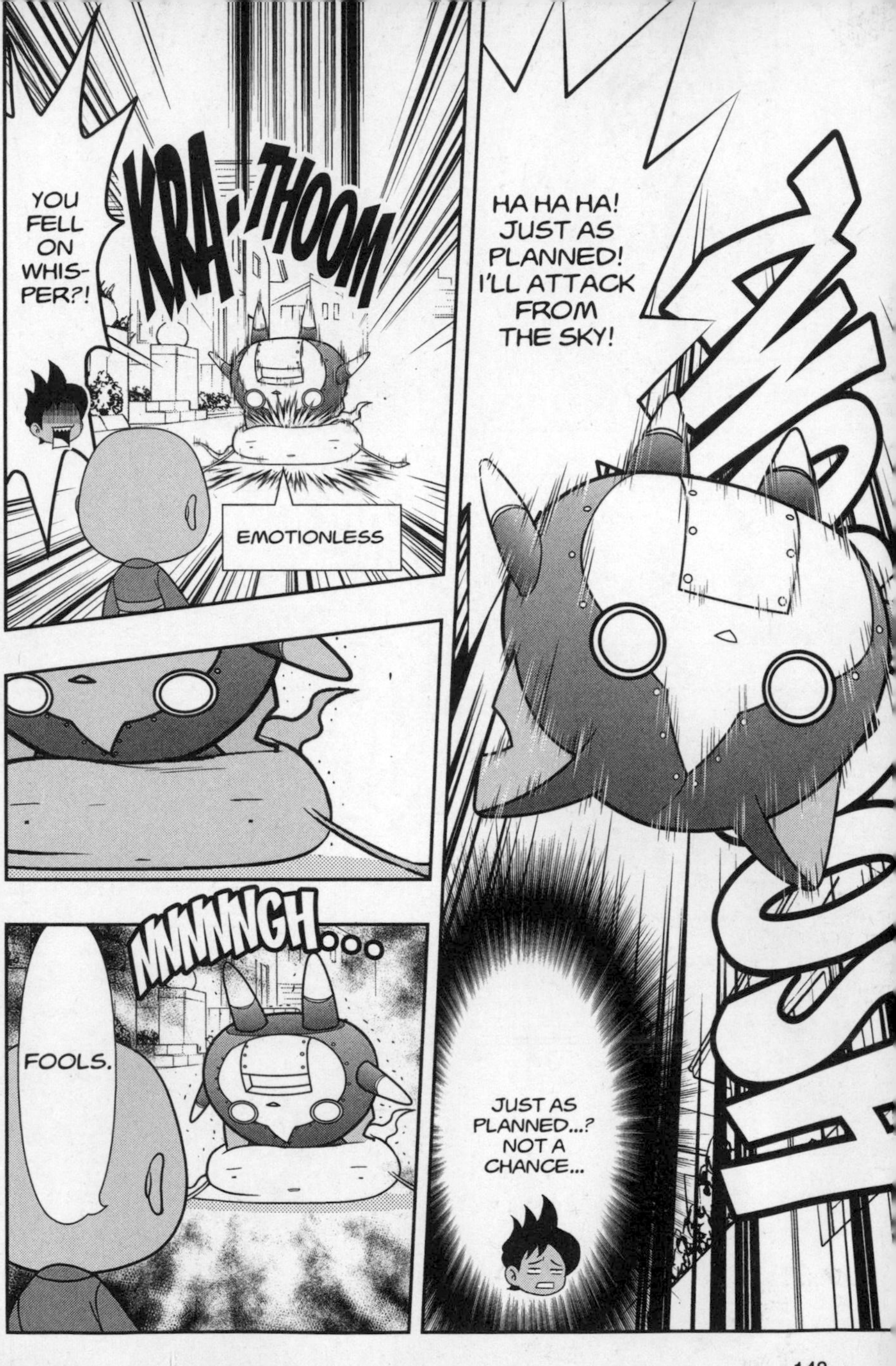
HA HA HA! JUST AS PLANNED! I'LL ATTACK FROM THE SKY!
ZWOOSH
JUST AS PLANNED...? NOT A CHANCE...
KRA-THOOM
YOU FELL ON WHISPER?!
EMOTIONLESS
NNNNNGH...
FOOLS.

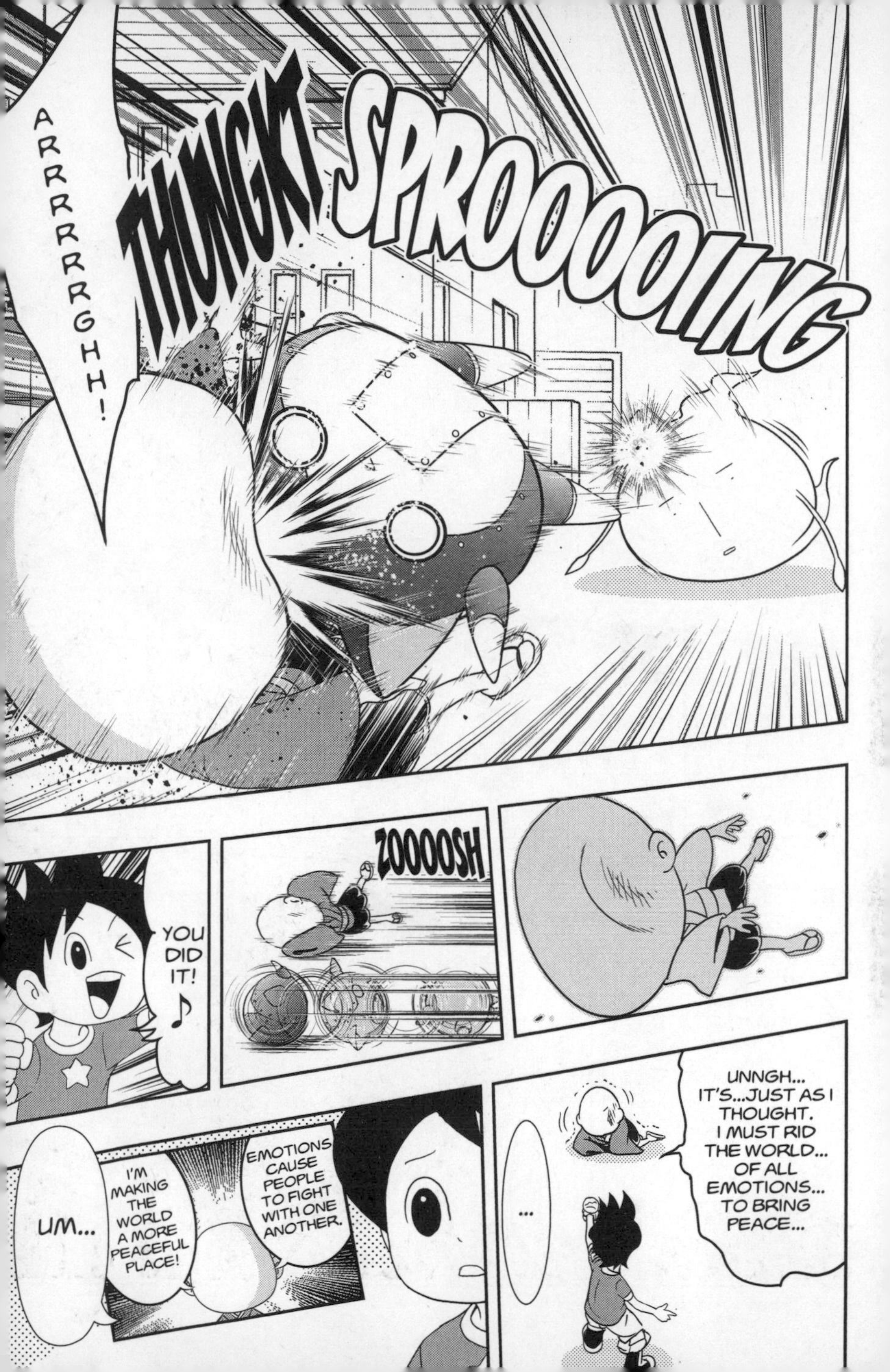
SPROOOOOING
THUNGK!
ARRRRRRGHH!
ZOOOOSH
YOU DID IT! ♪
UNNGH... IT'S...JUST AS I THOUGHT. I MUST RID THE WORLD... OF ALL EMOTIONS... TO BRING PEACE...
...
EMOTIONS CAUSE PEOPLE TO FIGHT WITH ONE ANOTHER.
I'M MAKING THE WORLD A MORE PEACEFUL PLACE!
UM...

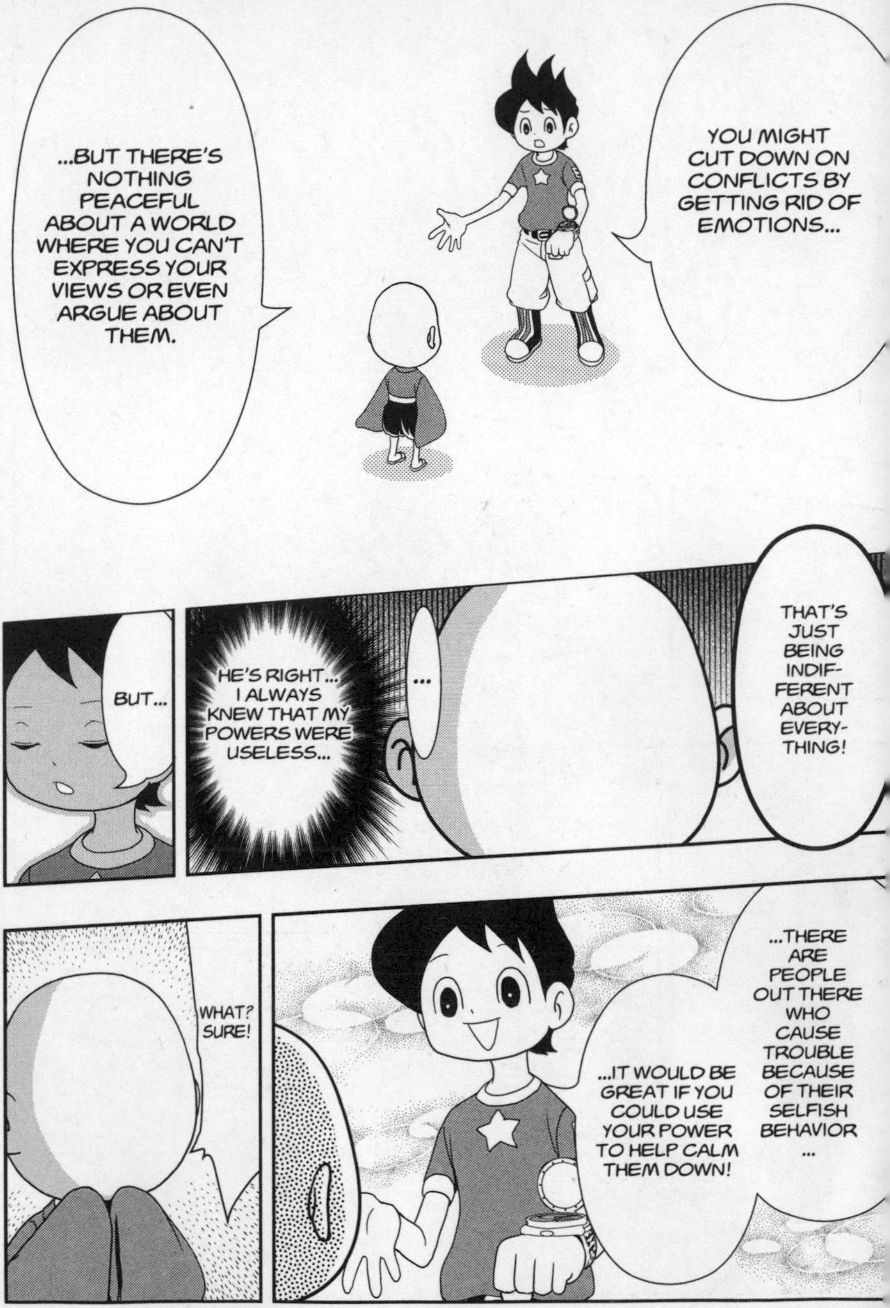
YOU MIGHT CUT DOWN ON CONFLICTS BY GETTING RID OF EMOTIONS...
...BUT THERE'S NOTHING PEACEFUL ABOUT A WORLD WHERE YOU CAN'T EXPRESS YOUR VIEWS OR EVEN ARGUE ABOUT THEM.
THAT'S JUST BEING INDIF-FERENT ABOUT EVERY-THING!
...
HE'S RIGHT... I ALWAYS KNEW THAT MY POWERS WERE USELESS...
BUT...
...THERE ARE PEOPLE OUT THERE WHO CAUSE TROUBLE BECAUSE OF THEIR SELFISH BEHAVIOR ...
...IT WOULD BE GREAT IF YOU COULD USE YOUR POWER TO HELP CALM THEM DOWN!
WHAT? SURE!

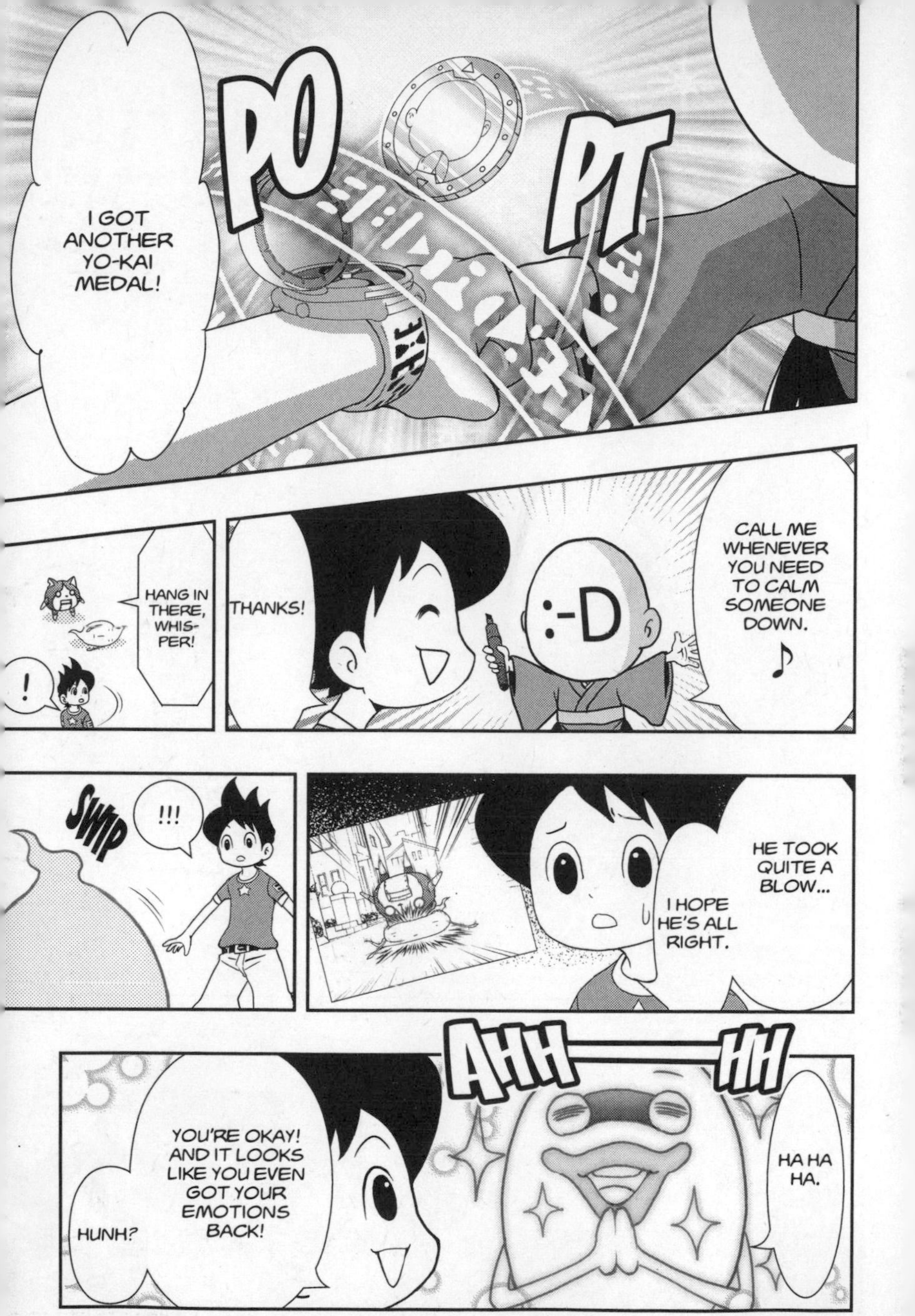
PO
PT
I GOT ANOTHER YO-KAI MEDAL!
CALL ME WHENEVER YOU NEED TO CALM SOMEONE DOWN. ♪
:-D
THANKS!
HANG IN THERE, WHISPER!
!
HE TOOK QUITE A BLOW...
I HOPE HE'S ALL RIGHT.
!!!
SWIP
AHH——HH
HA HA HA.
YOU'RE OKAY! AND IT LOOKS LIKE YOU EVEN GOT YOUR EMOTIONS BACK!
HUNH?

CHAPTER 42: YOU CALL THAT AN APOLOGY?!

FEATURING MAKESHIFT YO-KAI SO-SORREE

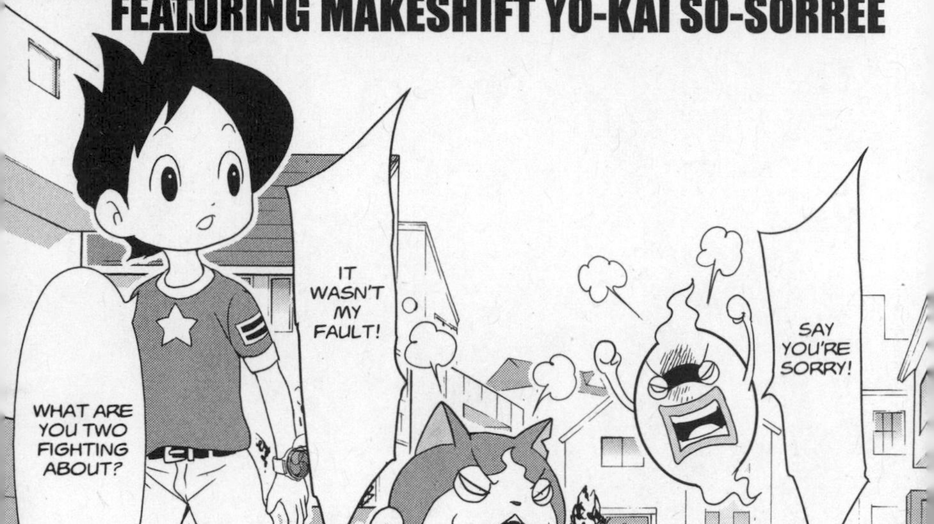
SAY YOU'RE SORRY!
IT WASN'T MY FAULT!
WHAT ARE YOU TWO FIGHTING ABOUT?

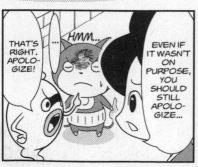

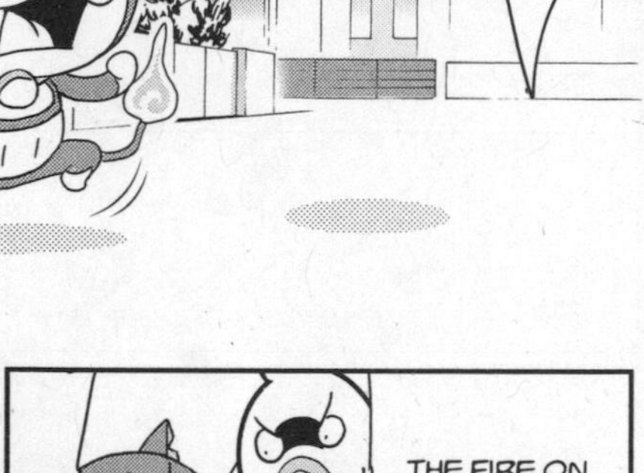
THE FIRE ON JIBANYAN'S TAIL HIT ME, AND IT WAS REALLY HOT!
BUT I DIDN'T DO IT ON PUR-POSE!

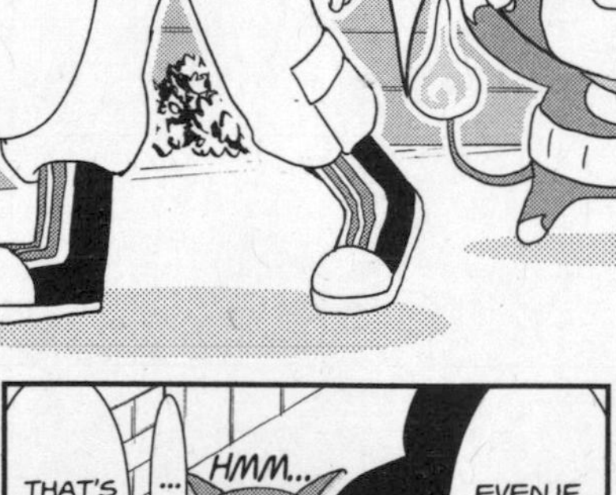
EVEN IF IT WASN'T ON PURPOSE, YOU SHOULD STILL APOLO-GIZE...
HMM...
...
THAT'S RIGHT. APOLO-GIZE!

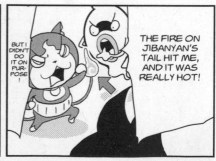

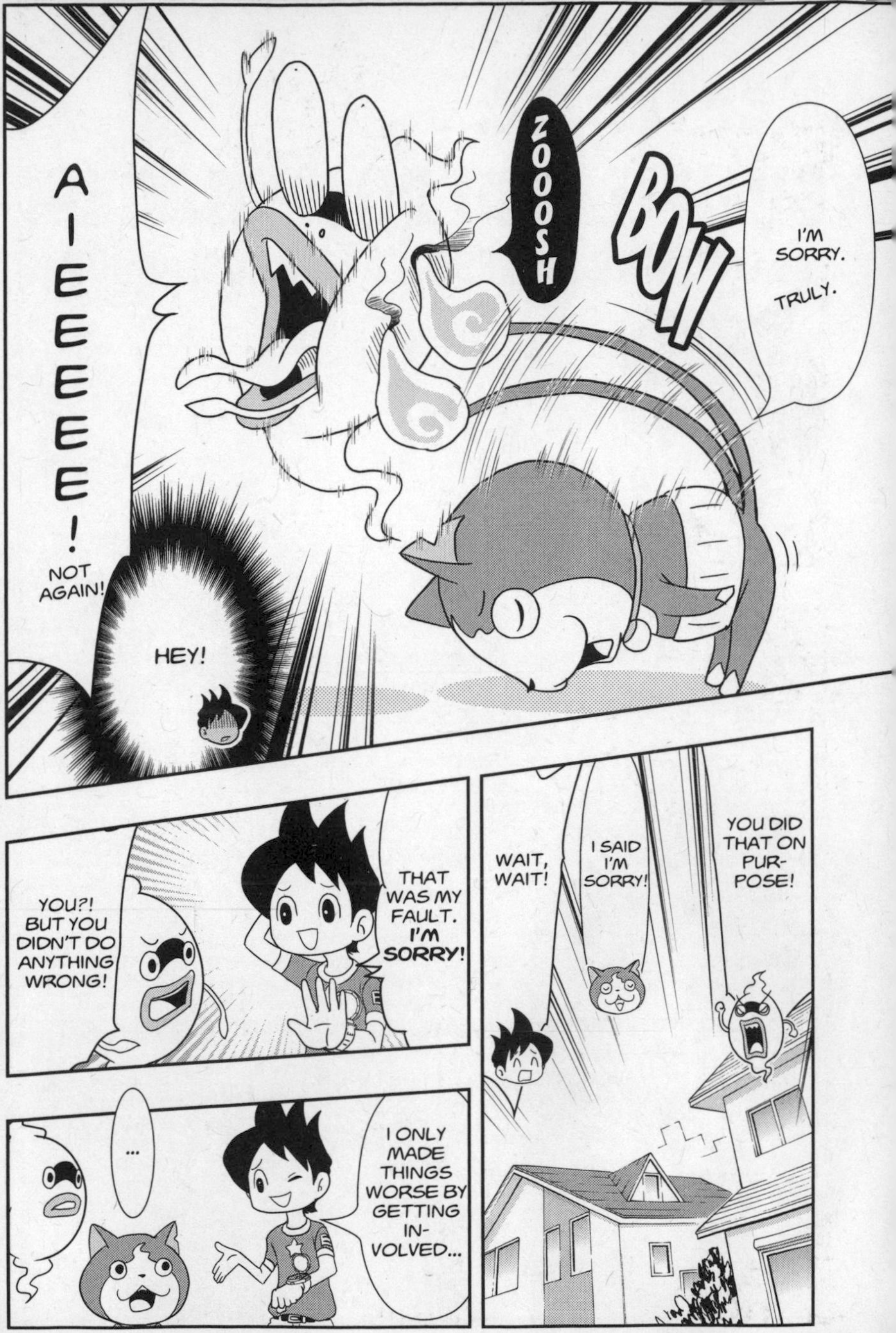
I'M SORRY.
TRULY.
BOW
ZOOOSH
AIEEEEEE!
NOT AGAIN!
HEY!
YOU DID THAT ON PUR-POSE!
I SAID I'M SORRY!
WAIT, WAIT!
THAT WAS MY FAULT. I'M SORRY!
YOU?! BUT YOU DIDN'T DO ANYTHING WRONG!
I ONLY MADE THINGS WORSE BY GETTING IN-VOLVED...
...

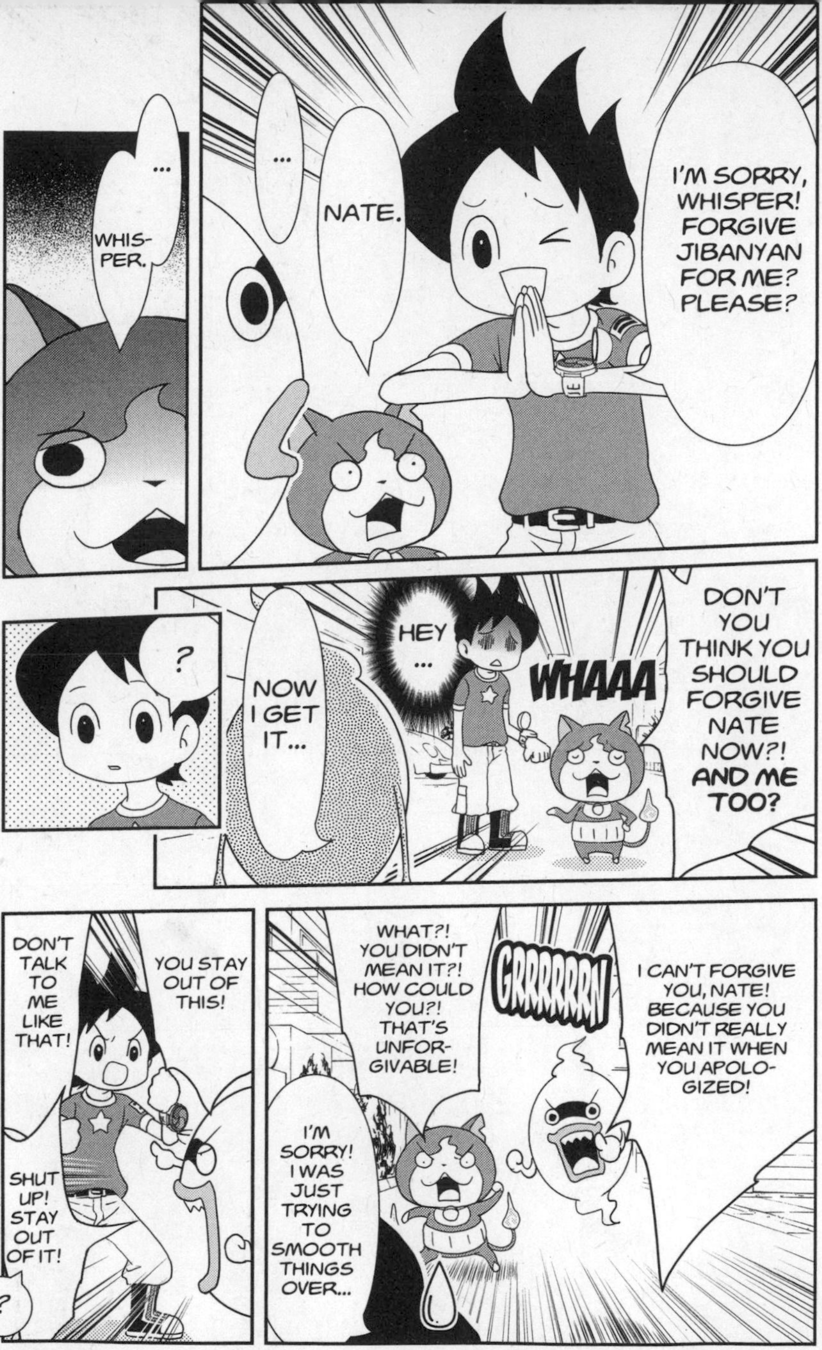
I'M SORRY, WHISPER! FORGIVE JIBANYAN FOR ME? PLEASE?
NATE.
...
...
WHIS-PER.
DON'T YOU THINK YOU SHOULD FORGIVE NATE NOW?! AND ME TOO?
WHAAA
HEY ...
NOW I GET IT...
?
I CAN'T FORGIVE YOU, NATE! BECAUSE YOU DIDN'T REALLY MEAN IT WHEN YOU APOLO-GIZED!
GRRRRRRN
WHAT?! YOU DIDN'T MEAN IT?! HOW COULD YOU?! THAT'S UNFORGIVABLE!
I'M SORRY! I WAS JUST TRYING TO SMOOTH THINGS OVER...
YOU STAY OUT OF THIS!
DON'T TALK TO ME LIKE THAT!
SHUT UP! STAY OUT OF IT!
?

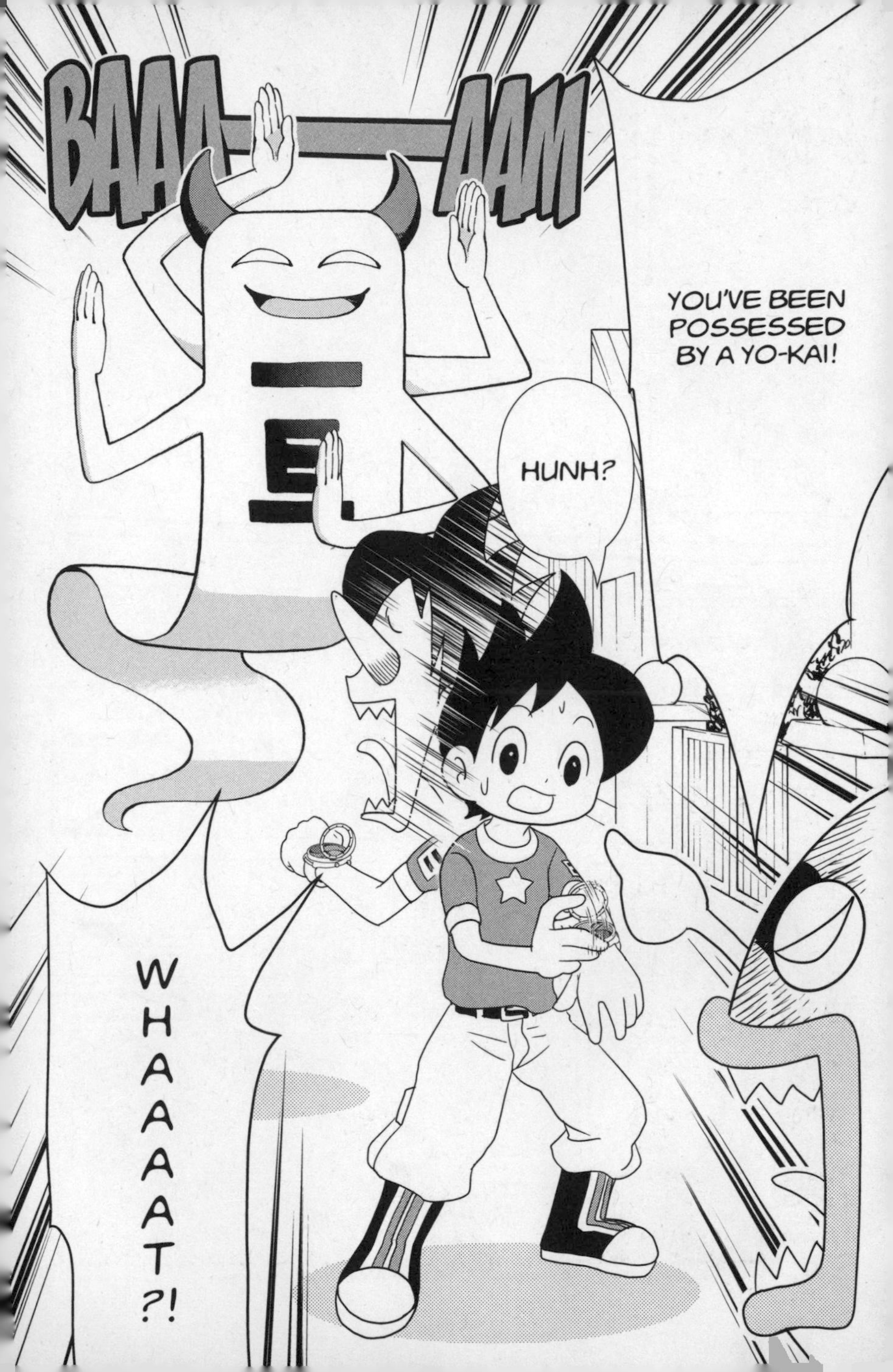
BAAA—AAM
YOU'VE BEEN POSSESSED BY A YO-KAI!
HUNH?
WHAAAAT?!

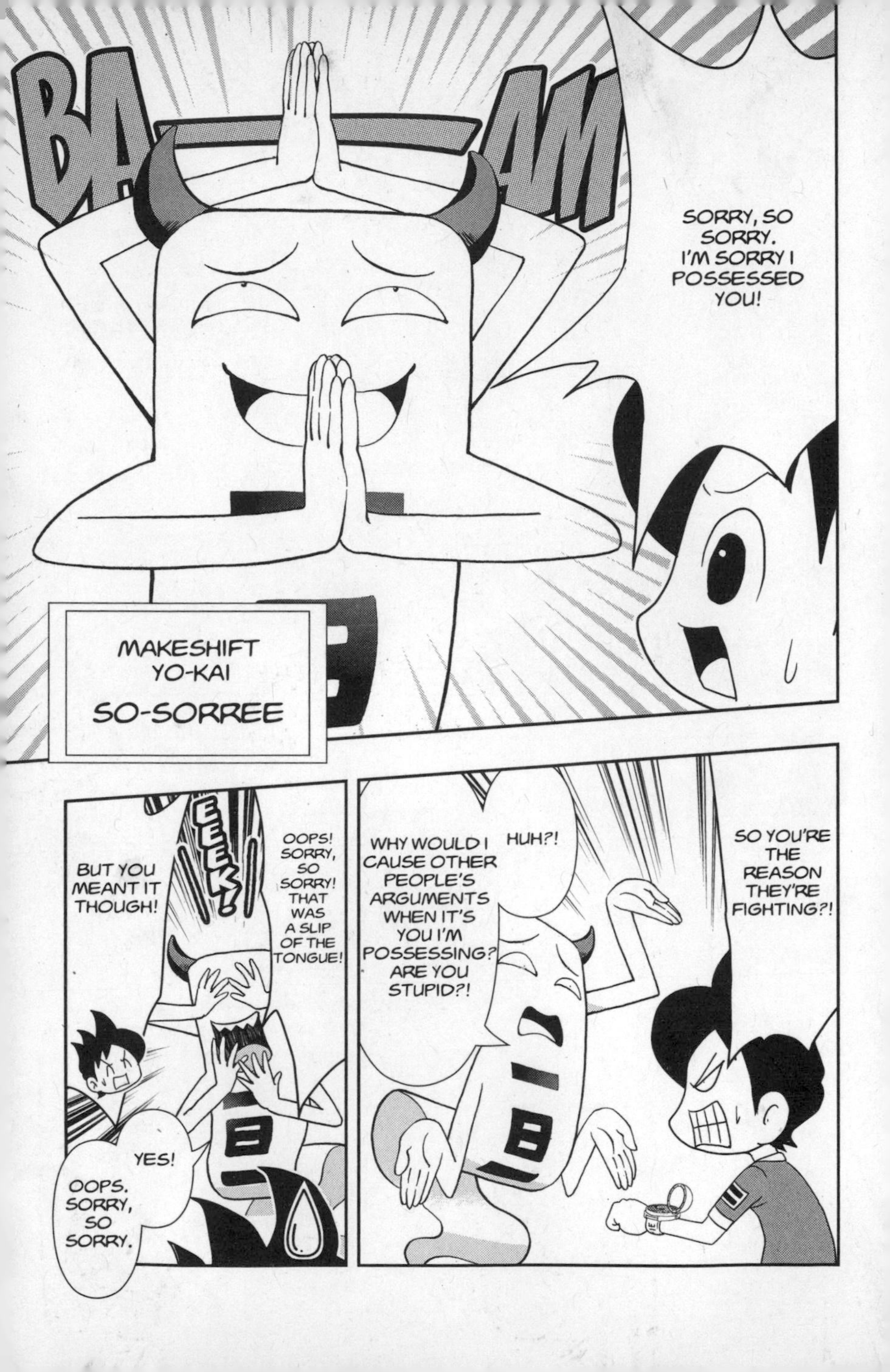
BA AM
SORRY, SO SORRY. I'M SORRY I POSSESSED YOU!
MAKESHIFT YO-KAI
SO-SORREE
SO YOU'RE THE REASON THEY'RE FIGHTING?!
HUH?!
WHY WOULD I CAUSE OTHER PEOPLE'S ARGUMENTS WHEN IT'S YOU I'M POSSESSING? ARE YOU STUPID?!
OOPS! SORRY, SO SORRY! THAT WAS A SLIP OF THE TONGUE!
EEEK!
BUT YOU MEANT IT THOUGH!
YES!
OOPS. SORRY, SO SORRY.

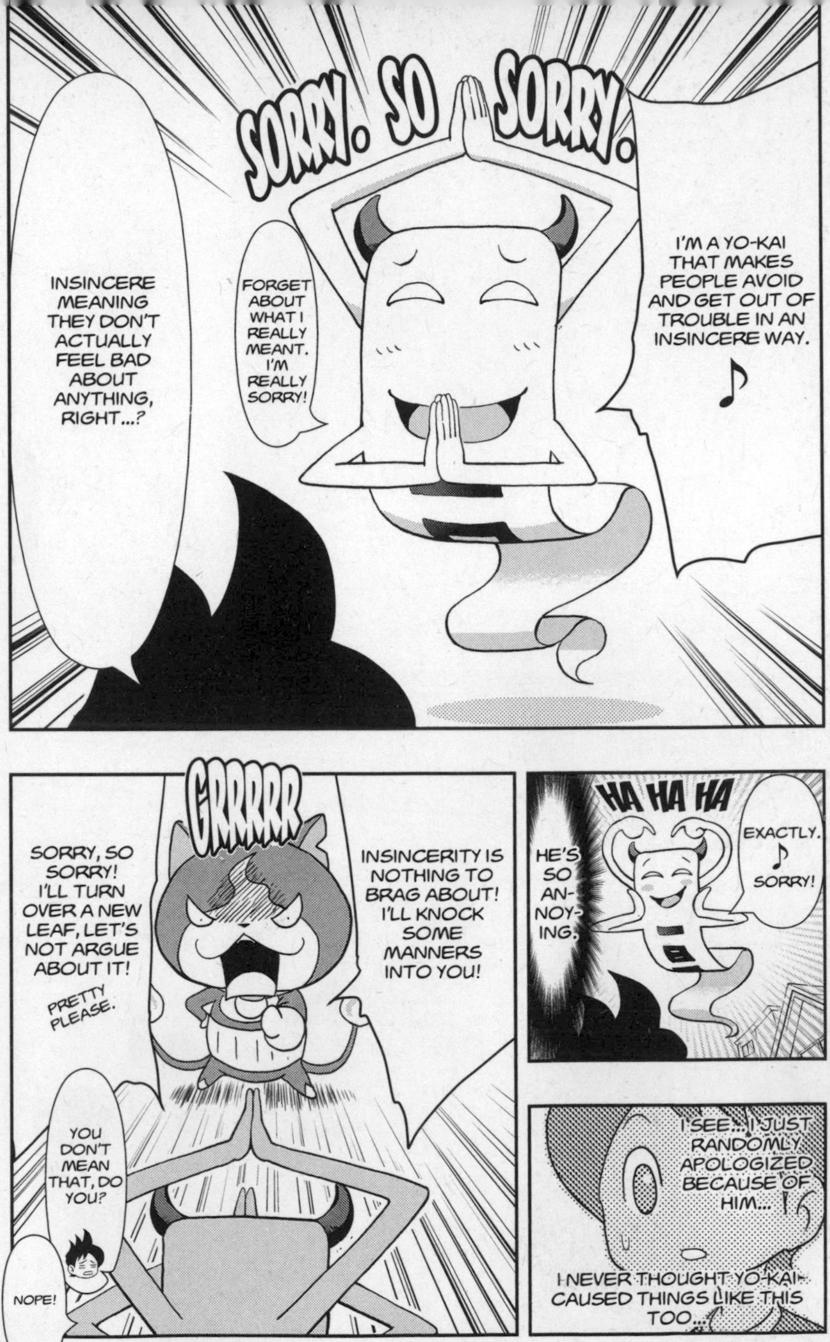
SORRY. SO SORRY.
I'M A YO-KAI THAT MAKES PEOPLE AVOID AND GET OUT OF TROUBLE IN AN INSINCERE WAY. ♪
FORGET ABOUT WHAT I REALLY MEANT. I'M REALLY SORRY!
INSINCERE MEANING THEY DON'T ACTUALLY FEEL BAD ABOUT ANYTHING, RIGHT...?
EXACTLY. ♪ SORRY!
HA HA HA
HE'S SO AN-NOY-ING.
I SEE... I JUST RANDOMLY APOLOGIZED BECAUSE OF HIM...
I NEVER THOUGHT YO-KAI CAUSED THINGS LIKE THIS TOO...
GRRRRR
INSINCERITY IS NOTHING TO BRAG ABOUT! I'LL KNOCK SOME MANNERS INTO YOU!
SORRY, SO SORRY! I'LL TURN OVER A NEW LEAF, LET'S NOT ARGUE ABOUT IT!
PRETTY PLEASE.
YOU DON'T MEAN THAT, DO YOU?
NOPE!

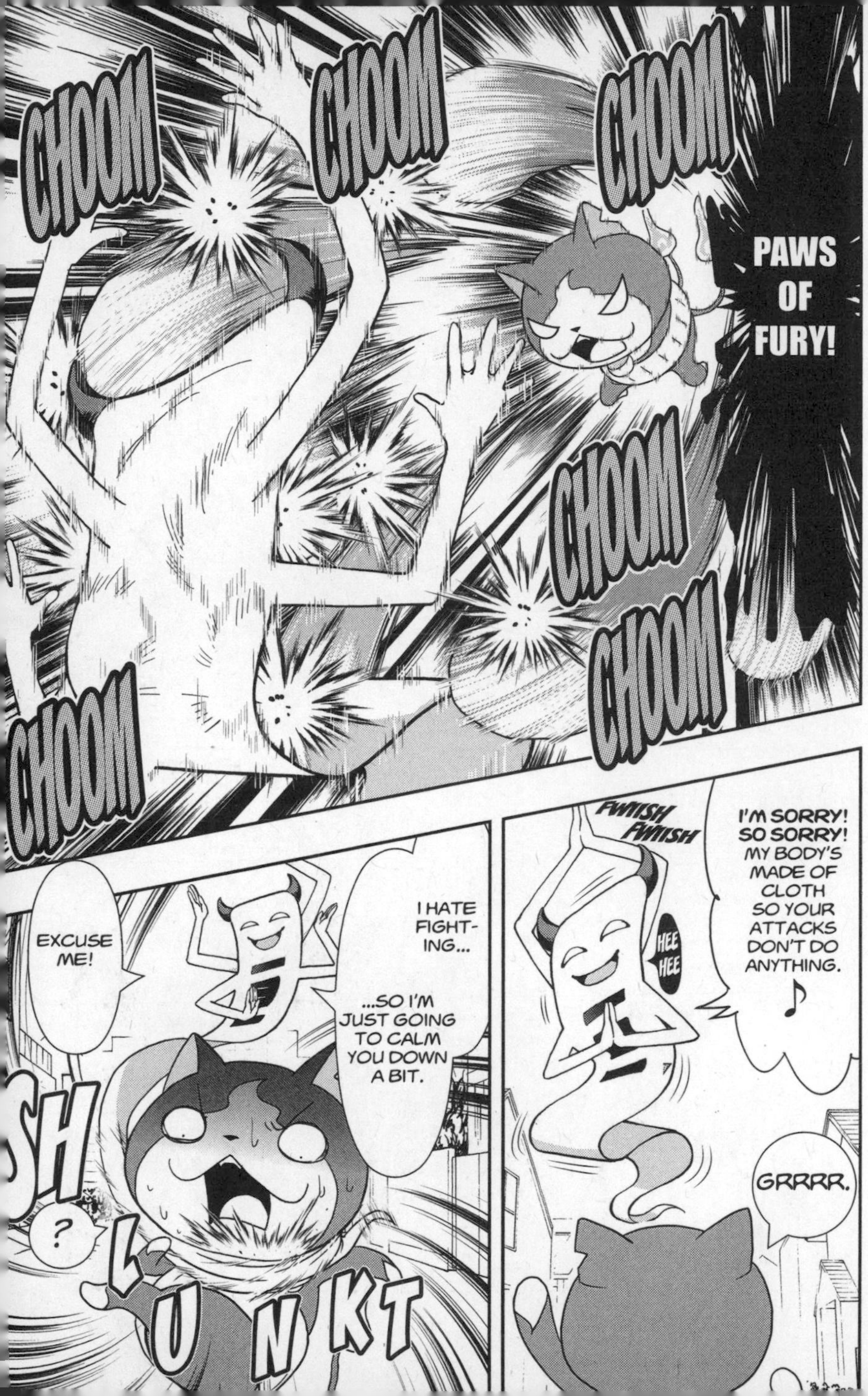
PAWS OF FURY!
CHOOM
CHOOM
CHOOM
CHOOM
CHOOM
CHOOM
FWISH FWISH
I'M SORRY! SO SORRY! MY BODY'S MADE OF CLOTH SO YOUR ATTACKS DON'T DO ANYTHING. ♪
HEE HEE
GRRRR.
I HATE FIGHT-ING...
...SO I'M JUST GOING TO CALM YOU DOWN A BIT.
EXCUSE ME!
SHLUNKT
?

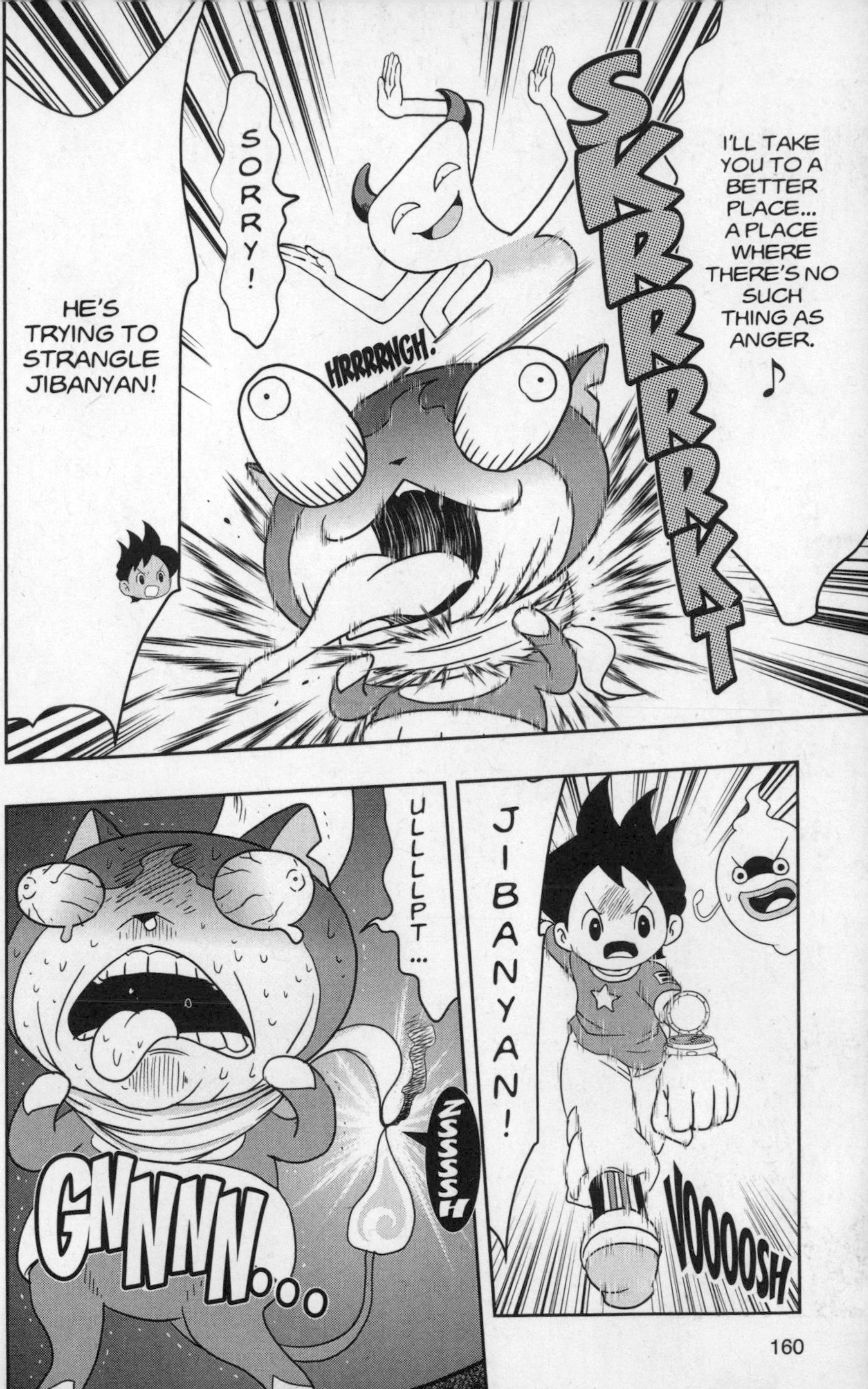
I'LL TAKE YOU TO A BETTER PLACE... A PLACE WHERE THERE'S NO SUCH THING AS ANGER. ♪
SKRRRRKT
HRRRRNGH.
SORRY!
HE'S TRYING TO STRANGLE JIBANYAN!
JIBANYAN!
VOOOOSH
ULLLLPT...
NSSSSH
GNNNNN...

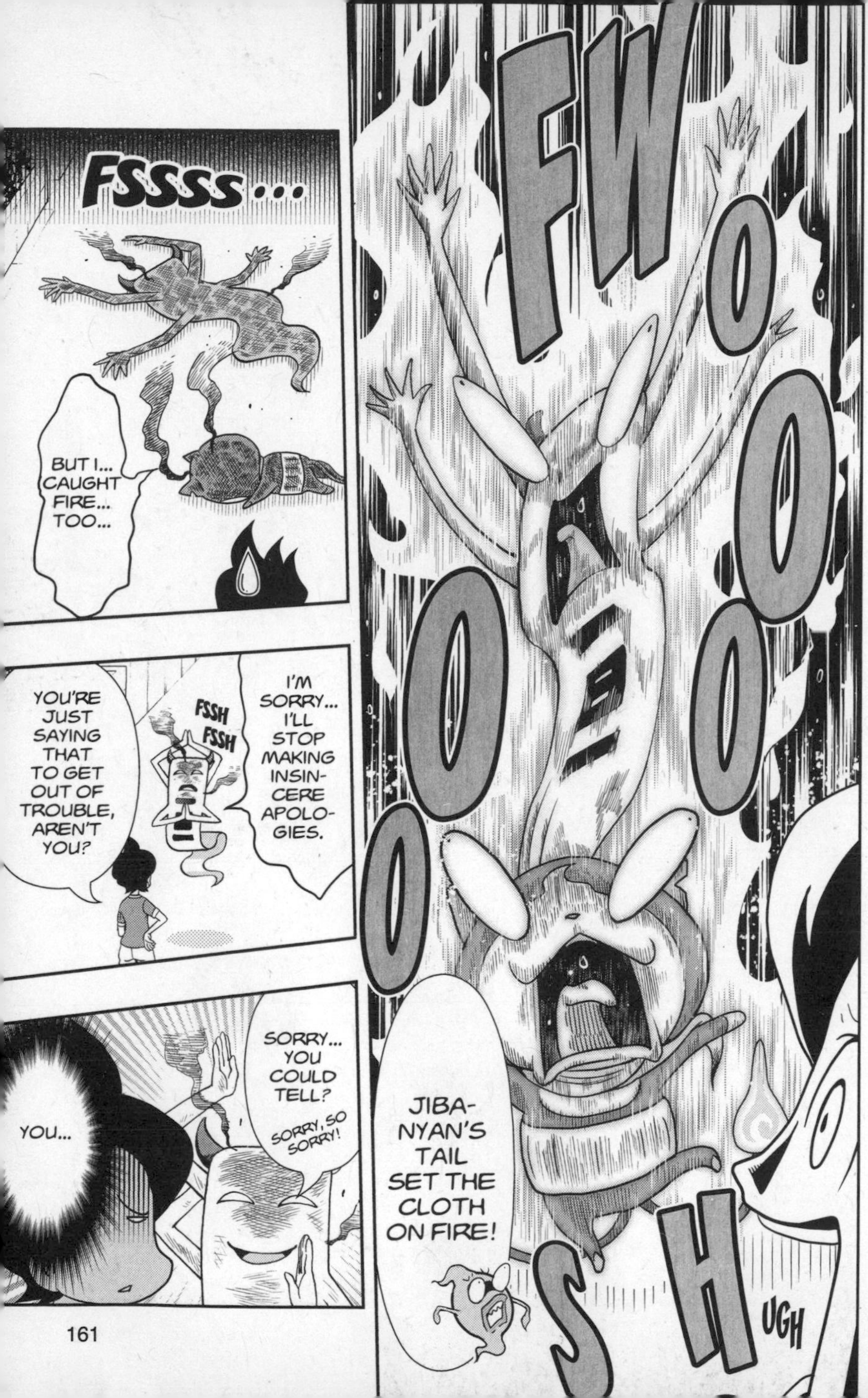
FWOOOOOOO
UGH
SH
JIBA-NYAN'S TAIL SET THE CLOTH ON FIRE!
FSSSS...
BUT I... CAUGHT FIRE... TOO...
I'M SORRY... I'LL STOP MAKING INSINCERE APOLOGIES.
FSSH FSSH
YOU'RE JUST SAYING THAT TO GET OUT OF TROUBLE, AREN'T YOU?
SORRY... YOU COULD TELL?
SORRY, SO SORRY!
YOU...

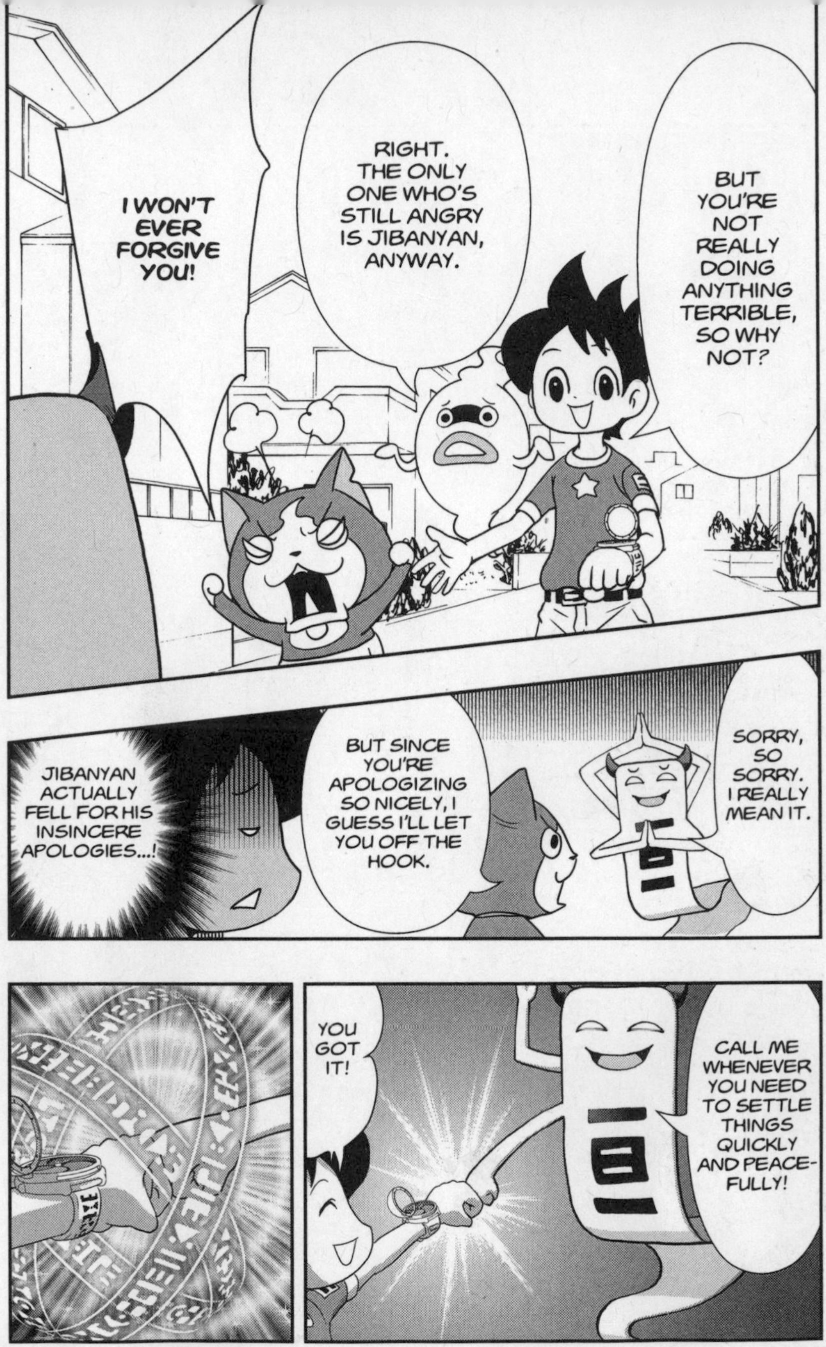
BUT YOU'RE NOT REALLY DOING ANYTHING TERRIBLE, SO WHY NOT?
RIGHT. THE ONLY ONE WHO'S STILL ANGRY IS JIBANYAN, ANYWAY.
I WON'T EVER FORGIVE YOU!
SORRY, SO SORRY. I REALLY MEAN IT.
BUT SINCE YOU'RE APOLOGIZING SO NICELY, I GUESS I'LL LET YOU OFF THE HOOK.
JIBANYAN ACTUALLY FELL FOR HIS INSINCERE APOLOGIES...!
CALL ME WHENEVER YOU NEED TO SETTLE THINGS QUICKLY AND PEACE-FULLY!
YOU GOT IT!

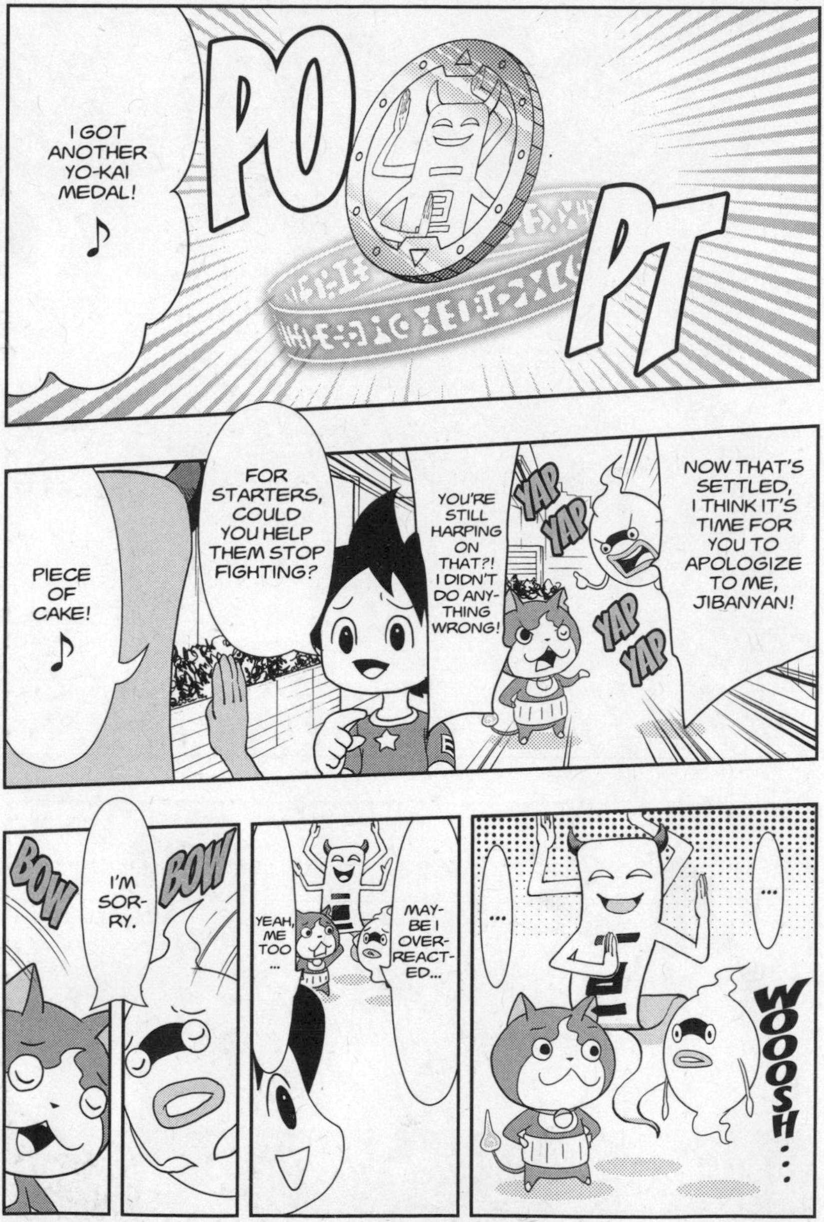
PO
PT
I GOT ANOTHER YO-KAI MEDAL! ♪
NOW THAT'S SETTLED, I THINK IT'S TIME FOR YOU TO APOLOGIZE TO ME, JIBANYAN!
YAP YAP
YAP YAP
YOU'RE STILL HARPING ON THAT?! I DIDN'T DO ANYTHING WRONG!
FOR STARTERS, COULD YOU HELP THEM STOP FIGHTING?
PIECE OF CAKE! ♪
...
...
WOOOSH...
MAY-BE I OVER-REACT-ED...
YEAH, ME TOO ...
BOW
I'M SOR-RY.
BOW

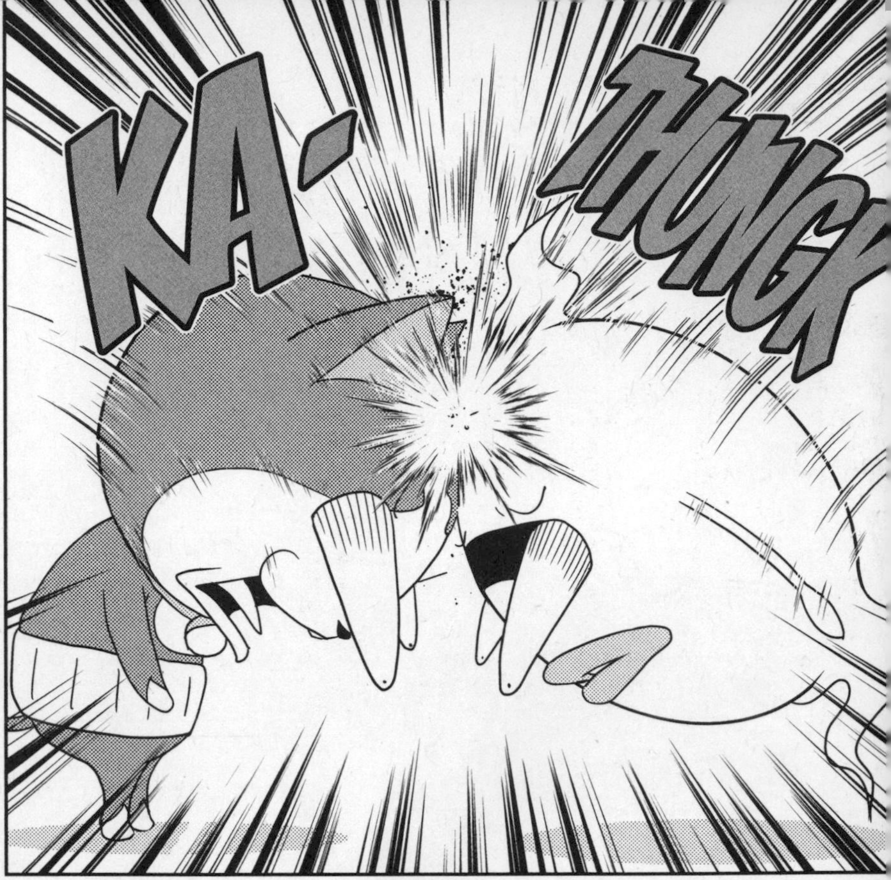
KA-
THUNCK

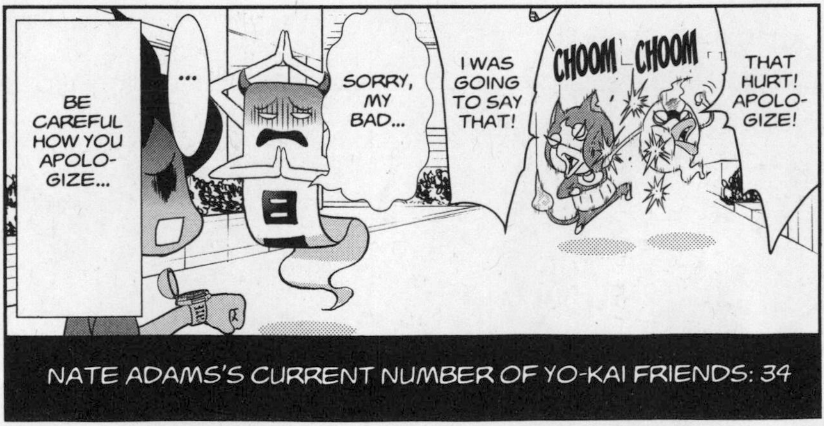
THAT HURT! APOLOGIZE!
CHOOM CHOOM
I WAS GOING TO SAY THAT!
SORRY, MY BAD...
...
BE CAREFUL HOW YOU APOLOGIZE...

NATE ADAMS'S CURRENT NUMBER OF YO-KAI FRIENDS: 34

CHAPTER 43: ALWAYS LOOK ON THE BRIGHT SIDE!!

FEATURING LIGHTHEARTED YO-KAI HAPPYCANE

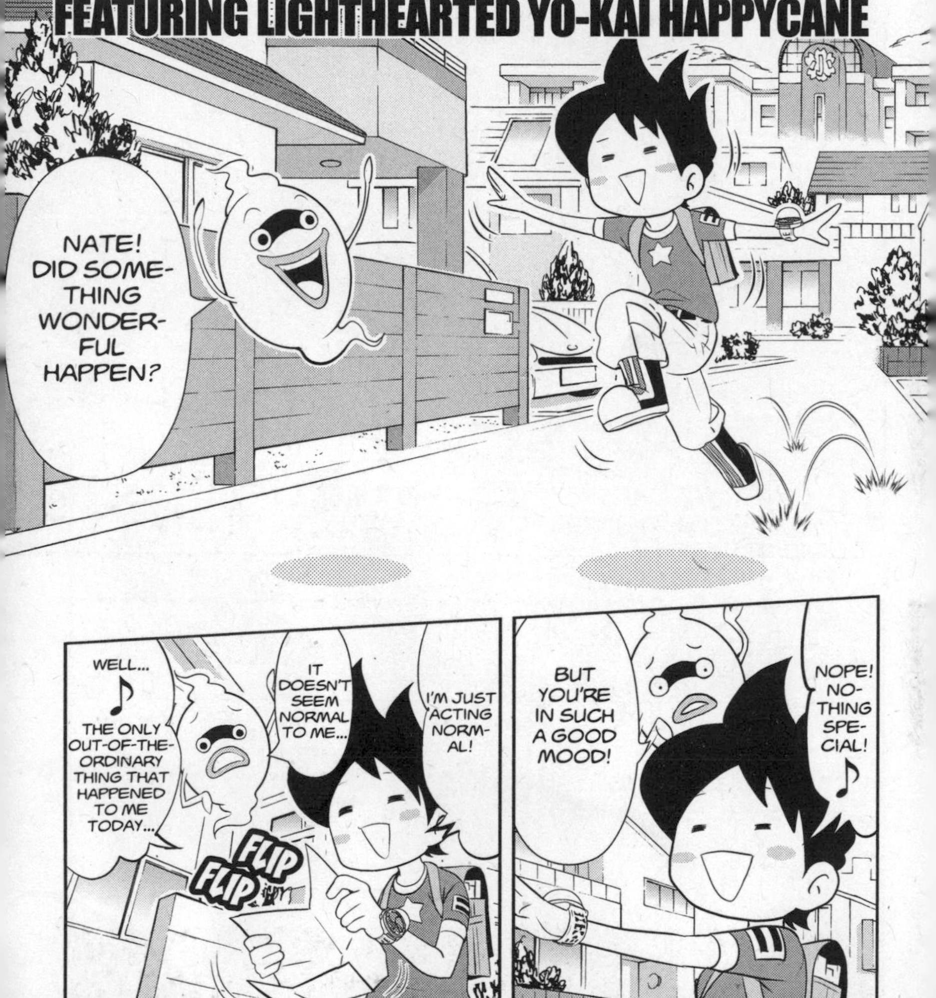
NATE! DID SOME-THING WONDER-FUL HAPPEN?
NOPE! NO-THING SPE-CIAL! ♪
BUT YOU'RE IN SUCH A GOOD MOOD!
I'M JUST ACTING NORM-AL!
IT DOESN'T SEEM NORMAL TO ME...
WELL... ♪ THE ONLY OUT-OF-THE-ORDINARY THING THAT HAPPENED TO ME TODAY...
FLIP FLIP

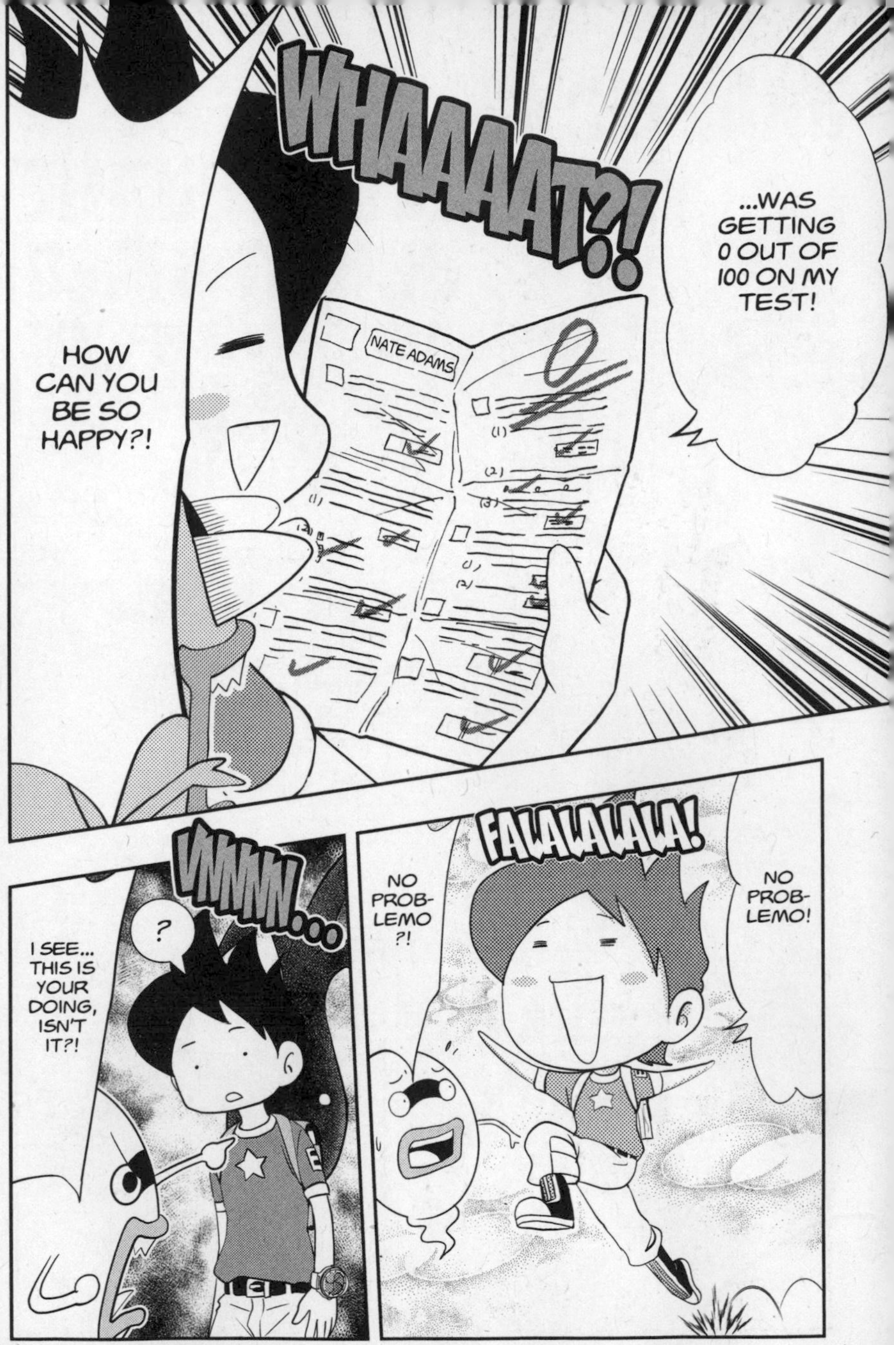
...WAS GETTING 0 OUT OF 100 ON MY TEST!
WHAAAAAT?!
NATE ADAMS
HOW CAN YOU BE SO HAPPY?!
FALALALALA!
NO PROB-LEMO!
NO PROB-LEMO ?!
VNNNN...
?
I SEE... THIS IS YOUR DOING, ISN'T IT?!

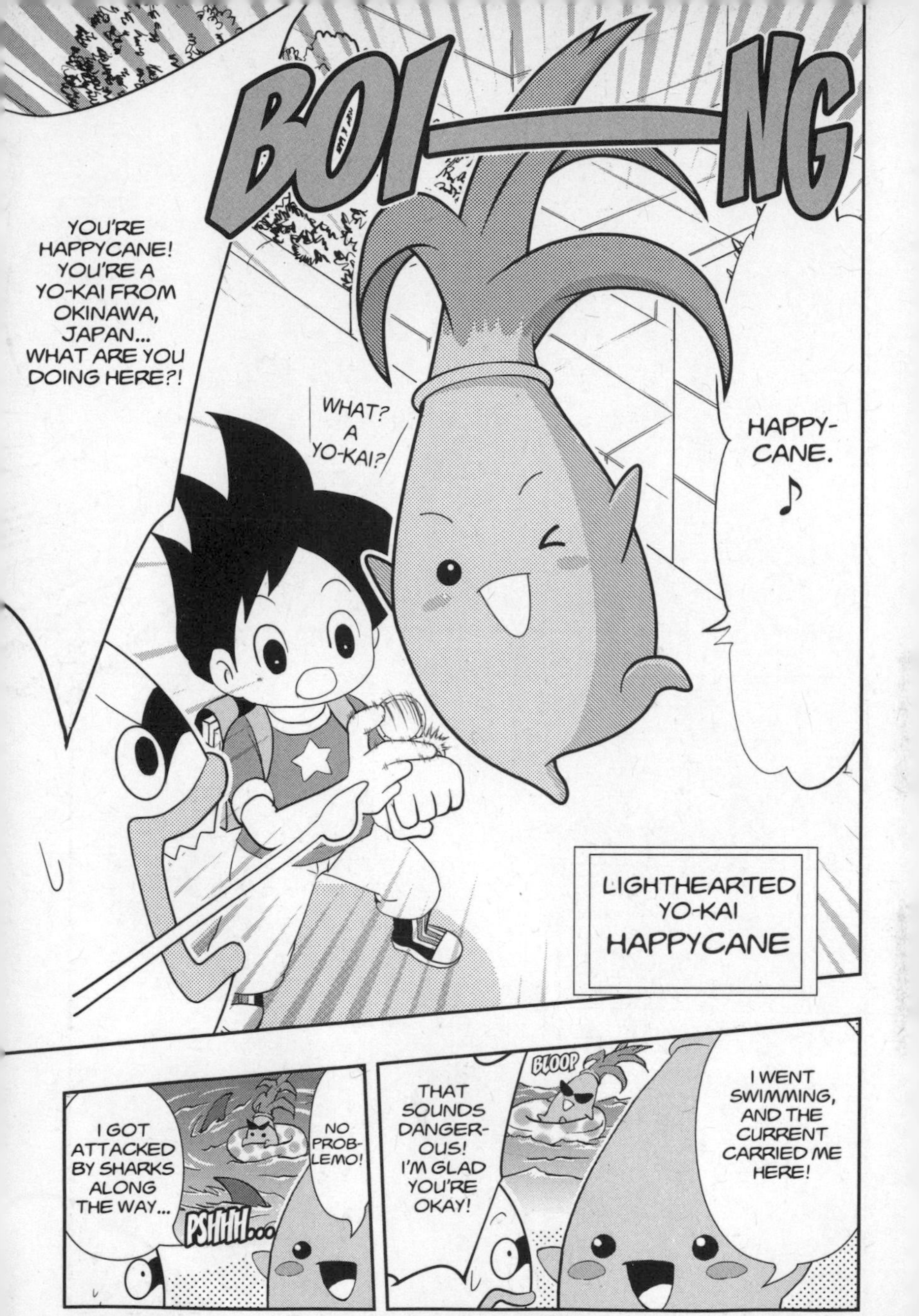
BOI—NG
HAPPY-CANE. ♪
WHAT? A YO-KAI?
YOU'RE HAPPYCANE! YOU'RE A YO-KAI FROM OKINAWA, JAPAN... WHAT ARE YOU DOING HERE?!
LIGHTHEARTED YO-KAI HAPPYCANE
I WENT SWIMMING, AND THE CURRENT CARRIED ME HERE!
BLOOP
THAT SOUNDS DANGER-OUS! I'M GLAD YOU'RE OKAY!
NO PROB-LEMO!
I GOT ATTACKED BY SHARKS ALONG THE WAY...
PSHHH...

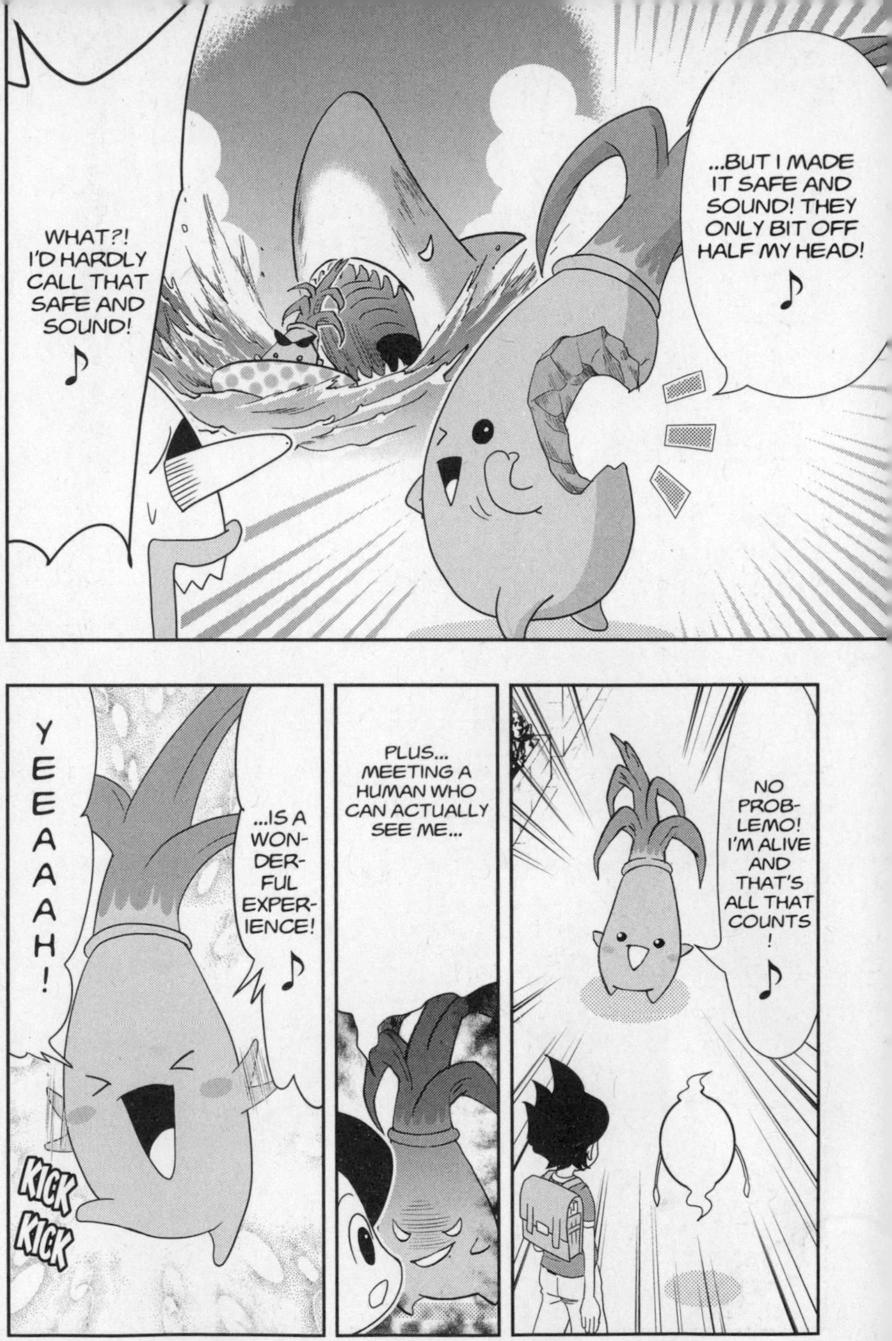
...BUT I MADE IT SAFE AND SOUND! THEY ONLY BIT OFF HALF MY HEAD! ♪
WHAT?! I'D HARDLY CALL THAT SAFE AND SOUND! ♪
NO PROBLEMO! I'M ALIVE AND THAT'S ALL THAT COUNTS! ♪
PLUS... MEETING A HUMAN WHO CAN ACTUALLY SEE ME...
...IS A WONDERFUL EXPERIENCE! ♪
YEEAAAAH!
KICK KICK

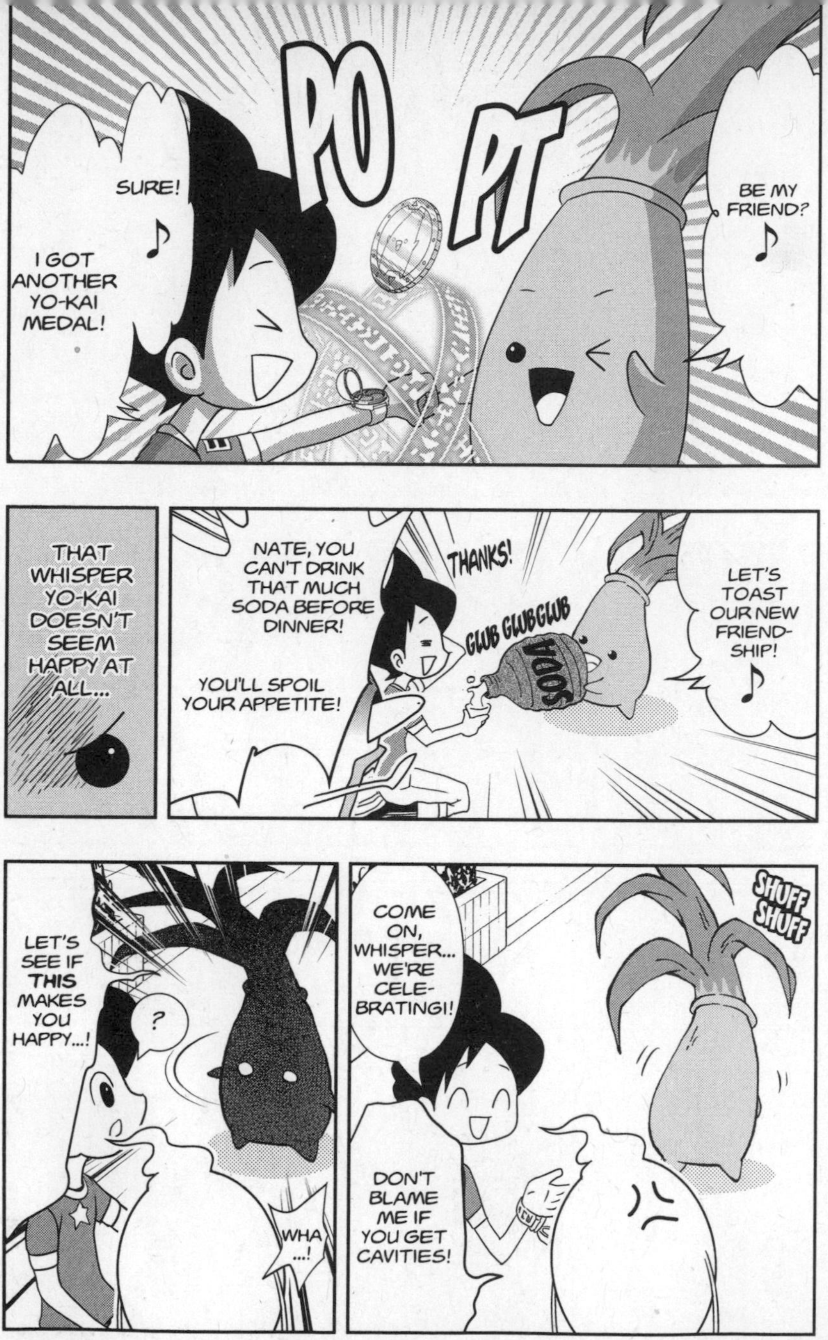
BE MY FRIEND? ♪
POPT
SURE! ♪
I GOT ANOTHER YO-KAI MEDAL!
LET'S TOAST OUR NEW FRIEND-SHIP! ♪
THANKS!
GLUB GLUBGLUB
SODA
NATE, YOU CAN'T DRINK THAT MUCH SODA BEFORE DINNER!
YOU'LL SPOIL YOUR APPETITE!
THAT WHISPER YO-KAI DOESN'T SEEM HAPPY AT ALL...
SHUFF SHUFF
COME ON, WHISPER... WE'RE CELE-BRATING!!
DON'T BLAME ME IF YOU GET CAVITIES!
LET'S SEE IF THIS MAKES YOU HAPPY...!
?
WHA...!

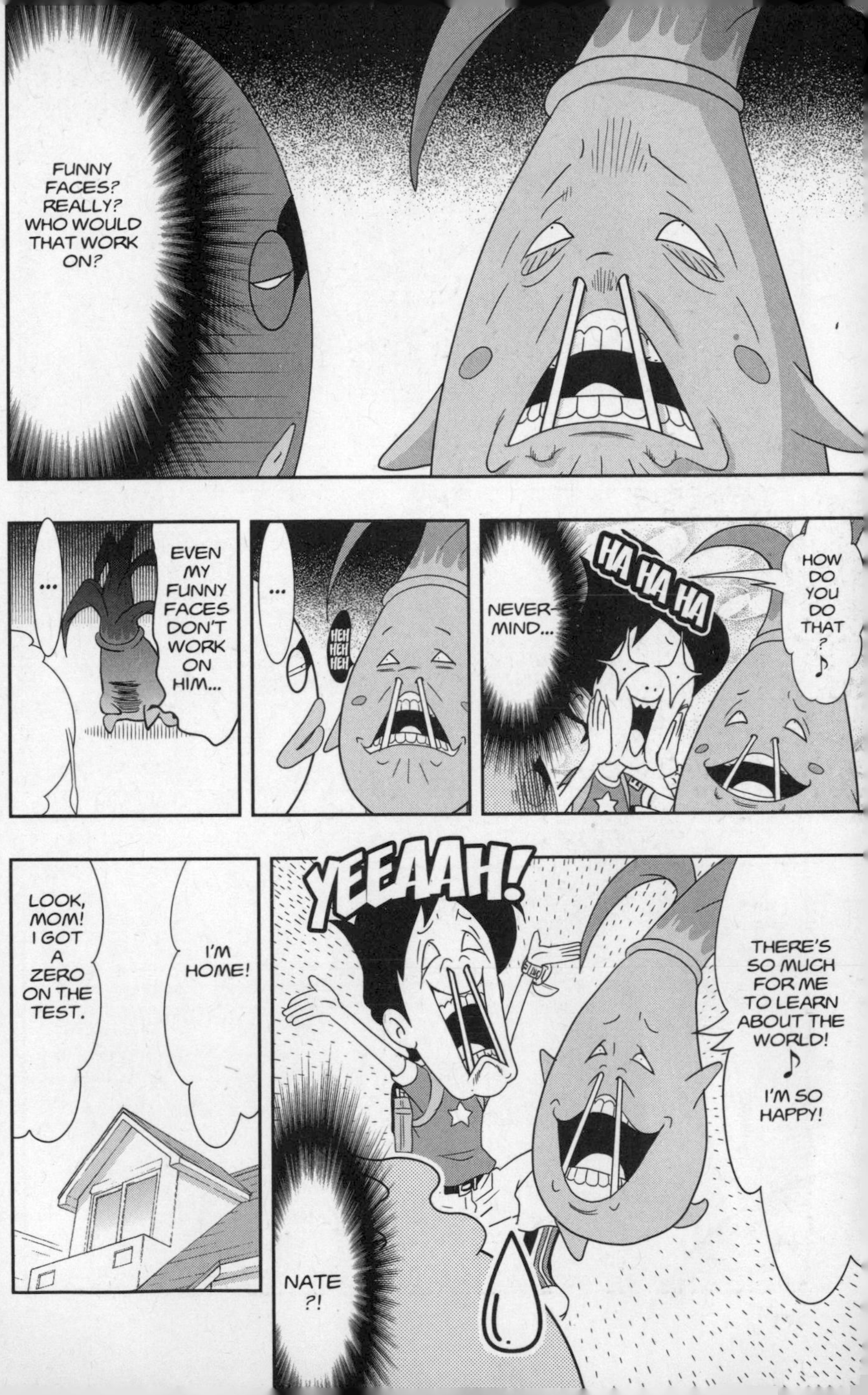
FUNNY FACES? REALLY? WHO WOULD THAT WORK ON?
HOW DO YOU DO THAT? ♪
HA HA HA
NEVER-MIND...
...
HEH HEH HEH
EVEN MY FUNNY FACES DON'T WORK ON HIM...
...
THERE'S SO MUCH FOR ME TO LEARN ABOUT THE WORLD! ♪
I'M SO HAPPY!
YEEAAH!
NATE?!
I'M HOME!
LOOK, MOM! I GOT A ZERO ON THE TEST.

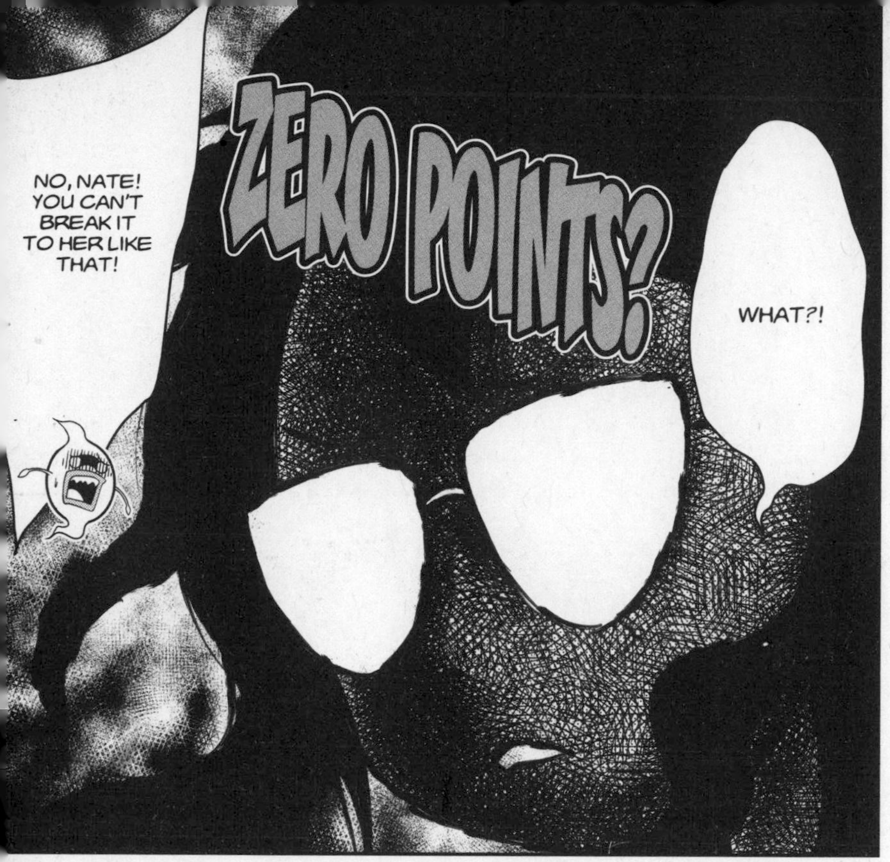
WHAT?!
ZERO POINTS?
NO, NATE! YOU CAN'T BREAK IT TO HER LIKE THAT!

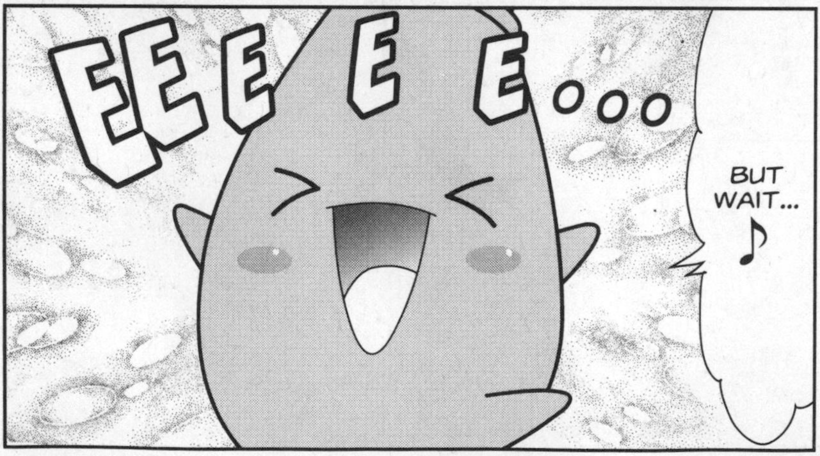
BUT WAIT... ♪
EE E E E...

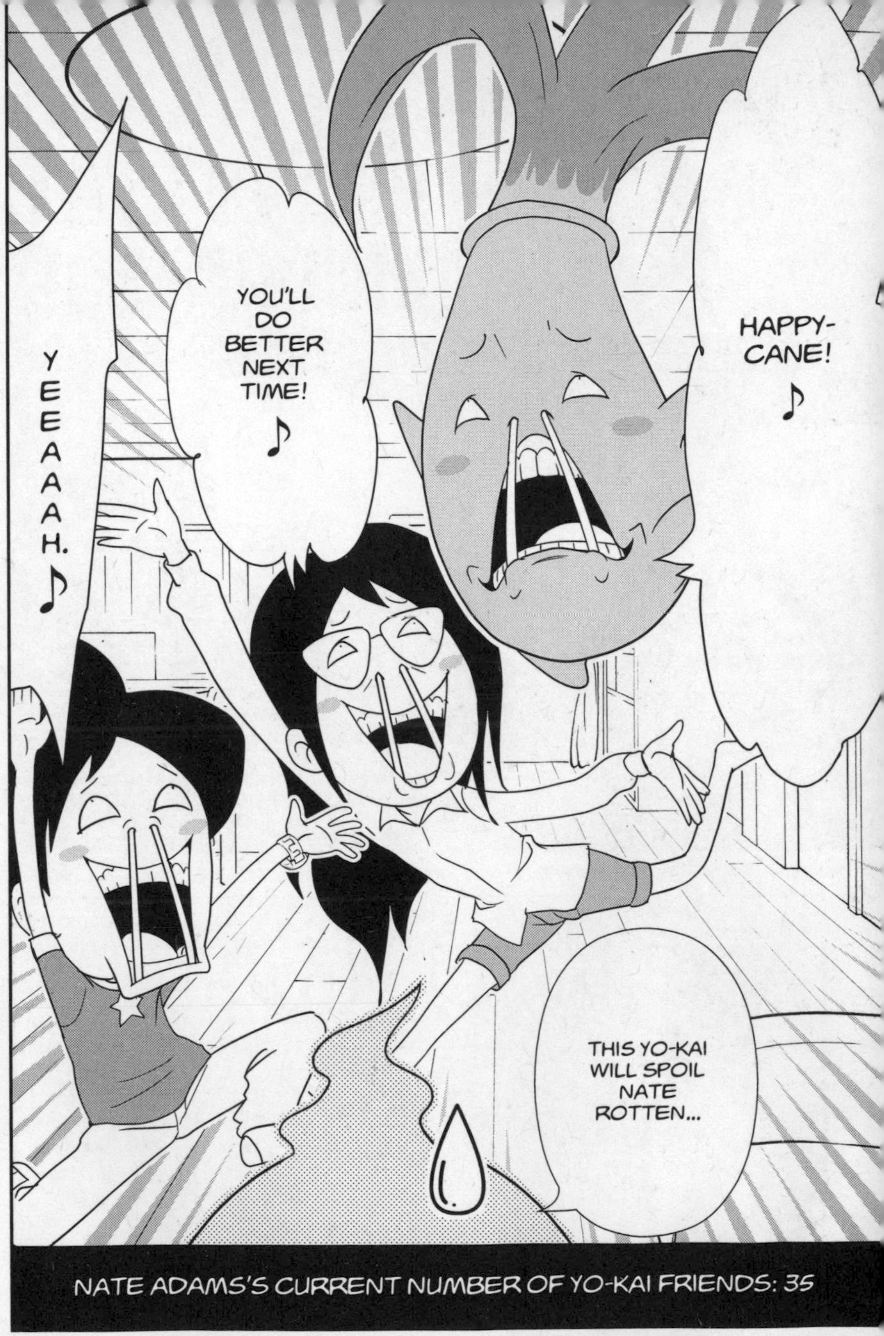
HAPPY-CANE! ♪
YOU'LL DO BETTER NEXT TIME! ♪
YEEAAAAH. ♪
THIS YO-KAI WILL SPOIL NATE ROTTEN...
NATE ADAMS'S CURRENT NUMBER OF YO-KAI FRIENDS: 35

CHAPTER 44: SICK AND TIRED OF STIFF SHOULDERS!!

FEATURING STIFF-SHOULDER YO-KAI AKE

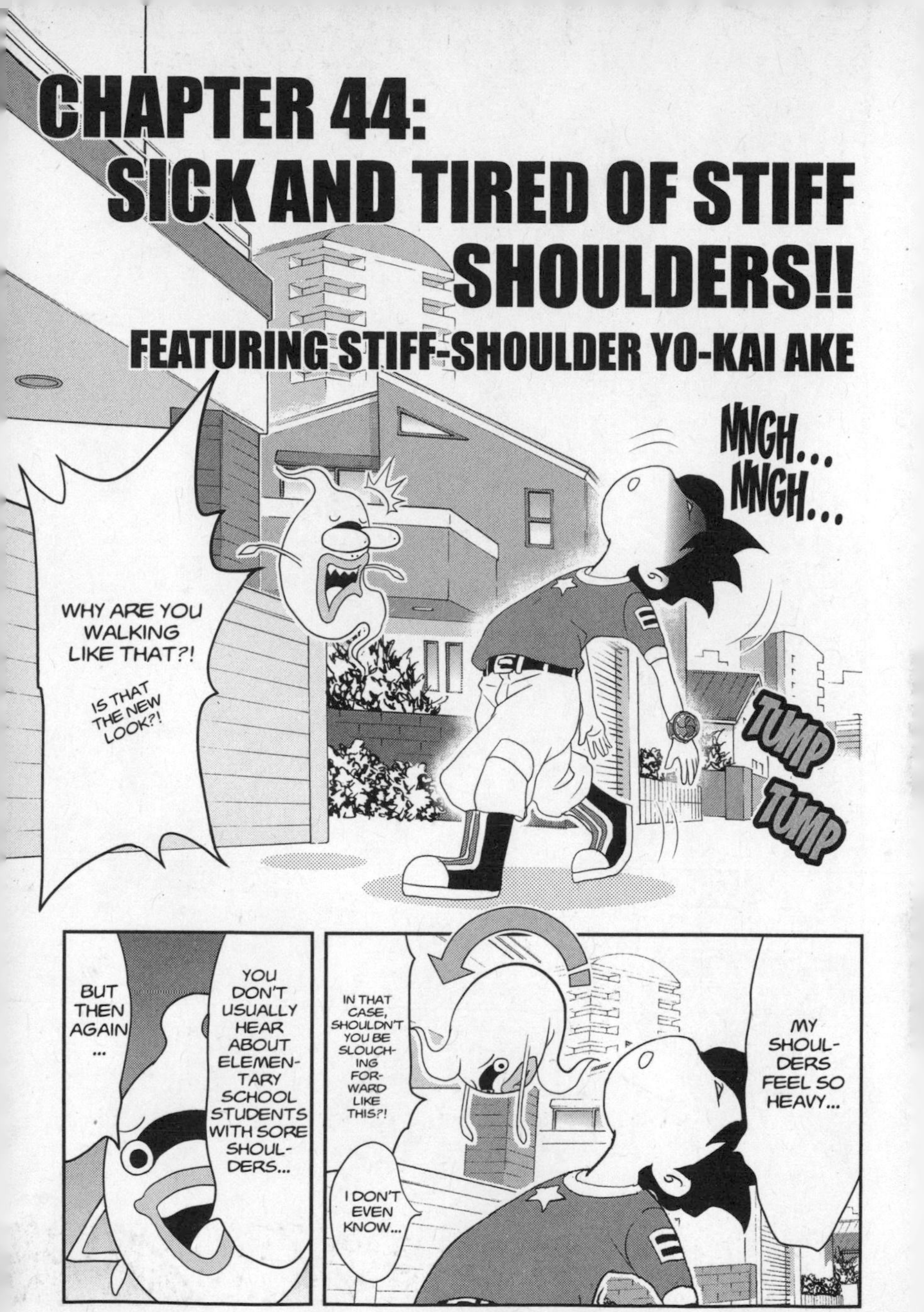
NNGH... NNGH...
TUMP TUMP
WHY ARE YOU WALKING LIKE THAT?!
IS THAT THE NEW LOOK?!
MY SHOUL-DERS FEEL SO HEAVY...
IN THAT CASE, SHOULDN'T YOU BE SLOUCH-ING FOR-WARD LIKE THIS?!
I DON'T EVEN KNOW...
YOU DON'T USUALLY HEAR ABOUT ELEMEN-TARY SCHOOL STUDENTS WITH SORE SHOUL-DERS...
BUT THEN AGAIN...

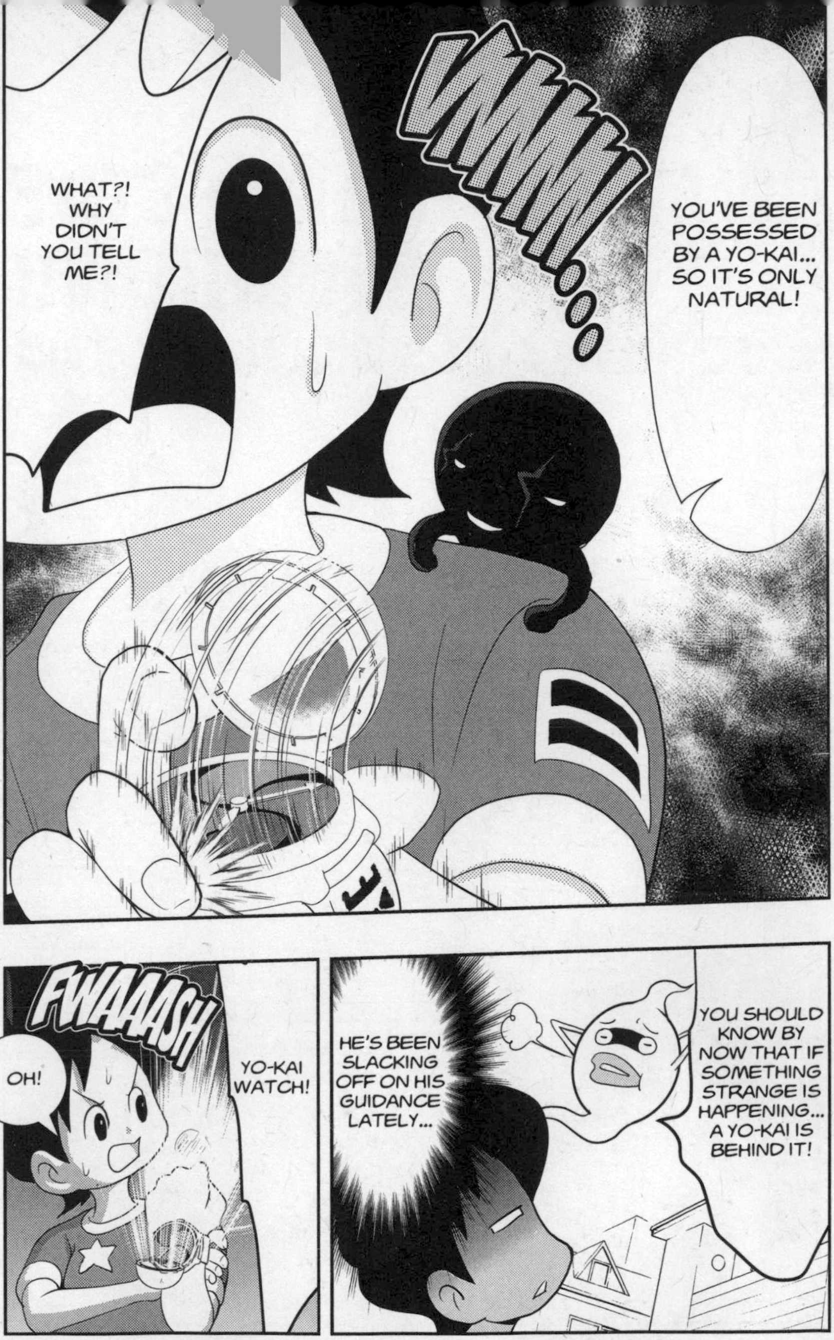
YOU'VE BEEN POSSESSED BY A YO-KAI... SO IT'S ONLY NATURAL!
VMMMN...
WHAT?! WHY DIDN'T YOU TELL ME?!
YOU SHOULD KNOW BY NOW THAT IF SOMETHING STRANGE IS HAPPENING... A YO-KAI IS BEHIND IT!
HE'S BEEN SLACKING OFF ON HIS GUIDANCE LATELY...
YO-KAI WATCH!
FWAAASH
OH!

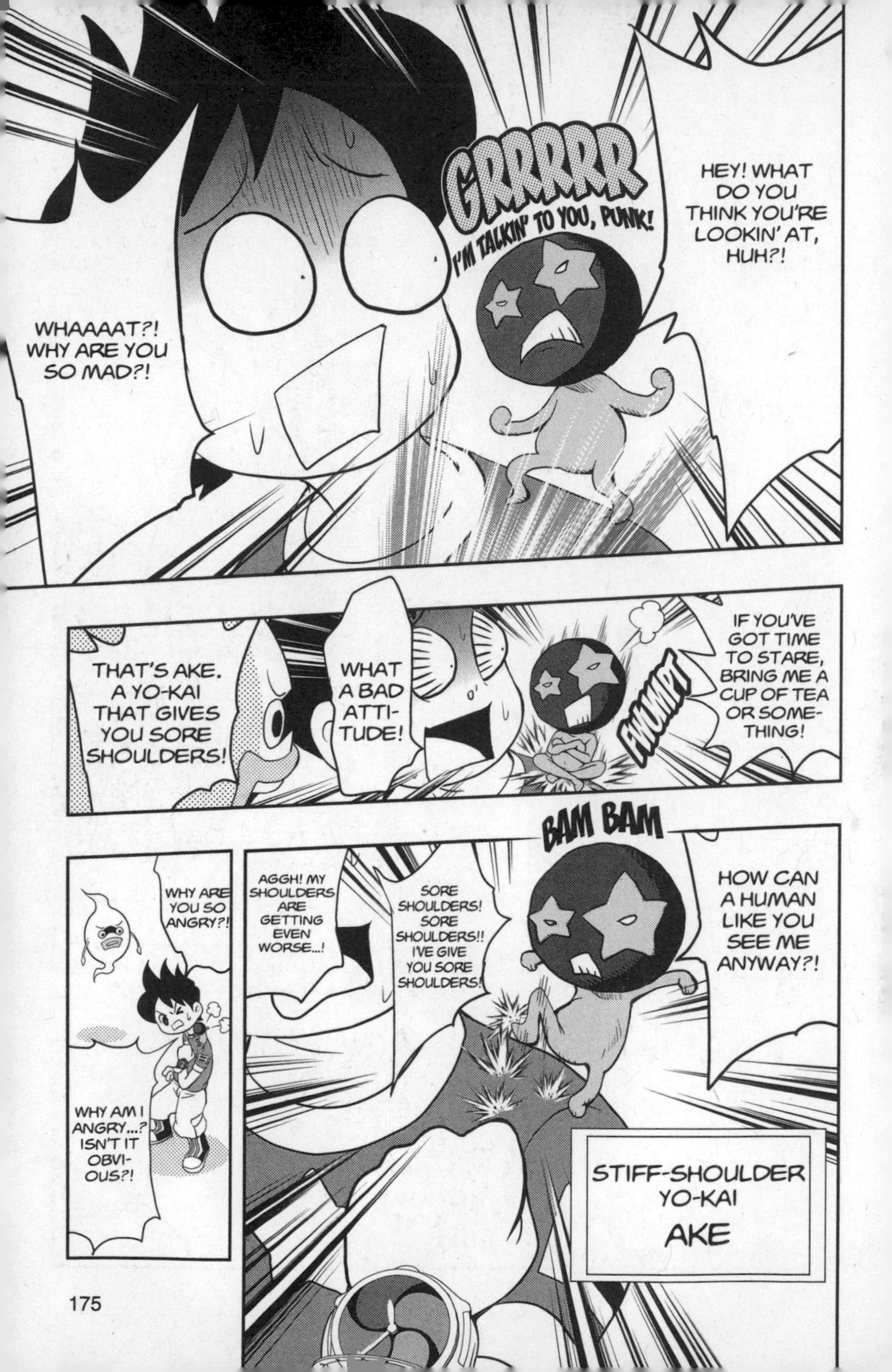
HEY! WHAT DO YOU THINK YOU'RE LOOKIN' AT, HUH?!
GRRRRR
I'M TALKIN' TO YOU, PUNK!
WHAAAAT?! WHY ARE YOU SO MAD?!
IF YOU'VE GOT TIME TO STARE, BRING ME A CUP OF TEA OR SOME-THING!
FWUMP!
WHAT A BAD ATTI-TUDE!
THAT'S AKE. A YO-KAI THAT GIVES YOU SORE SHOULDERS!
BAM BAM
HOW CAN A HUMAN LIKE YOU SEE ME ANYWAY?!
SORE SHOULDERS! SORE SHOULDERS!! I'VE GIVE YOU SORE SHOULDERS!
AGGH! MY SHOULDERS ARE GETTING EVEN WORSE...!
STIFF-SHOULDER YO-KAI AKE
WHY ARE YOU SO ANGRY?!
WHY AM I ANGRY...? ISN'T IT OBVIOUS?!

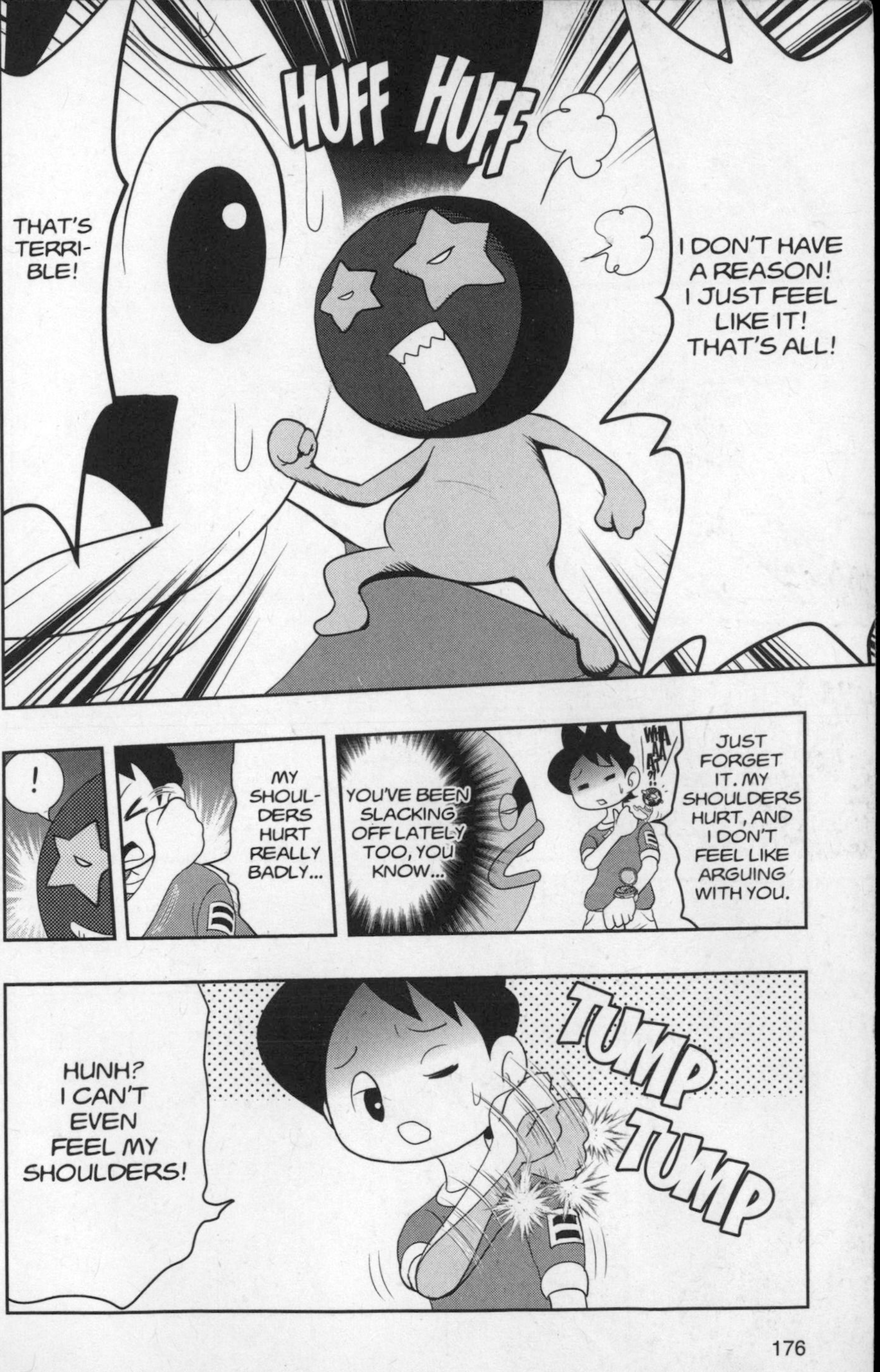
HUFF HUFF
I DON'T HAVE A REASON! I JUST FEEL LIKE IT! THAT'S ALL!
THAT'S TERRIBLE!
JUST FORGET IT. MY SHOULDERS HURT, AND I DON'T FEEL LIKE ARGUING WITH YOU.
WHAAAT?!
YOU'VE BEEN SLACKING OFF LATELY TOO, YOU KNOW...
MY SHOULDERS HURT REALLY BADLY...
!
TUMP TUMP
HUNH? I CAN'T EVEN FEEL MY SHOULDERS!

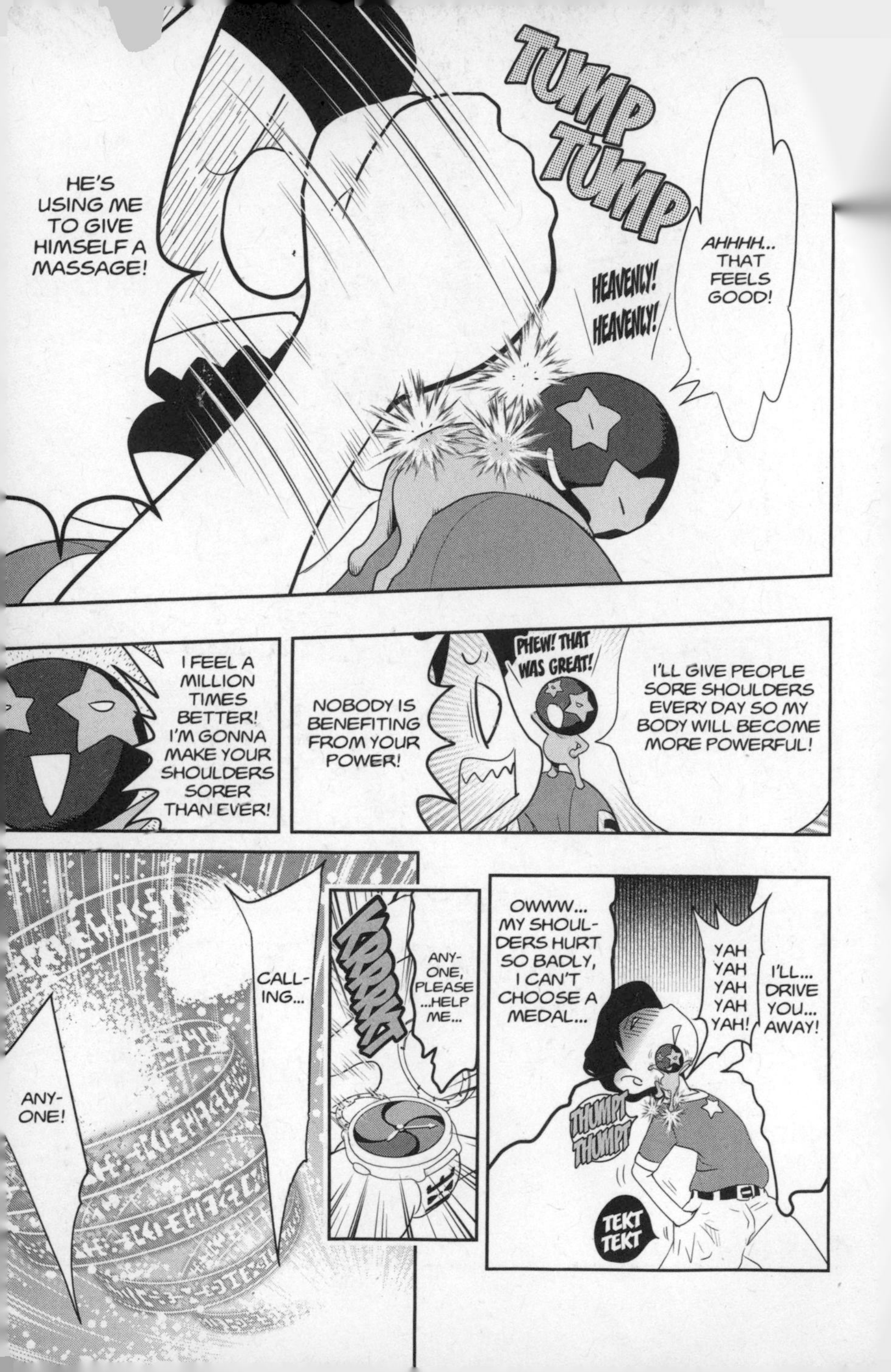

TUMP TUMP TUMP
AHHHH... THAT FEELS GOOD!
HEAVENLY! HEAVENLY!
HE'S USING ME TO GIVE HIMSELF A MASSAGE!
PHEW! THAT WAS GREAT!
I'LL GIVE PEOPLE SORE SHOULDERS EVERY DAY SO MY BODY WILL BECOME MORE POWERFUL!
NOBODY IS BENEFITING FROM YOUR POWER!
I FEEL A MILLION TIMES BETTER! I'M GONNA MAKE YOUR SHOULDERS SORER THAN EVER!
I'LL... DRIVE YOU... AWAY!
YAH YAH YAH YAH YAH!
OWWW... MY SHOUL-DERS HURT SO BADLY, I CAN'T CHOOSE A MEDAL...
THUMPT THUMPT
TEKT TEKT
ANY-ONE, PLEASE ...HELP ME...
CALL-ING...
ANY-ONE!

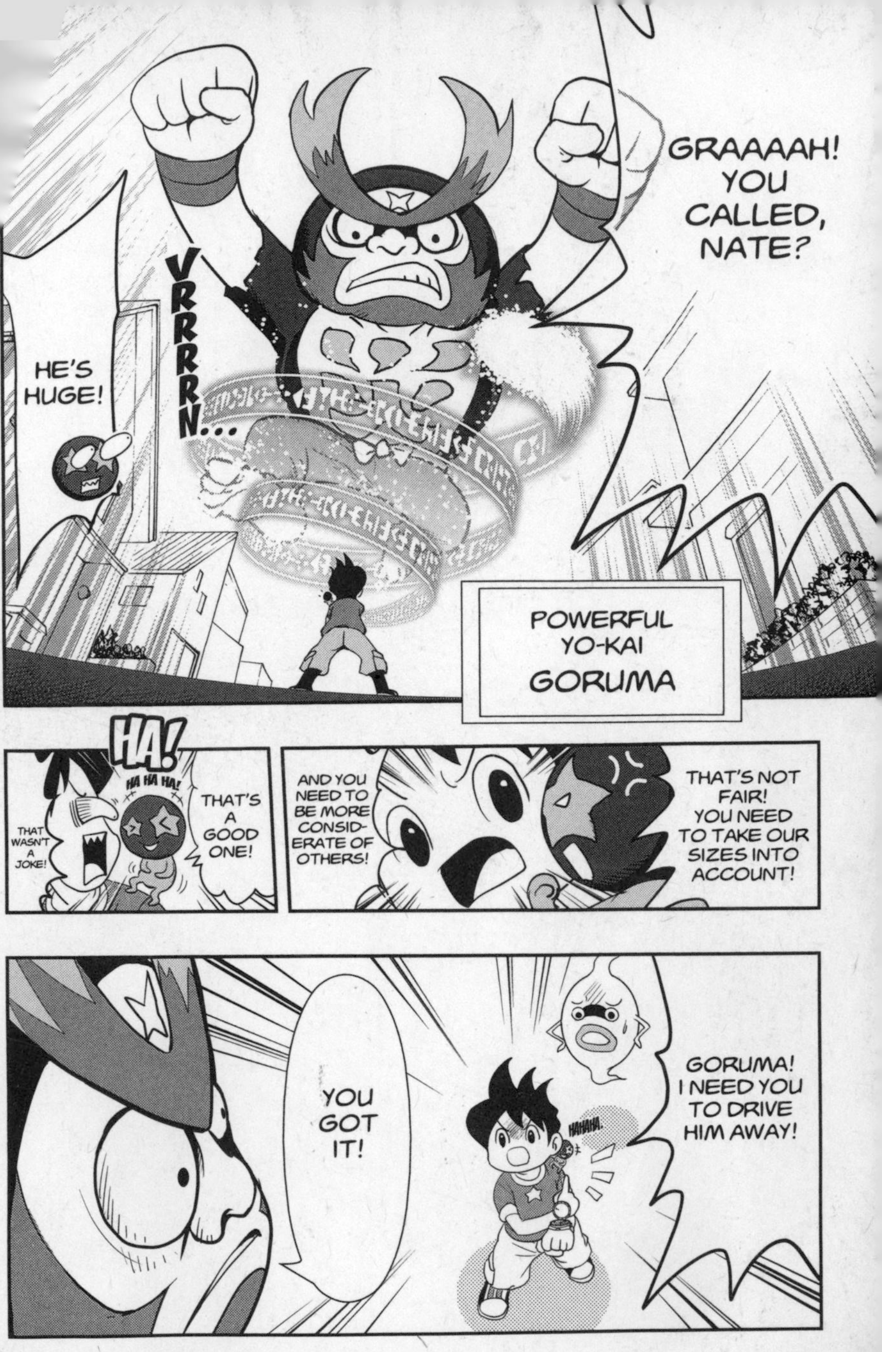
GRAAAAH! YOU CALLED, NATE?
VRRRRN...
HE'S HUGE!
POWERFUL YO-KAI GORUMA
THAT'S NOT FAIR! YOU NEED TO TAKE OUR SIZES INTO ACCOUNT!
AND YOU NEED TO BE MORE CONSID-ERATE OF OTHERS!
HA!
HA HA HA!
THAT'S A GOOD ONE!
THAT WASN'T A JOKE!
GORUMA! I NEED YOU TO DRIVE HIM AWAY!
HAHAHA
YOU GOT IT!

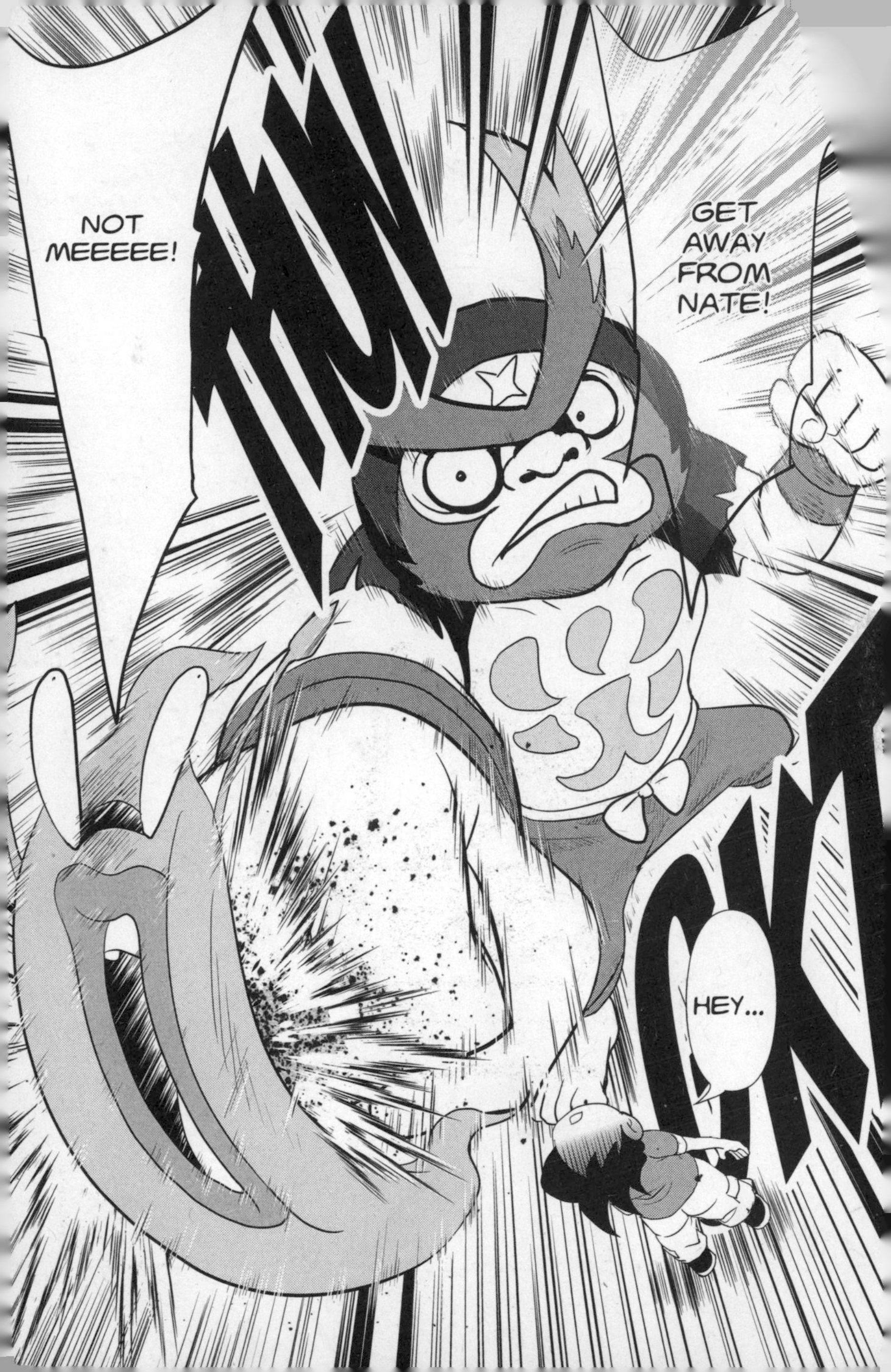
GET AWAY FROM NATE!
NOT MEEEEEE!
HEY...

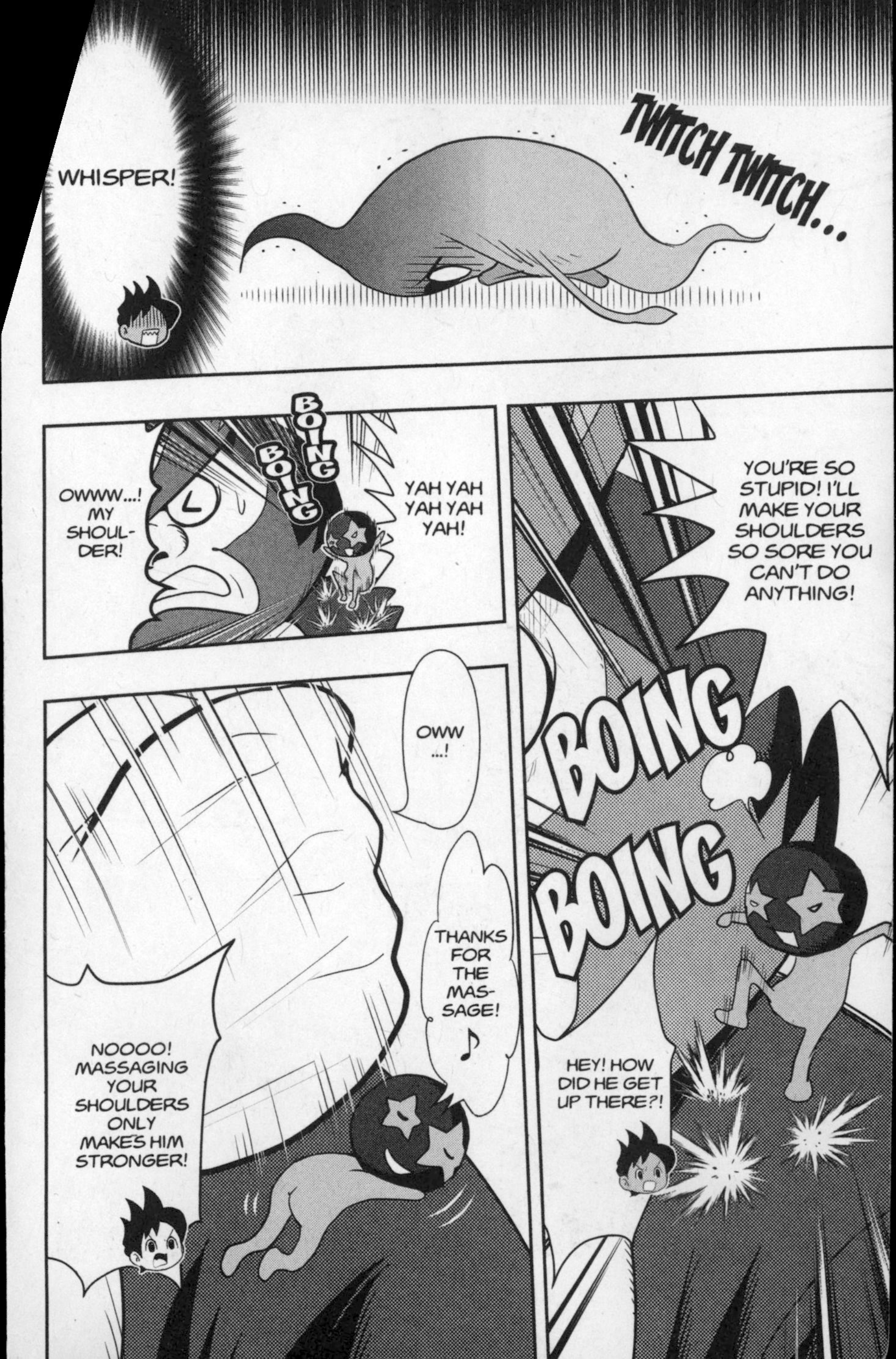
TWITCH TWITCH...
WHISPER!
YOU'RE SO STUPID! I'LL MAKE YOUR SHOULDERS SO SORE YOU CAN'T DO ANYTHING!
BOING BOING
HEY! HOW DID HE GET UP THERE?!
YAH YAH YAH YAH YAH!
BOING BOING
OWWW...! MY SHOUL-DER!
OWW ...!
THANKS FOR THE MAS-SAGE! ♪
NOOOO! MASSAGING YOUR SHOULDERS ONLY MAKES HIM STRONGER!

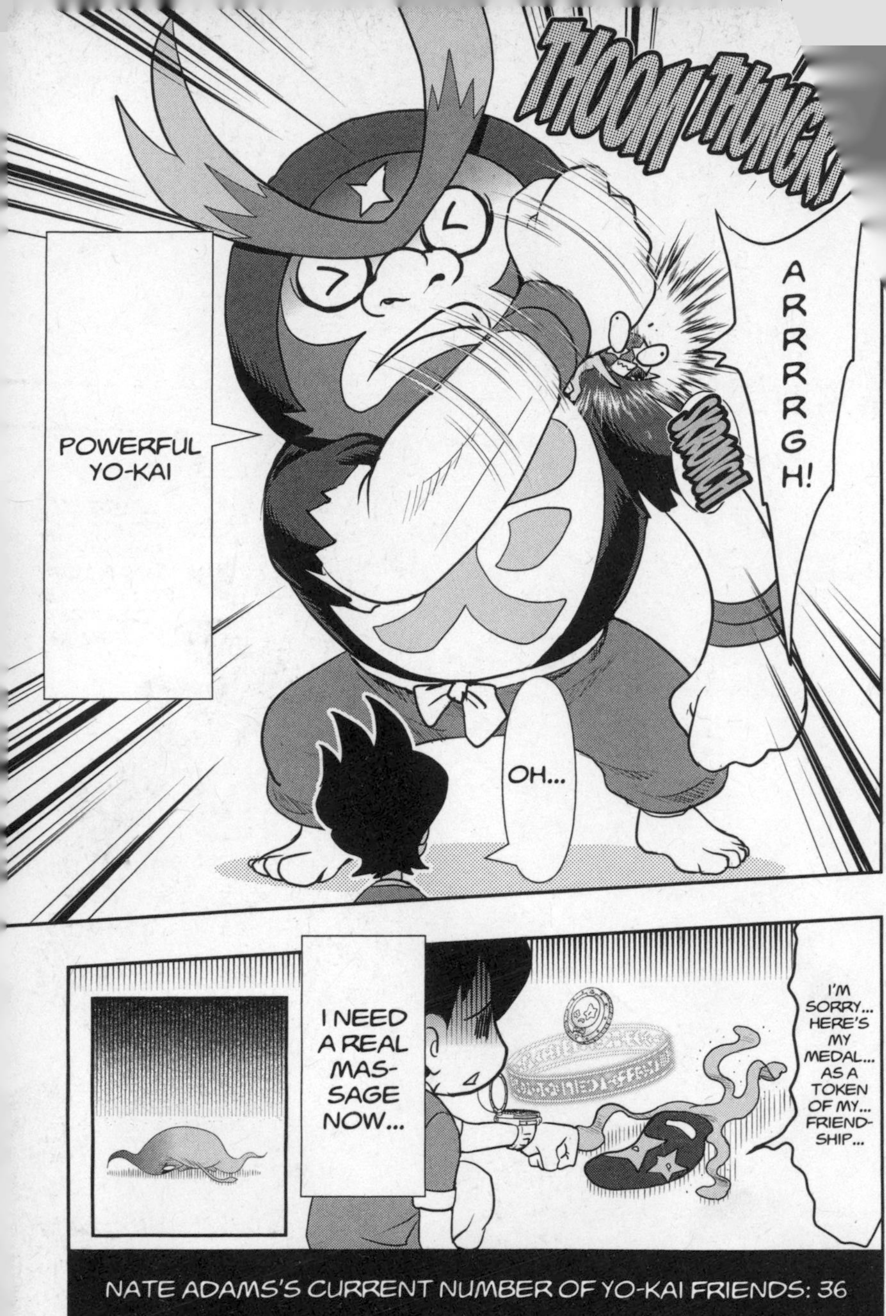
THOOM THUNCK
ARRRRRGH!
SKRUNCH
POWERFUL YO-KAI
OH...
I'M SORRY... HERE'S MY MEDAL... AS A TOKEN OF MY... FRIEND-SHIP...
I NEED A REAL MAS-SAGE NOW...
NATE ADAMS'S CURRENT NUMBER OF YO-KAI FRIENDS: 36

DANKE SAND COMETH

ZOOOSSH
WHOA!
THAT'S DANKE SAND! A YO-KAI THAT SWALLOWS EVERYTHING WITH ITS MASSIVE MOUTH!
ZOOOSSH
BE CARE—AGH!
LET'S EAT!
NOOOO! WHISPER!
YUCK! PTOO!
NNGH!
WHISPER, ARE YOU OKAY?! DO YOU TASTE BAD OR SOME-THING?
FWUMPT
PTOO! PTOO!
NAH...
I JUST SWAL-LOWED A BUNCH OF SAND.
WHAT?! YOU'RE MADE OF SAND?

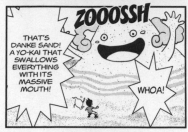

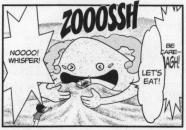

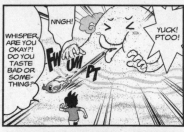

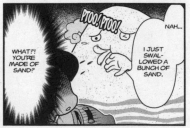

THIS IS THE END OF THIS GRAPHIC NOVEL!

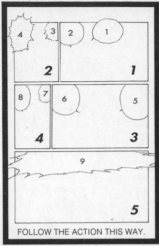

FOLLOW THE ACTION THIS WAY.

To properly enjoy this Perfect Square graphic novel, please turn it around and begin reading from right to left.

AUTHOR BIO

Thanks to everybody, the YO-KAI WATCH manga received the 38th Kodansha Manga Award. Thank you very much.

—Noriyuki Konishi

Noriyuki Konishi hails from Shimabara City in Nagasaki Prefecture, Japan. He debuted with the one-shot *E-CUFF* in *Monthly Shonen Jump Original* in 1997. He is known for writing manga adaptations of *AM Driver* and *Mushiking: King of the Beetles*, along with *Saiyuki Hiro Go-Kū Den!*, *Chōhenshin Gag Gaiden!! Card Warrior Kamen Riders*, *Go-Go-Go Saiyuki: Shin Gokūden* and more. Konishi was the recipient of the 38th Kodansha manga award in 2015.